The Secret
At
Beckham Manor

A Novel

By

Thomas J. Morrow

A continuation of his previous novel,

"Nebraska Doppelganger."

Edited By

James H. Martin

The Secret at Beckham Manor

ISBN: 978-0-9779119-2-9

E-Mail: Quotetaker@cox.net

Author's Note:

While there are some real historical characters referenced in this novel, all other characters, including the Beckham and Krauss families are fictitious. Any similarities between actual persons living or dead are purely coincidental.

Printed in the United States by Morris Publishing
3212 East Highway 30
Kearney, NE 68847
1-800-650-7888

About the author

Thomas J. Morrow lived in Nebraska and Iowa during his youth. His great-grandparents homesteaded on a sand hills homestead around the turn-of-the 20th century, living in a "soddie" in Box Butte County north of Scottsbluff.

His mother graduated from Hemingford High School in the small farming community where his grandparents operated a bakery during the early '30s.

His father's family was in the meat business in Seymour, Iowa some 7 miles north of the Missouri border, 180 miles east of the Missouri River and Nebraska.

During World War II, the Morrow family lived in Lincoln where his father worked as a foreman at the Goodyear Rubber Company's Havelock plant where rubber gas tanks for B-29 super fortress bombers were built.

The author graduated from high school in Seymour, Iowa, and through the years earned three college degrees.

For the past 40 years, he has enjoyed life as a newspaper reporter and editor, with the past 18 years spent as the daily community columnist for the *North County Times* in Oceanside, just north of San Diego, California. He is semi-retired from the newspaper life in 2007.

The author spent a lifetime interviewing and listening to the stories and experiences of veterans of World War II, in particular those who served in the European theater of operations.

Other than the leading German and American historical figures, all characters this book are fictional.

As an award-winning newspaper reporter and columnist, the author interviewed dozens of Allied and German combat veterans of World War II while doing research for this book.

Dedication

I dedicate this novel to someone I had never met until I'd worked with him nearly a year – my editor, **James H. Martin** of Rocky Mount, N.C.
For a lay wordsmith, Jim is the best editor I've known during my 40 years as a writer.

The Internet is a fascinating creation and, for me, a very valuable and beneficial device. In early 2008, Jim e-mailed me a note of praise for my first novel after discovering it on my Web site.

His father, **Carroll F. Martin**, Jr., had been a U.S. Army first lieutenant fighting in Germany during World War II. Jim had written his father's biography and was curious about my novel, "Nebraska Doppelganger."

Over the last year we've formed a close e-mail friendship and working relationship. I finally visited him at his and wife, Trudy, in their lovely home.

We're a good team. I write and he edits. Jim knows what I am trying to convey, removes unwanted commas, corrects my spelling, and moves my errant grammar when necessary. He's a wonderful researcher and probably knows more about Nazi Germany than those who lived through that terrible time.

Jim, I'll never be able to thank you enough for your good work.

Foreword

The directive from Germany's famed "Desert Fox," the beleaguered commander of the Atlantic Wall on the Western Front, was a one-word message: "Now."

The missive was delivered by special military courier to German Lieutenant Colonel Dieter Zeis at his bomb-shattered office bunker in Belgium. The message's authorship was unmistakable that of Erwin Rommel. The three-letter communiqué had the Field Marshal's familiar flourished scroll underlining it.

Dieter Zeis knew exactly what Rommel meant. It was the go-ahead signal to move on a last-ditch effort to save the Fatherland from total destruction. Dieter's orders had been detailed to him at a secret meeting before the June landing by the Allied forces: "Make your way to England at all costs and personally contact British Prime Minister Sir Winston Churchill or Supreme Allied Commander General Dwight Eisenhower."

The proposal was Field Marshal Erwin Rommel's personal plan for surrendering the German Wehrmacht. While other senior German officers concurred, only Rommel had the courage to attempt such a bold and drastic move.

During their last meeting, Rommel left little doubt with Dieter that the old warrior's days were numbered; nevertheless, the young officer continued to hold hope his general's plan would work and the country he loved so dearly could be spared from further destruction. The German High Command in Berlin was at the mercy of a madman—Adolf Hitler. He had to be stopped. The July 20, 1944 assassination attempt on Der Führer had failed. Rommel knew sooner or later his part in the plot, albeit a minor one, would be discovered. Dieter Zeis was one of the few remaining men the Field Marshal could trust.

Geographically, Zeis was well positioned on the Western Front facing Rommel's old nemesis—British Field Marshal Bernard Law Montgomery, now Commander of the 21st Army Group consisting of the British Second

1

Army, the Canadian First Army, and the American Ninth Army. And, Zeis was prepared for the occasion. His English accent was well groomed for the Royal Army officer's uniform he was about to don. Dieter had learned to speak, read, and write English fluently from an Oxford graduate student he had befriended and roomed with back in 1937 at Heidelberg University. From this point on he would be British Major Derek Eaton-Jones—at least until he could find his way to Whitehall or Grosvenor Square in London. As dramatic, ambitious, and foolhardy as it was, this was Rommel's last command to his most trusted friend and fellow German soldier.

Chapter

1

It was the news from Kearney, Nebraska, Cindy Krauss was dreading but expecting. Her Grandmother Harriet Krauss was dead at the age of 86. The rigors of Alzheimer Disease had taken its toll, erasing the many historical events the family's matriarch had witnessed.

Few people living today knew Grandma Krauss' full story. Her husband, John Krauss had confided in his granddaughter two years earlier as to the true identity of his wife, the mother of his children and grandmother of their offspring. As far as Cindy knew, few people were aware her grandparents were once members of Adolf Hitler's Wehrmacht.

Grandma Harriett was born Marlene Harriet Hink in 1921 near Potsdam, Germany. She was from a long line of Prussian Aristocrats. As a teenager, Harriet became a medic in the German Heer (Army) where, in 1938, she met her future husband and fellow medic, John Krauss.

Cindy Krauss was an accomplished journalist, graduating from the University of Missouri. But a strange twist of historical events culminated with her becoming the national correspondent for the New York Bureau of Beckham World News Service. Ironically, it was Grandpa John Krauss who was the key to her good fortune.

She didn't let any colleagues know it was pure nepotism that landed her such a prestigious job. Besides, that would take a bit of explaining. How do you tell anyone that Sir John Beckham, chairman of the board for one of the world's largest newsgathering organizations, is the bastard son of a simple Nebraska farmer; and that old farmer being her grandfather.

She pondered that particular thought for a moment. Simple Nebraska farmer? Now, that was a laugh. This octogenarian was anything but "simple." If the world only knew what she knew. Grandpa John gave permission to write his story two years earlier;* but Cindy still contemplated telling the old man's odyssey, which began in Nazi Germany in 1936 and continuing on to the end of World War II.   There   were questions. Before she could begin detailing her Grandfather's story, one glaring piece was missing. However insignificant it seemed at the time, Cindy pondered the whereabouts of Lieutenant Colonel Dieter Zeis, the good and decent German officer who had protected her grandfather during the war. Without Dieter Zeis, John Krauss' story would have been far different. Her reporter's "nose for news" told her there was far more to his disappearance near the end of the war.

Dieter Zeis had been the administrative officer and close confidant to Germany's famed Field Marshal Erwin Johannes Eugen Rommel during the North African campaign. He had accompanied Rommel back to Germany when the end was nearing for the Deutsches Afrika Korps in 1943. On July 20, 1944, within hours of the attempt on Hitler's life, Dieter vanished into thin air.

More and more questions kept bombarding Cindy as she pondered her grandfather's story. Was this enigmatic officer killed, or did he survive the final days of Germany's collapse? If so, where did he go? Was Dieter Zeis part of the plot to assassinate Adolf Hitler and, as a result, caught up among the more than 5,000 military officers and civilians who were rounded up and murdered by the Gestapo? Did Grandpa John really return from the war to take over the family farm in

---

* "Nebraska Doppelganger"

4

Broken Bow, Nebraska, or did he continue serving his country as an intelligence officer for the OSS—or maybe the CIA?

She discovered periods of time in 1947 through 1955 when Grandpa John was gone from the farm. These were quickly explained away by her father as extended trips John Krauss had taken as a member of the US State Department's agricultural delegation to get Europe back on its feet and restoring farm production. Cindy didn't believe it. However, a little research told her that being part of an "agricultural delegation" during the Cold War often was a cover of choice for CIA agents.

Maybe she was hoping for something more dashing and romantic than increasing the grain output of the Netherlands and Germany so more beer could be brewed.

Cindy sat at her newsroom desk preparing to book her flight online for the trip back to Nebraska when the e-mail flag popped upon her screen. The e-missive was from Sir Jack, her boss—her uncle—well, sort of.

"I'll be landing at LaGuardia Wednesday at 3 pm. Let's have dinner, and then fly to Kearney on Thursday for your grandmother's funeral."

How could a girl refuse free dinner with the boss plus a flight back home in the company's private jet?

As his e-mail announced, Sir Jack's Boeing 737 touched down at exactly 3 pm. Cindy was picked up by the company's limo at the downtown Manhattan office and whisked to La Guardia International Airport to meet the 68-year old company chairman. As the handsome Englishman bounded from the plane, he was holding a dark leather briefcase and his ever-ubiquitous brolly. Cindy didn't have to squint to see a younger version of Grandpa John in the image of Jack Beckham. Tall with more than six feet in height, he was dressed and looked the part of typical English gentry; his head held flowing gray hair with traces of blond.

He wasn't the son of Grandma Harriet; but, out of respect for his biological father, Sir Jack would attend her funeral. Sir Jack had never met Marlene Harriett Hink but knew her story as well as Cindy. His mother, German-born Greta von Carlsen-Beckham, was John Krauss' first love back during the late '30s in Berlin but duty and war prohibited anything more. Sir Jack would be 16-years old before he learned his real father was John Krauss, Nebraska farmer, former German medic—a strange doppelganger, indeed.

That evening at dinner, Cindy sat across from her boss at the Waldorf Astoria, Jack's favorite place to stay when he was in New York. Of course he wanted to know all the latest office gossip and how Cindy was doing with her assignment as the national correspondent "for the colonies," as Jack would tease her. During the dessert, the conversation turned a bit more solemn.

"I have a special assignment for you and it may not be something you will want to do," he began. "I don't think the ol' man has been all that truthful with us about his life since the war."

Cindy looked puzzled.

"You mean my Grandpa John?"

"Yes. I believe he has been a long-time agent for your Central Intelligence Agency," Jack continued. "His gentleman farmer role has been a mere ruse."

Cindy was dumbfounded. She didn't know what to say.

"Why are you saying this? What makes you think Gramps had been a CIA agent?" Cindy had a slight edge to her voice.

"I began suspecting it some time ago after an off-hand remark my mother made," Jack replied. "I didn't think much of it at the time, but it kept gnawing at me so I made some quiet inquiries with a friend at MI-6."

"Your Secret Service told you?"

"No, but it was what my man didn't say that got me even more curious," he said. "I figure if there is anyone who can get him to talk it would be you."

"Well, first of all, if he was an agent after the war, what of it?" Cindy countered. "I mean, it was the 'Cold War' and our two countries were engaged in a lot of intelligence work against the Soviets. I'm sure there was a good reason for secrecy."

Jack took a sip from his snifter of Courvoisier.

"I don't disagree, but now that the Cold War is over, a lot of great stories are being written and, after all, we're in the news business. If there is a story to be told, wouldn't you want to write a sequel to your grandfather's first book?"

The conversation hit Cindy by surprise. She caught herself staring, thinking, and wondering all at once.

"There's one question about your Grandfather's story that hasn't been answered"

"What?" she quipped.

"What happened to Dieter Zeis?"

Jack was right. Grandpa John pretty much glossed over that question leaving the impression that Lieutenant Colonel Zeis had been killed during the final days of the war. Dieter had accompanied Field Marshal Erwin Rommel back to Germany in 1943 before the fall of the Deutsches Afrika Korps in North Africa. He wasn't heard from again after Rommel was forced to commit suicide in October 1944.

"I got the impression that Dieter was caught up in Hitler's purge of the conspirators in the July 20, 1944 assassination attempt on his life," Cindy replied.

"Yes, that was my understanding as well," Jack said. "We'll go back to Nebraska for your grandmother's funeral. I'll clear it with your boss in the office so you can spend a few weeks on special assignment. I would think you will need to spend time in Washington with some contacts I have … and also in London. You might be able to get something from my mother as well. If there is anyone other than your grandfather who knows the story, it would be Greta."

The maitre d' suddenly appeared at their table as Sir Jack began to light a large Cuban Cohiba cigar.

"I'm sorry sir … but we no longer allow smoking in the restaurant," he said in a polite, but firm manner.

"Ah, you Americans. You've started something that has caught on over on my side of the pond," Jack chuckled. "And, I went to great lengths to smuggle this Cuban beauty through your customs."

Jack replaced it into his jacket humidor.

"It's one of the few little pleasures I still allow myself that isn't fattening or immoral," he joked.

"Yeah, but just think ... you might get an extra five years of good living instead," Cindy replied.

Cindy said goodnight to Sir Jack in the hotel's lobby and promised to be back for the trip to the airport the following morning for their trip to Kearney.

She had a lot to think about and doubted whether she would get much sleep. Grandpa John a CIA agent? It sounded too incredible. Cindy knew him as a kindly old farmer who always seemed to wear bib overalls. Grandpa John sleuthing as an undercover CIA agent wasn't a picture she could quite get into focus. If he did serve the CIA, it would have to have been 50 or maybe even 60 years ago. Today, he was 89-years old. She had no idea what the retirement age was for the Central Intelligence Agency but was pretty certain they didn't have many field agents in their 60s or 70s.

If John Krauss was a secret agent, what of it? Why would Jack be so interested in this story now after all those years?

At 8 am sharp the following morning, Sir Jack emerged from the Waldorf Astoria's lobby elevator where Cindy was waiting. Not much was said between them on the way to the airport. The British press tycoon made a passing comment about the change in the New York skyline with the missing twin World Trade Center towers.

"How will I ever ask Gramps about him being an agent for the CIA?" Cindy asked, breaking the quiet ride to the airport.

Jack continued gazing out the limo's window.

"Ask him about Reinhart Gehlen," he said.

That name sent shivers through Cindy. When Grandpa John revealed he had been a member of the Office of Strategic Services (OSS) during World War II, she did some research and found that after the war the intelligence-gathering agency morphed into the CIA. German SS Major General Reinhart Gehlen became a key source for the CIA in building its body of information against the Soviet Union during the early days of the Cold War.

"If you don't know that name, try 'Googling' it on the Internet," Jack offered. "You'll find dozens of pages of information. He was one very treacherous man."

"I know," Cindy acknowledged. "I've read a little about him but ... what would he have to do with Gramps?"

"That's what I want you to find out," Jack said as he opened a copy of the Financial Times.

Cindy had the distinct feeling Jack Beckham knew more about this question than he was telling her, but what?

The flight to Kearney took just over three hours in the Beckham World News Service's executive aircraft. The Kearney airport's long runway had no problem in welcoming the 737 executive jet. The facility had been created back in 1942 to handle heavy Boeing B-17 bombers during World War II when it was a US Army Air Corps base.

As expected, John Krauss, the family's patriarch, was standing outside the airport's terminal building waiting for his son and granddaughter.

"I'm so glad to see you both" the old sage said, giving his granddaughter a big hug and kiss. "Thanks Jack for being here."

On the short ride west into town along US Highway 30, Grandpa John told how many family members had gathered for his wife's funeral. John was in an unusually good mood for someone who had just lost his wife. Still, Cindy understood her grandfather's state of mind. Grandma Harriet hadn't been herself for a couple of years after suffering from Alzheimer Disease. She had left a long time ago. The burden of caring for her had rested upon Grandpa John; and he was no doubt relieved her days of living in a memory-less void had finally ended.

The next day, Harriet Krauss' funeral was held in typical Midwestern American fashion—an open-casket viewing with an overflowing crowd at the Lutheran Church and later at the gravesite in the cemetery. Of course, there were a few questions about Sir Jack. The old man hadn't really told anyone exactly who this younger version of himself was. Cindy thought it was funny. She could just imagine the curiosity in everyone's mind.

Back at her grandparents' home, family and friends gathered for the ever omnipresent after-funeral feed. Cindy hated these gatherings. People seemed more interested in eating and talking than the reason for which they were there. John saw her sitting by herself on the patio.

"Everything all right, Sissy?" he asked.

"Sure, Gramps ... just hate these things ... don't you?"

"Yeah ... but the family more or less expects to endure this ritual," the old man reckoned. "It won't be that long before you'll be reconvening here for me."

"Grandpa ... don't say that," she snapped. "You're gonna be with us for a long time to come."

"Well ... we both know that once you reach my age, you don't buy any green bananas," John said slightly chuckling.

Changing the subject, John asked how long she would be staying.

"I've got to get back to New York," she replied. "I'll be leaving tomorrow with Jack, but why don't you come with us and take a rest away from all of this? I've got a few days off from work."

John looked out at his backyard.

"Well ... I could use a break, there's no doubt about that."

"Good, then it's settled. You're going home with me and we'll have some fun, maybe go to the theater," Cindy said.

Cindy enjoyed the luxury of executive travel—the seamless ease of bounding from a limo into a private jet, avoiding the hassle of long security lines. While she knew this privilege would be fleeting, Cindy was savoring the opportunity while it lasted. Her grandfather didn't seem all that impressed. It was as if he had been on private jets many times before.

Could there be any truth to Jack's concerns about Grandpa John? The problem, as Cindy saw it, was approaching her grandfather. How do you broach the subject?

She pondered: *"Oh, by the way Gramps ... are you or have you ever been a CIA spy?"* The thought seemed ludicrous. Still....

The flight back to New York was smooth. Jack had some of those famous Midwestern rib-eye steaks from Grampa John's freezer thawed and put in the plane's galley for the steward to prepare for their in-flight meal. Jack was immersed in a thick Clive Cussler novel at the front of the cabin. Cindy sat with her grandfather, who was lightly dozing with a headset of soothing elevator music covering his ears.

Little discussion took place among the three passengers until after dinner. It was getting darker as the plane knifed through the stratosphere into the eastern United States toward New York. Jack had returned to his book while Cindy began small talk with Grandpa John.

"Gramps … I'm making pretty good progress on your biography, but from what you've told me so far, the book falls short after the war," Cindy began. "I mean … we haven't discussed what your life has been like since 1947."

The old man sat across from her studying Cindy's face with a slight smile.

"What else do you want to know?" he replied. "Being a farmer isn't very exciting."

Cindy paused, and then took a deep breath.

"When you were on those various agricultural missions for the government, were you working for another branch of the government, say … the CIA?"

The slight smile turned into a chuckle, and then all expression disappeared. John looked out through the plane's portal at the quickly darkening clouds. Then he looked back.

"What would cause you to ask me such a thing?"

"Gramps, as a former OSS officer, not to mention your knowledge of Europe, you would have been a natural for the CIA. Besides, wouldn't the OSS or CIA hang on to someone like you for as long as they could?"

More silence. The old man shuffled his feet; then he looked back out the plane's portal again. It was nearly pitch black now.

Cindy took another deep breath.

"Does the name 'Reinhart Gehlen' mean anything to you?"

Now she had the old man's full attention.

"Who have you been talking to?" Grandpa John asked, looking straight into Cindy's eyes.

"Remember Gramps, I'm an investigative reporter. I'm doing a piece on the early days of the CIA and your name came up," she lied.

"I doubt that very much, young lady," he replied smiling and looking back at the blackness of night.

"Seriously Gramps … you know more than you're telling me," she continued with her quest. "You couldn't have been just talking about corn and wheat on all of those trips with the State Department."

"I'd like to know if you ever found Dieter Zeis. Did he survive the war?"

More silence. Then Grandpa John looked back at Cindy who was waiting for her answer.

"Well … if he did survive it'd be interesting to talk with him," Grandpa John mused with that sly smile returning.

Cindy didn't say anything to the obvious comment. John was looking straight at her again.

"Is this what my stay with you is going to be like?" he asked.

"Probably. Inquiring minds want to know."

"Yes, but whose inquiring minds? I have the feeling the sudden interest in this isn't something you came up with yourself."

"Gramps, I don't reveal my sources."

"Yeah well … I don't like talking to the press," he countered with a smile. "Besides, if I were a spy, would I go around blabbing my mouth?"

"I'm your granddaughter, dang it! You're supposed to tell me stories of your life. That's what grandparents do."

The conversation had evolved into a sparring match of words and neither was getting the upper hand.

"Let's just relax and enjoy the rest of the flight," the old man suggested.

Chapter

2

When Cindy awoke the next morning at her apartment, she found a note from her grandfather on the breakfast counter. *"Gone for my morning walk. I'll fix breakfast when I get back."*

As much as she loved her Gramps, the conversations with Jack about the old man possibly being a CIA agent was disconcerting. She especially was distressed at the thought that her kindly grandfather would have had anything to do with the former Nazi spy Reinhart Gehlen.

Cindy had only to "Google" Gehlen's name on the Internet whereupon page upon page of information immediately popped up on the screen of her laptop.

The United States Freedom of Information Act allowed thousands of dark secrets from the CIA and National Security Council to be exposed to the public light of day.

The National Security Archive posted the CIA's secret history of the government's relationship with General Reinhard Gehlen. The former Nazi was the German Army's intelligence chief for the Eastern Front against the Soviet Union during World War II. It was because of his intimate knowledge about the Soviets that made him such an attraction to the OSS-CIA. Gehlen quickly seized upon the paranoia the Americans had toward the Soviets and established a close relationship which allowed him to successfully maintain his intelligence network that ultimately became that of the West German Government during the Cold War. It wasn't just Gehlen, but those who worked for him. The ranks of the Gehlen Organization were filled with numerous Nazi comrades, many of whom were known war criminals.

The US Congress established the Interagency Working Group on January 11, 1999, giving it a commission life until March 2005 to oversee the declassification of about eight million pages of documents from multiple government agencies.

The documents uncovered revealed extensive relationships between former Nazi war criminals and various American intelligence organizations—including the CIA. Records show at least five associates of the late Nazi SS Colonel Adolf Eichmann had worked for the CIA; more than 23 other Nazis were approached by the CIA for recruitment, and no less than 100 officers within the Gehlen Organization were former Gestapo agents.

As she browsed the many Internet pages on the Nazi spy, Cindy was mystified as to how American intelligence officers had been so easily duped by Gehlen.

Gehlen was the son of a Catholic bookseller. He joined the Reichswehr's 100,000-man Army (to which Germany was restricted by the Treaty of Versailles after World War I) in 1920 and entered the German Staff College in the 1930s. He was promoted to captain and was attached to the Army General Staff. In 1940, after being promoted to major, he became the liaison officer to Field Marshal Walther von Brauchitsch. He was then transferred to the Army Chief of Staff under General Franz Halder. In July 1941, Gehlen was promoted to lieutenant colonel. He worked extensively on the Eastern Front and, because of his superior talents and expertise, was promoted to senior intelligence officer with the German General Staff on the Russian Front.

In 1942, Gehlen was approached by three high ranking German Army officers to participate in a minor role in an assassination attempt on Adolf Hitler. When the bomb plot failed on July 20, 1944, Gehlen's role was covered up, allowing him to escape Hitler's brutal retaliation.

"Trying to kill that maniac is the first good thing I've read or heard about the man," Cindy thought to herself as she poured over the volumes of files on Gehlen.

In December 1944, Gehlen was promoted to major general and, as head of Fremde Heere-Ost (Foreign Forces-East) was assigned to gather concentrated intelligence on the political and battlefield tactics of the Soviet Union.

Knowing the end was near, Gehlen made plans to be captured by the approaching American forces. He concealed his voluminous files of the Soviet Army and political leaders in a steel drum and then buried it in the Bavarian Alps.

On May 22, 1945, Gehlen surrendered to the US Army Counter Intelligence Corps. The first American recognition of the importance of Gehlen as a prisoner of war was made by US Army Intelligence Corps' Brigadier General Edwin Sibert of the US 12th Army Group.

Gehlen impressed General Sibert with his knowledge of Soviet military and political affairs. To further impress his American captors, Gehlen revealed a number of OSS officers as being secret members of the US Communist Party.

Using his newfound influence with the Americans, Gehlen offered to hand over Soviet resources in exchange for his freedom as well as that of his fellow colleagues imprisoned in American POW camps in Germany.

General Sibert contacted his superior officer, Lieutenant General Walter Bedell Smith, Eisenhower's Chief of Staff, who then worked with OSS chief, General William Donovan and his OSS Station Chief in Bern, Switzerland, Allen Dulles. Arrangements were completed on September 20, 1945, for Gehlen and three close Nazi associates to be flown to the United States where they began working for the US Government in a quasi house arrest status.

"Dulles? Wasn't he a brother of a Secretary of State?" Cindy pondered.

In July 1946, Gehlen was officially released from American captivity and flown back into Germany where he began his intelligence work setting up an organization of former German intelligence officers, which became known as the "Gehlen Organization." He set up a dummy organization in

Munich called the "South German Industrial Development Organization" to mask his undercover operation and spy ring.

Initially, Gehlen personally selected 350 former German intelligence agents; but that number grew to 4,000 undercover agents. These secret German agents were known as "V-Men." For many years during the Cold War, the V-Men were the only eyes and ears of the CIA inside the various Soviet Bloc Nations. The spy group, which became the intelligence arm of the West German Government, was called the "Gehlen Org."

Cindy heard Grandpa John puttering in the kitchen making omelets as she finished browsing the various pages on the Internet regarding Gehlen. There were too many to read at one sitting.

"Do you want bacon or sausage?" said Grandpa John's voice from the kitchen.

"Bacon of course," she replied. "Sausage is fattening.

Cindy heard a big laugh echoing from the kitchen.

"Potatoes?"

"Naw … just an omelet and some bacon will be 'nuff. Thanks, Gramps."

Cindy sat down at the kitchen table as her grandfather served breakfast. He had brought home some nice fresh croissants from the corner bakery.

She couldn't contain herself. After reading all those various pages on Gehlen, Cindy continued her probe.

"Did you *ever* meet Gehlen?"

The old man didn't look up from buttering his croissant.

"C'mon Gramps … I gotta know?"

"Why? But let's just say for argument's sake that anything I might or might not have done after the war was supposed to be a secret. If I had anything to tell you, it wouldn't be a secret anymore … now would it?"

He still didn't look up while buttering his croissant.

"The fact that I told you about me being an OSS Agent might have been a mistake because no matter what I say … you'll just want more."

Cindy couldn't argue with that. But, something told her to just sit there and be quiet.

"I did make a number of overseas trips for the State Department and they were classified. Unless I'm told differently, which I haven't, they still are."

He was testing his coffee. Cindy didn't look up from her omelet, but that didn't mean she wasn't listening very closely.

"If I were an enterprising young writer wanting to know what really happened over there, I'd go to a better source than me."

The old man was unfolding the New York Times.

"Who could Gramps be talking about besides himself?" Cindy started to ask, but continued her silence.

"Okay … forget about the CIA for now. What about Dieter?"

"Same advice," he countered.

"Who would know such things?" she thought.

"GRETA?" she exclaimed with her mouth full.

"Don't talk while you're eating," Grandpa John said as he lightly scolded her in a mockingly manner.

"That's it … isn't it? Greta. She knows … doesn't she?"

John Krauss was tearing off a piece of croissant, putting some strawberry jam on with a knife. He didn't look up, but Cindy detected a very slight smile on his normally stoic face.

"I'm not saying that you're correct … but, maybe that could be a way to have a lot of questions answered."

Of course, Greta. She and Dieter were tight in-laws by marriage. Dieter knew of her espionage activities in the '30s when she was in Berlin. If Dieter did survive the war, Greta would be the one he would return to if he needed help. What was it that Jack told her: maybe his mother had answers? She had to get to London. Maybe Jack would let her fly back with him. Why hadn't he asked this question of his mother himself?

There's definitely more going on than anyone is saying.

Chapter

3

Cindy was convinced Greta von Carlsen-Beckham was the key to a number of mysteries. The 99-year old mother of Sir Jack Beckham was a perspicuous and headstrong woman whom John Krauss first met when he was an 18-year old college student at Berlin University. She not only was John's first love, but also a British secret agent reporting Nazi activities back to Whitehall by shortwave radio.*

Greta would be the logical one for Dieter Zeis to turn to if he needed help. But, why was Jack so interested, and what did Reinhart Gehlen have to do with anything? Somehow Cindy had the feeling everyone, including her grandfather, was connected.

Jack had corporate business to attend to in Manhattan that would keep him busy for about a week. Cindy now had time to pal around with Grandpa John before she would leave for England. They would fly into Hatfield Airport just north of London where Jack had a hanger for his jet.

Cindy decided not to quiz her grandfather anymore on the subject of the CIA, Gehlen, or Dieter Zeis. She would make the next five days as enjoyable for the both of them as much possible. John Krauss was relaxing for the first time in several years. The ordeal of taking care of his wife had been a great strain. It wasn't that she had to be waited on for nearly everything, but he couldn't remember when he had gotten a full night's sleep. Harriet would get up in the middle of the night and wander about the house. On one occasion, John found her walking down the middle of the street in her nightgown at 2 am.

---

* "Nebraska Doppelganger," Chapter 4.

He couldn't afford to go into a deep sleep for fear his wife would hurt herself in some way.

Now, all that was behind him. John felt as if the weight of the world had been lifted from his shoulders. He said this to Cindy no less than a dozen times over the next few days. While he was sad that Harriet was gone, he knew she was in a better place. He was in a better place.

After five days of sightseeing, which included a couple of nice dinners, an evening at Radio City Music Hall, a cruise around New York Harbor, and a quick trip to the top of the Empire State Building, Cindy was saying goodbye to her grandfather as he climbed into an airport limo to take him back to La Guardia for the flight home.

"I'm sorry I couldn't give you what you wanted," he said, looking down at Cindy, giving her a kiss on the forehead. "I think you know what you need to do and I'm sure things will work out. It just can't come from me. I hope you understand."

Whatever "it" was, Cindy shook her head in agreement.

"I love you, Gramps. Take care of yourself," she urged. "If I get in a rut can I call you?"

"Well, I hope you'll call me even if you're sailing along on a super highway."

"You bet," she said. "I love you!"

"I love you too," he said through the limo's window as it pulled away and drove out of sight.

There went the one man she loved and trusted the most in her life. More so than her own parents; Grandpa John Krauss was her anchor. The one person she truly believed in. He helped her financially through the University of Missouri and has been her biggest fan throughout her journalistic career. So, it was odd how quiet this complex man had been during his week's visit with her in New York. They talked about everything *but* what was really on their minds—his past. Or, at least that part which he wasn't about to talk.

The flight to London was seven long hours. It didn't seem like it should take that long, but Cindy utilized the time to finish up a couple of articles she had been working on, and more importantly, quiz Sir Jack a bit more on just what it was she's supposed to be working on.

Cindy got the distinct feeling Jack knew more about what it was he was prodding her toward than he was letting on. The corporate jet took off around 9 pm so as to arrive at Hatfield by 9 am London time the next morning. After taking off, Cindy and Jack were served a gourmet meal after which they briefly relaxed in the living compartment having idle chitchat about the day's news. After about an hour, Jack retired to the master suite in the forward compartment while Cindy stretched out on the bed in the rear compartment. The plane's steward assured Cindy she would be awakened 90 minutes before landing at Hatfield.

She had no idea what Jack had told Sam Hightower, her editor in New York. He sent her an e-mail saying that she was considered "on assignment" until the first of August. That's one month from now.

When Cindy awoke, the sun was brimming through the portal of her compartment suite. She quickly made herself presentable, changed into a business suit, and went forward for some breakfast. Having a short hairstyle had its advantages. Jack was already at the dining table reading overnight e-mails he had received via the plane's Internet connection. He looked up over his reading glasses, nodded good morning, and then went back to reading his missives.

The steward served her coffee and a light breakfast of Corn Flakes and fruit. Jack put away his laptop and began preparing himself a cup of English breakfast tea. Cindy realized she may never get the chance to talk with Sir Jack like this again. They were alone. The steward was back in the galley stowing away gear for landing. Now was her chance to poke back at Jack about what she was really looking for.

"What is it that I'm really looking for, Jack?" she began in the most direct manner she could.

"You're looking at why the Cold War really started. You're looking to amplify a lot of that information you've already uncovered via the Internet," he replied, not looking up from the cup of tea he was stirring.

"Yes, but why? A lot of this already has been written about. What is it you think I might find that will be a new angle?"

Now he was looking straightforward into her eyes from across the table.

"We know the Soviets and the Americans divided up the German intelligence and scientific spoils after the war. My country, Britain, got a few scraps. We were more or less in the middle, riding on the backs of Uncle Sam, who, as it turned out, wasn't very honest with us as his *most-trusted* ally." Sir Jack's British accent was, well, accented. Cindy could tell he was somewhat miffed about something.

"Cindy ... you have to realize that one ... for a short time I was an MI-6 agent. That's the equivalent of your CIA. Two ... I'm bound by oath not to reveal certain facts. Three ... if this story is ever to be told, it must be uncovered by an American. An English journalist wouldn't get the respect in your country that someone like yourself would ... and besides, it would only come off as you Americans would say ... *sour grapes!*"

"But why are you and Grandpa pointing me toward your mother?" Cindy asked. "Wasn't she a British Secret Service Agent during the war?"

"Yes, but as far as the Secret Service was concerned, anything they think she might know has long since been declassified ... pre-war stuff." Jack was sipping his tea.

Cindy sat there looking at him; then she smiled. It was as if a hundred watt light bulb had just been turned on.

"Ah, but she knows things MI-6 or the CIA doesn't know she knows ... right?"

Jack sat down his cup, tapped his mouth with his white cloth napkin, turned, and asked the steward for more hot water.

"You're getting the picture, young lady," he said without looking up as he prepared himself a second cup of tea. "You've met my mother. You know she's a tough ol' bird who doesn't suffer fools lightly. She and I have discussed her chatting with you. In fact, I've already made arrangements for you to spend the week with her at the estate."

Cindy was back at wanting to pinch herself for being in such a position of luxury. Two years ago she was a police reporter on the Nebraska State Journal. Then her grandfather tells her one fantastic story about how he had gone to the 1936 Berlin Olympics after graduating from Broken Bow High School.

He enrolled in pre-med at Berlin University where he met Greta, a widow 10 years older than him. Then, Grandpa John found himself being drafted into Hitler's Army after refusing to join the Nazi Party and ironically ending up being a valet for Field Marshal Erwin Rommel, Germany's famed "Desert Fox."

But John Krauss didn't get assigned to Rommel without the help and influence of one Lieutenant Colonel Dieter Zeis. Of the friends Grandpa John had in Germany, including Grandma Harriet, only one was unaccounted for—Dieter Zeis. Why?

The weather in London was, as usual, gloomy. It was July 1 and time for tennis at Wimbledon; so naturally, it would be raining. Why the English continue holding one of the world's greatest tennis classics during a month that historically brings daily showers was lost to Cindy.

Of course, the Rolls Royce Silver Cloud limo was waiting at Hatfield Airport for Sir John and his newest New York investigative journalist. The drive to Greta's palatial home near High Wycombe would take about 45 minutes.

Part of the drive was along M-40, Britain's idea of an Interstate Super Highway. The short trip gave Jack an opportunity to give Cindy a brief history lesson about the section of Buckinghamshire County they were traveling through. While High Wycombe is one of the larger towns in Buckinghamshire, the smaller West Wycombe was steeped in history.

When threatened by destruction back in 1929, the entire town of West Wycombe was bought by the National Trust for historical preservation. The picturesque village boasts several vintage buildings dating back to the 16th century.

Jack told Cindy about the area's most famous historical character, Sir Francis Dashwood, who founded the Hellfire

Club. Nearby are the West Wycombe Caves. In the 1750s the caves were excavated from an old quarry by Sir Francis, partly to give work to unemployed locals, and partly to create an out of the way spot for his debauching club to gather. One of the club's most distinguished members was Ben Franklin. Jack told Cindy that Sir Francis and old Ben used to hold some pretty wild parties in the caves.

The estate of Greta's late first husband, German-born Paul von Carlsen, was located in the historic county of Buckinghamshire just west and a bit north of London. It looked every bit like one of the many English country estates Cindy had seen in movies and slick magazines.

As they drove along the two-lane country road, the mile long row of thick trees served as a veiled curtain depriving passing motorists from seeing the wonderfully manicured lawn and gardens of the Beckham Manor. Passers-by could only steal a quick glimpse through the iron-gated entryway to the sprawling square graystone mansion at the end of what seemed like a mile long driveway. After her second husband Sir Lawrence Beckham died in 1947, Greta decided to rename the estate.

The Rolls Royce meandered up the long entryway and around the circular drive where a formally dressed butler with thinning white hair was waiting. Cindy reckoned his age was well past retirement, maybe late 80s.

"Welcome home, sir," the elderly butler said opening the limo's rear door, greeting Jack. "Your mother is in the library."

"Thank you, Somes. You remember Miss Krauss, don't you? She'll be visiting here with Mother for the week. Let's make her as comfortable as possible." *

"Yes sir… and very good, sir."

Cindy was back pinching herself. It was a scene right out of Agatha Christie. It was all simply too wonderful. It was elegant. It was grand. It was, well, English!

Walking through the huge 10-foot high doorway of the mansion was like entering an English aristocrat's home of the 19th century. The entry hallway had two large shiny suits of

---

* "Nebraska Doppelganger," Chapter 24.

armor standing at attention as they guarded each wall. The hallway then opened into a large circular foyer where a 14th Century Yuan Dynasty white cloisonné vase, half filled with fresh-cut Graham Thomas golden roses and a half dozen of the Fair Bianca, adorned the center table. Cindy just knew the vase had to be a valuable antique. The center circular table looked as though it also had some history based on the dark glowing rosewood patina.

There were two stairwells, each hugging the side of the foyer leading to the second floor. On the right side of the circular foyer was a double set of doors leading to the library.

Somes, the butler, quietly summoned two housemaids to take the luggage up to Cindy's room. Jack gingerly guided Cindy through the double doors into the library where Greta was sitting in her wheelchair by the largest fireplace she had actually ever seen. She remembered seeing a large fireplace in the movie, "Where Eagles Dare." But eventually Clint Eastwood blew it up. Good spy movie she thought.

"There's my little friend," Greta exclaimed, holding her arms open to embrace Cindy. The old sage's greeting was purely genuine and Cindy truly felt welcome and at home in what had to be the biggest house she had ever been in. It honestly was a breathtaking experience.

"I was so sorry to hear about your grandmother," Greta solemnly said. "Is your grandfather okay?"

"He's doing fine. Thank you for asking," Cindy replied. "I believe Grandpa John is actually relieved that it's over. He's been through a lot over the past couple of years."

Jack had gone up to the second story study while the two women chatted and reacquainted themselves. Cindy had previously met Greta two years ago when her grandfather brought her to London to meet Sir Jack and also resulting in her landing the New York job at Beckham's as the US National Correspondent.[*]

Cindy was amazed at how young Greta looked compared to her nearly 100 years. Her bright violet eyes were as sparkling as ever. While she could walk on her own, Jack insisted his mother use a wheelchair ensuring she wouldn't fall. He had an elevator installed behind the circular stairwells that could accommodate her wheelchair and lifting her to the second floor and her bedroom. The house had a third floor accommodating six large bedrooms. They were reserved for guest when large numbers were invited for weekend retreats.

The two women chatted, exchanging small talk for about 20 minutes.

"You're probably tired from your trip, so why not go up to your room and get some sleep," Greta suggested. "We'll meet this afternoon about 4 pm for tea. That will give you a few hours to get some rest."

Greta assured Cindy if there was anything she needed, Somes the butler would take care of it.

The old butler, who walked smartly as if in a military procession, escorted Cindy to a second floor guestroom, which adjoined Greta's large bedroom suite. The guestroom was more like a hotel suite with a king-size bed. A small sitting room overlooked the rear of the mansion where a huge patio and swimming pool was located. The neatly manicured lawn stretched far beyond the patio and pool seemingly rolling all the way to the North Sea—or would that be the Irish Sea.

Cindy learned from her first trip to England not to go to sleep after flying across the Atlantic. The jet lag can be uncomfortable and throw your personal time clock haywire. A shower would be helpful, but she decided against one.

"I'm just going to relax after a small snack and try to stay awake until my regular bedtime tonight," she thought.

Her best intentions melted away when she stretched out on the bed. The next thing she knew, Greta was knocking on her door.

"My dear, you need to get up and have some tea with me out on the patio," Greta said through an open door that adjoined with her suite.

Cindy was groggy from her four-hour nap. After finally taking a quick shower, she was now fully awake and felt surprisingly good. She slept for three hours on the plane, and together with the last four hours, she was ready to go.

Greta was sitting on the patio beside the pool when Cindy joined her. As expected, it had rained earlier in the afternoon; now the sun was putting a bright, sparkling sheen on the brilliantly green countryside. To Cindy the English landscape seemed surreal and something out of a Jane Austen novel.

She forced herself to focus on why she had come to England. Cindy learned early on in her journalistic career that the best approach was the direct approach.

"Has Jack told you why I'm here?" she began.

Greta smiled, put down her cup of tea, reached over, and took Cindy's hand.

"Yes dear, I know. So … why don't we begin? Ask me what you want. I'll try to answer as best I can, but I'm not guaranteeing you'll get what you want."

Cindy thought it was all too easy. The question she really wanted to ask was *"What the hell is going on?"* But, Cindy reckoned she'd go along and play this game.

"Well, as you know, Grandpa John told me his story about being with you in Germany and how he had been drafted into Hitler's Army," Cindy began. "He then told me how he had been the valet to Field Marshal Rommel and how he was sent back to the States as a prisoner of war."

Greta sat quietly, smiling, shaking her head in acknowledgement.

"I know that Grandpa had an easier time of it in Germany primarily due to the help he got from you and Lieutenant Colonel Dieter Zeis. I know what happened to you; but my compelling question is *what ever happened to Dieter Zeis?*"

Before speaking, Greta curtailed her smile as she prepared herself another cup of tea. "Well, as you know, Dieter was my brother-in-law," she began. "He was married to my first husband's sister. Although he was never a member of the Nazi Party, he managed to rub shoulders at the highest levels. Dieter became one of the few officers Rommel trusted.

"I've never told anyone this, but it was Dieter whom Rommel assigned to make a plea for an honorable peace with the Allies."

"I'm not familiar with that," Cindy said. "What was he supposed to do?"

"About a month and a half after the D-Day landing in June 1944, a group of officers, including Rommel, tried to kill Hitler," Greta continued. "In the first few hours when they thought they were successful, Rommel sent Dieter a message to proceed with their plan. Dieter was stationed near the front in Belgium. His orders were to somehow make it to England and contact directly with Churchill or Eisenhower as Rommel's personal representative.

"Dieter showed up here in Buckinghamshire dressed as a Royal Army Major," Greta said. "He had slipped behind the lines as a British officer and managed to get across the Channel aboard a Dutch fishing trawler. Of course the fishermen had no idea they were taking a German to England. They thought he was just some poor chap trying to get back to his unit."

"So … what happened when he arrived here in England?"

"Well … by the time he finally got to my place, Rommel was dead … so now, Dieter had no one to represent and nothing to bargain with. The original plan was for Rommel and his comrades to deliver an end to hostilities on the German side. When their assassination attempt on Hitler failed, so did their plan."

"So … what did Dieter do?" Cindy asked.

"Well … nothing. What could he do? Dieter thought about surrendering himself, but I talked him out of it, or at least until after the war. But in the meantime, he stayed here with me. After a few days, it was thought we should still make some plans to deliver Rommel's message even though he was dead. With my connections, I then tried to figure out a plan to get him in to see Eisenhower. He would be easier. Churchill would be impossible."

Chapter

4

Lady Greta Beckham didn't look her 99-year age. Born in Dusseldorf in 1908, she has outlived two husbands and enjoyed citizenship in three countries. Cindy remembered Greta's basic biographical information given to her by Grandfather John Krauss. She immigrated to the United States in 1923 to live with an aunt, then returned to Germany in the 1930s and married playboy flier Paul von Carlsen, a Prussian Aristocrat. Paul was a test pilot for noted aircraft designer and builder Willy Messerschmitt.

Paul was wealthy and, because his mother was English, he inherited her family's estate here in Buckinghamshire. When he died in a mid-30s plane crash, Greta suspected foul play on the part of the Nazis. She didn't believe the *accident* report given to her. Paul was not a believer in the Nazi line, nor what Hitler was doing. He was convinced Germany was headed down a path of destruction and didn't hide that opinion.

After his death, Greta was approached by a diplomat from the British Embassy in Berlin about serving as an espionage agent. She was secretively performing this task when she first met young John Krauss in 1936.

When Greta returned to England in late 1938, she continued working for the British Secret Service, even though she was pregnant with John Krauss' son. After "Little Jack" was born, she became involved with a program that eventually led to *assisting* the United States with its new intelligence agency—the Office of Strategic Services, better known as OSS.

From 1939 until 1943, Greta briefed British and OSS agents about the German culture, customs, and language. She gave classes outlining the various levels of power from the lowest Gestapo agent to the many tiers of generals in the German High Command.

In early 1943, OSS Director William Donovan created the counterintelligence branch known as "X-2" to provide the British Secret Service with a liaison office in OSS for sharing intercepted and deciphered German intelligence information gleaned from Project "ULTRA." Without the Allied intelligence gathering information from ULTRA, intercepts from Germany, and "MAGIC" intercepts from Japan, the war might have been lost.

In those early days of the war, the OSS didn't enjoy the confidence of the US Military. While the Army and Navy had their own intelligence-gathering mechanisms, the uniformed services shared only a small portion of their intelligence information. With the Pentagon's approval and backing, the Army and Navy refused to give Donovan and his OSS a role in procuring or analyzing enemy signals; however, there was an important exception. The X-2 made good use of ULTRA intelligence from Germany; by the end of the war the OSS had established itself as a formidable practitioner of clandestine operations.

Because of her position with the British Secret Service, Greta became acquainted with various key figures between both the British and American intelligence services. For a time she was assigned as a liaison officer to the OSS. On a number of occasions, she attended briefings, meetings, and after-hour cocktail socials where top US Military leaders were in attendance, including Supreme Allied Commander for Europe, General Dwight D. Eisenhower and his staff.

Greta's primary job was to not only serve as a senior go-between for the British, but also keep an eye on the Yanks who were new to the war and intelligence gathering. She soon discovered the cousins from the west side of the Atlantic learned how to play the spy game quite quickly and proficiently.

The ULTRA intercepts by the OSS from the Third Reich greatly assisted the British in capturing every German agent in the United Kingdom. Some of the arrested Nazi spies were turned into double agents; who, as a result, sent a flow of plausible, albeit bogus, information back to Berlin. The ones who refused to turn were shot. At this point, it was all part of war.

While the British certainly wanted American assistance, they didn't quite trust the OSS as an organization. The British insisted the Americans mirror their own security practices of keeping colleagues in the dark and on a "need-to-know" basis in order to protect the intelligence-gathering techniques of ULTRA. This was done so the Germans wouldn't be tipped off and change their message procedures or codes. The Brits mistrust only made the Americans more efficient at espionage.

October 15, 1944: Lieutenant Colonel Dieter Zeis was fully dressed out in a British Royal Army disguise making his way to the coast of the English Channel. Obtaining a uniform and identification tags was easy. There were plenty of dead soldiers from both sides littering the battlefield. The plan was to blend into one of Monty's smaller British units in order for him to somehow make his way across to England. His opportunity came sooner than expected.

Near the French-Belgium border just south of Calais, France, which was the closest point across the English Channel to Dover, Dieter encountered a squad of eight British enlisted infantrymen who had taken two German Waffen SS officers as prisoners.

Dieter found himself being the only British "officer," so the English soldiers gladly turned to him for leadership. The two SS officers, one a lieutenant and the other a captain, were sitting on the ground with their hands tied behind their backs. They were visibly frightened—not because of the Englishmen, but because of the two French Maquis resistance fighters that were standing nearby. Dieter knew if the Germans were handed over to the

French, their fate would be sealed in agonizing torture. The Maquis was notoriously brutal in their interrogation tactics, almost to a point the Gestapo and SS could take lessons. Dieter was in a precarious position. He had to be careful lest he found himself joining the two SS officers.

The British tommys were quite proud they had captured their enemy, and the two Frenchmen were quite eager to take them away. Dieter found himself going into a mode that was unknown to him. He knew what had to be done.

They were in a small gully with a creek and surrounded by a strand of trees. Automatically, Dieter ordered the two Frenchmen and six Brits to fan out and protect their perimeter. Two soldiers stood guard over the Germans. Dieter was furtively surprised when everyone instantaneously followed his orders.

"The Geneva Convention requires we be treated with utmost courtesy and with humanity," the English speaking German pleaded.

"Yes … I've seen some of that *humanity* your Gestapo and fellow SS Guards have dealt to British captives," Dieter replied.

Hearing that, the two German captives were clearly getting nervous. The other German was sobbing telling Dieter he had a wife and child waiting for him back in Germany. Dieter acted as though he didn't care what he was saying.

If he allowed the French to capture them, they surely would be tortured. If the Brits took over them, they would undoubtedly be humanely treated; but what if Dieter was discovered? Would he later be recognized by the two SS officers? He could not take that chance; immediate action was required.

Dieter quickly walked behind the German officers and without hesitation, pulled out his service revolver and fired one shot each into the back of their heads. One man fell forward burying his face squarely into the ground. The other officer fell to the right; distortedly positioned, his face half cocked on the ground, his eyes wide open, blood oozing from his open mouth. The gory scene was indelibly fixed in Dieter's mind.

The action was quick and to the point. The Brit guards were startled, then relieved. It was the first time Dieter fired shots in anger at anyone—and it was at his own countrymen. He wanted to get sick.

"Unbelievable? Surely. Unforgivable? Never!" Dieter thought.

"Monty says we don't have time nor facilities at this time for prisoners," Dieter authoritatively declared in his best English accent. "Bury them as quickly as possible. I need to get to the port of Calais. The essence of time demands it!"

Dieter didn't allow time for regrets. That would come later during many sleepless nights. Those brief seconds of deliberate action would haunt him; the scene would forever be etched in his memory.

The two Frenchmen became visible angry when arriving back at the gully.

There it was—nothing left but to carry out Rommel's order.

The two French fighters stomped off, grumbling as they headed south; the squad of Brits accompanied their new leader north to Calais. Somehow, Dieter would figure a way to get across the Channel. It was now time to perform.

October 19, 1944: It was 2 o'clock in the morning when Dieter Zeis arrived at Greta's mansion in Buckinghamshire. He had hitchhiked from the coast and it was, he thought, surprisingly easy. Englishmen were quite proud of their uniformed servicemen, especially officers. The rank of major he wore on his shoulders obviously helped.

Not knowing who might be present in the mansion, Dieter made himself comfortable in the pool house in the rear.

The following early morning sunlight cascaded through the pool house window gently prodding Dieter from slumber. After sitting on the edge of the bed to fully awaken, he then went into the small bathroom where he splashed water on his face. He washed his hands and then looked into the mirror, straightened his British green combat uniform and black beret realizing if he was caught in this uniform he was a dead man. After several moments of thought, he smartly walked toward the mansion. Through the drawing room window, he could see Greta sitting, reading a newspaper. Her peripheral vision caused her to turn. She couldn't believe her eyes when she saw her old friend standing at the window. He walked to the rear door.

"Mrs. von Carlsen, I'm Major Derek Eaton-Jones," Dieter said professionally as Greta opened the door. He didn't know who might be with Greta, so he continued his ruse.

"It's all right Dieter … I'm alone," Greta said, embracing her brother-in-law and giving him an affectionate kiss on the cheek. "I've been so worried about you. I was beginning to think you had been caught up in that nasty little paper hanger's assassination attempt."

"No … I managed to elude notice," he replied. "I'm here on orders from the Field Marshal."

"Rommel? Haven't you heard?"

"Heard what?"

"German radio reports Rommel died as a result of wounds he received from that strafing incident back in July," Greta told him.

"Nonsense," Dieter brusquely replied. "If he's dead … they've killed him! I saw him four weeks ago and he was well recovered from his wounds. No … if he's gone, it wasn't at the hands of the Allies or any war wounds."

Dieter sat, staring out the window toward the sprawling manicured lawn and garden at the rear of the Dames mansion. He didn't say anything for several minutes. Greta sat quietly, waiting for him to speak again.

"Well … I'm behind enemy lines wearing a British uniform … so if I get caught now, I'll probably be shot as a spy," Dieter said, half chuckling. "With my commanding officer dead … who's going to believe anything that I have to say now? I'm here on a diplomatic mission … but with Rommel gone, there is no one to deal with. The rest of the German officer corps won't have the fortitude to stand up to Hitler."

"What sort of diplomatic mission?" Greta asked.

"I was ordered to talk directly with either Winston Churchill or General Eisenhower to tell them there could be a ceasefire … however, that depended largely upon getting rid of Hitler and his gang," Dieter explained. "I really don't know exactly how Rommel planned on arranging such a peace, but he felt confident there was enough sanity left among the officer corps on both sides to make that a possibility."

Greta thought for a minute. She knew Dieter was right. He was definitely in danger of being assumed a spy, portraying himself as a British officer—an officer that had been killed in action somewhere in Belgium.

"I want you to stay here with me," she said. "There's only my maid and butler with me and my son. My husband.…"

"Husband … son? I didn't know.…"

"Yes … I'm married to a British Army Officer. Lawrence is a major in the Black Watch. He's assigned in Scotland and doesn't get home but about once a month."

"You said something about a son," Dieter probed.

"Yes. That's why I left Berlin. I got a bit careless."

"John?"

"Yes. Oh … he's here in England you know!"

"No, I didn't know. The last time I saw him he was in North Africa. I left with Rommel and returned to Germany. And the Korps … well, they had to surrender. I assumed he was taken prisoner of war."

"Well … he's here in England," Greta told Dieter. "He's a member of an American intelligence unit. They call it the Office of Strategic Services."

Dieter was dumbfounded. How did John end up in England with the Americans and assigned to a unit with such a mundane moniker?

Greta told him what she knew of John's odyssey that followed after being taken prisoner by the Allies in North Africa. His trip across the Atlantic and long railroad trip to a POW camp in the American Middle West—a far off place called Clarinda, Iowa. She told Dieter about how he escaped to his home near Broken Bow, Nebraska, only to find a military conscription summons waiting for him from the US Army.

Dieter softly laughed.

"Poor John. He hasn't had very much luck over the past few years … has he?"

"Well, he considers his time with the Field Marshal as one of his best experiences … and you as one of his best friends."

"Yes, I suppose he's right. But, he never should have been pulled into the German Army in the first place. I tried to protect him as much as I could."

"Yes, I know you did … and John knows you did as well," Greta said.

"Does he know about his son?"

"Yes, I told him just the other day," she replied. "I saw him for the first time since leaving Germany. He's training for some sort of mission, but that's all I know." [*]

Greta ordered breakfast from her maid while they continued talking and catching up with more than five years of their respective lives.

She didn't exactly know what to do about Dieter, or to whom she would talk, but she knew he couldn't present himself to the British until there was a plan.

Greta had her butler, James, put "Major Eaton-Jones" in one of the second floor guest rooms. She brought in some of her husband's clothes: underwear, toiletries, and personal gear, since her houseguest arrived with only the clothes on his back— a British officer's uniform.

Later, Greta gathered James and the housekeeper, Helspeth, into the drawing room, telling them Major Eaton-Jones was an old family friend on leave from the war—none of which was a lie—except for the phony name. Dieter actually was a relative, an understandable situation; but being a German officer absent from the war probably wouldn't be fully understood by Greta's servants, no matter how loyal they may be.

James' oldest son was a downed Lancaster bombardier airman POW being held in Stalag Luft I near Barth, Germany; Helspeth lost her only child on D-Day somewhere on a beach in

* "Nebraska Doppelganger," Chapter 20.

Normandy. Both were loyal service staff; they had definite opinions about Der Führer and his attempt at world conquest.

Greta drove herself into London where she had a meeting with intelligence officials at Whitehall. She was to attend a briefing in one of the Cabinet War Rooms that were built underground along King Charles Street near Downing Street. Sir Winston was known to have spent many sleepless nights prowling the various offices that were constructed there beneath Clive Steps.

Her mind wasn't on the briefing that was attended by both the Americans and British. What was she to do about Dieter? While she had a number of friends and acquaintances in the British Secret Service, Greta didn't have a clue as to whom she should trust with this problem.

"Maybe the best way to handle things was the direct approach," she thought. *"Besides, Dieter could be of tremendous help to the intelligence services of both the British and Americans. But, would he be willing to cooperate?"*

Greta thought about the problem further. She began going over the various officials who might be interested in helping. The more she thought about it, the more she realized this could be a valuable intelligence coup for her and the Service.

During the meeting at Whitehall Greta was only half-aware of what was being said. She continued to ponder Dieter's fate. He had information on the inner workings of the various top German commands, but would he betray the Fatherland? It might be the only way to save Germany and ensure the defeat of the Third Reich. It might also be the only way to save his own fate.

When Greta returned to the mansion, she found Dieter sitting beside the pool reading the daily newspaper. The German Army was in retreat towards the Rhine and the Allies had stepped-up day and night bombing raids all over major German cities.

"The end can't be far away," he said, not looking up from the paper. "The Germany we knew is gone, Greta. What the Allied bombers haven't destroyed, Hitler and his henchmen have. I don't know if I ever want to go back."

Greta didn't say anything. She slowly sat down. Dieter looked up.

"What is it?" he inquisitively asked.

"I've been thinking about your situation and what to do," she began. "Would you be willing to talk with someone at Allied Headquarters?"

"Well … that is what I came here to do … but I was directed to talk only to Churchill or Eisenhower. How can I do that?"

Greta sat studying Dieter's face.

"I can get you in to see Bedell Smith," Greta finally said.

"Who?"

"General Walter Bedell Smith. He's Ike's Chief of Staff. No one gets to Eisenhower without going through Bedell. It'll be easier than trying to get to Winston … too many politicians around that ol' charmer. Ike is different. He's a no-nonsense chap. You'll like him … that is, if he likes you."

Dieter pondered the suggestion.

"How are we going to make this approach? I mean, I just can't waltz in and say 'Hi General Smith, I'm a Lieutenant Colonel from the German Heer and I'm here to talk to you about ending the war'."

Greta laughed.

"No … I think we'll be a bit more clever than that," she replied. "But … maybe not much."

Chapter

5

Compared to the British, the American OSS agents were neophytes in intelligence gathering. When the United States joined the war after the attack on Pearl Harbor, President Franklin Roosevelt was anxious to develop US intelligence services, both civilian and military.

William Donovan was brought to Roosevelt's attention in 1940 by the new US Secretary of the Navy, Frank Knox. Although FDR didn't know him when they were in college, Donovan had been a fellow classmate at Columbia Law School many years earlier.

Donovan's first intelligence assignment was to test the resolve of the British. Prime Minister Sir Winston Churchill was urging FDR to support his nation in its desperate battle against Nazism. Without any of his staff's knowledge, FDR secretly requested Donovan visit England and report on how well Whitehall's staying power would be against Hitler. It didn't take long for Churchill to catch on to Donovan's mission. The Prime Minister granted Donovan unconditional access to many of Britain's defense and intelligence secrets, even taking him on a tour of their outposts in the Mediterranean—including "Fortress Gibraltar."

Upon his return to Washington in 1941, Donovan reported directly to the White House assuring the President that the British, if properly supported, could hold out indefinitely against Germany. FDR was impressed with Donovan's report and grasp of intelligence and its use during wartime. Soon after Donovan's return trip from England, Roosevelt made a decision that would force the Army and Navy to cooperate with US civilian intelligence gathering efforts by creating the Office of

Coordinator of Information later named the Office of Strategic Services.

As the Director of the OSS and a representative of the Joint Chiefs of Staff at the Pentagon, FDR saw fit in March of 1943 to commission Donovan a brigadier general. By November 1944, Donovan commanded thousands of OSS civilian and military personnel and was summarily promoted to major general.

October 25, 1944: Greta had thought about the problem of getting Dieter into General Eisenhower's office. However, she had another problem. As a senior member of the British Secret Service, she was obligated to bring Dieter's presence to Whitehall's immediate attention before introducing him to the Americans. But, she knew Dieter would never get to talk to Churchill. If she could get him in to see General Walter Bedell Smith, it would be the same as talking to Ike himself.

Dieter would have to continue his masquerade as a British officer in order to get inside Smith's office. Greta couldn't get past her original thought that maybe the direct approach was probably the best approach.

General Smith was the heavy hand of General Dwight Eisenhower—the enforcer and a general officer with whom to be reckoned. Though Ike himself could be tough, his reputation was that of an affable military commander. Having a tough-minded Chief of Staff like Smith was the perfect fit for the most powerful military commander of the Allied Forces. General Bedell Smith quickly became known as Ike's hatchet man.

He entered the military service as a private in the Indiana National Guard before World War I. Bedell acquired his salty manner from his early days as an enlisted man. In 1917, Smith joined the US Army as an officer in the Infantry Reserve, serving in France with the 4th Infantry Division.

In 1940, General George C. Marshall became the Army's Chief of Staff. In 1941 Major Smith was promoted to an Assistant Secretary on Marshall's Staff and then later to lieutenant colonel when he became a secretary on the Joint

Chiefs of Staff. In December 1942, when Supreme Headquarters, Allied Expeditionary Force Headquarters (SHAEF) was instituted, Smith was promoted to major general and assigned by Marshall to be Ike's Chief of Staff at SHAEF. In January 1943, he was promoted to lieutenant general. Ike would later call Bedell Smith the "greatest general manager" of the war.

At 10 o'clock every Wednesday morning, Greta personally delivered a Whitehall briefing packet to Ike's office at 20 Grosvenor Square.

Supreme Headquarters, Allied Expeditionary Forces was located in a simple, but elegant civilian graystone residence on the northwest corner of Grosvenor Square. This unique weekly access to Ike's Headquarters gave Greta an idea. She made note of the time on her next visit as to exactly how long it took her to walk from the street curb past the bevy of armed Military Police sentries stationed at the front of the mansion as well as the three different armed guards inside layered to the offices leading up to General Smith's office—one sanctuary removed from Ike himself.

To get to General Smith's office, the corridor took you through the front door past a US Army master sergeant, up the stairway to another sergeant, and then to 1st Lieutenant Bruce Durham's office, who was an aide to Bedell. Greta noted that during her weekly visits, Lieutenant Durham was occasionally interrupted from checking her in by taking outside phone calls. This meant it was possible to call his number directly from outside the building. And, she determined that Bedell was a man of strict habit. He was always there on Wednesday mornings during her visits. She knew this because when Durham received calls for Smith, he would clear them and then forward the caller directly into his office.

At her office on King Charles Street, Greta easily obtained Durham's direct phone number from the classified Allied liaison directory. On the following Wednesday, she made her usual visit to Grosvenor Square. Once she was past the two sergeants, she was cleared to Lieutenant Durham's office in exactly three minutes—the same time as the two previous visits.

The information that Greta carried was usually non-classified. Now that she new the time frame for getting to

Durham's office, she thought of a new angle that might work to get Dieter inside SHAEF.

"Lieutenant, I'll be sending a courier with a special classified packet tomorrow that will be 'Eyes-Only' for General Smith," Greta told Durham, a 25-year-old rusty-haired lad with tan freckles on a boyish face.

"What's it all about, ma'am?" Durham inquired.

"I'm not at liberty to say, but General Smith will definitely want to see the package immediately," Greta assured.

Greta knew she was taking a chance handling the situation in this manner, but she was positive Dieter's visit would not be received by her own government in the same way she could expect at SHAEF. Because she lost count of all the wartime violations she was committing by aiding and abetting a German officer, albeit on an unorthodox diplomatic mission, her career, maybe even her freedom, was at risk.

On Thursday morning at 9:59 sharp, Major Derek Eaton-Jones, aka Lieutenant Colonel Dieter Zeis, stepped from a black London cab in front of 20 Grosvenor Square carrying an attaché case chained to his wrist. He marched smartly up to the armed sentries, presented authentic-looking credentials, and was immediately passed inside to the master sergeant in the foyer of the mansion. By the time Dieter got to the second floor sergeant, it was 2 minutes, 30 seconds. As he approached Lieutenant Durham's desk, 3 minutes had exactly elapsed. Before he could speak, the telephone rang. Durham held up his hand in a pausing motion while he answered the phone. Dieter prayed it was Greta on the other end of the line.

"Yes?" Durham answered into the telephone.

Greta was on the other end of the line telling the American officer the British Major standing in front of him was carrying vital diplomatic information that must be handed directly and personally to General Smith.

"This is irregular ma'am … are you sure it has to be this way?" Durham asked in a puzzled way.

"To authenticate the officer of who he is supposed to be, tell General Smith to ask the Major what his relationship might he be to me?"

"And … what's the response?" Durham inquired.

"The Major should say 'brother-in-law'."

Durham held the receiver away from his head, making a frown as if not to believe what he was hearing, but then shrugged.

"You Limeys and your cloak and dagger routines," he chuckled. "All right, I'll send him in."

The lieutenant hung up, then called in to General Smith telling him about the courier who was there to deliver diplomatic information. Durham stood up, holding the phone in one hand and opening the door to the General's office with the other, motioning with his head for the visitor to go on in. Once the door was closed, Durham continued talking to the General, telling him about the instructions Greta had given him.

General Smith was a tall, stern-looking man who looked several years older than the 49 he had just turned back on the fifth of October. Dieter stood at attention, waiting for Ike's Chief of Staff to address him. Dieter had studied the British Army mannerisms, which weren't all that different from his own army. Of course he would have to refrain from the Prussian heal-click. That wouldn't go over well.

The General was leery of the situation. Without speaking to his visitor, he told Durham, who was still on the line, to call Greta von Carlsen at Whitehall.

"I want to speak to her personally!"

With what seemed like an eternity, General Smith began speaking again. It was obvious from his intonation and effervescent facial grin that he was well acquainted with Greta.

"Yes … all right," he said, abruptly hanging up the phone.

"Young man … what relationship are you to Greta von Carlsen?"

Still at attention, looking straight ahead, Dieter replied, "I'm her brother-in-law."

"I know Major Lawrence Beckham, but I was led to believe he has no brothers or sisters.…"

"I'm her brother-in-law from her first marriage … to the late Paul von Carlsen.

43

"He was a kraut … wasn't he?"

"Jawohl, Herr General. As am I."

"What the hell.…"

"Herr General … I am Lieutenant Colonel Dieter Zeis, personal representative of Field Marshal Erwin Johann Eugen Rommel sent here on a mission of peace."

"Rommel's dead!"

"Yes sir I know … but he was very much alive when I left the continent."

"Son, you know you could be shot for being here in that uniform!" General Smith said with a growl.

"I'm very well aware of my precarious position … but it was the ardent belief of the Field Marshal that something had to be done to stop the war and save what is left of Germany."

Bedell was now standing behind his desk with an even bigger scowl on his face.

"So … why did you come here to see me?" he demanded.

"My orders were to directly contact either Prime Minister Churchill or General Eisenhower. I'm here to report my General's request to your General," Dieter replied.

"Then what?" Smith probed.

"I'm to advise you of the growing numbers of German officers who wish to end this madness our Führer has gotten us into."

"Before that can happen, I'm afraid you're going to have to endure a rather harsh debriefing by our G-2 boys," Smith said, picking up the telephone.

"Have a couple of MPs get in here right away!" he snapped into the phone.

Within seconds two husky MPs arrived just outside General Smith's door.

"Escort this officer down to the basement conference room and hold him there until I give you further orders," he told the MPs. "And, make damn sure he's treated with respect. But make no mistake … he's under arrest until further notice!"

Dieter nodded with acknowledgement of General Smith's order. "I understand, Herr General. I will cooperate anyway that I can."

The two MP guards escorted their charge out of the office. General Smith immediately got on the phone, calling back Greta von Carlsen.

"What in the *hell* is going on here Greta?" Smith snarled into the phone.

"General Smith, you have before you a good, decent, and loyal officer who is trying to carry out the wishes of his commander," Greta replied.

"And what does that make you?"

"General ... I've been fighting the Nazis in my own way since 1935. Dieter Zeis, who was married to my first husband's sister, has been aware of my activities since I began working for the British Secret Service. If you know anything about the sort of man Rommel was, you'll have some idea of who Colonel Zeis is."

"How are you going to square this with your own people? I mean ... why didn't you just hand him over to the Brits?"

"Sir, only you and Lieutenant Durham are aware that I'm involved. If, after you're satisfied as to the validity of Colonel Zeis's mission, one way or the other, I'll leave it to you as to decide whether my name is brought up in connection with this affair. However ... it won't take a genius to figure out our former relationship."

"Well ... we'll see what your friend has to say," Smith said, slamming down the phone. He was irked that an enemy officer was able to penetrate SHAEF; and, with the help of a British agent no less!

"It's a goddamned strange war," General Smith mumbled to himself as he got back on the phone to call his top G-2 Officer about the situation.

"It's a goddamned strange war."

Chapter

6

For the next month Dieter was treated like a guest; but, nonetheless, he was a prisoner of war. The American G-2 interrogators were convinced Lieutenant Colonel Dieter Zeis was being truthful in what he was telling them—as far as it went. Allied Intelligence verified that Dieter was indeed Field Marshal Erwin Rommel's trusted administrative officer during the North African Campaign, and was the logistics specialist along the "Atlantic Wall" for the defense of Germany's conquered territory in France, Belgium, Luxembourg, Denmark, the Netherlands, and Norway. For the most part, what he was telling the Americans could be verified. It was what he wasn't telling them that perplexed his inquisitors.

Dieter insisted he had valuable, top-secret information that could bring an end to the war; but, if not handled properly, it could extend the slaughter indefinitely. Nevertheless, he would only talk to the very highest officials, as directed by Rommel.

Within days of surrendering himself, Bedell, at Ike's direction, reluctantly informed the British of the high ranking German officer's presence.

From SHAEF at Grosvenor Square, Dieter was taken to an isolated mansion on the Thames River north of Oxford University and told the British they had limited access to him. He made no mention of how the German officer got to SHAEF. For the time being, Greta was safe.

December 16, 1944: Bedell was hopping mad. The Germans had launched a massive counteroffensive in the Belgium's Ardennes Forest taking the Allies by surprise. Ike's Chief of Staff made a personal visit to where Dieter was being held.

Dieter no longer wore the British officer's uniform. Instead, was given a used suit of civilian clothes. The pants and jacket were bland brownish tweed; the shirt was gray, the tie non-descript, the shoes dark brown. So much for what Dieter had envisioned about the fashion of an English gentleman.

When informed of the massive German assault, Dieter shook his head.

"I could have told your Supreme Commander about this build up if you would have only trusted me," Dieter said solemnly.

"Why in the *hell* didn't you tell *me*?" Smith demanded.

"I was ordered to talk only with General Eisenhower or Prime Minister Churchill," Dieter replied. "My orders were very specific."

"Yeah, by a dead man. How do we know Rommel gave you such an order?"

"You don't. It was a verbal order. Such a directive would have been a death sentence for the both of us if the Gestapo or the SS found out," Dieter explained. "As it turned out, Herr Field Marshal has lost his life anyway."

"I can definitely tell you right now son … you are *never* going to meet with either Ike or Churchill. It just ain't gonna happen!" Smith said emphatically."

"Then I pray that the information I possess never becomes your nightmare," Dieter deadpanned his reply.

The December counteroffensive launched by the German Army became known as the "Battle of the Bulge." With 500,000 Germans and 600,000 Allied troops, the battle was the biggest single combat engagement in modern world history. There were more than 81,000 Allied troops wounded, 23,000 captured, and 19,000 killed. The Germans suffered more than 100,000 casualties.

Bedell Smith didn't believe Dieter had prior knowledge of the German counteroffensive, but when a G-2 officer pointed out the German already revealed he had been a logistics officer in Belgium, the General realized that maybe a different tact was needed in dealing with this prized enemy captive.

Dieter was having second thoughts about stubbornly sticking to his original orders of addressing either one of the two Allied leaders. Rommel *was* dead. Could the terrible Ardennes Battle been prevented if he had told SHAEF about the impending German offensive before the 16th of December? Probably not, but he did know about the massive buildup. He was part of it.

General Smith had his hands full managing the war. One daunting task was keeping prima donna commanders Field Marshal Bernard Law Montgomery of the British 21st Army Group and General George Smith Patton Jr. of the US Third Army separated. This in itself had become a full time job. And in between those two commanders were General Omar Nelson Bradley of the US 12th Army Group and General Charles De Gaulle, a symbol of the Free French. It was like juggling a three-ring circus with all participants fighting for center stage and the spotlight.

The US Army had what Smith thought were more important concerns. Thus, the disposition of Dieter Zeis, reluctantly, was transferred to the joint custody of the British Secret Service and the OSS.

February 2, 1945: The wind was bitter cold in Kiel where the U-234 was being refitted for a special mission transporting a very important cargo. The submarine was an XB Class Boat, the largest in the German Kriegsmarine (German Navy). Lieutenant Johann Fehler was its commander.

Of the six big mine-laying boats Germany built, only the U-234 and the U-219 remained. The 1,600-ton XB Class U-boats were slow and hard to maneuver. The other four became easy prey to Allied destroyers and patrol planes. Even the U-234 didn't escape the wrath of enemy bombers. It was badly damaged in

1944 requiring months of refitting. Now, an entirely different and highly secret mission was scheduled for her.

The berthing quarters aboard the 294-foot vessel was being adapted to carry a number of VIPs. Commander Fehler bristled at the thought of having to handhold so-called important personnel aboard his submarine—people who weren't going to be carrying their own weight, simply going along for the ride.

"There's barely enough room in this fish to breathe the way it is, let alone jamming unnecessary personnel and equipment into the boat's hull," Fehler thought.

Commander Fehler was an experienced seaman. He served as a senior officer aboard the infamous surface raider "Atlantis" before receiving his U-234 command.

The Atlantis was known in the Kriegsmarine as "Schiff 16;" to the British it was known as "Raider-C." The ship was a converted auxiliary cruiser. From 1939 until November 21, 1941 when she was sunk by HMS Devonshire, it traveled more than 120,000 miles in 602 days sinking 22 Allied vessels luring them close-in with its various disguises.

The Atlantis was a masquerade ship altering its superstructure outline with a dummy funnel almost at will. The crew numbered 350 consisting of 328 enlisted Marine-type troops. The raider carried a large supply of paint, canvas, and other materials for quickly altering the ship's appearance. This also included a supply of costumes for the crew and various national flags. The Atlantis was capable of being modified to mimic 26 different silhouettes on the ocean's horizon to unsuspecting Allied vessels.

Given its mission, the raider was one of the best-armed vessels in the German Kriegsmarine. The ship had four torpedo tubes, a 90-plus mine compartment, and two Heinkel built seaplanes. It was equipped with six 150-mm guns, a 75-mm bow-gun, two twin 37-mm guns, and four 20-mm automatic cannons.

All of the Atlantis' armament was hidden behind pivotal false decking. To top off the ship's disguise, a phony crane and deckhouse were located on the aft section where four 150-mm guns were hidden.

When Fehler arrived aboard the U-234, he was well trained and experienced in the art of deception and escaping enemy destroyers. Because of his skill and craftiness, he was handpicked by Admiral Karl Dönitz to lead this mission.

As various compartments of the boat had already been refitted, countless truckloads carrying top-secret cargo was methodically and carefully loaded starting deep within its bowels. There was so much matériel, it forcible displaced the usual storage for torpedoes; makeshift stalls had to be improvised—two were stored in the boats tubes, three were put under the deck plates, and the last two were stored on top of the deck plates. But the lack of a normal torpedo stock really didn't matter; this voyage was destined for transport—not pursuit.

Hans Uhlman, Chief of the Boat, estimated more than 235 tons of documents had been loaded on board, and it was still weeks before they were to sail. But to where? It was Fehler's first U-boat command and he had no idea when he was going to disembark.

One morning in March, Fehler heard a commotion of laughter and yelling coming from the ship's crew on deck. The Commanding Officer left his small compartment amidships and preceded topside where he found workmen making ready to load two disassembled Me-262 Jets and one Me-163 Rocket Fighter into the hold of his submarine. But, there were other items: one Henschel HS-293 glider-bomb, four Junker jet engines, ten canisters of uranium oxide, a ton of diplomatic mail, and more than three tons of technical drawings, fuses, armor-piercing shells, and one extra torpedo. It was all marked for Japan.

"Are you crazy?" Fehler screamed. "That cargo will never fit aboard unless you plan on having the boat run itself!"

"Herr Capitan, you will load everything aboard and all will be fine," said a thin, bespectacled man in civilian clothes. "Our loadmasters have made all of the necessary calculations for your refitting. I assure you that everything will fit with room to spare."

Fehler didn't know who the man was, but he was sure he really didn't want to know if the long dark trench coat and black fedora was any indication. These were desperate times. Good men were being shot for questioning less than this.

"Here are your orders, Herr Capitan," the man said, handing Fehler a packet sealed with the High Command's crest. It wasn't from Hitler himself but close enough. Heinrich Himmler had countersigned the orders. Fehler didn't want to know anymore.

The U-boat Commander went below to his compartment and, against Kriegsmarine policy, unsealed the packet. Fehler would not only be carrying the cargo stuffed inside his vessel, but there would also be nine passengers: Luftwaffe Lieutenant General Ulrich Kessler, two Luftwaffe Colonels, two Japanese officers, and four civilian rocket and jet experts.

The scheduled departure date was in three days—March 25, 1945.

Dieter Zeis was moved to yet another location just north of London. He wasn't quite sure where he was, but the German officer knew it was close to the city because he could hear an occasional explosion to what must be to the south of his location. He was told by his handlers that V-2 bombs were still falling on London.

His interrogators changed once again. There were two principal inquisitors: one Brit and one American. Occasionally other men and women entered the room to bring coffee and tea, and sometimes sandwiches. Dieter was now in a library of what seemed to be another mansion not all that different from Greta's. He had been blindfolded again when moved, so he wasn't quite sure where he was.

The two interrogators' mood was more relaxed than their uniformed counterparts from the US Army's G-2 branch. Still, they were dead serious to learn what Dieter could tell them; but, he was just as stubborn not to reveal anything important until he knew he could talk to someone who might make a some terrible weapons that, if unleashed, could kill thousands of people," Dieter began. "I'm not talking about soldiers in the field, but innocent civilians here in England and even in America."

"Go on," the American urged.

"Our scientists have developed a rocket that is capable of reaching New York."

The two agents looked at each other, somewhat astonished. The V-1 and V-2 rockets had played havoc here on England. There had been rumors of more powerful weapons, but nothing confirmed.

"Well, if such rockets were able to reach America, and, I emphasize 'if,' it wouldn't make much of a dent, would it?" Philby inquired. "Maybe a building or two."

"That's the part you don't understand," Dieter said, pausing and breathing heavier. He was about to reveal a well-kept secret.

"Are you familiar with atomic energy?"

Philby shook his head. The American had a somewhat blank look, and Greta started shaking her head from side-to-side—not from knowing what he was talking about but realizing such a weapon could be devastating.

"Our scientists have developed a way to mount a powerful, but terrible bomb atop a rocket that could kill several hundred thousand people."

"Impossible," Philby said in astonishment.

"Such a terrible weapon is possible," Dieter insisted. "It wouldn't kill many people from the initial impact or explosion, but because of the deadly gases emitted into the air, something called 'radiation poisoning,' it would infect thousands of innocent civilians. This deadly atmospheric poisoning would be carried by the prevailing winds over large populated areas and even as much as a third of the United States."

"Just where is this terrible weapon being built?" Philby asked in bewilderment.

"Well, that's one of the big problems we all have," Dieter replied.

"We?"

difference in the outcome of the war—specifically whether Germany would be brought to its knees or given an opportunity to surrender non-conditionally. Still, Dieter realized that as long as Hitler continued to live, surrender would never happen. After the bungled July 20th assassination attempt, he seriously doubted there would ever be another organized effort.

At his new location, Dieter was allowed a better grade of food. In fact, he was given a menu of choices with which to select. There was a lamb, fish, pork, and eggs—but no beef or butter. For their toast, the English used an unsweetened horrid-smelling fruit jam they called "Vegemite."

"We're in a war, ol' chap," the Brit told Dieter as he scanned what looked like a delightful menu.

"Don't get too excited," the American broke in. "We are, after all, in England and as you probably know, they have no cuisine."

All three men chuckled.

"That's fine," Dieter replied. "I've already eaten far better since I've been in your care than I have in the past two years. The last good meal I had was in North Africa … it was a fine leg of lamb roast prepared by a sergeant friend of mine. What a wonderful meal that was … yes indeed!"

The initial tactics used by the two civilian agents were more of a get-acquainted style and a review of the war to date. Dieter discussed his duties and role as administrative officer and confidant to Rommel during the North African Campaign. Dieter speculated that vast pieces of real estate probably could have ended up in Axis hands had it not been for Hitler cutting the Deutsches Afrika Korps' supplies.

"You don't think ol' Monty could have still won, do you?" the Brit asked.

"Do you?" Dieter countered. "Let's face it. We ran out of gas, we ran out of ammunition, and we ran out of food. All our supplies went to the Eastern Front. If it hadn't been for that, we would have ended up in Cairo and maybe even as far as Baghdad."

The American agent reckoned Dieter had a point. He acknowledged that until General Patton took over the US II Corps, things weren't going very well for the Yanks.

Dieter recognized this tactic of befriending and agreement. Why not go along? It had been a long time since he'd been involved in good conversation with intelligent men who weren't trying to conquer the world.

"If it weren't for those fanatics in Berlin, the war would be taking a far different turn," Dieter offered. "First of all, many of our general officer corps were not members of the Nazis Party … and, if they were, it'd merely be for expediency of their careers. It's the same with our technological industries and our scientific community. Many go along with the Nazi line just so they can do their work."

"What sort of work?" the American agent inquired. "Things like your buzz bombs and jet airplanes?"

"Ja, those … and many other things."

Dieter realized he was being probed. He had already made up his mind to reveal what he knew, but he thought taking his time and playing the game a bit longer wouldn't hurt—and it may even earn him a bit more respect. No one likes a quitter, or even a traitor. Would what he was about to reveal about his country make him a traitor? No, if given the right circumstances; he had information ordered by Rommel to be conveyed to the highest Allied authorities.

"My name is Philby," the Brit finally said, extending his hand. "You and I have more in common than you might think."

"And how would that be?" Dieter asked.

"Well … I'm married to an Austrian, whom I believe, would now be a fellow countryman of yours," Philby replied.

"Is she safe?" Dieter inquired.

"Very much so. We met in Vienna when I was with the British Embassy. I got her to safety before things got sticky," Philby replied. "Unfortunately … we're now divorced."

Philby was a dark haired, slight man with a pleasant face. He wore a typical English business suit with vest and gold chain that probably had one of those pop-open gold watches attached to the end.

54

The American didn't identify himself even when asked his name. He continued to make an occa comment about the war, usually one of compliment, to get the German to drop his guard. Dieter recognize understood this tactic. He was going to play along.

Just then the door opened to the study where Dieter a two agents were talking. Dieter couldn't believe his eyes. Greta.

"Gentlemen … my I have a word in private wi Colonel," she asked.

Philby looked at the American, nodded, and the two l room and closed the door; Greta entered, walked over, and the table.

"Dieter … you must cooperate in anyway you can, pleaded. "The Allies are closing in on Germany and it's (matter of time now. Is there *anything* you can giv Americans to help bring an end to all of this madness?"

He knew, of course, she was right. And, he did something that, while it might not help end the war, it coul(well prevent an expansion of hostilities.

"Do they know about us?" Dieter asked.

"Who?"

"Your people and the Americans."

"Not to the extent General Smith knows, but thes(agents are aware I have a *special interest* in you," she re| nodding her head toward the door. "They just don't kno\ what that might be."

"All right … bring them back in and we'll talk," he with a sigh. A feeling of remorse and relief hit Dieter all ; same time. It was as if the breath had been taken from hin the weight of the world lifted from his shoulders.

With the Brit and the American back in the library Greta remaining, Dieter began telling them of secret plans missions he was aware of that, if carried out, could chang(directions of the war in favor of the Germans.

"In spite of what you might believe about our indı being obliterated, which much of it has, Germany has devel(

55

"Yes. I'm not even sure Hitler is aware of exactly what's going on, not that he'd try to stop it. There is a group of fanatics in the German High Command who know the end is near, but they think Japan has a good chance of continuing the war and even winning it if they have this terrible weapon. The atomic technology our scientists have developed is being transferred to Tokyo where Japanese scientists are working on their own atomic weapon."

"How?" Greta asked.

"By submarine. I don't exactly know when or where, but it may have already happened," Dieter continued. "The Nazis are sending uranium oxide ore, all of our scientific data, and some key technicians to help the Japanese develop their own atomic weapon to drop on the United States.

"In nature, uranium is found as an oxide, such as in the olive-green-colored mineral pitchblende. Uranium oxide also is the chemical form most often used for atomic fuel, and that is what would be needed to build this terrible weapon," Dieter explained.

Greta was beginning to understand what Dieter's mission was. Rommel knew such a terrible weapon not only would extend the war, but also plunge Germany into a depth of criminality such as the world has never known. This had to be stopped.

Chapter

7

The U-234 departed Kiel, Germany, and headed north for the Norwegian harbor of Kristiansand. The sub would be escorted partway by two other Kriegsmarine U-boats, which would serve not only as protection, but also as decoys in case Allied spies were trying to track the secret mission.

In Norway, still more critical materials would be loaded onto the U-234 before departing on its long voyage to Japan. Commander Johann Fehler knew that, in order to avoid detection, he would have to stay submerged 22 hours a day and only surface for two hours in the dead of dark to recharge the batteries. If it was a moonlit night, running on top could be dangerous. Cloud cover would certainly help. The mostly underwater voyage to Japan would take many more weeks than a surface vessel, especially since a course had to be charted so as to avoid known Allied task force positions.

March 26, 1945: The English manor where Dieter was detained was guarded by a company of British and US Military Police, who were stationed both inside as well as patrolling the surrounding grounds. While these men were uniformed, only civilian agents came in contact with Dieter. As far as he knew, no other prisoners were being held at this location. He couldn't help but feel fairly important.

Agent Philby found Dieter and Greta in the dining room having breakfast.

"Our agents in Germany reported three U-boats left Kiel last night," Philby said with excitement in his voice. "Could one of these boats be the one you were talking about?"

"I don't know, but it's highly unusual for three submarines to be leaving port at exactly the same time," Dieter replied.

Harold "Kim" Philby was an experienced British Secret Service agent with overseas experience in Austria and Spain. A graduate of Cambridge University, Philby was born in India, the son of a British diplomat. He was the epitome of a highly educated English Aristocrat. Somewhat of a snob, Philby knew when to turn on the charm or when to be cleaver—even deadly.

Philby despised the Germans and, despite what he thought of the German Colonel in his charge, he was intrigued with the information Zeis had imparted. It was this type of knowledge that was valuable to the Allies and the winning of the war. Though, Philby had more personal reasons for finding this information of value.

April 1, 1945: In his Munich office, Major General Reinhard Gehlen was feeling fortunate; yet all the black uniformed SS officers with their dreaded Totenkopf insignias scurrying about the compound reminded him of rats running from a fire. The end was near and Gehlen knew it. The thousands of documents being collected from the offices for burning confirmed his thoughts.

Since the miserable failure of the Ardennes offensive in Belgium back in January, it was apparent that, anyone with common warfare knowledge, Germany could not hold out much longer. Gehlen's only hope for survival was to sell the Americans on his personal value as an intelligence expert—particularly his knowledge of the Soviet Union.

There was very little evidence Gehlen had ever bought into the Nazi Party. Although he joined The Party, it was a designed career move. He convinced himself of that; now he would have to convince the Americans when they arrived. Gehlen could ill afford capture by the Russians—not with his background.

Major General Reinhard Gehlen was Germany's foremost expert on Soviet affairs. He was directed by Hitler to head up all eastern intelligence. Gehlen was in a unique position to know exactly what to expect from the Russians and of their plans for dominating all of Europe once the war was over. After all, for the past two years, it was General Gehlen's gathered intelligence that Hitler used for directing all German battlefield tactics against the Russians. There would be no place for him with the Russians except in front of a firing squad—if he was lucky.

Since late December, Gehlen was carefully making plans for his postwar career. It had to be with the Americans, and it's doubtful they would take his word at face value. He needed proof. Gehlen was appreciative of the efficiency of his nation's pride and zeal for keeping records. All of the intelligence research gathered since the late '30s on the Soviet Union was carefully documented and in his possession.

Gehlen went about sifting through the countless pages of documents; extracting those he would need in the months to come convincing the Americans their need for his expertise. Documentation, after all, was validation, even if some of it were, well—exaggerated. If he knew anything about the Americans, he knew this: if they could read it, they could believe it.

Gehlen narrowly escaped being tied to the infamous July 20th attempt on Hitler's life at his East Prussian "Wolf's Lair" Headquarters in Rastenburg, Poland. He had known all along about the plot since first being approached back in 1942. Colonel Klaus von Stauffenberg, Colonel Henning von Tresckow, and General Adolf Heusinger revealed their plan to Gehlen for killing Hitler and installing a military tribunal government. Such a move could quickly bring an end to the war.

Gehlen tacitly approved of eliminating Der Führer but dared not expose himself anymore than necessary. Later, as a senior intelligence officer with privilege of office, Gehlen made available to the plotters certain conditions allowing them to carry out their plan. But when the effort failed, Gehlen covertly managed to cover up his involvement—thus escaping Hitler's wrath. Some 5,000 other *suspected* conspirators, including Field Marshal Erwin Rommel, weren't so lucky.

Gehlen's present task was assuring himself he had a saleable product. He would present himself along with a number of his colleagues as well as a great deal of valuable intelligence information. Plans had to be designed so his documents would not be captured. If that happened, there was nothing with which to bargain.

Gehlen carefully selected certain documents on the Soviet Army and political apparatuses he deemed would be useful to the Americans in the postwar period. He was fully aware of Josef Stalin's grand plan of European domination—possibly even the world.

He packed these microfilmed documents in a 55-gallon watertight steel drum and later buried it in an undisclosed location near a small mountain cabin retreat in the nearby Bavarian Alps of Southern Germany. He later in similar fashion buried backup materials just across the border into Austria. Gehlen trusted no one and did everything by himself. In the coming days, there would be no one to betray him. The reams of intelligence would be his and his alone for bargaining with the Americans; for they were the ones that had emerged as the strongest world power.

Gehlen figured his biggest problem was getting to the Western Front in all the chaos. That's where the Americans were. At the moment, he was too close to the east and that's from the direction the Russians were approaching. But, it would be the Americans with which Gehlen wanted to stake his future.

April 5, 1945: Major General Leslie R. Groves was receiving distressing reports from Los Alamos. There may not be enough enriched uranium to fuel more than one "gadget." A test would have to be performed to see whether or not the damned thing would even work. Oakridge had processed only a certain amount of uranium oxide up to this point, and Groves was told there may not be enough ore available for the test. The fuel of course could be processed, but it was questionable if there was enough time—and the lack of time was the essence of this problem.

Groves looked and dressed like a middle aged, overweight Army sergeant. His ill-fitting uniforms were always disheveled, and he sweated like a Bronx meat cutter. Of course, he had a $2 billion project resting on his shoulders—the most expensive single project ever undertaken in the history of the world. And, it may not even work. Groves was an Army engineer. He understood building things; but, for all he knew, what his small army of scientists and technicians were constructing in the mountains of New Mexico, the gadget *could* destroy the world.

General Groves reckoned his top-secret assignment came to him because of his ability to get things done while keeping his mouth shut. Groves was a no-nonsense, gruff-talking West Point graduate who had received his promotion to brigadier general when he was handed the assignment for carrying out the Manhattan Engineering Project. His office was at the Pentagon, but he was seldom there. He spent most of his time on a B-24 flying between Washington, New Mexico, Tennessee, and various Army Air Corps bases throughout the nation.

The secret OSS dispatches, courtesy of Bedell Smith at SHEAF Headquarters in England, reported the possibility that the Allies might capture some amount of uranium oxide ore from the Germans. This news elated General Groves as well as distressed him.

"The goddamned Germans are ahead of us building their own gadget," he thought to himself. *"Now they want to give it to the Japs! Great! And we don't even know if ours will work."*

But, if the OSS reports were true, and if the Navy could track down and capture the German submarine carrying this uranium oxide ore, then his worry of having enough fuel for the gadget would be alleviated. Nonetheless, those were two very big "ifs."

Gestapo Agent Conrad Krueger had just returned to Munich from Kassel where he had interrogated a captured American agent. He was now assigned as a Gestapo representative to General Gehlen. He found Gehlen in his office sifting through a pile of documents.

"Where have you been?" the general asked.

"On a mission to Kassel," Krueger replied. "We captured an American OSS agent. He was caught trying to destroy the engine and gun factory for our Tiger Panzers. He is a traitor of the worst kind—a former soldier of The Reich who betrayed the Führer by changing uniforms." [*]

"I doubt if he'll be the last to do that," Gehlen said.

"I fear you are right, Herr General."

"Krueger ... have you thought about what you'll do after the war," Gehlen asked, not looking up from perusing the papers in front of him.

"You mean after our glorious victory?"

Gehlen looked up at the Gestapo agent with a dull stare.

"You don't seriously believe we will be on the winning side ... do you?"

"The Führer has promised to unleash many secret weapons and...."

Gehlen held up his hand interrupting this fake zealot. A conversation such as this would normally be impossible, but Krueger and Gehlen have known each other since childhood, attending the same Catholic schools. The agent owed his position in the Gestapo to Gehlen.

Krueger wasn't able to pass the physical examination for the Wehrmacht; the "Geheime Staatspolizei" (Gestapo) was an alternative. Because of Gehlen's assistance to his old friend, there was a close personal relationship allowing them for frank discussions.

"I'm not waiting for the Führer to unleash his secret weapons. I'm making arrangements to be on the right side ... and I think we both know who that will be."

"How will you do that?" Krueger asked his friend.

"My dear Krueger, in times such as these, we must make ourselves indispensable to the victorious ... and to the victors belong the spoils, as the saying goes."

---

[*] "Nebraska Doppelganger," John Krauss, Chapter 22.

"I don't understand."

"With the knowledge I have collected on the Russians, I am in a unique position to be of value to their future enemy," Gehlen explained.

"What future enemy?"

"America! Do you not see it, my dear friend? There has always been a hatred for communism in the United States. Such a philosophy is a threat to America's precious capitalistic system. The Americans now find themselves allied with the Soviets only because of our illustrious Führer ... who in all his infinite wisdom, chose to pursue a two-front war. Adolf should have read 'War & Peace' before striking out into the east. If he had, he would have known it was impossible to win a land war against mother Russia."

"Maybe he did read that book," Krueger fathomed.

"I doubt it ... his ego is such that if he had studied history, he'd be convinced that he could do what Napoleon couldn't."

"So ... what makes you believe the Americans will be poised against the Russians?" Krueger's interest was piqued.

"The Americans are not our natural enemy as are the Russians," Gehlen replied. With our help, the Americans will be better equipped to combat communism in their next great struggle."

"How can you be sure such a struggle will occur?"

"It will happen," Gehlen said, resuming his examination of the papers on his desk. "Of course, I shall do what I can to assure it will."

"Whatever happens, Herr General, I would be honored to be at your side."

"Of course my old friend ... but maybe just a bit to the back of me, if you will. I'll need some protection!"

The two men chuckled together, although Krueger's laugh was a bit forced. He knew Gehlen was right about everything and certainly didn't want to be left behind. Being left behind would mean prison and maybe even a firing squad as a war criminal. General Gehlen could help ensure that it won't happen. Krueger stood ready to be of service to the general, *his* old friend, in anyway he could.

Friendship among Nazis was indeed a rare quality. In fact, it barely existed. A friendship with a comrade was simply for convenience. Loyalty was another matter.

Chapter

8

"Whatever can go wrong will go wrong." Kapitanleutnant Commander Johann Fehler wasn't sure whether the Irish had a coin on that phrase or not. On the night of March 28th, while approaching the Viking Bank off the Shetland Islands in the North Sea, a navigational glitch caused the U-219 to collide with the U-234 causing severe damage to the U-234s rudder. Fortunately for Fehler, he was able to steer his boat to Kristiansand Harbor in Norway. They were due to stop there anyway for more supplies, but now a repair was on the agenda.

After a lengthy delay, on April 15 the U-234 and the U-219 quietly slipped out of the Norwegian port to continue its long voyage to Japan. The third remaining sub was recalled back to Germany and returned just after the accident.

Their new charted course would take them west through the dark green waters of the North Atlantic, then south across the equator with a stop-off in Buenos Aires, Argentina. From there they'll continue onwards around the tip of South America into the cold deep blue Pacific.

Fehler was notified by the Kriegsmarine Command in Berlin that Allied Navies, patrolling the North Sea and the North Atlantic, had been tipped of the U-234's secret mission. So for at least the next two weeks, Fehler would remain submerged 22 hours each day, surfacing only two hours in the dead of night to recharge his batteries.

At the Mittelwerk rocket factory in the Southern Hartz Mountains near Nordhausen, thousands of slave prisoners were hard at work producing the dreaded "Vergeltungswaffen" (Revenge Weapon); or, as it was more commonly known—the V-2 Rocket. It was the brainchild of Germany's foremost rocket scientist, Wernher Freiherr von Braun. Though he held the rank of an SS major, von Braun had little or no interest in politics. SS Reichsführer Heinrich Himmler had *invited* von Braun to join the elite SS ranks, which he did, albeit reluctantly.

Nevertheless, von Braun's mission in life was sending rockets into space with the vision of exploring its vastness. Still, political disinterest or not, his current wartime mission was to build and launch his V-1 and V-2 rockets against Allied targets. It was a mission von Braun knew would end badly for Germany unless he did something to stop the rockets from raining death on its targets.

The V-1 rocket was the forerunner of the more devastating V-2 rocket; although, it still caused tremendous damage to the English population. Six days after the D-Day allied landings, the first V-1 was launched from a rail platform in the Pas-de-Calais region where it descended on a startled London population. From that day onward until June 20th, 8,000 rockets landed on the British capital killing 5,479 people and injuring 40,000 more. Better than 75,000 buildings were destroyed.

Because of the buzzing sound the rocket made while flying, Londoners coined it the "buzz-bomb." The rocket itself was a small pilotless jet-propelled plane that traveled at 400 mph on a predetermined course. It carried 2,000 pounds of explosives that detonated after it ran out of fuel and crashed. Considering the relatively slowness it traveled, swift airplanes, and antiaircraft guns were able to shoot 630 out of the air before falling on a target.

The V-2, on the other hand, was a supersonic rocket launched from secret bases located in and around the Netherlands. It was 48-feet long with a diameter of five and a half feet. It weighed 13-tons including a one-ton explosive warhead. The rocket could reach a speed of 3,500 mph with a 116-mile ceiling and a range of 225 miles making England an easy target. On September 8, 1944 the first V-2 was launched toward England, and by the end of the war over 1,000 had landed on the island with 600 directly hitting London causing 10,000 casualties.

Because of the speed and height with which this weapon could fly, it was virtually impossible to see or shoot down before crashing and exploding. When one of these weapons crashed and exploded, to Londoners, it literally came out of nowhere. It made no noise whatsoever beforehand.

In recent years, thousands of prisoners from nearby concentration camps had already been worked to death producing the V-1 and V-2 rockets; yet von Braun seemed oblivious to that fact. How much he knew and participated in this wholesale slave labor movement would be debated long after his death.

As brilliant and valuable as he was, the rocket master wasn't universally popular among the Nazi hierarchy. In 1944, he spent two weeks in a Gestapo prison, and for what he was about to do in order to save his people, von Braun could have been shot or hung.

Himmler had approved von Braun's 1944 arrest the previous year for having a defeatist attitude. Top Nazis thought he was paying too much attention to the moon, planets, and stars instead of focusing on defeating the enemy. With the Red Army closing in, von Braun was having the same postwar thoughts as was Reinhard Gehlen. Defeat was imminent—and it was coming fast. Walking to the Americans seemed much more comforting than running from the Russians. It was the clearest of choices and von Braun knew it. To accomplish this feat, it would require the cleverness of a thief and the dexterity of a sleuth. It was the direst of circumstances.

For the first time, being an SS officer had its advantages. It gave him a way to save his staff as well as himself. Von Braun assembled his senior scientists and asked them to whom they would rather surrender. Because of the known cruelty of the

Russians, nearly everyone von Braun polled voted to surrender to the Americans.

In an effort to save his valuable team of technicians and scientists, von Braun covertly swiped numerous blank sheets of official SS stationery and expertly forged a set of transportation and transit orders. This ruse enabled him to convoy the entire group by truck southwest through bombed out cities and towns where they could rally with the American forces near the Elbe River.

In the ensuing days, the SS quickly discovered von Braun's plan. In a desperate attempt to keep personnel, equipment, and records from falling into Allied hands, the Elite Guard was ordered to find and capture him and his fellow scientists, execute them on the spot, and destroy all vital records in their possession.

Von Braun and his huge 5,000-man team finally managed to evade the approaching Waffen SS troops and escape to safety. They had hidden delicate equipment and records deep inside mineshafts, keeping them from the pursuing German troops tracking them down. Meanwhile, rocket engineer Magnus von Braun, brother of Wernher, managed to reach the American lines ahead of the main convoy telling a young private who he was and what his brother was trying to do.

Realizing the importance of the scientific treasure-trove stashed in the all too hidden caves, the American area military commander immediately responded by sending two regiments of troops to Peenemünde and Nordhausen, just days ahead of the Russians, to seize control of the left over spoils. The technical prize netted 300 fully loaded railcars of assorted equipment, which eventually was transferred to the United States. Von Braun, along with many top scientists, went from portrayal as inhuman war criminals to top-secret government employees of the nation that defeated them.

Moving some 5,000 personnel was no small feat. Though, not all of the German scientists and technicians escaped to the American lines. Many ended up being captured by the Russians.

May 6, 1945: After the suicide of Adolf Hitler on April 30th, Admiral Karl Dönitz, the onetime top chief of the Kriegsmarine U-boats, was given the role of Supreme Reich Commander. As the top military authority, Dönitz notified the Allied Forces he was prepared to sign the Articles of Surrender. There was much to be done in the way of passing the news of the impending surrender to the thousands of German troops, airmen, and seaman across much of Europe and the high seas.

Admiral Dönitz was especially mindful of the secret mission of the U-234. He began sending out messages to his troops to surrender to Allied Forces effective May 8, 1945, when the official surrender was to take place.

Meanwhile, the U-234 continued submerged somewhere in the North Atlantic on its way around the world to the far Pacific. On May 10, Fehler surfaced to recharge batteries and check for radio messages. There was an important one waiting for him. When he received the transmission from Admiral Dönitz to cease all hostilities and surrender to the nearest Allied port, Fehler contemplated it might be a trick. The submarine commander was duly suspicious of deception upon the high seas having become a master of such tactics from his days aboard the Atlantis.

Kapitanleutnant Commander Fehler immediately submerged to consider if Admiral Dönitz' surrender message was valid. He immediately fired off a coded interrogator to the U-219 to see if that boat's captain had received any unusual messages from Berlin.

"Have we surrendered?" Fehler asked in the coded message directed to the captain. When the reply returned in the affirmative, Fehler, as directed, made preparations to follow orders of the Kriegsmarine by raising his periscope with an attached black flag. His next move, as ordered, was to contact by radio the nearest Allied port.

However, before he did this, he uncharacteristically polled his crew about whether they had any preference to whom they wanted to surrender. The reaction was mixed. Several of the younger crewmembers wanted to nix surrender altogether and head for the South Pacific and find some island paradise; the older seamen just wanted to go home and be with their families.

Imperial Japanese Navy Lieutenant Commander Hideo Tomonaga was a leading Japanese submarine designer, and Lieutenant Commander Genzo Shoji, an aircraft expert, had been in Germany studying the weaponry of the Third Reich. They became overtly despondent when told the U-boat must surrender. The two officers each retired to their cabins and took a powerful barbiturate. To them, committing suicide was a far better alternative than surrendering to the Allies.

When Fehler made his decision to surrender, the U-234 was positioned in the North Atlantic exactly where the Allied territorial zones of the United States, Canada, and Great Britain converged. He could take his boat to any port of the three—or return to a German port. But, Fehler quickly dismissed returning home because he was afraid the Russians might be there to greet them and that was a fate he didn't exactly relish.

The U-234 was able to contact Halifax, Nova Scotia, and was summarily ordered to proceed to that Canadian port. However, Fehler's choice was to an American port. He radioed back that he was proceeding on a northwesterly course toward Halifax at eight knots, when in fact he was going at double that speed in a southwesterly direction toward the American port of Newport News, Virginia.

One passenger of note on the U-234's VIP list was Lieutenant General Ulrich Kessler of the Luftwaffe. Kessler was the stereotypical German officer portrayed so many times in movies: black high-top polished boots; an impeccably tailored uniform; one eye sporting a monocle. He was the epitome of an arrogant Prussian Aristocrat. During the voyage, the officers and crew avoided him like the plague as they had nothing in common and were repelled by his aloof manner.

June 1, 1945: The mood of the Allied agents interrogating Colonel Dieter Zeis had dramatically changed since Admiral Karl Dönitz announced May 8 the surrender of Germany ending all hostilities in Europe. To ensure that all German units, including all U-boats at sea, surrendered quietly, new Reich

President Dönitz was allowed to continue the government for two more weeks. On May 23rd, what was left of the German government evaporated when the entire administration was arrested, including armament czar Albert Speer. Of course, many of its members would be tried for war crimes; all except Heinrich Himmler, the evil commander of the concentration camps, who died on this date when he bit into a cyanide capsule shortly after the British arrested him. In the meantime, nearly every high ranking American officer on the British Isles left and descended upon Germany.

The Potsdam Conference held July 17 thru August 2, 1945 was the final meeting of the "Big Three:" the United States, Britain, and Soviet Union, and was basically designed to implement the decisions reached at the Yalta Conference on February 4 – 11, 1945. One key decision was the subdivision of Germany into zones of occupation, which was a matter of convenience so the country could be governed by a central control council where all four powers would be represented. While France was not invited to the Potsdam Conference, and not originally assigned a zone in the occupation, it heartily clamored for one. With subtlety, the United States and Great Britain finally relented and decided to cede certain parts of their zones to France. Though, by the *first* of July 1945 and except for France, all zones were occupied by their respective governments.

The Eastern sector, which included Berlin, would be controlled by the Soviet Union; the South and Southwestern sector by the United States; the far Western portion of the country, known as the Rhineland, would be the French sector; and the North and Northwestern sector would be controlled by Great Britain. Even though the city of Berlin was in the Soviet zone, it also was subdivided into smaller zones by the Big Three and France.

Near Munich, General Reinhard Gehlen reached his goal and was being interrogated by US Army Intelligence (G-2) officers. Gehlen had done his homework. He was well aware of the various aspects of the Yalta Agreement made by President Roosevelt, Prime Minister Winston Churchill, and Marshal Josef

Stalin. According to the agreement, all German officers involved with the Eastern Front against the Soviet Union were to be turned over to the Russians. Gehlen was at the top of that long list of high ranking German officers.

Because of the information Dieter already had imparted to the Americans and British, particularly the secret mission of U-234 loaded with technology and equipment being sent to Japan, he was afforded the freedom of house arrest in the mansion and surrounding property as long as he didn't try to leave. In fact, whenever he would interact with any of the Allied agents and officers, he was treated as an equal—almost. He still was an enemy officer and it would take time for real trust to be acquired.

Dieter was all too aware that he was a prisoner of war from a defeated nation. Still, someone must think he has value because a high ranking officer from the US Army's G-2 Intelligence was about to quiz him on a number of subjects—namely the value of certain captured assets and personnel.

Introducing himself with a quick handshake, Colonel Howard "Bud" Hildabrand met Dieter in the manor's library. He invited the German officer to have a seat. In the room with them were two OSS agents and a British Secret Service agent. Accompanying the American G-2 officer was Captain Homer Van Dyke, an aide to Hildabrand. Noticeably absent was Greta and the Brit who had interrogated him the most, Agent Philby.

"Colonel Zeis … General Smith advises me you're someone we can trust," Hildabrand began. "I hope you won't be offended if I take my time with that."

"No … not at all, sir. If I were in your position, I'm sure I'd be just as cautious," Dieter replied.

"A certain number of SS officers have come under our control and we're having trouble sifting through all the bullshit they're feeding us," Hildabrand began. "I think it's bullshit, but we have a couple of generals who think otherwise."

"What are you being told?" Dieter asked. He could just imagine the scurrying for cover that hundreds, maybe even thousands of officers, particularly SS officers, were going through at the moment.

"Well, we have one kraut general … ah … pardon the expression.…"

Dieter smiled, shook his head, and waited for the officer to continue.

"This guy claims to be the foremost authority on the Soviet Union, their military and political organizations," Hildabrand continued.

"That would be Major General Reinhard Gehlen," Dieter offered. Hildabrand immediately beamed a surprised look on his face.

"Well … what'a ya know … that's the guy we have in Munich. Can we believe him?"

"Ah … Colonel Hildabrand. Can a wildcat cornered in a cage be trusted?"

"I see what ya mean," the American replied. "Well, the guy claims to be able to prove who he says he is and how much he knows about the Russkies."

"I thought the Russians were your allies," Dieter said cynically with a sly smile.

"Well yeah … but there's been a school of thought that says we should have been fighting the Russkies instead of you Krauts," Hildabrand said with a laugh. "Anyway, we'd like to make you an offer."

Dieter was faintly stunned but not overwhelmed. He wasn't quite sure what was next, but he suspected the Americans and the Brits were about to ask him for help. He was trying his best to repress any emotion for the next few minutes.

"I think I've made it quite clear that I'm at your service in anyway I can to help my country get back to sanity. That was the final order I received from my commander. You are, of course, well aware of that."

"And … who was that?" Hildabrand inquired.

"Field Marshal Erwin Rommel," Dieter answered.

"Good god … I was told you were highly placed among the Krauts, but I didn't know it was that high. I really didn't know."

"Well … let's just say I was in a position to rub elbows, as you Americans say, with some rather influential leaders," Dieter concluded.

"Nevertheless, we'd like to take you to the good ol' US of A. We want to talk further in dept with you." Hildabrand boasted.

"America?" Dieter asked knowing full well what he meant.

"Yeah. The Army has taken General Gehlen back to Fort Hunt ... in Virginia ... for further debriefing."

"Vat ist das?" Dieter said, catching himself reverting to his native language.

"Debriefing? Oh, that's a fancy word for interrogation. Even though I haven't been able to convince the powers-to-be this guy may be blowin' smoke up our butts ... they've given me permission to try and vet him with one of his own."

Dieter was lost. *"Blowin' smoke? Vet? What was this officer talking about?"*

The young captain standing nearby interrupted, explaining to the colonel that he wasn't sure whether Gehlen was lying to them, and they needed verification, one way or the other, in order to validate him as a valuable or phony asset.

"I understand," Dieter said, smiling.

"I have to ask this of you sir ... but were you a member of the Nazi Party?"

"No ... no I was not," Dieter said.

"Yeah, I figured that's what you'd say," Hildabrand said with a smirk. "I haven't met a *Nazi* yet. As near as I can tell from interrogating hundreds of your fellow countrymen, there aren't any *Nazis* in Germany."

"Well Colonel ... I think you're aware of our preciseness for record keeping. Finding The Party membership rolls shouldn't be too hard. They're probably deep in some bunker, or in a Swiss Bank. You won't find my name on any Nazi membership roll. I'm sure I was on at least one of the SS lists, but not as a member of The Party."

"That's okay Colonel ... I've already vetted you ... I'm satisfied you are who you say you are. My sources tell me you're a loyal German officer, but you're first a good and honest man.

Damned, it's hard to find that combination nowadays," Hildabrand said, laughing aloud.

Dieter suspected Greta had been able to influence the situation. How else would anyone be able to describe Dieter in those terms? But, there was more.

"Colonel, I thought you'd want to know that the information you gave us about that secret mission to Japan has been verified," Hildabrand added. "One of our Navy destroyers intercepted your U-234 in the Atlantic and escorted her to Portsmouth Naval Shipyard in New Hampshire. The cargo and passengers on board that sub were most interesting."

"I do hope you've got everything secured in a safe place," Dieter said with concern in his voice.

"Yeah … it's all taken care of," Hildabrand confirmed. "We're gonna take very good care of it all."

Colonel Hildabrand thanked Dieter for his cooperation and left him with his aide to go over travel arrangements to the United States. Dieter would be leaving the next day aboard a B-24 Liberator Bomber bound for Washington where he'd be met and taken to Fort Hunt. Dieter wasn't exactly clear on what it was he was supposed to be doing for the Americans, and he had the distinct feeling they didn't either.

Greta had dinner with Dieter that evening. It would be the last time they'd see each other for quite some time, he feared.

"I never dreamed I would end up in this situation," Dieter solemnly said as they sat over a meal of English cold pork pie and Yorkshire pudding.

"You're here because this is where you can do Germany some good," Greta said consoling her close friend.

"Why do you think that? How is my going to America going help Germany?"

"Look … Germany is on her knees. America and Britain are in a position to help rebuild your country," Greta explained.

"It was your country too … at one time!" he countered with emotion.

"I know. I feel torn … but I have knowledge you don't. There's another war coming. It may not be right away, but some day in the future, we're going to be pitted against the Russians.

Moscow has vowed to make the entire world one big Communist State and it appears they've got a good start by conquering Eastern Europe."

"Communists ... Nazis ... to me they're all the same," Dieter deadpanned.

"What would *he* want you to do?" Greta asked.

"Who? Rommel?"

"Yes. You're here because he had faith in you."

"I'm here because I was following orders and with the belief that Rommel's message could help end the war," Dieter replied.

"Yes but now with the information you've already revealed ... you just might have prevented another war from happening."

"I never thought of it that way," he admitted.

"If science can create a terrible weapon like you described, we must do everything possible to make sure no one else gets it," Greta said.

"Yes. You're right ... of course," Dieter said with a sigh. "I'll do what I can."

Chapter

9

The commotion surrounding the arrival of the U-234 at the Naval Shipyard was a media circus. The jubilation of the Nazi defeat was enhanced even more by the arrival of a Luftwaffe General emerging from the Coast Guard Cutter as the crew and passengers disembarked at the American Naval Base.

The U-234 was intercepted by the destroyer escort USS Sutton (DE771) just south of the Newfoundland Banks as it approached the coastal waters off the shores of the United States. While at sea and prior to arriving at the naval shipyard, the 41 German crewmembers, six officers, and seven VIP passengers were transferred from the U-234 to a US Coast Guard Cutter outside the naval port. The two dead Japanese passengers were later removed from the sub wrapped in blankets. Commander Johann Fehler stayed aboard his vessel with armed American sailors as they eased the huge sub into an oversized berth inside the port harbor.

Upon Fehler's arrival, the Portsmouth US Naval Shipyard was looking reminiscent of a German submarine pen at St. Nazaire, France as the U-805, U-871, and the U-1228 had already surrendered and arrived ahead of the U-234.

American newsmen were so busy getting photos and interviews with General Kessler, contents of the huge submarine were of little or no interest to the media. But, there was interest. A tall, slender man wearing a tan, wide-brimmed hat was escorted aboard the submarine to inspect the 1,235 pounds of uranium oxide ore.

J. Robert Oppenheimer was concerned about having enough fuel for the two nuclear weapons he was constructing at

Los Alamos, New Mexico. The arc-welded sealed boxes of ore cargo remained unopened and were carefully and quietly loaded aboard a US Naval destroyer escort and spirited away to the more secure Norfolk Naval Station in Virginia. Under the supervision of U-234 First Officer Lieutenant Karl Pfaff, the metal cigar-box type containers of oxide were carefully opened for inspection. When it was determined the boxes weren't booby-trapped, civilian government officials quickly moved in and took charge of the uranium booty.

Once Oppenheimer was satisfied the cargo contained the precious uranium, he immediately ordered it shipped to Oak Ridge, Tennessee, for processing. It meant the Manhattan Project could now go forward with enough fuel to complete two of the top-secret atomic gadgets.

Dieter frustratingly thought the flight across the Atlantic would never end. Flying in a bomber was cold, noisy, and uncomfortable. He thought it ironic how he ended up riding in one of the airplanes responsible for so much death and destruction upon his homeland. Accompanying him on the flight were OSS Agents James Henry and Horace Grossman.

Dieter had been acquainted with Agent Henry during his confinement at his last location in England, but the other agent was a new face—and not a particularly friendly face at that.

When the three men arrived at the US Army's Fort Hunt late in the evening, Dieter was taken to the Bachelor Officers' Quarters (BOQ) and given his own room. The two agents roomed on either side of Dieter's quarters, with two MP guards posted outside in the hallway.

He immediately knew he was in another world once he settled into his quarters. A pile of magazines on the end table next to the bed revealed the richness of America. Each was filled with advertisements for the latest appliances and the new 1946 automobiles. Dieter learned later that the heralding of many of these luxuries were the first in four years as American factories had been turning out guns and planes instead of refrigerators and Cadillacs.

The next morning, breakfast was brought to Dieter's room. It was a service he hadn't had in England, and for that matter, a long time before. He thought back—yes, it had been at least three years since he enjoyed room service. The meal was unbelievable: real pork bacon, fresh scrambled eggs, yellow butter, and cream and sugar for fresh Columbia coffee. The German officer was delighted at such extravagance, but he barely had time to enjoy this early morning feast; some 15 minutes later the two OSS agents escorted him to a non-descript, two-story wooden building on the edge of the base. There was a high, barbwire fence surrounding the structure with armed guards walking about its perimeter. Once inside the gate, Dieter saw Colonel Hildabrand, the army officer who invited him to America, standing at the building's entrance.

Hildabrand was slightly balding with a pockmarked face. His temples, like Dieter's, were showing slight signs of gray, but unlike the German, Hildabrand had developed a slight paunch in his stomach. Dieter reckoned the officer was doing a little more administrating and a little less fieldwork, but he could be wrong. Hildabrand revealed little of himself.

"This place looks like a prison or maybe a bunker," Dieter audibly mumbled under his breath as the four men walked passed the guards into the building.

"Both," grunted Agent Grossman. It was the first words Grossman had uttered since they left England. This agent's attitude toward Dieter was slightly disturbing. The German didn't expect friendliness from his former enemies, but Grossman acted as though there was something personal between them.

"Maybe he lost someone in the war," Dieter thought to himself. *"That's probably it."*

The two agents, Colonel Bud Hildabrand, and Dieter walked down a hallway and into a dark room. The area was small with a one-way observation window adjoining a larger room. In that room was a slender, tired looking man shabbily dressed in an old rumpled suit. Hildabrand identified the man as German Major General Reinhard Gehlen. Dieter had never met General Gehlen, but he did recognize him.

He was seated at a long table with two US Army officers: one sitting on the end and the other on the opposite side. They were sifting through huge stacks of what appeared to be personnel files. Dieter immediately recognized them as German files. The swastika on several covers was the dead giveaway. As the two American officers took each file folder from one pile to another, they briefly discussed each person with Gehlen, and then selected a particular pile to place it on. Dieter noted some of the file folders had paperclips placed upon them for easy future reference. Hildabrand reached up and turned on a small speaker allowing them to hear what was being said in the room. The entire conversation between Gehlen and the two officers was conducted in German.

Dieter listened to the German general comment on each of the folders as they were held up by the Americans. Gehlen talked with apparent authority on nearly every folder presented. Gehlen was saying such things as, "He … has indispensable knowledge of Soviet espionage tactics," and "He … worked closely with military leadership in planning attacks on the Red Army," or "He … supervised espionage operations on the Eastern Front."

Depending upon the particular value judged by the US officers depended whether or not a paperclip was placed on the folder. Dieter could see Gehlen's so-called knowledge and expertise was being relied upon by the Americans. He later discovered the OSS would use Gehlen's information and recommendations to develop a future intelligence network that monitored the Soviet Union. Most of the results from the Gehlen investigation was folded into what would to be known as "Operation Paperclip."

"There's another room I'd like you to see," Hildabrand said, motioning for Dieter and the other two agents to follow. The men walked into a similar viewing room where another German was being interrogated by two other US Army officers. Only one of the American officers was interrogating the dark-haired man who looked to be maybe 35 years old. Like Gehlen, he was dressed in a cheap, ill-fitting civilian suit.

"I know this man," Dieter offered. "I can't remember his name, but I had dealings with him before … it's been a number of years."

"His name is Conrad Krueger ... a Gestapo agent," Hildabrand said.

Dieter looked harder at the figure, sitting slumped in a chair, leaning on the table. The black, penetrating eyes behind the round, steel-rimmed glasses were unforgettable. "Ah yes ... now I remember."

Dieter recalled Krueger coming into the Berlin Medical Supply Depot several years ago throwing his weight around trying to intimidate Dieter and his staff. He chuckled to himself, recalling how Sergeant Werner Schroeder had summoned everyone to surround Krueger with the intention of counteracting his intimidation.*

"We're being told by General Gehlen this particular agent is a valuable asset who could be important to our future intelligence operations," Hildabrand explained.

"I wouldn't know, but I do remember him as not being a very pleasant man," is all Dieter could offer. "I couldn't begin to imagine what value he would be to anyone."

The men walked back out into the hall.

"Colonel ... I'm really not sure what I'm doing here," Dieter posed to Hildabrand. "I know what you told me, but the more I've thought about it, the less I'm sure if I can ever be of any value."

"Well, Colonel Zeis ... right now, I'd like you to spend the next few days just observing and listening to these two men and several others who we'll be bringing in from Germany," Hildabrand replied. "We'll talk later about future assignments we may have to offer you."

That evening, Hildabrand took Dieter to dinner at the base Officers' Club. Like guard dogs, the two OSS agents were across the dining room sitting at another table, occasionally glancing over. Dieter was struck by the relaxed atmosphere of the club where several officers, accompanied by women, were enjoying dinner. A few were standing at the bar smoking cigarettes. Everyone seemed to be enjoying themselves in a very comfortable

---

* "Nebraska Doppelganger," Chapter 7.

atmosphere. The exception, of course, was the stiff demeanor of Agents Henry and Grossman.

Dieter continued to be amazed at the abundance of fresh foods so readily available. The one thing he hadn't had in a number of months was a good piece of beefsteak. There were several cuts of meat offered on the club menu. So many, in fact, Dieter had never heard of half of them: Steak Diane? Kansas City? New York? Delmonico? All were listed under servings of beef. Dieter thought to himself that it might be a ruse. Berlin restaurants would present fabulous menus listing exotic fare, most of which were unavailable due to the needs of the war.

"I find it interesting how much food you have available compared to the shortages in England and Europe," Dieter said.

"Well … we do have a few privileges here on base that you won't normally find in many of our civilian restaurants," Hildabrand replied.

During the sumptuous dinner, the two men continued passing their time talking about the one thing they had in common—the war. Hildabrand talked of how he joined the army out of college and was later recruited into the OSS. It was the first time Hildabrand identified himself as OSS.

Dieter recounted how he had first met Field Marshal Rommel. It was obvious Colonel Hildabrand admired the German General. He asked a number of questions about what it was like to be with such a great man.

Dieter finally got around to asking Hildabrand a question that had been nagging him for sometime. "What's bothering Agent Grossman?"

"What do you mean?"

"He doesn't seem to care too much for me," Dieter explained.

"Maybe it's because he lost some relatives in your death camps," Hildabrand replied.

"I don't suppose it would do any good to tell you, or him, that I knew nothing of such things."

"Nope. We've both heard that one before," Hildabrand said, taking a sip of coffee. "Seems as though no one in Germany knew anything about those camps."

"Oh, I knew about Dachau and a couple of the others … Buchenwald south of Berlin, but I knew nothing of the mass exterminations the SS carried out against the Jews," Dieter honestly replied.

"Well, that's part of your job here," Hildabrand continued. "We're convinced you weren't involved in such things, but we want you to help flush out those who were. We'll start with Major General Gehlen. He claims he wasn't even a Nazi, that he went along with Hitler's sinister program just to get along and improve his military career. Gehlen has quite a lot of documentation to back up his boast that he's an expert on the Russians."

Dieter was putting some sugar into his coffee. Having this small luxury was something he hadn't enjoyed for quite some time. Even in England, sugar was rationed; but here at the Fort Hunt Officers' Club, there was a large bowl filled just waiting to be scooped up.

"I'll do what I can to help you," Dieter said, taking a sip of coffee. He had been accustomed to drinking tea since being a guest of the British. Black English breakfast tea was more his cup, but the Americans were coffee drinkers. He really didn't like coffee but, with real cream and sugar in abundance, Dieter was enjoying this cup as much as ever.

"Smoke?" Hildabrand asked, holding a pack of Camel cigarettes, offering them to Dieter.

"No thank you. I stopped many years ago," Dieter replied. "The Field Marshal … well … he didn't approve of such things."

"Herr Rommel and ol' Monty at least had that in common," Hildabrand said, chuckling as he lit his Chesterfield.

"You might consider looking for Heinrich Müller," Dieter offered as the two men sat chatting over their after-dinner coffee.

"Yes, we know all about Müller but haven't caught up with him just yet," Hildabrand replied. "As far as we've been able to determine, Mueller was a pretty nasty fellow who was head of Gestapo operations and a driving force in the killing of Jews."

Dieter nodded in agreement. In the fall of 1942, Müller, under the direction of Heinrich Himmler, set forth the construction of concentration camps all over Germany and Poland for the "Final Solution" to the Jewish question that resulted from the Wannsee Conference on January 20, 1942.

In January 1943, Müller rounded up 45,000 Jews from the Netherlands, 3,000 from Berlin, 30,000 from the Bialystok ghetto, and 10,000 from Theresienstadt, a former "humane" concentration camp located in northern Bohemia but later designated as a transit station for the "inhumane" death camp at Auschwitz.

"If we ever do catch up with him, Müller is certainly headed for the hangman's noose," Hildabrand reckoned.

"Isn't that what this is really all about," Dieter asked.

"This was a dirty war. Not everyone fought as honorably as your late commander," Hildabrand offered, motioning for a waiter to bring more coffee. "As I see it, there's a difference between the loyal German soldier and the fanatical Waffen SS guard. One was fighting for Germany … the other for Hitler and the Nazi regime."

Dieter waited until his coffee cup was refilled.

"That's quite a blurry line, Colonel," Dieter replied. "There was a time in the beginning when most of us believed Hitler's vision … even Rommel."

"When did everything start coming apart?" Hildabrand asked.

"December 18, 1940 when Hitler issued War Directive 21 renaming "Operation Fritz" to "Operation Barbarossa," Dieter replied.

"The attack on the Soviet Union?" Hildabrand clarified.

"Yes … on June 22, 1941. Until that time, most of us thought Hitler was an absolute political genius. He left the strategic planning of the war to those of us who knew what we were doing. But, when the Eastern Front was launched, he began playing little Napoleon and everything became unraveled.

"We could have taken all of the Middle East with our Deutsches Afrika Korps if the Führer would have kept his promises and sent us the supplies and equipment we needed," Dieter concluded. "We had enough manpower, we just ran out of everything to keep an army moving."

Hildabrand pondered that last point for a moment.

"Didn't Allied ships and planes have something to do with your supply lines being broken across the Mediterranean?"

"True, but not to the extent we suffered because of Hitler's neglect," Dieter countered. "My opinion ... of course."

"Well, you certainly were in a position to know firsthand what affect that had."

"Your Normandy invasion wouldn't have gone quite so successfully as it had been if Hitler would have left the defense strategy to our generals," Dieter surmised. "As it was, his hesitation to release our Panzer divisions allowed your forces to overwhelm us. If the Führer had listened to Rommel and Rundstedt and moved the Panzers near and along the beach, things would have turned out much differently. Rommel knew exactly where you would land ... Normandy where an attack was least expected ... but alas, our glorious *Führer* would not listen to them!"

Dieter was savoring the taste of another cream and sugar-laden cup of java as he continued with his historical speculation.

"It was a few days after the Normandy landing both Rommel and I knew we had lost the war," Dieter continued. "Did you know we had less than 100 Tigers in Northern France at the time of your invasion?"

"Panzers ... er ... tanks?"

"Yes ... but, those 90-some panzers would have been devastating to your forces, if only they would have been in the right place. A good Tiger commander can knock out an Allied tank at 1,000 yards, whereas the American Sherman or British Matilda would have to have a very lucky shot at 200 yards."

"What about 'The Bulge'?" Hildabrand offered.

"Our counteroffensive in the Ardennes Forest?"

"Yes."

"Really a desperate, last-ditch effort on our part, which I must say ... nearly worked," Dieter chuckled. "But, as you Americans would say, 'we ran out of gas' ... and we did ...

literally! Our Tigers get very thirsty. They'll only go 30 or 40 miles and then need refueling."

Hildabrand acknowledged what Dieter was saying with a quiet nod and smile.

"You Yanks literally outmanned us, out-built us, outspent us, and outgunned us." Dieter added. "The world has never seen such a military machine built so quickly and maneuvered so skillfully. My compliments, sir."

The two officers lifted their cups in a small toast to Dieter's compliment.

As the two men walked back to the Bachelor Officers' Quarters, Hildabrand startled the German colonel by telling him he had freedom of the base.

"You won't be able to leave because you don't have an ID or a pass, but you're free to walk about ... enjoy the Officers' Club and the Post Exchange," Hildabrand said. He then handed him a set of papers.

"These are your orders that will admit you to anywhere that might require an ID. If you have any problems ... just have them call me," Hildabrand explained. "Also, here are a few bucks to give you some walking around money."

Dieter had never seen American currency. Hildabrand had given him $20. He thought such base freedom was interesting in light of the fact that Fort Hunt was but only a few miles from the American national Capitol City of Washington, DC.

"Just who am I now?" Dieter inquired. "I mean, am I a prisoner of war trustee? A civilian displaced person? What?"

"Well for now ... you're a VIP guest of the United States Army and the Office of Strategic Services. If all goes well, I may be able to further clarify your status within the next few days."

The two men bade good night and went to their separate quarters.

Chapter

10

Project Paperclip, also known as "Operation Paperclip," was an American scheme to import selected Nazi scientists, technicians, and intelligence personnel from Germany. At war's end, the United States anxiously competed with the Russians in scooping up the cream of Germany's scientific community.

Harry S. Truman, the new American President, was adamant about not allowing ardent Nazis into the United States. He publicized a directive stipulating that no known Nazis be allowed to participate in any government projects of the United States. However, despite Truman's edict, the US Army and OSS officials cautiously ignored the diktat and continued processing the key scientists, technicians, and German officials. There *were* more ardent Nazis captured than nonmembers; but in the interim, the alternative would be to allow the Russians to land these experts. With that thought in mind, it was obvious to the American intelligence community that it had no choice but to resist the presidential order.

Among the more notable scientist allowed to emigrate from Germany to the United States under Operation Paperclip was Dr. Wernher von Braun. From 1937 to 1945, von Braun was the Technical Director of the Northern German rocket center known as Peenemünde; a wooded island located in the Baltic Sea 115 miles due north of Berlin. It was here that von

Braun's "Wunderwaffen" (Wonder Weapon), the V-1, and V-2 (Vergeltungswaffen) was developed.

Since von Braun *was* considered an ardent Nazi, under Operation Paperclip, the rocket scientist's dossier was surreptitiously revised portraying him as an unenthusiastic Nazi who openly deplored Der Führer. While this was basically true, his new file simply verified those feelings. All he really wanted to do was build rockets for space. He never liked the idea of sending his bomb-laden rockets to kill innocent people.

Once in the United States, he knew he could develop his dream. He enthusiastically worked with the US Army and developed its guided missile program. It was this development that eventually led him and his fellow scientist into the launching of the United States into space.

Because of his expertise, he was named director of the National Aeronautics and Space Administration's Marshall Space Flight Center in Huntsville, Alabama. His rocket research and development efforts helped the Americans to be the first on the moon in July of 1969. The following year, von Braun became NASA's Associate Administrator. He and many of his colleagues eventually became American citizens.

But, probably the most far-reaching impact Operation Paperclip had on America's future was the relationship between the OSS, later to become the Central Intelligence Agency, and former German Major General Reinhard Gehlen.

For 10 solid months in the backrooms of Washington's Fort Hunt, Gehlen and American agents diligently scoured the personnel files of former Nazi SS officers and Gestapo agents; especially those who were considered experts on Soviet affairs. In spite of the fact that many of Gehlen's top aides were known to have committed war crimes before and during World War II, they, nonetheless, were hired to organize a spy network against the Soviet Union; all with the tacit blessing of the American intelligence community.

Gehlen's intimate knowledge of the Soviets was derived from his role as head of the German Army's intelligence arm for the Eastern Front. Reportedly, Gehlen was directly responsible for the torture and the starvation murder of some four million Russian POWs.

Soviet prisoners, who refused to cooperate with Gehlen's agents, were often tortured and then executed. Many POWs were murdered after they gave information. Others were left to starve to death. So, it's no wonder Gehlen was keen on surrendering to the Americans rather than the Russkies.

In Munich during the closing days of the war, Gehlen carefully microfilmed vast files of documents he had accumulated on the Soviets. The German general carefully packed this highly important information into watertight steel drums and buried them in the nearby Bavarian Forest with the hope of using it as bargaining chips with the American intelligence community.

The OSS Senior Station Agent in Bern, Switzerland during the war was Allen Dulles—who became well acquainted with General Gehlen's expertise in espionage against the Soviet Union. Dulles convinced OSS Director William Donovan of Gehlen's intelligence value when he learned the German spymaster wanted to surrender to the Americans. Gehlen did so on May 22, 1945.

The availability of Gehlen immediately created a tug of war between the US Army's Counter Intelligence Corps and the OSS for authority and control over the Nazi general and his microfilmed treasure.

Dieter was sure President Truman had no idea of what was going on, or how many Nazi war criminals were being allowed into the United States. He attempted to advise Hildabrand on numerous occasions about various individuals known to be *less than desirable* human beings. Each time, as Dieter was told, any objections he or Hildabrand might have would be overruled by Dulles and other top officials in both the Army and the OSS.

After months of debriefing at Fort Hunt, Dulles arranged for General Gehlen's return to Munich in the American sector of Germany where he was allowed to form a private intelligence organization later known as "The Gehlen Org."

Two of Gehlen's early recruits were Emil Augsburg and Dr. Franz Six, who had been part of the mobile "Einsatzgruppens" (Nazi killing squads) which murdered Jews, intellectuals, and Soviet partisans whenever and wherever they could be found. Other early Gehlen recruits included Willie Krichbaum, the former Senior Chief Gestapo Agent in Paris, Southeastern Europe, and later Kiel.

With the encouragement of the OSS, then later the CIA, the Gehlen Org set up so-called "rat lines." This was a list of Nazi war criminals who were escaping Europe for South and Central America to avoid capture and the war crimes tribunals. This secretive operation was known as the "Odessa File" Through transit camps and phony passports, the Gehlen Org assisted in the escape of more than 5,000 ardent Nazis.

Those relocated Nazi agents and officers included all sorts of mass murderers as well as one well-known Klaus Barbie, "The Butcher of Lyon." Barbie later assisted a number of South American Governments in setting up death squads in Chile, Argentina, El Salvador, and other South and Central American nations.

August 6, 1945: Dieter was awakened in his BOQ room at 5 am by an excited Hildabrand. Dieter's worst fears were realized. The United States had just dropped an atomic bomb on Japan. A single explosion reportedly destroyed the entire city of Hiroshima populated by 350,000 citizens. Reportedly, more than 60,000 were killed.

"If this doesn't bring those Japs to their knees, nothing will!" Hildabrand exclaimed with trepidation.

Dieter immediately thought of the U-234. Had the uranium ore aboard the German sub gone to fuel the American bomb? If it did, would it have happened if Dieter hadn't revealed the secret German mission? It was a question that would trouble him for years.

Three days later, an American B-29 dropped a second bomb on Nagasaki. Another 10,000 civilians were dead. The two atom bombs left more than 120,000 people badly injured and dying of burns and radiation poisoning.

By August 12, more than 190,000 Japanese citizens were dead. Hildabrand was right—it did bring Japan to its knees where they finally agreed to an unconditional surrender on August 15, 1945. At last, the long seven-year nightmare was over. Since September 1, 1939, the world was at war—now it was at peace.

Dieter pondered his future. What did he have? There was nothing for him back in Germany. Maybe his future was with the Americans—or maybe the British. Only time would tell.

Chapter
11

On a warm gray day in Tokyo Bay on September 2, 1945 aboard the American Battleship USS Missouri, the Japanese formally surrendered. Now the hard part was ahead—rebuilding structures ripped by war; but repairing peoples' lives, that was another matter.

Dieter spent weeks, which quickly turned into months, listening and observing the interrogation and vetting proceedings at Fort Hunt. He had to hand it to General Gehlen. The German spymaster was one of the world's greatest bullshit artists—and the Americans were lapping it up. He was telling them what they wanted to hear because it validated what Army and OSS officials were telling the powers in Washington. The threat of the Soviet Union taking over all of Europe was very real, and Gehlen confirmed those fears. The Gehlen factor was the OSS ticket to more funding, more manpower, more influence, and certainly more power as a government organization.

Frequently, Dieter cautioned Hildabrand about claims Gehlen was making, but he had no proof to contradict the German's assertions.

During his time at Fort Hunt, Dieter became more familiar with American society; albeit from a military point of view. His British accent was waning, taking on a more American style as he interacted with clerks at the base Post Exchange, the man in the kiosk at the Fort Hunt Theater, and most every evening at the Officers' Club with the bartender. All the while Dieter kept his true identity to himself. Only a small circle of OSS officials knew he had been a lieutenant colonel in the German Heer.

During the months at Fort Hunt, Dieter had the opportunity to develop an amiable relationship with Bud Hildabrand and was even able to strike up a few cordial conversations with Agent Leonard "Len" Grossman; though at first, they were edgy exchanges.

Grossman was born and raised in New York to a second-generation German immigrant family. His grandfather came to the United States before World War I where he became a banker with an older brother—who had previously immigrated to America. Len Grossman was a Harvard graduate with a law degree. Being an agent for the OSS was a choice for a career, Dieter thought; but the more he got to know Grossman, the more apparent it became that being an espionage agent was the best way for this rather angry man to partake in the war. The subject of politics occasionally arose and it was apparent Grossman had socialistic viewpoints. Could he be a Communist? Maybe he was a member during the Great Depression. Every modern country in the world had it share of communist sympathizers, especially in the '30s when the capitalistic system imploded.

As the weeks passed into months, Grossman gradually warmed to Dieter when it became apparent he wasn't a die-hard Nazi. Still, Agent Grossman was a man with little to say and kept to himself.

By early 1946, Dieter and Hildabrand were on their way back to England. Dieter was now designated as a temporary "Special" OSS Agent—whatever that meant! He had been sponsored by Colonel Hildabrand, who, as it turned out, was one of America's earliest and most senior intelligence agency members. He was in "Wild Bill" Donovan's most inner-circle of agents along with Allen Dulles. At first, Dieter didn't realize how high Hildabrand was placed in Washington. He quickly learned his presence meant something.

Now that Dieter was a "Special Agent," he had questions. Up until now, he refrained from being inquisitive—biding his time.

"Do you know an agent by the name of John Krauss?" Dieter asked Hildabrand during their flight back to London.

"Sure. Say, now ... there's a strange story," the colonel replied with interest.

"Yes, I know. He's an old friend."

"Are you the one who covered his ass when Hitler drafted him into the German Army?"

"That would be me," Dieter admitted. He then began to tell Hildabrand how he had met young Krauss, who at the time was an 18-year-old Nebraska farm lad from Broken Bow, Nebraska. He had come to Germany with his father in 1936 to see the Berlin Olympics. He ended up staying and going to medical school that year. Later, he rented a room from Greta von Carlsen, Dieter's sister-in-law. After a couple of years, the Nazis drafted him into the army when he refused to join The Party.*

"You know, that's the first time you've actually verbalized your relationship to Agent von Carlsen," Hildabrand said.

"You didn't know?" Dieter replied.

"Yes ... of course we did, but we just never heard it from you," said Hildabrand smiling. "She told us who you were months ago after you showed up on her doorstep. That's one of the reasons we began thinking you'd make a good agent. Did I ever tell you I thought the British officer disguise was a good ruse ... risky but good. You know you could have been put in front of a firing squad?"

"Yes, I know ... but at the time, it seemed like the most logical thing to do. The situation I was in ... it just seemed to warrant it." Dieter replied and then changed the subject

"So ... where's John Krauss now?"

---

* "Nebraska Doppelganger," Chapter 3.

"He's in Germany, somewhere, looking for a friend of his in the POW camps. You might know him … a Sergeant Werner Schroeder?" Hildabrand replied.

Dieter's eyes brightened.

"Werner Schroeder … yes … he was my top sergeant when I ran the Medical Supply Depot in Berlin. He later became the Field Marshal's personal chef and a good friend of ours," Dieter replied. "I was able to bring him and Krauss along with me when I became part of Herr General's personal staff in the 7th Panzer Division and later in the Afrika Korps. He was a great cook! Rommel certainly enjoyed his culinary abilities, especially the way he cooked the leg of lamb."

"Yes … I know," Hildabrand said, smiling.

"Is there anything you don't know about me?" Dieter responded, smiling.

"I don't know … is there?" Hildabrand countered.

As the plane glided through the air, the drone of the four-engine C-54 Douglas transport was the only sound for several minutes.

"Zeis, I want you to remember that you're one of us now," Hildabrand said with a serious look.

"Pardon?"

"You are now a *full* OSS Agent," he replied. "I know you're close to your former sister-in-law, but she's on the other team, so to speak. We can't go sharing everything we know with ol' 'John Bull'."

Dieter was a bit confused. *"John Bull? Who the hell is John Bull?"*

"I'm not sure I follow you, sir," Dieter said. "Who's 'John Bull'?"

Hildabrand explained that it was less than a flattering moniker the Americans have long called the British. "John Bull," "Limey," both slang references to the American cousins across the pond in England.

"It has to do with their stubbornness and tendency to be a bit on the cheap side of things. I mean … have you ever seen a Limey pick up a dinner or drink tab?" he asked.

Dieter thought for a moment and then chuckled to himself. He hadn't had that many social opportunities with his former enemies.

"Well sir … I haven't exactly been out that much socially over the past few months," he wryly said. "I was treated quite nicely on my last trip to England … especially at Greta's."

"That doesn't count … she's German," he laughed. "Seriously … from now on out, we have to be very cautious of what we share with the Brits. After all, Uncle Sugar *is* paying for most of everything. The Brits are so poor … they're still on rationing of almost everything from coffee to beef."

Dieter quickly pointed out that all of Europe was on the dole.

"Yes … and America is paying for it," Hildabrand reminded Zeis.

Dieter almost shot back that it was American bombers that had pretty much obliterated German industry and its capacity to feed and clothe itself, but he thought better of that—the Yanks didn't do it without provocation.

Although he was now working for the Americans, in his heart, Dieter still considered himself a proud and loyal German soldier even though there was no army for him to report—no uniform to wear, no flag to salute. Oh, the Allies were making some sort of attempt to resurrect a nation of sorts from the ashes of the Third Reich, but it would never really be the same. Right now, the Fatherland was occupied and split four ways by the Allied victors. How it all emerged remained to be seen.

The C-54 landed at some unknown Army Air Corps base in England where an olive-drab-painted sedan was awaiting the two agents. They were whisked away to what Dieter was told was Devonshire Hall near Cambridge. It was yet another one of those three story graystone mansions of which England was famous.

"It's one of our training facilities," Hildabrand explained. "We're going to teach you a few tricks of the trade. You'd be surprised how many ways there are to kill a man with your hands."

Dieter didn't react. He just stared out the sedan's rear seat window as the lush green English countryside rushed by.

"It seems the Americans have something specific in mind for me," Dieter thought. *"Why else would I be going to a training facility?"*

Dieter was correct. He was being trained in the martial arts. Hildabrand was right; there are countless ways to kill someone with your hands.

Instead of a finely manicured lawn in the rear of the mansion, an obstacle course and shooting range were among the numerous training modules.

The more the training progressed, the more Dieter realized it wasn't so much about how to kill a man; but how to keep from being killed. It was a very intensive self-defense course. If the attacker was killed while you were trying to stay alive, so be it.

After three weeks of intensive training, Dieter was told he would finally be going back to Germany. If this was the case, he wondered what all the martial arts training had to do with it.

It was over a quiet dinner at a nearby English tea house where Hildabrand gave Dieter his new orders. "You'll be advising and observing the prosecution of a war crimes tribunal in Dachau," Hildabrand explained. "Because you were stationed in Belgium, we want you to sit in on the 'Malmédy Massacre Case'."

"Malmédy?"

"Yes, I'm sure you were aware that Lieutenant Colonel Joachim Peiper's Kampfgruppe [Combat group] of the 1st SS Panzer Division murdered 86 US troops after they had surrendered … and several days later murdered another 350 American POWs and a hundred or so unarmed Belgian citizens," Hildabrand said.

Dieter got mad. This isn't what he expected to do as an OSS agent.

"Tell me Colonel, will there be a trial for those who ordered the bombing of Dresden?" Dieter deadpanned in a higher octave.

"Dresden? Of course not … that was war," the colonel shot back.

"You and I know perfectly well that Dresden was not a military target and that it had no value to Germany's war effort. It was just a beautiful city full of civilians," Dieter retorted. "That was murder, as well."

"I take it you're not very happy with your first assignment."

"No sir … definitely not!" Dieter said, angrily.

"Well, there is a reason I want you to go to Munich," Hildabrand reasoned. "General Gehlen, who will be setting up his organization there, has made some rather interesting claims."

Dieter subtly calmed himself after his brief surge of anger.

"According to the good general, the OSS has a few communists in our midst," Hildabrand said. "He claims a few of them are rather high-placed."

"What could I possibly do about that?" Dieter sardonically asked.

"I would like for you to play the 'man in the middle'," the colonel positioned to Dieter. "As a fellow German officer, we want you to get close to Gehlen. Find out if he is as knowledgeable as he claims. I know Dulles is high on him, but I don't trust him. Still, if there is a chance one or two Reds are in our midst … I want them ferreted out as quickly as possible."

Dieter pondered the thought for a moment. This was more to his thinking of what he should be doing.

"Has Gehlen given you any names?"

"Naw … not really … just a few. The Nazi bastard is holding out. Before he gives us anymore names, he wants more security, more money … and more jobs for his buddies," Hildabrand replied.

Dinner was over. Hildabrand asked about a digestif.

"Schnapps would be in order … I believe," Dieter replied feeling a bit more relaxed. The last few minutes had really curled the hairs on his neck.

When the waiter returned, Hildabrand ordered two schnapps not specifying a brand name. Dieter was a connoisseur of this spirit and asked particularly for the German "Doornkaat." The waiter acknowledged it was a staple item for them.

As the two men sat sipping their schnapps, Dieter asked the obvious.

"Well ... will I be going to Munich and Dachau for the war crimes trial ... or to spy on Gehlen?"

"Both," Hildabrand answered, taking a sip of his liqueur. "God, I've never been able to figure what you Jerries see in this stuff. It tastes like nitroglycerin!"

Dieter just smiled and remarked, "Maybe next time, I'll order the Peach!"

"So ... I'll be more or less a spy within a ring of spies ... right?"

"Something like that ... I suppose. As far as our little *club* is concerned, you're there to observe and advise the prosecution on the trial. Whatever else you find out you'll be reporting directly to me and only to me. No one else needs to know about this," Hildabrand said with caution in his voice.

"Does Washington know about it?" Dieter asked.

"The man himself knows ... but that's all," Hildabrand replied.

"The man," of course, was OSS Director General William Donovan. Throughout the service, all agents referred to Donovan as "Wild Bill," "Big Bill," "The Man," or "The Boss," so Dieter didn't have to inquire further.

"What about Dulles?" Dieter inquired. "How tight is he with Gehlen?"

"Quite!" Hildabrand responded. "He's so enamored with Gehlen that Donovan doesn't quite trust that relationship."

"Then, why me?" Dieter probed.

"You wouldn't believe it if I told you," Hildabrand said, chuckling.

"Please ... try me!"

"Well, Donovan was a great admirer of Herr Rommel. He figures anyone 'The Fox' trusted, like you, could be trusted by us. It's a rather well known fact that Rommel didn't tolerate hardcore Nazis ... or the SS. That leaves you with a pretty clean bill of health."

Dieter smiled at the comment. Being known as a trusted agent could go a long way in his new career. He liked that moniker.

"When do I leave for Germany?"

"There will be a car picking you up in the morning at 8 o'clock and taking you to the airfield."

"Will you be going with me?"

Hildabrand upended the snifter, swallowing his last few drops.

"No. Except for the Station Chief in Munich, Edgar Jansen, I don't want anyone down there to know about our association," Hildabrand explained.

"How will I communicate with you?" Dieter inquired.

"Don't worry ... I'll be the one getting in touch with you. You're not to make any effort to contact me. If you're being watched by a Commie in our midst, I don't want any foul ups. I may not be in contact with you in person, but whomever I send will ask you one simple question: 'The water in Munich makes better beer, don't you think?' And, you'll reply, 'Not as good as in Düsseldorf'."

Dieter chuckled to himself. It was obvious these Americans hadn't been in the spy business very long. But, then again, what did he know. This was his first experience as well.

As they left the teashop, Hildabrand handed Dieter an envelope.

"Here are your credentials and some money," he said.

"Won't I need some travel documents or orders?" Dieter asked.

"Son, you're with the American Forces. All you have to do is show your credentials. It has your photo ID, the works. Anyone who questions it, have them call the OSS Office in Munich to verify."

"Will they know who I am?" Dieter inquired.

"Don't worry … you'll be greeted quite warmly down there with the build-up I've given Jansen."

"What about General Gehlen?"

"How you get close to him is your business. Hell Dieter … I can't do everything for you! Use some of that 'Desert Fox' ingenuity and initiative he taught you! Hide in plain sight and see what you come up with."

Hildabrand had one caution: "You're probably going to be shocked at what you see when you arrive in Munich," he said. "The city is pretty much destroyed from all of the bombing raids … I believe there were something like 77 in all."

Back at Devonshire Hall, Dieter examined his envelope more closely. The black wallet-like cardholder had his OSS photo ID along with some business cards. There also was $500 in US currency; mostly one, five, and ten dollar bills. He hadn't given money much thought in months. He had been the guest of Uncle Sam and hadn't really needed a lot of cash. In Germany, though, he'll be on his own; the Reichmarks weren't worth the paper they were printed on.

The next morning, as promised, an American sedan was waiting for Dieter as he walked out the mansion. He was carrying a small satchel with some belongings. He was returning to his homeland with far more than when he left.

Chapter

12

Hildabrand was right. The devastation to Munich was shocking. Dieter could not believe this once-beautiful Bavarian cultural city was now a series of rubble heaps. Little of the city center was recognizable, but it was hard to tell from the air.

So much of 20th century German history had occurred in Munich. It was here where Adolf Hitler and his gang first organized. On November 8, 1923, the Munich Beer Hall Putsch was staged with Hitler leading the coup. It was designed to overthrow the weak Weimar Republic—Germany's attempt at democratization following World War I. The overthrow failed; Hitler was arrested. At his trial, he represented himself mesmerizing the judges with dazzling displays of oratory taking full responsibility for the attempted coup. He was sentenced to five years in Landsberg Prison; but actually spent just nine months before he was summarily released. During his sentence, he dictated to Rudolf Hess the first volume of "Mein Kampf" which later became the political bible of the Nazi movement.

In those early days of the Nazi Party outside of Munich, the Nazis were fairly obscure. Hitler's imprisonment stalled The Party's progress—temporarily. When Hitler was released, Munich again became central to the Nazi movement. When in 1933 enough members of The Party were elected to the German Parliament in Berlin to forge power at the Reichstag, Hitler was named Chancellor. Because of Munich's importance to the rise of Nazism, Party loyalists always referred to Munich as their "Capital of the Movement."

It was in Munich where British Prime Minister Neville Chamberlain received his assurances from Hitler no further demands of territory would be made if only the German-speaking Sudetenland of Czechoslovakia were ceded to Germany. The now infamous 1938 Munich Agreement promised "Peace in our time," Chamberlain assured the world—the ultimate in famous last words.

A year later on November 8, 1939 and on the 16th Anniversary of the Beer Hall Putsch at the Bürgerbräu Keller, there was an attempt on Hitler's life. While delivering a contemptuous speech on British perfidy, he uncharacteristically cut short his pontification. Within minutes of leaving the hall, a bomb exploded near a large column causing the roof to collapse killing seven people and injuring 63.

Dieter wasn't sure he wanted to land. As the C-47 twin-engine transport droned over the city, the structural obliteration of war became even more apparent. Little was left. Where were the more than half a million people living? There was little left standing.

Aboard the US Army aircraft were a dozen or so military personnel. Dieter and three others were the only personnel in civilian clothes. Thanks to Hildabrand, Dieter was outfitted with the latest in men's fashion when the Fort Hunt Post Exchange received its first shipments of civilian clothes just after the war.

Dieter felt privileged to have the new wardrobe; although, wearing it made him feel a little odd. Not many former German officers were so honored. With shoes, gray flannel suit, and black fedora, no one would ever guess he was a German—he was dressed as American as possible; but for Europe, he could pass for a millionaire playboy in hot pursuit of heavy action on the French Riviera.

As the aircraft taxied to the partially destroyed terminal, Dieter observed dozens of US Army aircraft in various stages of unloading to the army-green deuce-and-a-half trucks. Civilian workers were scurrying about removing valuable cargo to mostly unclassified destinations. Dieter could only imagine the thousands of fellow countrymen waiting to receive what he hoped were life saving commodities.

In a Quonset hut serving as a transportation office, Dieter presented his credentials asking for some conveyance into the city. There was no one waiting for him. For the first time since presenting himself at Greta's mansion more than a year ago, the former German Army officer was, indeed, on his own.

"Ya got a choice, Mac," grunted an American sergeant with a heavy northeastern accent. "Youse can take a Jeep and drive yerself right now … or, youse can wait until one of our drivers gets back from town with a sedan."

Dieter didn't hesitate.

"I'll take the Jeep," he replied.

Evidently, the OSS ID Dieter presented held guarded privilege because he could hear grumbling from the other men in the room who were trying to hitch a ride into the city. Dieter was rather embarrassed to receive such VIP treatment but only for a moment. In an earlier life, such courtesies would have been expected of a high ranking officer of the Third Reich. Dieter had to keep reminding himself, though, the Third Reich no longer existed—he was in another capacity all together.

Before leaving the building, Dieter got directions to the Munich area military commander's headquarters. And, as a gesture of friendship, asked if anyone wanted a ride. No one took his offer. Evidently the civilian clothes were a dead giveaway for the secret service. Apparently, none of the uniformed personnel wanted any part of being seen with him.

An OSS office was temporarily set up in the US Army Headquarters building halfway across town. That's where he was to report according to the verbal orders given to him by Hildabrand.

An American sergeant gave him directions. The trip was approximately five miles, but it turned out to be the longest five miles he had ever traveled. Almost immediately after leaving the airfield, Dieter began driving past bombed out rubble that once had been part of an architecturally proud city. Old men and young women were everywhere picking through debris looking for something to salvage. Children were running about, sometimes chasing Dieter's Jeep. Because of the traffic of trucks and other army vehicles, he could only travel about 10 mph making it easy for youngsters to run alongside. A couple of the older, bolder youths tried to jump inside the Jeep. Only a sharp scolding in German frightened them off.

Dieter finally figured out that driving along in an American vehicle, dressed like a New York stockbroker, was an invitation for children to ask for money. He thought he would dress less conspicuous in the future.

American bombardiers did their job well. While nearly all of the city's industrial areas and much of the commercial districts were pounded into piles of shattered bricks, the outer residential areas of Munich remained relatively undamaged. However, several huge apartment complex buildings near the center of town were no more. Apparently, many of the people Dieter watched as they sifted through the rubble were former residents. It was a tiring sight to observe.

Where were the returning soldiers? Many were being sent home by the Americans; but with this being a US controlled sector, there should be former members of the Wehrmacht milling about.

After what seemed like 50 miles, Dieter finally found his way to the US Army Headquarters. Curiously, it was located in the old Gestapo Building at the center of Munich. An MP at the door to the huge four-story former hotel directed Dieter to a second floor office.

"How ironic this dreaded Gestapo building could survive 77 Allied strategic bombing missions over Munich," Dieter thought as he climbed the stairway.

He reached Room 243, a former hotel room made into an office by joining rooms together. A painted makeshift sign on the door read "US Office of Strategic Planning." It was an odd name for a spy headquarters, Dieter chuckled to himself. *"First, 'strategic bombing,' now 'strategic planning'."*

Dieter walked into the office where two women were seated at typewriting desks. One of them looked up.

"May I help you?" she said in English with a heavy German accent.

"I'm looking for the Station Chief," Dieter replied in English.

"I'll get Mr. Jansen," she said, getting up and walking to another office door across the room. After a few seconds, a tall, slightly balding man of about 40 years of age appeared in the doorway.

"Are you Dieter Zeis?" he asked.

"Yes sir," Dieter replied, walking over and shaking his hand.

"I'm Edgar Jansen," the man said cordially.

Jansen ushered Dieter into his office, closing the door behind them.

"I've been expecting you," Jansen continued. "Agent Hildabrand filled me in on your background. He puts a lot of stock in your abilities to assess the situation."

Dieter chortled.

"I'm not really sure what situation you're referring to, sir," he coyly replied.

"Well … we've got to figure out what Gehlen's up to, whether we can really trust him," Jansen said in a concerned way.

Dieter was confused. He thought that part of his mission was just between him and Hildabrand. He pondered a response, but thought it best to keep his mouth shut and observe. After all, observing was his primary mission.

"Do you have a place to stay?" Jansen asked subconsciously knowing the answer. "Of course you don't," he quickly added, answering his own question. "I'll have one of the girls out front set you up with a room somewhere close by."

Jansen appeared to be a rather affable American; sure of himself and his surroundings. He seemed to be a likable fellow with a good head on his shoulders.

"You'll want to shed the Brooks Brothers suit," Jansen said with a titter. "You stick out like a sore thumb. That get-up has 'Government Agent' written all over you. You'll blend in better with something a bit more casual."

Dieter believed Jansen was right figuring a less conspicuous outfit was in order. Though, after the slight at the airport, then driving from the airport into town, Dieter had that one already figured out.

"You'll be going out to Dachau later this week," Jansen said. "Ever been there?"

Dieter hesitated, and then replied: "I was in Munich many years ago … however, I've never actually been to Dachau."

Jansen began describing Dachau to Dieter.

"Dachau is a small village on the outskirts of Munich," he began. "The concentration camp itself is just west of the village. It was one of the first camps the Nazis set up back in the '30s … but, you probably already knew that didn't you?"

Jansen stood, looking at Dieter with a fairly accusatory stare.

"Yes, I was aware of the camp, but I wasn't aware of what really went on there."

"Right. I'm sure you weren't," Jansen said cynically with a forced smile.

"The war crime trials will begin soon. I'm sure you'll want to sit in on those. As for General Gehlen, you won't have to look far for him. He's set up an office here in the hotel. You might want to make yourself known to him, unless he already knows who you are."

"No sir, I've never actually met the man," Dieter assured.

Dieter had to face reality. He was a former German Army officer. No matter what he might say, the stain of the Third Reich would be forever etched on him so he might as well just get used to it.

Jansen pressed a button on his desk intercom.

"Ruta … would you come in here please."

Within seconds, the woman Dieter first spoke appeared in the doorway.

"Would you show Agent Zeis where he can find a room," Jansen said to her. "You might try the Hofzeller. I believe they should have a room that would be adequate."

"Yes sir," she said. "Would you come with me, Colonel?"

"Oh, and Ruta ... you can to drop the 'Colonel' bit. Those days are long gone for Agent Zeis, so we wouldn't want to give our local friends the wrong idea ... or any hope."

Dieter wasn't sure what that meant; but nevertheless, he wasn't anxious to let anyone know his background anymore than necessary, so he had no objections to Jansen's remark.

When returning to the Jeep, Ruta hopped into the passenger seat and Dieter got behind the wheel. *"The woman was probably about 30 or so, close to his age,"* Dieter thought. *"Not bad to look at—dark blonde and slender; even though her dress was plain and her open-toed shoes were about to fall apart, she still managed to make them work nicely for her."*

"How are the Americans to work for?" he asked in German, making small talk as he followed her directions to the hotel.

"I have no complaints," she replied in German, keeping the conversation to a bare minimum. The woman gave further directions for Dieter to follow to the hotel.

With a rustic nondescript front, the Hofzeller Hotel wasn't much to look at. Somehow, the building miraculously survived intact all the air raids. It was one of those 19th century-style hotels complete with a grand, ornate central lobby. Dieter imagined elegantly dressed patrons wandering about for a formal ball. Today, however, there was one shabbily dressed bellhop looking well past retirement age guarding the front door. A large oversized reception desk covered most of the left side of the room where an older woman was performing her daily paper work.

"Guten Tag, mein Herr," the woman offered.

Dieter responded in perfect German bringing a friendly smile to the receptionist's face. Then Ruta began to speak explaining whom Dieter represented, when suddenly he tactfully interrupted her describing himself as a war trials observer. He figured the best way to begin making friends among the locals was to keep his true business to himself. He might need the help of these people down the road.

After Dieter registered, he asked Ruta how she would return to the office. "I live nearby," she offered. "It's close to my quitting time, so I'll walk home from here. Auf Wiedersehen, Herr Zeis."

The trip up the hotel elevator was an adventure. It stopped twice on its way to the third floor. Dieter was unsure whether it was faulty equipment, an interruption of electricity, or both.

The room the bellhop ushered him into was woefully sparse looking as though it hadn't been used in quite awhile. Dieter handed the old man a few American coins at which he stared for a moment, then retreated with a faint smile. Before closing the door, Dieter asked him if there was a place nearby to get a beer or some schnapps.

"Next door is such a place, but be careful. They're usually old soldiers in there looking for handouts," the old man replied. "They are more hungry than thirsty."

When the bellhop closed the door, Dieter realized he wanted to be anywhere but in this depressing room. It was lit with a single light bulb hanging from the ceiling. He imagined at one time there must have been a very nice elaborate fixture hanging in its place; but that would have been several bombings ago. In the corner was a desk chair that had no desk. Off to the center of the room was an old pedestal bed nearly covering an old worn out carpet that had seen better days. Next to the bed was a makeshift nightstand made from a wooden crate that was fitted with a drab iron lamp with a torn fabric shade. The light was just bright enough to illuminate the wallpaper by the bed that must have been quite the fashion many years ago. The tall, large-paned window without curtains faced out over the front of the hotel. It had been nailed shut.

The reality of truly being alone finally hit Dieter Zeis. After leaving Belgium on orders from Field Marshal Rommel, he had been caught up in a whirlwind of activity with the British and Americans; the hollowness of being by himself lay heavy in the pit of his stomach. He didn't like that feeling. Most of all, he missed his beautiful wife. He tried not to think about her; much of the Dresden populace was incinerated—to hold out hope for her survival was pure folly.

Dieter left the room and descended the stairs back to the lobby. He didn't care to chance the elevator. Being trapped in a small dark box would not have been pleasant. For some reason, his thoughts drifted back to North Africa and Rommel's panzer divisions. Being trapped in an iron coffin was frightening. He wanted no part of such claustrophobic spaces. Being with Rommel, he had the chance to experience a panzer, and he could only imagine the horror of trying to escape.

As he walked across the lobby from the stairway, the lady receptionist at the front desk hailed Dieter.

"Herr Zeis, there is a man in the bar next door asking for you," she told him.

Dieter was puzzled as to whom this was. He could only fathom.

"Did he leave a name?"

"No, he just asked if you had checked into the hotel," she replied.

The bar next door was not much more than a long hall with a few tables and chairs. The bar itself, if one could call it that, was just big enough to hold a couple of bottles and some glasses. Two people would have a hard time standing and leaning against it.

The room was dark, lit only by a couple of those hanging bulbs—one at each end. Four men were sitting at a table near the front, each with a mug of beer in front of them. They were unmistakably former soldiers. Dieter recognized their shabby boots. Two of the men were wearing their Heer tunics. The original green color was badly faded, except for where the eagle and swastika patches had been ripped from their right breast. He wondered how many other German soldiers were lurking about in such places around the city. Except for members of the SS, most enlisted men and officers under the rank of captain had been freed to return to their homes. The French and the Russians were still holding hundreds of thousands of German troops using them for nothing more than slave labor. This was the American Zone, so most of the POWs had been repatriated.

Sitting at a table in the rear of the room was a well-dressed man. He had his chair propped back leaning against the wall. His fedora was half cocked barely covering his eyes. As Dieter stepped closer, a familiar face suddenly emerged.

"John ... is that you?"

The fellow got up from his chair and extended his hand.

"Colonel yes ... it's me. How are you!"

It was John Krauss, the American farm boy Dieter befriended eight years ago.

"I heard you were over here somewhere. My god, how long has it been?"

"Thousands of miles and scores of trials," John poetically replied.

John no longer was the fresh innocent looking young farm kid from Midwestern America. Today he was a veteran OSS agent pushed well beyond the 28 he was.

"Schroeder?"

"Yes sir ... I found him in a POW camp near Bonn. I found Marlene as well. She was working in a hospital in Kassel."

Dieter was overjoyed to see his friend. It was the best he had felt in two years. John quickly brought him up-to-date. Through his contacts with the OSS, John was able to get both Schroeder and Marlene to America. The old sergeant was reunited with his wife in New York. Marlene Harriet Hink was waiting in Nebraska at his parent's house for John to return so they could be married.

"Schroeder is opening up a restaurant," John proudly said. "He's finally going to prepare those fabulous dinners for paying customers!"

The two men heartily laughed, reminiscent of the old times.

"So ... what the *hell* are you doing here in Munich?" Dieter inquired.

"I'm trying to get food to these people and soldiers back to work," John replied. "Uncle Sugar is trying his best to get beans, flour, and meat to these poor people. But with the black market all around us ... it hasn't been easy."

John described in detail of how he was taken prisoner in 1943 in Tunis, transferred to the United States on a Liberty ship, and later *escaped* a train while being transferred from Camp Clarinda, Iowa to Fort Robinson, Nebraska.*

"Believe it or not, I jumped right off that POW train into a ditch just as it was pulling out of my hometown!"

"Broken Bow?" Dieter said, chuckling along with John.

"The OSS knew all along who I was ... and they covertly designed my own escape!" John continued, laughing. "I thought I had 'em fooled. As it turned out, they had me fooled! At least I got to see my parents before heading back here.

The two friends chatted for several more hours, drinking beer, sipping schnapps, catching up on each other's lives.

When Greta's name arose, John immediately asked about "Little Jack."

"He was with her husband's parents in Scotland," Dieter replied. "With all the upheaval arising in London, she felt it best he be put out of harm's way."

"Is she happy?" John inquired.

"She seems quite content. Greta is heavily involved with the British Secret Service, so she doesn't have much time to think about herself," Dieter replied.

John then got very quiet before speaking again.

"I don't know how much longer I'm going to be over here. It's all a matter of how much trouble the Russians give us," John continued. "On the surface, I'm working to feed the German refugees ... but ... I have other assignments as well."

Dieter revealed a slight smile.

"Yes ... I understand," Dieter replied. "What do you know about General Gehlen?"

"Just enough to know that I don't trust the son of a bitch."

"Well ... some of the Yanks don't either," Dieter countered. "He says he can identify a number of communist spies within our ranks."

"The OSS?"

Dieter nodded his head.

---

* "Nebraska Doppelganger," Chapters 14 – 17.

"I wouldn't be surprised," John added. "I have my suspicions with a few agents myself."

"Anyone I should be concerned about?" Dieter asked.

"I'm not sure just yet, so I'm not saying anything," John replied. An old friend once advised me to, 'Be careful what you say and to whom you say it'."

Dieter smiled, recalling his warning of many years ago when they were dealing with hardened Nazi members, SS troops, and Gestapo agents.

"Who's your controller?" John asked.

"Bud Hildabrand at Devonshire Hall."

Quietness prevailed over John.

"What's wrong?" Dieter asked, slightly alarmed.

"Not sure. Just remember your own sage advice," John replied.

"Was ist der, 'sage'?" Dieter said in a jokingly manner.

"It means 'wise' you ol' fool!"

"You Americans! You have too many words with too many meanings," Dieter chuckled.

"Blame it on the damn English!" John chortled.

Dieter now turned serious. The shooting incident that happened near Calais many months back was gnawing at him. He had to confide in someone.

"I performed a very deplorable act," Dieter confessed to his friend.

"Just one?" John interjected.

"Yes. I was forced to shoot two Waffen SS officers during the time I was making my way to England," he replied.

"Why?"

Dieter related the story to his friend.

"Look Dieter … you had no choice," John said in a comforting tone. "Your mission might have been compromised. Welcome to the underworld of intrigue and espionage!"

Somehow, those words didn't comfort Dieter. Even though John was of direct German descent from his parents, John was born an American with a different set of values. Dieter didn't think John fully understood Dieter's feelings. But then again, John was a warm, compassionate human being; so maybe he did.

The two men parted, promising to meet the next evening.

Back in his room, Dieter sprawled on the bed; it was squeaky—but for the most part, comfortable. Before he drifted into slumber, Dieter reflected on his few hours back in Germany.

"I must follow my own advice. Be careful what you say and to whom you say it."

Chapter

13

July 8, 2007: Cindy could see that Dieter Zeis' story was taking its toll on Greta. She wasn't sure just why, but there had to be more as to why she was going through all of this ancient history—more so than what Jack was telling her.

Up until now, the story was quite interesting but admittedly routine; maybe even a bit boring to someone her age. Cindy decided upon a new tactic with her boss before proceeding with Greta.

Jack returned home from his London office around 6:30 that evening. Cindy, Greta, and Jack had a pleasant dinner with his mother excusing herself around 9 o'clock for bed. The opportunity was perfect for seriously grilling Jack. She was, after all, supposed to be an investigative reporter; so starting with her best source at this point seemed logical.

"Jack, I've spent the last several days listening to Greta … but I have to tell you, I'm still in the dark about what I'm really looking for…" Cindy began.

Jack looked up from his snifter of Château Guynot ready to respond but wasn't fast enough. Cindy quickly continued.

"…and don't tell me it's simply a matter of the Americans keeping the British in the dark about spook secrets during the

Cold War," she continued in a rather offensive fashion. "You can read any of that shit by Googling the Internet!"

Cindy learned early on that almost any name, subject, or event could be rapidly researched by simply typing into the Google web site the sought after information. Whether any of it was true was certainly another matter.

Jack looked at Cindy and smiled.

"Do you know what a double agent is?" Jack asked quizzically.

"What?" Cindy was incredulous. She could see Jack was deadly serious.

"It's a simple question."

"Well yes ... of course. Doesn't everyone?"

Jack took a long, slow draw from the Cuban Cohiba he was coddling.

"We suspected that Dieter may have been working for the Russians." he said, after releasing a cloud of blue smoke.

Cindy started to speak and then caught herself. Jack tackled an angle that slightly puzzled her. But the revelation was startling. She walked over to the bar and poured herself a full glass of Siegerrebe 2005—a wonderful dry white wine from the Three Choirs Vineyards in Gloucestershire County. She took a sip.

"What's your point? What are you saying, Jack?"

"I'm saying that, despite my mother's very close relationship, not to mention your grandfather's association, there was some evidence to suggest he was spying for the Russians while he was supposedly spying for the West."

Cindy began digesting Jack's words. Maybe there were facts! She was toying with the rim of her wine glass, shaking her head.

"I don't get it. Why? Why would Dieter do such a thing?"

"Who knows? Things were rather chaotic after the war. His home was in the Russian Zone, East Germany, and maybe he felt a loyalty to help. We're not even sure if that was true ... but I believe my mother knows."

"Have you tried asking her?" Cindy asked.

"Yes, but she always avoids giving me a straight answer by diverting the discussion in another direction. You seem to have a special relationship with her … you know, that girl to girl thing!"

Cindy no longer felt she was grasping at fireflies on a dark summer night. Thanks to her conversation with Jack, at least Cindy now had a direction—if nothing else. The best thing to do at this point was continue listening to Dieter's story from Greta.

"The secrets the ol' gal must be keeping in her head," Cindy thought. *"And, to be torn between her native Germany, her adopted America, and her inherited home of England. The woman was one hell of a juggler. What was Dieter? Was he a juggler as well?"*

The following morning Cindy was greeted on the patio by Somes, the butler, who had morning tea ready. For the first time, she noticed Somes had a slight limp in his left leg.

"Probably an old war wound," she thought. *"He's definitely of World War II age."*

By now, she was accustomed to English breakfast tea, forsaking America's favorite morning caffeine fix. Coffee was available; but, when in England, join the natives and indulge in their daily rituals—consumption of hearty black or white tea being central to most in their habits. Conversation, work, social grace; everything revolved around the serving of tea in one form or another.

Cindy quickly learned what it means to be "mother," taking it "with or without," and having it "black or white." Translation: "who'll serve, with or without sugar, straight or with cream." It's a time-honored tradition at which no one pokes fun—or at least not noticeable so. Besides, Cindy was growing rather fond of this cultured ritual. She certainly could see how a bunch of colonial fanatics dumping tons of precious tea into Boston Harbor would piss-off the sons of Mother England.

But, the Boston Tea Party was just the beginning of a nearly 300 year old strained love-hate relationship between the United States and Great Britain. Ben Franklin was right: two nations separated by a common language—or was that Mark

Twain? Cindy would have to "Google" that one when she had time.

Today, she was prepared for another long session with Greta, who appeared on the patio, well rested and ready for a sunny day—or maybe a bit of rain. It was, after all, July—and this was England.

Chapter

14

There was much more to Dieter Zeis' story than Greta was allowing. For most of his life, the enigmatic German officer relied on his own counsel; but secrets were what he kept best.

Dieter was born April 11, 1914, in Dresden, Germany. He was the son of a German financier. His mother was of Prussian Aristocracy. Her brother, Karl Rudolf Gerd von Rundstedt, was a top general in the German Heer. It was through Uncle Karl that Dieter was able to move rapidly through the ranks. From 1926 to 1930, he attended a military preparatory academy in Bonn; then went on to receive his formal college education at Heidelberg University, graduating with a degree in business and finance.

General von Rundstedt saw to it his nephew received an officer's commission in the Heer Reserves and by the time Dieter graduated from Heidelberg, he was a captain. During the Great Depression, only those who had financial stability were able to succeed and stay in the army. Pay was not always reliable and only officers of independent means could afford a military career. Dieter was fortunate his father and mother were both wealthy and could ensure that their son receive the best education, have the prestige of military rank, and be placed correctly in upper German society.

It was during his years at Heidelberg that Dieter met Marta von Carlsen. They fell in love and, upon their graduation, were married. They made their home in Dresden; but when Hitler came to power in 1933, the Wehrmacht began expanding, taking Dieter on a career path as a logistics and administrative officer. Dieter had little to do with actual warfare; rather, he provided the implements and supplies for his comrades to wage war.

"His mother asked her brother, General von Rundstedt, to promise to keep Dieter out of combat situations," Greta recalled. "I presume that is why his army career was primarily one of paperwork."

This was the first time anyone had really told Cindy anything personal about Dieter Zeis.

"What happened to Marta?" Cindy asked.

Greta didn't answer. She just stared at the horizon at the rear of her lawn. She was quiet for several minutes before replying. Cindy had learned to be patient with the old sage. An answer was forthcoming.

"She was in Dresden during the firebombing," Greta responded choking back a tear. "That was primarily a British bombing mission, so I've felt particularly guilty since that dreadful deed was done by the RAF. Oh (to be sure!) the Americans did their part, but it primarily was a British show.

"It was so unnecessary, but the British and the Americans needed to show ol' Uncle Joe [Stalin] that we were doing our part in bringing the war to a close."

A couple of times in the past, Cindy had heard Grandpa John and Jack mention Dresden, but she was unaware of the psychological impact and loss of life the bombings had on the German people.

Greta tearfully described the Royal and American Air Force's tactics of dropping incendiary bombs in clusters over strategic targets, primarily German cities. Incendiary bombs were bombs filled with highly combustible chemicals such as magnesium and phosphorus, and then petroleum jelly was added to make a hotter fire. This combination was later known as napalm.

"After the targets were set ablaze, the air above became extremely hot and rose rapidly," Greta explained. "Cold air then rushed in from ground level and people were literally sucked into the fire. And to compound those matters, the people able to avoid the flames were, unfortunately, killed when the oxygen feeding those massive flames was extracted from the air suffocating them where they stood. It was a very horrible and agonizing death."

She went on to describe Dresden as one of Germany's most beautiful medieval cultural centers. It had no military value whatsoever; in fact, it had not been attacked during the war—not until February 13, 1945. The city had swollen in population from its normal 600,000 to close to 1 million; many were refugees from the eastern part of Germany fleeing the approaching Red Army.

"There were 773 RAF Lancaster Bombers over Dresden on that horrific night," she recalled. "To make matters worse, the Americans sent more than 500 of its B-17s and B-24s over the next two days just to make sure the job was done."

"And, Marta?"

"As far as I know, Dieter never found her," Greta solemnly replied. "He, of course, tried. He went there to find their home, but there was nothing left except burned out rubble."

Cindy felt Greta's remorse. It was a sad story indeed; but there was hesitation in her voice as she told the story. Saying Dieter never found Marta seemed rather indefinite.

"How many lives were lost?" Cindy asked, changing from Marta.

"Well my dear, that's a question … isn't it?" Greta replied. "Allied statistics say maybe 35,000, but German estimates have it closer to over 100,000. Whatever the figure, it was an absolutely unnecessary attack on innocent people who had no military value whatsoever. In fact, there were a lot of Allied POWs who perished during the bombings. But, hell … that's war!"

The Allied POWs worked civilian jobs in Dresden as well as other cities because so many of the German men were away fighting the war. Nevertheless, the bombing raids were just another attempt at demoralizing the German people into surrender. It wasn't their choice to surrender, but they wish it had.

Chapter

15

The fog of war was just that—a haze where no two people saw the same action in the same way. Whatever actually occurred at the Baugnez crossroads near Malmédy, Belgium on the early afternoon of December 17, 1944, probably no one will ever really know.

The war crimes tribunal Dieter observed at Dachau would be one of the toughest assignments he's ever had. Luckily, decisions for the outcome weren't his responsibility.

This story might have been more confusing had it not involved the Kampfgruppe (Battle Group) of the 1st SS Panzer Regiment—under the 1st Waffen SS Panzer Division—commanded by Lieutenant Colonel Joachim Peiper, who was the former adjutant to Heinrich Himmler. Peiper was renowned as a brilliant officer and was decorated with the Knight Cross. Still, his association with Himmler makes the German version of the story suspect.

The Baugnez crossroads was known to the Americans as "Five Points" since it was a junction of five different roads some two miles southeast of Malmédy. Despite being told about an approaching Panzer Division, American artillery officers ignored the warning and continued sending more than 100 soldiers of Battery B of the 285th Field Artillery Observation

Battalion in convoy, which subsequently landed into the hands of the Germans.

Of course, the story isn't that simple. The brume of war demands confusion to the point that no one really knows what happened; yet an Associated Press news report by a "Stars and Strips" reporter turned the incident into an international war crimes trial. Reporter Hal Boyle wrote a month later: "Nazis turned machine guns on GI POWs."

The Germans captured 113 GIs from the convoy, plus another 26 who came along later. Five of the Americans in the front of the convoy managed to escape; one other GI in the last vehicle also escaped.

The Americans were assembled by the Germans near a café adjacent to Five Points, and according to a young Belgium boy, who witnessed the event, were shot by German machine-gunners *in cold blood.* Later, some 60 Americans, who were not killed by the initial strafing, attempted to escape; but German soldiers still in the area, opened fire. At least 18 more were killed and another was never heard from again. The rest managed to escape, later to be witnesses at the post-war trial.

After the Battle of the Bulge was over, more than 70 American bodies were found frozen beneath the snow by US Army Engineers using mine detectors.

While GI survivors swore the Germans stripped the Americans of their valuables, the majority of recovered bodies had rings, watches, money, and other valuables on them. However, many of the bodies had gunshots to the head and several were beaten about the head. At least nine of the men still had their arms raised above their heads where they fell.

[Writer Michael Reynolds wrote about the Malmédy Massacre in the February 2003 issue of *World War II Magazine.*]

"Twenty-one American survivors made statements to US authorities in Malmédy on December 17, the day of the massacre, as well as on the following day, before there was any possibility of collusion or anybody putting ideas into their heads.

"The American survivors all told the same story: After surrendering to a German armored column and being disarmed, they were assembled in a field just south of the crossroads. The Germans then opened fire on them with machine guns and rifles. In most cases, the survivors mentioned two pistol shots before the main shooting started.

"They said German soldiers then entered the field and shot anyone who showed signs of life and many of the bodies were kicked or prodded in order to get a response. Then, the German column continued onward, with some of the vehicle crews taking potshots at the bodies lying in the field.

"All but one of the survivors insisted no attempt to escape had been made before the Germans opened fire; and the escape attempt came at a much later stage when they thought the Germans had left."

But the real question in front of the tribunal was judicious: while there was little doubt the Germans fired upon the soldiers en masse, did the Americans attempt to escape *before* the Germans opened fire?

By the time Dieter got to Dachau, the trial had already begun. Lieutenant Colonel Peiper, his senior staff, and 70 of his men were facing multiple charges before a US Military Court. Charges included "willfully, deliberately and wrongfully permit, encourage, aid, abet and participate in the killing, shooting, ill treatment, abuse and torture of members of the armed forces of the United States of America."

The old adage: "To the victors belong the spoils," that winners are right because they won, turned out to be the case for this particular trial. It came as no surprise that all of the German defendants were found guilty.

Dieter was stunned at the speed in which the trial was conducted. Had he arrived an hour later, he would have missed everything. With a tribunal of seven American officers, and a brigadier general as President, it took less than three minutes on each of the charges before them.

Peiper, the senior officer, and 39 of his men were sentenced to death by hanging—the ultimate disgrace for a military man. Another 22 of the accused were sentenced to life in prison; the rest received sentences of 10 to 20 years each.

Later, Dieter learned none of the death sentences were carried out due to inconsistencies in witness statements, faulty investigations, and a general appearance of "rush to judgment." All of the prisoners, including Lieutenant Colonel Peiper, were free men by the mid-1950s.

So much for American wartime justice.

The sign read on the door just down the hallway from the OSS Office in Munich: "The South German Industrial Organization." Dieter was about to meet Major General Reinhard Gehlen face-to-face. He remembered observing the former German spymaster at Fort Hunt through a two-way mirror. But because of diverse conditions, he never met him. As far as Dieter knew, Gehlen was unaware of him; nevertheless, the circle of power in the Third Reich was interesting, at best, and there was a chance Dieter *was* known to him.

Dieter entered the small front office where there were several secretaries typing and answering the phones. Everyone seemed busy, but one lady approached him asking if she could be of help. Dieter showed her his OSS credentials and requested to see General Gehlen. Without hesitation, she whisked him straight into his office. Dieter marveled at the *magic* his credentials possessed.

"Colonel Zeis, how good of you to stop in," Gehlen said, standing up from behind his desk, extending his hand. "I've heard so much about you."

This did not make Dieter feel welcome.

"Good to meet you too … General," Dieter straightforwardly replied.

"So … you're working for Uncle Sam," Gehlen said in a gesturing manner.

"I'm trying to help Germany the best way I can," Dieter said.

"And so you should my boy … so you should."

Gehlen motioned for Dieter to have a chair.

"What do you think of the Americans' intelligence service?" Gehlen probed.

"Well … I'd say they learned well from the British."

Gehlen coyly smiled.

"They still have a lot to learn. I would hope that, as a loyal German officer, you would consider coming home to work for me and my organization," Gehlen said. "We have a tremendous opportunity to rebuild Germany."

Dieter feinted a slight smile, saying nothing in reply.

"You realize I knew Field Marshal Rommel quite well," Gehlen continued. "We went through a strategic planning course together."

Dieter doubted just how well someone like Gehlen would know Herr General; but, then again, maybe he did know Rommel.

"Those final days on the Atlantic Wall must have been horrendous."

Gehlen was probing. Dieter simply shook his head in agreement reiterating past knowledge of what was known; any useful information, Gehlen would have to probe elsewhere.

After about 15 minutes, Gehlen mentioned he had another appointment he had to attend but wanted to continue his meeting with Dieter during lunch. He had someone he wanted him to meet.

"You must come and have lunch with me today if your schedule permits," Gehlen said cordially.

"Yes … I would like that very much," Dieter replied.

"Good, then I'll meet you downstairs in the dining room around noon. They have a marvelous array of fresh foods and drink. You won't believe how well our captors eat … but, you already know that, don't you?"

The two men shook hands and Dieter parted.

Dieter had little more than two hours before meeting back with Gehlen for lunch, so he decided to drive around the city to kill some time and to look at all the devastation. He finally managed to find less conspicuous clothes—a GI field jacket, a cap, khaki slacks, and a wool shirt. Somewhat military but not to the point of being ostentatious. It was just enough to alert the populace that he wasn't one of them but just enough to make him feel like an outsider. Why should *he* feel like an outsider? He was German-born, educated, and served his country with distinction, yet....

Driving through the rubble-filled streets was reminiscent of driving through an army obstacle course; except this time the obstacles were real. In the sluggishness in passing, numerous children scampered about the Jeep begging for food. It was a heartrendingly situation that made him sad. Although he and Marta had talked about children, they never had any. In a terrible sense, he was probably lucky. Dieter could just imagine his children running alongside an Allied Jeep in another city—Dresden, for example. Yes, he was lucky.

"I'll smuggle something from lunch to pass along," he thought. *"But, of course, that would be tossing a crumb into a cavern of swarming swallows. Maybe John can help."*

As he continued driving through the maze of debris, Dieter noticed dozens of US Army vehicles and men. The 65th and 71st Infantry Division had set up their headquarters in and around Munich. Near the end of the war, these two forces occupied Southeastern Bavaria and Northern Austria and were seemingly destined to be here for a while.

Dieter drove past a group of US Army Engineers and numerous German civilians who were talking and looking at maps and plans. He later learned the Americans were planning to help the Munich residents completely rebuild their city as near as possible to its prewar condition. It was to be a major undertaking.

"Not many conquering nations would do such a thing," he thought, remembering the devastation left by the Wehrmacht in Poland, Belgium, France, and North Africa.

But quiet desperation pierced their faces. All their heads were hanging—doing anything and everything possible to better themselves. At the moment, just sifting through rubble, piling useable bricks, and occasionally finding food was about all they could do. Germany was starving. They needed help. Would it arrive in time?

Chapter

16

At noon sharp, Dieter parked his Jeep and walked back into the American Army's Headquarters. It was one of the surviving hotels from the 77 bombing raids—much nicer and more elaborate than the one where he was staying. What little damage sustained from the bombings, the GIs had already repaired, painted, and cleaned up. During the war, it had been used as the Gestapo Headquarters.

After Dieter showed the MP his identification, he walked through the huge double doors. Upon entering the foyer, he arbitrarily glanced back and noticed General Gehlen's black sedan pulling up in front of the building. Apparently he was just returning from his appointment. As the spymaster emerged from the car, he was closely followed by someone who looked familiar. As the two walked up the steps, he realized it was former Gestapo agent Conrad Krueger. Dieter walked back through the doors and greeted Gehlen. He in turn introduced Krueger. They conversed in German.

Dieter made no mention of recognition of the former agent, but Krueger himself had a puzzled expression on his face pondering Dieter's identity. He looked familiar but couldn't quite place where he'd seen him before.

The dining room was bustling with some 100 mostly uniformed American officers. Several others besides Dieter, Gehlen, and Krueger were in civilian attire.

Dieter quickly noticed a number of German men and women working the room as waiters, waitresses, and busboys. He could only hope the same was true in the kitchen. He subconsciously thought of Werner slaving over a hot oven baking a leg of lamb for one of Rommel's staff gatherings.

In less than a minute, a middle-aged German hostess warmly greeted them in English and took them to a table near one of the large front windows.

After common pleasantries were exchanged, General Gehlen pointedly asked Dieter what assignment he was given in Munich.

"I'm here to monitor the war crimes trials in Dachau," Dieter insipidly replied.

Krueger grunted and smiled as his cold black eyes focused on the OSS agent. "Why would they send you here to do that job?" Kruger subtly asked.

"I don't know ... I suppose someone thought I might have some sense of fairness ... a sense of understanding the crimes that were committed."

Gehlen slightly grinned, but Kruger kept a straight face.

"Yes ... I'm sure that's it," Gehlen replied.

Krueger continued looking at Dieter with Gestapo scrutiny.

"The Malmédy trials didn't take that long," Dieter continued as a waitress brought them a loaf of Pumpernickel bread and each a glass of chilled water.

After their food orders were taken, Gehlen continued to probe.

"How did you come to be an OSS agent?"

Dieter tore a piece of the freshly baked bread from the loaf that was being passed. Pumpernickel was one of his favorite breads because of the unique sweetish taste. It was rarely found in his hometown of Dresden. He discovered this bread while on a trip to Düsseldorf back in the '30s. It was quite popular in the Westphalia region of Germany. Dieter figured the bakery chef must be from that area. It's doubtful anyone in Bavaria would know how to steam it properly.

"I happened to be in the right place at the right time," Dieter replied, now speaking in English. "I would think it more polite, considering where we are, that we speak the language of our hosts."

"But, of course," Gehlen replied in English, smiling.

Krueger continued studying Dieter.

"Can't remember where you know me?" Dieter said looking sternly at Krueger with barely a trace of a smile.

"Sir, you have the advantage," Krueger finally spoke.

"Yes, I'm sure that I have." Dieter took his time with another piece of bread. The waitress, a middle-aged, brown-haired woman, brought the three men their meals, curtseyed politely and left.

"It was 1938," Dieter finally replied. "I was Commandant of the Berlin Medical Supply Depot. You came in one day trying to impress me and my soldiers with your long, dark leather coat and black fedora. I notice you don't wear that wardrobe anymore."

"Ah, yes. You had a rather large and loud sergeant, as I recall," Krueger smartly replied, continuing to gaze at Dieter with a sinister stare.

Gehlen realized the tension was building between the two men.

"Gentlemen, gentlemen ... we are all working together on the same side," Gehlen interjected. "Let us have peace and enjoy this fine meal."

"If I recall correctly, you were protecting some American farm boy. Krauss ... wasn't that his name?" Krueger continued probing.

"A good and loyal German soldier, who gave you no reason for harassment!" Dieter vociferously replied causing nearby patrons to look his way.

Gehlen stayed quiet as he relished the American roast beef au jus, mashed potatoes with garlic, and green beans.

Dieter recognized Krueger's tactic—the snarling guard dog being held at bay by an ostensible master. As the Americans would say, "Good cop, bad cop."

Dieter regained his composer and didn't reveal anymore than he had to while they continued their lunch. Because of the close working relationship the OSS had established with the Gehlen Org, Gehlen invited Dieter back to his office for further conversation. But what he really expected was a further interrogation.

Krueger excused himself and did not go upstairs to Gehlen's office. When Dieter returned with Gehlen, he began discussing the reconstruction of Germany. Gehlen seemed interested, but Dieter sensed he was more concerned about building an empire for himself and his cronies rather than worrying about the welfare of the German people.

Gehlen abruptly changed the subject getting to more pressing matters concerning the OSS. He felt Dieter should be apprised of certain issues.

"You know the OSS has a number of communists within its ranks," Gehlen posed, looking for a reaction. "The Americans don't seem to believe me."

Dieter was aware of the situation but allowed Gehlen to continue his probe.

"Some of them are here in Germany and some of them are in England," Gehlen continued thinking he should get an answer now.

"Have you identified these people to the Americans?" Dieter inquired.

"No … not yet. I'm not going to play all my cards at once," Gehlen replied. "I've already turned over a vast amount of Soviet intelligence … but I'm holding out some of the more important aspects including names of agents and communist sympathizers until a more prudent time."

This last piece of information was an obvious plant intended for delivery back to the Americans. After 30 more minutes of conversation, Dieter left.

Dieter learned that German men and women working in American mess halls and supply depots were the lucky ones— they were permitted a certain amount of rations to take home to their families; some of the sergeants looked the other way when outright pilfering occurred. Other American officers and difference in the outcome of the war—specifically whether Germany would be brought to its knees or given an opportunity to surrender non-conditionally. Still, Dieter realized that as long as Hitler continued to live, surrender would never happen. After the bungled July 20th assassination attempt, he seriously doubted there would ever be another organized effort.

At his new location, Dieter was allowed a better grade of food. In fact, he was given a menu of choices with which to select. There was a lamb, fish, pork, and eggs—but no beef or butter. For their toast, the English used an unsweetened horrid-smelling fruit jam they called "Vegemite."

"We're in a war, ol' chap," the Brit told Dieter as he scanned what looked like a delightful menu.

"Don't get too excited," the American broke in. "We are, after all, in England and as you probably know, they have no cuisine."

All three men chuckled.

"That's fine," Dieter replied. "I've already eaten far better since I've been in your care than I have in the past two years. The last good meal I had was in North Africa … it was a fine leg of lamb roast prepared by a sergeant friend of mine. What a wonderful meal that was … yes indeed!"

The initial tactics used by the two civilian agents were more of a get-acquainted style and a review of the war to date. Dieter discussed his duties and role as administrative officer and confidant to Rommel during the North African Campaign. Dieter speculated that vast pieces of real estate probably could have ended up in Axis hands had it not been for Hitler cutting the Deutsches Afrika Korps' supplies.

"You don't think ol' Monty could have still won, do you?" the Brit asked.

"Do you?" Dieter countered. "Let's face it. We ran out of gas, we ran out of ammunition, and we ran out of food. All our supplies went to the Eastern Front. If it hadn't been for that, we would have ended up in Cairo and maybe even as far as Baghdad."

The American agent reckoned Dieter had a point. He acknowledged that until General Patton took over the US II Corps, things weren't going very well for the Yanks.

Dieter recognized this tactic of befriending and agreement. Why not go along? It had been a long time since he'd been involved in good conversation with intelligent men who weren't trying to conquer the world.

"If it weren't for those fanatics in Berlin, the war would be taking a far different turn," Dieter offered. "First of all, many of our general officer corps were not members of the Nazis Party ... and, if they were, it'd merely be for expediency of their careers. It's the same with our technological industries and our scientific community. Many go along with the Nazi line just so they can do their work."

"What sort of work?" the American agent inquired. "Things like your buzz bombs and jet airplanes?"

"Ja, those ... and many other things."

Dieter realized he was being probed. He had already made up his mind to reveal what he knew, but he thought taking his time and playing the game a bit longer wouldn't hurt—and it may even earn him a bit more respect. No one likes a quitter, or even a traitor. Would what he was about to reveal about his country make him a traitor? No, if given the right circumstances; he had information ordered by Rommel to be conveyed to the highest Allied authorities.

"My name is Philby," the Brit finally said, extending his hand. "You and I have more in common than you might think."

"And how would that be?" Dieter asked.

"Well ... I'm married to an Austrian, whom I believe, would now be a fellow countryman of yours," Philby replied.

"Is she safe?" Dieter inquired.

"Very much so. We met in Vienna when I was with the British Embassy. I got her to safety before things got sticky," Philby replied. "Unfortunately ... we're now divorced."

Philby was a dark haired, slight man with a pleasant face. He wore a typical English business suit with vest and gold chain that probably had one of those pop-open gold watches attached to the end.

The American didn't identify himself even when Dieter asked his name. He continued to make an occasional comment about the war, usually one of compliment, trying to get the German to drop his guard. Dieter recognized and understood this tactic. He was going to play along.

Just then the door opened to the study where Dieter and the two agents were talking. Dieter couldn't believe his eyes. It was Greta.

"Gentlemen ... my I have a word in private with the Colonel," she asked.

Philby looked at the American, nodded, and the two left the room and closed the door; Greta entered, walked over, and sat at the table.

"Dieter ... you must cooperate in anyway you can," she pleaded. "The Allies are closing in on Germany and it's only a matter of time now. Is there *anything* you can give the Americans to help bring an end to all of this madness?"

He knew, of course, she was right. And, he did have something that, while it might not help end the war, it could very well prevent an expansion of hostilities.

"Do they know about us?" Dieter asked.

"Who?"

"Your people and the Americans."

"Not to the extent General Smith knows, but these two agents are aware I have a *special interest* in you," she replied, nodding her head toward the door. "They just don't know yet what that might be."

"All right ... bring them back in and we'll talk," he said with a sigh. A feeling of remorse and relief hit Dieter all at the same time. It was as if the breath had been taken from him; yet the weight of the world lifted from his shoulders.

With the Brit and the American back in the library and Greta remaining, Dieter began telling them of secret plans and missions he was aware of that, if carried out, could change the directions of the war in favor of the Germans.

"In spite of what you might believe about our industry being obliterated, which much of it has, Germany has developed some terrible weapons that, if unleashed, could kill thousands of people," Dieter began. "I'm not talking about soldiers in the field, but innocent civilians here in England and even in America."

"Go on," the American urged.

"Our scientists have developed a rocket that is capable of reaching New York."

The two agents looked at each other, somewhat astonished. The V-1 and V-2 rockets had played havoc here on England. There had been rumors of more powerful weapons, but nothing confirmed.

"Well, if such rockets were able to reach America, and, I emphasize 'if,' it wouldn't make much of a dent, would it?" Philby inquired. "Maybe a building or two."

"That's the part you don't understand," Dieter said, pausing and breathing heavier. He was about to reveal a well-kept secret.

"Are you familiar with atomic energy?"

Philby shook his head. The American had a somewhat blank look, and Greta started shaking her head from side-to-side—not from knowing what he was talking about but realizing such a weapon could be devastating.

"Our scientists have developed a way to mount a powerful, but terrible bomb atop a rocket that could kill several hundred thousand people."

"Impossible," Philby said in astonishment.

"Such a terrible weapon is possible," Dieter insisted. "It wouldn't kill many people from the initial impact or explosion, but because of the deadly gases emitted into the air, something called 'radiation poisoning,' it would infect thousands of innocent civilians. This deadly atmospheric poisoning would be carried by the prevailing winds over large populated areas and even as much as a third of the United States."

"Just where is this terrible weapon being built?" Philby asked in bewilderment.

"Well, that's one of the big problems we all have," Dieter replied.

"We?"

enlisted men, alike, used foods and supplies as bartering materials for the black market. Everything from jewelry to war souvenirs were exchanged. Women prostituted themselves in order to have food for their children.

That evening, Dieter and John met at a small downtown family owned beer garden where homemade food was prepared daily. It certainly was a better joint than the one they visited the previous evening. Ready to talk and relax, they ordered a pitcher of Weizenbier (Wheat beer). They later would order from the menu for something to eat.

"I met an old friend of yours today," Dieter said as he sipped his beer.

"Oh ... and who might that be?"

"Conrad Krueger," Dieter replied.

Solemnness creased John's face. He became angry but controlled it well.

"I don't think I ever told you, but I was captured during the last days of the war when I was on my first mission for the OSS," John said. "I went through a rather painful reception, courtesy of Herr Krueger. I would think he might get a bit nervous if he knew I was still alive.[*]

"During captivity, I rather well got the distinct impression he expected me to be executed after his men tortured me. But I believe the American Army was closing in at the time and they themselves disappeared to save their own necks. I guess timing is everything!"

Dieter took another sip of beer pondering what he had just heard.

"Stay away from Gehlen's office at 22 Janningstrasse in the US Army Headquarters building," Dieter told him. "I don't know how Krueger would react if he sees you. During our brief encounter, I reminded him about that day at the Medical Supply Depot. He remembered 'the American farm boy.' His comments weren't very kind."

John acknowledged the caution.

---

[*] "Nebraska Doppelganger," Chapter 22.

"What can we do to help feed these folks around the city?" Dieter asked, changing the subject.

"We're due to start distributing flour, beans, salt, and sugar next week from three distribution points," John replied. "Of course, that's a long way from solving the problem, but it's a start. There's a massive food program being organized back in the States. Though, I really have no idea when it'll begin."

"I watched people sifting through garbage from behind the American Army Headquarters this afternoon. People are starving," Dieter said sadly.

"I know," John confirmed. "But, whatever we do, without massive aid, it's going to be a drop in the bucket."

The talk of food finally settled in on the two friends and each asked for a menu. Although Dieter had a full meal for lunch, he was really only interested in just a sandwich. He ordered the Leberkäse on a Kaiser Roll and Kartoffelsalat with a side of süß Senf. Even though John was of German descent and could speak the language fluently, he was unfamiliar with what kind of sandwich Dieter ordered. He did know that Kartoffelsalat was potato salad and süß Senf was sweet mustard. But the sandwich was a mystery.

"Leberkäse is a mixture of corned beef, bacon, and onions finely ground together and baked in a bread pan to make a 'meatloaf'," Dieter enlightened his friend. "When baked properly, it has a crunchy brown crust. You can then slice it to make a sandwich, and with sweet mustered added to the roll, it is quite tasty. It's been quite a while since I've had one. I hope it still taste as good as I remember!"

John was tired of sausages and sauerkraut. Dieter's description sounded tasty and John ordered the same thing. They also ordered another pitcher of Weizenbier and toasted to the good evening they were enjoying.

As days turned into weeks, Dieter became better acquainted with Gehlen even though neither fully trusted the other. Krueger seemed to go out of his way to avoid Dieter. His role in the Gehlen Org wasn't quite clear. At least one OSS name was revealed to Dieter as being a communist. He wasn't surprised to hear that Agent Grossman was on Gehlen's list—a record that came from the 1930s. Whether or not Grossman was still a communist was questionable; or even worse—a Russian agent. It wasn't his place to report such rumors; he'd let the general handle that part. If it were true, so be it. If it wasn't, then Dieter Zeis would not be the one to point an erroneous finger.

John had been reassigned back to Paris. For what, Dieter didn't know and John wasn't at liberty to discuss.

While he didn't trust Gehlen, Dieter admired him in a way. The man knew what was going on in the Soviet sector. Dieter asked about Dresden, which was in the Russian Zone in Eastern Germany.

"My home was in Dresden," he told Gehlen.

"Any family?" Gehlen asked.

"Just my wife. After the fire bombing I wasn't able to learn any information about her, but our home was destroyed. None of the displaced persons agencies were of help. I've pretty much given up hope, but, then again...."

"Have faith, my friend," Gehlen said in a comforting tone. "Let me see what I can do in the way of finding out more information."

Dieter gave the general Marta's full name and description and their address. He didn't have much faith that Gehlen would give the search a great deal of effort. But they had been getting along with each other, so maybe he would.

Dieter had been in Munich three months now and still no word or new orders from Hildabrand. Other trials had taken place at Dachau, with the same swift American justice the Waffen SS had received from the Malmédy incident. Dieter dutifully observed the proceedings, made his reports, and sent them to Devonshire Hall via a diplomatic courier servicing the Munich OSS Office. As ordered, he made no written report or comments on Gehlen. Dieter simply made mental notes of information he thought might be of interest to the OSS.

Gehlen was a very shrewd character. He had the ability to turn on the charm when needed; but could just as easily turn vicious at the drop of a hat. Even though Dieter was an OSS agent, he had the gut feeling Gehlen was revealing certain information to him that he normally wouldn't. Dieter reckoned it was because he was a fellow German. He doubted the general would be as revealing to the Americans, but then again, maybe he was using Dieter as a conduit. Either Gehlen had underestimated Dieter's loyalty to his new employer, or he was setting a trap. Whichever, he would have to be on guard.

Chapter
17

As devastated as Munich was from the Allied bombing raids, it wasn't any worse than 95 percent of the other German cities. Nearly all the other larger cities, regardless of military value, had been pummeled into rubble.

Dieter wasn't aware of the war of words and political struggle festering in the United States. Henry Morgenthau, Jr, the American Secretary of the Treasury, put forth a memorandum known as "The Morgenthau Plan." Quite simply, it called for the de-industrializing of Germany by stripping its resources and keeping them from producing anything viable other than fodder and foodstuffs. Morgenthau, a Jew, was advocating a German agricultural nation thus eliminating the likelihood of them ever restarting World War III.

By the time Dieter could fathom what had been planned, President Truman authorized Secretary of State George Marshall to implement his "Marshall Plan," which called for the feeding and rebuilding of Europe, including Germany, which had been virtually destroyed by the war. Ironically, it was Marshall, the top American General during the war, to direct Allied forces to dismantle the German war machine.

At 3 am, there was a knock at Dieter's door stirring him from a deep sleep. As he stumbled to the door, he asked who it was. It was the night bellman from the lobby. "A message for you, Herr Zeis."

The message simply read for Dieter to report to the American Army Headquarters building as soon as possible with his bag packed and ready to travel.

He knew the message was valid and came from Hildabrand. His OSS controller was very clear about not following any instructions other than his.

It took Dieter 30 minutes to pack and carry his small bag of belongings and walk to the American Headquarters building. Sure enough, there was Hildabrand standing in the doorway, waiting for him.

The two men nodded at each other, shook hands, and went inside to a small room off the foyer of the reception area. Hildabrand closed the door and motioned for Dieter to have a seat.

"What's going on?" Dieter said with a quizzical look.

"I have a new assignment for you, but it's something that requires me to present it in person," Hildabrand began. "This mission is optional for you. You don't have to take it. There is considerable risk involved."

Dieter said nothing, but all sorts of thoughts began flying through his head. He focused on the words "considerable risk." Dieter thought those days were behind him along with the war.

"What I'm about to tell you is not to be repeated to anyone else," Hildabrand continued. "I'll continue as your sole contact. Any and all orders you receive during this mission will come through me ... and me only! At this time, we want you to allow yourself to be recruited as a spy by the Soviets. We will put you in a position for that to happen."

As an OSS agent, Dieter never really thought of himself as a spy—but then again, that's pretty much what he's been doing with his reports back to England and to Hildabrand. His observations on Gehlen have been that of a spy.

"That would make me a double-agent ... would it not?"

"That's exactly what you'd be. The friend and ally we thought we had in the Soviets have proved otherwise. It's now your turn."

Dieter pondered Hildabrand's words.

"Then your General Patton was right," Dieter concluded with a slight smile. "You should have re-armed us and kept moving east towards Moscow."

Hildabrand said nothing. He simply gave Dieter a firm look.

"How will I go about carrying out such a mission," Dieter asked.

"First ... you'll go back to England for specialized training. After that, you'll spend a few weeks in Washington for intensive briefings."

"Why Washington?" Dieter was curious why he couldn't get the necessary information in London. He wasn't all that anxious about flying back to Washington.

"We want the Soviets to identify you as one of our agents," Hildabrand replied. "The only way they'll ever approach you about working for them is knowing you're one of us ... which can be of value to them."

Many questions began filling Dieter's brain. *"Why go back to England? Why not go straight to Washington? Maybe I should just stay here in Germany!"*

"The Brits are way ahead of us in counterintelligence work and the training of agents to gather our enemy's secrets," Hildabrand answered. "We're novices compared to them. Of course, there are those in our agency who don't quite agree with that assessment, but it's the simple truth. They've been at it a lot longer than we have. We spent so many years with our heads in the sand that we have a lot of catching up to do. The Soviets have had a spy network across America for the past 20 ... maybe 30 years. There's some evidence they may have snatched our atomic secrets right out from under our noses."

"Can I have a few days to think about all of this?" Dieter inquired.

"A few days ... no. A few minutes ... yes. If you agree, then we leave shortly for England and you'll be ready to begin your new training. If you decide against this assignment ... we have something else for you." With a time restraint that short, Dieter knew damn well what they were asking and what his answer would be.

143

"Can I inquire as to what the alternative assignment would be?"

"No … but I will tell you the job we'd like you to have pays about five-times more money."

Dieter hadn't even thought about money. In fact, other than the small expense money he had been issued on a weekly basis, he had no idea what his salary was.

"I don't know what I'm making now, so what does 'five-times' mean?" Dieter asked with a slight chuckle.

"In addition to expense money … $5,000 US currency will be put into a Swiss bank account each and every month as long as you're on this assignment," Hildabrand replied. "The money will be sent to a numbered account that only you and a controller will know. Our disbursing people in Washington will have no idea to whose benefit the money will be going. Of course, you'll have access to your account should you ever need cash … but you would have to travel to Switzerland to retrieve it. Look on this money as a nice retirement fund when your spying days are over!"

Dieter didn't say anything.

"And as far as money is concerned … the Soviets will offer you something to spy for them, so you should be set in that regard also," Hildabrand continued.

"What information will I be giving them," Dieter asked?

"Exactly what *we* want them to have," Hildabrand replied. "That's all you need to know. You communicate back to me what assignment they've given you, and I'll see to it that you have something to give them."

Dieter thought for a minute. "There is one thing I'd like to do as soon as possible. I'd like to go to Dresden and search for my wife."

"I think that can be arranged," Hildabrand replied with a smile. "Remember … Dresden is in the Soviet zone. You might soon have the occasion to be there."

Hildabrand stood up and motioned for Dieter to follow.

"There's a plane waiting for us at the airfield. We should be back in England for lunch," he said. "At least for afternoon tea!"

Both men laughed as they exited the headquarters building where an olive-drab-colored Army sedan was waiting.

On the way to the C-47, Hildabrand leaned over and whispered in Dieter's ear, "By the way … we're no longer the OSS. We're now known as the 'Central Intelligence Group'."

That information really didn't mean much to Dieter. All he really knew was he was working for the nation that defeated his.

It was a five-hour flight to England. As the plane passed the white chalky cliffs of the southern end of the island, bright green fields hastily appeared before Dieter's eyes in the early morning sunrise. He hadn't seen such lush countryside in Europe for years. Much of Germany's fertile farmlands had been neglected due to the shortage of labor. During the final days of the war, most men of all ages had been conscripted for the defense of the Fatherland.

Their plane landed at a non-descript airfield about 50 miles past the metropolitan area of London. Dieter recognized it as being an American base because of the dozens of B-17 bombers lined up on both sides of the runway.

Dieter had mixed feelings as he watched the parked B-17s pass by his portal as the C-47 taxied to a stop in front of the flight office. America built more than 12,800 of these huge bombers, most of them launched against the Third Reich. German 88-millimeter cannons and the Luftwaffe took their toll knocking down more than a third of them in the skies over Europe. Still, these so-called "Flying Fortresses" dropped more than 600,000 tons of bombs, obliterating the Reich's cities, industrial complexes, and military installations.

Dieter pondered to himself. *"I wonder if some of these planes here ever dropped firebombs on Dresden? Very possible … very possible."*

Chapter

18

Hildabrand was looking hard out one of the plane's portals as the C-47 taxied up to the tarmac near the operations building. He suddenly jerked away from the window. "We're good to go," he said. "Our car is waiting for us."

From the airfield, the car took them even further north. Dieter estimated the trip was close to 50 miles, but it was hard to determine. He fell asleep for part of the way trying to recoup those lost hours from their early morning departure in Munich. Light sleep came easily when Hildabrand finally stopped what the Americans called "small talk."

While Dieter lightly dozed, the car casually sped through idyllic pastoral pastures occasionally passing large towering trees with trunk-like branches that overhung the slender two-lane road providing what seemed like a vegetational type tunnel partially blocking the morning sun. It was a soothing scene Dieter subconsciously felt. He was very relaxed.

Subtly, Dieter awoke when he smelled the acrid stench from a cheap cigar Hildabrand just lit. The Field Marshal didn't allow smoking in his presence, and so Dieter decided at the time just to give up the habit; besides, it was hard to get good tobacco during the war.

The car slowed and turned into a gated driveway where two white helmeted American Army Military Police were standing. Hildabrand extended his arm halfway thru the window and held up his identification. The two soldiers immediately snapped to attention waving the car to pass. They were now on a long, concrete paved driveway with well-manicured lawns embellished on either side. It was at least a quarter of mile before a huge mansion suddenly appeared. It was not unlike the one Dieter had previously stayed when he first arrived in England.

"We're here," Hildabrand announced as he bolted from the car before two well-dressed English servants could get to the vehicle's door. The driver directed them to bring in the luggage from the trunk of the sedan. Dieter slowly followed Hildabrand out of the car and up the steps observing the beauty of the palatial ivy-covered graystone.

"Well ... this is home for the next few weeks," Hildabrand quietly said. After entering the house, Dieter realized this house was considerably more formal than the previous mansion he stayed. A butler led the two men to their rooms situated across the hall from each other. The two servants carrying their luggage were close behind. Dieter remained silent continuously observing this wondrously large structure.

"Relax and get some rest," Hildabrand directed. "We'll meet downstairs in the library for cocktails around 4 o'clock. We'll talk more then."

A few hours later, Dieter found Hildabrand already in the library sipping a Scottish Glenlivet with ice. There were several other gentlemen in the room as well; but Hildabrand was noticeable the only American because he was drinking his scotch "on the rocks." The Brits frowned on "bruising" their whiskey in such manner. The English way of drinking malt was with a splash of water to enhance the taste.

Hildabrand was chatting with a tall, distinguished looking chap with soft, flowing gray hair. He was dressed in a finely tailored business suit standing out from everyone else in the room.

"Colonel ... let me introduce you to Lord Toynesby ... our gracious host," Hildabrand said, putting his hand lightly on Dieter's back guiding him toward the gentlemen's outstretched hand.

"Colonel Zeis ... late of the Deutsches Afrika Korps ... was one of Field Marshal Rommel's top staff officers," Hildabrand remarked, with a note of boastfulness in his voice.

"So happy to meet you, Herr Zeis ... especially under a bit more pleasant circumstances," Toynesby said, smiling and shaking Dieter's hand.

"The good English Lord here ... was one of General Montgomery's senior staff members during the North African campaign," Hildabrand said, holding back a laugh. "Odd that you never ran into each other while chasing about in the desert."

Dieter smiled. Even he knew enough about English protocol not to belittle a titled personage; but he was getting used to the Yankee sense of humor—crude and rude and sometimes sociable unaccepted. But tonight it seemed okay.

Dieter was certain Hildabrand could care less about offending anyone. The victors were always right; and, even though the British were allies of America, the Yanks still carried the biggest stick.

"Well Lord Toynesby ... I'm happy to meet you as well," Dieter replied. "Since working with our American friends, I have picked up the habit of taking my scotch with ice. I'm not sure General Montgomery nor Herr Rommel would have been able to accommodate that amenity."

The remark caused everyone to chuckle and brought the gathering to a more relaxed state.

Dieter glanced around the room remarking about the magnificent décor and architecture Lord Toynesby's manor possessed.

"Thank goodness for the almighty Yankee dollar or I might be living in some hovel in a London suburb," Toynesby jokingly replied in his strong British accent.

"Now Lord ... I'm sure that's not the case," Hildabrand said, trying to downplay the fact the Americans were occupying the mansion—but paying a hefty monthly fee for its rent. Nothing was mentioned about price, but Dieter gathered it *was* keeping Lord Toynesby in the style with which he had been accustomed to living.

"Just because I hold station in English society doesn't mean I have the wealth that is perceived to go with such status," Toynesby interjected. "You chaps enjoy my whisky while I make sure the servants keep a running account on how much you're drinking," he said, as he walked away gently laughing.

"He's not kidding," Hildabrand said quietly, taking another sip from his scotch. "If it wasn't for ol' Uncle Sugar, he and a lot of other nobles like him would be on their asses."

Dieter was learning England—like Germany—had suffered tremendous economic losses from the war. He recalled how well he ate and drank while he was in Washington at Fort Hunt, but even after the war was more than two years behind them, England was still rationing. However, they were definitely better off than his fellow countrymen; but not by much.

After mingling about, Dieter learned the other men in the room were from the British Secret Service. They were to be instructors at the mansion for American Intelligence Agents. Hildabrand told Dieter five more American agents would be joining them later that night.

"Their plane won't make it in time for drinks but should be here after dinner in time for cigars and brandy," Hildabrand mused, taking another slight poke at English tradition.

After a wonderful meal of Rosé Veal covered with a delicious Shallot Sauce, and followed by a digestif afterward in the library meeting the new American agents, Dieter retired to his room. It had been a long day.

As he lay there in his oversized bed, he continued pondering his future. Did he want to be a counter-spy, or did he want to consider the alternative assignment Hildabrand had eluded without describing its nature. Though, at the moment, it really didn't matter. He was too tired and his mind was foggy. The only thing clear to him was he wanted to get to Dresden.

Chapter
19

Dieter opted to stay in England and take the agent's course at the mansion but bargained with Hildabrand about the future. He wanted to get back to Dresden as soon as possible without making another trip to America and Washington. He thought Hildabrand agreed a tad too easy. Was that his plan all along?

The next five weeks were intense ones. Along with learning the various tricks of the spy game: making microdots, hiding cameras, concealing weapons; a crash course in Russian was most essential. In college, Dieter learned English and French, but Russian was a downright mystery. Speaking the language was a struggle; reading it was damn near impossible.

"Being able to understand the Russian language could save your life one day," the instructor impressed upon the students. But, as the weeks dragged on it was apparent to Dieter his training wasn't intended for spy work but for another reason—a hunter.

Hildabrand had just returned to the mansion after spending a month in Washington. He walked into the library, poured himself a Glenlivet, and was preparing to sit down. With a glass of bourbon dangling from his left fingertips, Dieter abruptly cornered him with his right forefinger poking Hildabrand in the chest.

"You led me to believe you wanted me to do counterintelligence work, yet the training I'm receiving has me preparing for one thing and one thing only … that of an assassin!"

Hildabrand slowly sipped another drink without taking his eyes off Dieter. He knew Dieter was upset but there wasn't much he could do about it right now.

"Can't fool you Germans, can we," he said with a grin. "If you'd had enough gas and less of a maniac for a leader, our positions could very well be reversed right now."

Dieter didn't find the remark amusing; although, he did see the irony.

"Just what am I really doing here?"

"Well ol' man … we want you to find someone and kill him for us," Hildabrand stoically replied.

"Who? Josef Stalin?" Dieter sarcastically replied.

"Ah now … that wouldn't be any fun … would it? That information is still on a need-to-know basis, and of course … until you're ready … you don't need to know!"

"How much more training does it take to do what I have to do?"

"Well," Hildabrand continued as he poured himself another generous portion of scotch. "It's not so much that it's going to be a problem finding your target and knowing how to do it … it's doing it and getting away clean."

"By 'clean' you mean returning without getting killed."

"Well, if you want to be so indelicate, yes," Hildabrand smiled. "Just pay particular attention to your small-arms training, and don't miss any lessons on the many ways to use a knife. And, if it makes you feel any better … I don't even know what your assignment *will* be."

Dieter didn't know whether to believe him or not. He realized trying to find out anything else was just a waste of time, so he changed the subject. Later that evening back in his room, Dieter contemplated how he had arrived at this place in time.

When he was a staff officer for Rommel, his life was simple—follow orders and keep records straight. Now that he was with the Americans and the Brits, he was, as one Yank recently said, "a crap shoot." Why did he spend all of that time in Munich going to the war crimes trials? What was he doing getting to know General Gehlen? Maybe he should have just ignored Rommel's orders and stayed in Belgium to be captured as a POW.

Dieter knew the war was over and Rommel's days were numbered. He himself was so close to the July 20th conspiracy to kill Hitler that he too risked being pulled in along with the other 5,000 so-called martyrs. Of course, many of those 5,000 had nothing to do with the attempt but were simply friends or acquaintances of people that were in the know. In fact, because of his loyalty and association to Rommel, the chances of him being hung or shot along with the others who had nothing to do with the operation was pretty much a foregone conclusion. Following Rommel's orders probably saved his life.

Dieter found aspects of his training fascinating. While he thought disguise and false identity would be a big part of his upcoming mission, none of his training addressed those aspects. Though, Hildabrand was right about firearms; he learned how to take apart and reassemble three different pistols with his eyes closed. Of course, he was already familiar with the German 9-millimeter Lugar. He carried it with him as a side arm on full uniform occasions. The American produced M1911 Colt .45 caliber automatic and the German produced Walther PPK .25 caliber were new to him.

To Dieter, after spending many hours with each weapon, there was no question of choice. It was the Walther PPK. The Lugar jammed a lot and the Colt .45 was heavy and clumsy. The PPK was small and easy to conceal; yet it could do its job within 25 feet—the closer, the better.

During map reading sessions, Dieter was given sectional maps of Germany. While others in the class received certain other locations throughout Europe, Germany seemed to be his mission's target. It was a guess, of course, but he thought it was a pretty good one.

One day during a map reading session, one of the associate instructors walked into the room carrying numerous fairly worn corduroy-type sports jackets. He distributed them to the agents in the room paying particular attention as to who got what jacket. He then left the room where another instructor entered with a similar type jacket. As the agents gathered around the podium, he tore out the lining of the jacket as a demonstration. "You will see that the inside lining is, what you'd expect, the inside lining of a jacket. However, if you take the left arm of the lining and rip it thusly, you'll see that the entire back of the jacket is covered with a map. The map is not designed to get you to the target … it is designed to get you out!"

"What's the map inside the jacket you gave me?" Dieter deadpanned.

"All of you will find out your assignments tomorrow," came the reply. "Don't try to tear anything apart because you won't be able to put it back together again. It's designed to be torn apart only once and that's only in an emergency, so button up your curiosity until you receive your assignment. You'll then know what your map will be."

While the instructor continued talking, Dieter and a few of the other agents donned their jackets for size. Dieter's jacket was about two sizes too small and any normal arm movement probably would have ripped the lining out on its own. Standing nearby was Agent Martin who, after putting on his jacket, found his jacket to be about two sizes too big. Obviously, they had each other's jacket and proceeded to switch with a slight chuckle.

Dieter pondered to the instructor, "Now, wouldn't that be the pits. You do all this work to complete your mission only to find out you're now in a 'pickle' and you need your map to escape only to discover you got the wrong coat for somebody who's 500 miles away! That's not exactly a comforting feeling."

The instructor was embarrassed knowing Dieter was right. Just to be sure, he retrieved all the jackets taking them to the back room where they could be verified one more time for absolute assurance. They would reissue them the following day.

Hildabrand had been missing from the mansion for the past two days. Dieter knew he wasn't in the building because his stock of Glenlivet in the library hadn't been touched. If he was on the property, he knew Hildabrand wouldn't be too far away when it came time for cocktails.

Dieter spent a restless night in anticipation of his assignment. If Hildabrand was true to his word, he still could change his mind and not go on a killing mission. Still, the intrigue of it all fascinated him. While he laid there in the bed, all sorts of thoughts plunged through his head. *"Is this cloak and dagger stuff really something I want to be involved with? Do I even want to go back to Germany? I could get killed out there. This is serious business."*

Dieter finally drifted off to sleep around four in the morning. Surprisingly, he awoke at his usually time of 6:30. By 8 o'clock he was having breakfast in the dining room and at 9 o'clock he walked to the small antechamber just off the library. He found Hildabrand and another man waiting for him. Hildabrand stood beside the desk while the other man, a slightly balding gray haired bespectacled man with chalky skin, was seated behind the desk. He was dressed in a dark suit, not unlike that of a banker. The moustache was a dead giveaway for a banker or stockbroker. Or at least that's what he thought.

"Colonel Zeis, this is Allen Dulles," Hildabrand said, introducing the man.

Dieter had heard of Dulles, of course. He ran the OSS operations from Switzerland during the war and was now one of those near the top of the American intelligence organization.

After pleasantries Dieter was invited to sit down. Hildabrand remained standing and silent. Dulles definitely had control of the meeting.

"Colonel, we have special task for you. Are you familiar with Artur Axmann?" Dulles began.

"Yes, I believe he was head of the Hitler Youth," Dieter replied. "He was one of Hitler's ... how do you say ... lackeys?"

"Yes, that's right. He evidently was one of those who didn't cross your Führer. Well, we have Axmann alive and well. He tells us he saw the dead body of Martin Bormann after they left Hitler's bunker on May 2, 1945. In short, we don't believe him. We think he's leading us astray."

Dieter pondered for a moment.

"I don't believe I understand what you want."

Dulles's words were almost inaudible. His eyes were steely cold.

"Well, from what I've learned about General Gehlen when I personally got to know him in Munich, a lot of the top Nazis fled Europe for South America," Dieter replied.

"That's true. Gehlen developed the Odessa File. We're not supposed to know anything about it, but it is the master plan for top Nazis to flee and stay alive for the resurrection of the Reich," Dulles said. There was a hint of a smile.

"Why would you think he's still alive? And, if so, what makes you think he's still in Europe?"

"We have information he's being protected by the German underground. We're not quite sure if that's the case, but he has been spotted in Dresden. I think you have some familiarity with Dresden ... do you not?"

"Yes, my wife and I lived there. Unfortunately, so I've heard, our house was totally destroyed."

"And ... your wife?"

"I don't know. I've been told she's dead, but I'd like to find out for myself."

"In this assignment you'll have that opportunity," Dulles said. "You are to go to Dresden, find Bormann ... and kill him."

"Just like that."

"Yes ... just like that."

"Do I have a choice?"

"No!"

Dieter didn't like the sound of Dulles' voice for that last retort.

"Sir, if you don't mind … why me? Aren't there more qualified, ah…"

"…assassins?

"Yes … of course, but you'll be above suspicion at all quarters. You were never a Nazi … you served a German hero, Herr Rommel … and you're from Dresden. You'll be returning home soon and you'll be free to move about as much as any German can these days in the Russian Zone."

"What do I say if anyone questions why I've been with you and the British?"

"Tell them you were an observer for Germany at the war crimes tribunals, which you were."

"And Gehlen?"

"You heard about the general working with the Americans on developing an intelligence service for the new Germany and you wanted a job."

Dieter pondered what he was hearing.

"You don't have to lie about any of those things. You witnessed the trials, and you had a few lunches and meetings with Gehlen. Even he couldn't say anything happened other than you were visiting."

"What about my trip to America?"

"You were there to be de-briefed about Field Marshal Rommel and what you knew about the July 20th attempt on Hitler's life. Its pretty mundane stuff. It makes you appear as an ordinary German officer who's trying to get on with his life."

"So, what is Bormann's location at this time?"

"You'll soon be given what you need to know. It is important that you memorize it. All that you'll have with you that needs guarding is that jacket you were issued … and your choice of weapon. By the way … what pistol did you choose?"

"I like the Walther PPK."

Dulles looked at Hildabrand and nodded.

"I told you he'd choose that one," Hildabrand smiled.

"You realize of course you'll have to get up real close to pull the trigger," Dulles cautioned.

"Yes … yes I know."

Chapter

20

Dieter still had an occasional nightmare from killing the two SS officers on the Belgium border with France while he was making his escape to England. He wasn't sure if he had it in him to pull the trigger a third time—especially on another fellow German, no matter how big a bastard he was.

Hildabrand summoned Dieter to another meeting the next day for a more thorough briefing on his mission.

"How'd you sleep?" Hildabrand inquired.

"What do you think? Not very well," Dieter replied. "I've only killed two men in my life and their pleading eyes still haunt me."

"Most of us never get used to it. Hopefully, you won't have but one more."

Hildabrand ushered Dieter into the sprawling English garden which seemingly stretched forever.

"These bloody English do love their flowers, don't they?" Hildabrand observed.

"Why is Bormann so important you want him dead? Dieter asked.

"It's not so much as who he is … rather, it's what he knows and what he may have," Hildabrand replied. "We think he's got a very important map the Russians would dearly love to have. If you can get this map, we don't want Mother Russia to know we have it, and the only way to ensure they never find out is to eliminate Bormann. It's really quite that simple."

Dieter pondered at what he had just heard as the two men strolled slowly past a long row of rose bushes. Each bush was in full bloom. "Ever wonder how the Limeys get so many different colors," Hildabrand remarked, observing each bush as they strolled by.

Dieter then casually noted many of the more than dozen bore blooms of different colors: the ever-beautiful Fair Bianca, the pink Kathryn Morley, the peach Sweet Juliet, the orange Evelyn, the golden Graham Thomas, the deep blush Geoff Hamilton, and the cream Perdita.

Hildabrand was impressed with his agent's knowledge of roses. But within seconds, Dieter stopped his floral oral and abruptly changed the subject.

"What is so damn important about this map?"

"Well, my boy, it should lead us to the location of a very large and valuable 'pot of gold'," Hildabrand replied matter-of-factly.

"And, that is…"

"Ah … the Amber Chamber … or Amber Room as it's better known today. When you chaps invaded Mother Russia, your army had several specialized units experienced in the looting of art and cultural artifacts. They knew exactly where those treasures were and, with careful precision, went after this precious wealth. Hitler was quite high on feeding his desire to have this sort of thing in his empire."

Dieter's curiosity began to wax. He had never heard of this chamber. But he was appalled at the plundering his army did. There was never any indication of this type of thing while serving with Herr Rommel. Taking over a mansion for headquarters was one thing, but plundering was another matter. The Field Marshal would never have stood for such travesties.

Hildabrand continued with the history showing Dieter its importance. They casually walked past a sculptured row of bushes that formed a fence separating the rose garden from a large plot of varietal flowers.

"Ironically, the Amber Chamber was originally conceptualized and designed in Berlin, then situated in East

Prussia back in the early 1700s. It was the brainchild of your Queen Charlotte, the second wife to King Friedrich I. Before he became King, he was known as Frederick III, the Elector of Brandenburg, and his wife was known as Sophia Charlotte. In the late 1600's she wanted a summer home built outside Berlin. I guess ol' Freddy didn't seem to mind. By 1699 it was finished off in the Italian Baroque style and he named it "Lietzenburg."

Dieter's past memory realized he had seen such a large palace but thought the palace's name was "Charlottenburg Palace." Hildabrand verified that was correct as he continued his story.

"In 1701, ol' Freddy the Third became Friedrich the First when he was crowned King of Prussia and Sophia Charlotte was renamed Queen Charlotte. I imagine in those days it was a mighty big step upward," Hildabrand interjected with a slice of levity.

"After Friedrich's coronation, Miss Charlotte decided it was time to upstage the neighbors. She knew her husband loved art so her idea for an opulent room in the palace wasn't misguided. I suppose when you're the king, the contents of a bank vault has no limitations. Anyway, she contacted this fellow named Gottfried Wolfram who was the master craftsman for King Frederick IV of Denmark. They approved a plan, and he pulled in other master craftsman to perform the work."

"I assume the theme for the room was amber," Dieter surmised,

"Yes … that's correct … and aside from amber, there was lots of gold leaf and mirrors. The art designs were incorporated on meticulously made panels and designed so the various sized sections would fit together like a puzzle. It was a long and arduous endeavor taking about eight years to complete and install. Unfortunately, Miss Charlotte died in 1705 so she never got to see the room finished … which was in 1709. Anyway, after her death, Friedrich decided to rename the mansion the 'Charlottenburg Palace' in her memory."

Dieter was getting the history lesson he had forgotten in his early high school days. He's now beginning to feel the magnitude of this job; but what he actually wanted to know was the real reason behind this mission.

"Later after the Amber Room was finished, I guess ol' Friedrich got antsy about the size of his palace and decided to have it enlarged … happening somewhere around 1712. If you remembered seeing the turrets and orangery, that's when these were added," Hildabrand pointed out.

"I'm beginning to remember now. Though, it was a few years back when I saw it. Yes … I do remember the turrets now that you mention it."

"Well, about now, the story picks up speed. In 1712 Russian Czar Peter I, better known as Peter the Great, stopped in on Friedrich to see if he could convince him to have his army join his in his fight against Sweden. But at the time ol' Freddy wasn't much interested in joining his army. His own army wasn't very big and he really didn't have a bone to pick with the Swedes. Freddy was kind of a peace-loving king. Anyway, while he was there, ol' Freddy shows Peter his Amber Room and Peter just about fell head over heels with its beauty.

"But, a few years later, the situation reversed. Friedrich died in 1715 and his 25-year old son was crowned King Friedrich Wilhelm I. By comparison to his father, he wasn't much of an art lover. He was more interested in building a bigger army. To help fund that, he started disposing of his father's art later picking up the nickname 'Soldier King.'

"A few years later, the Prussian relationship with the Swedes soured and in early January 1717, the Soldier King made a trip to Leningrad, well at the time it was known as Petersburg, to see if ol' Peter the Great would work with him in disposing of the Swedish problem in the province of Vorpommern on the Baltic Sea near where the present day border with Poland lies.

"Peter was a little miffed that the Prussians were returning to him for help when they turned him down several years before. But then again, Peter was dealing with the son's father and he was now dead and gone."

Dieter was becoming more intrigued with what he was hearing. He sort of wished he'd paid a little more attention to this history in the earlier years.

Hildabrand continued. "One of the aids to Wilhelm quietly reminded him how much Peter admired the Amber Chamber when he had visited his father a few years back. Needless to say, ol' Wilhelm put his thinking cap on and approached Peter about giving him the Amber Chamber if he would form a Russian – Prussian Alliance. The room didn't mean anything to him. That was his father and stepmother's cup of tea. So, as far as getting what he wanted, he thought this was a perfect idea. He believed Peter would go for it.

"After whatever negotiations there were, Peter informed his wife to prepare herself for a rather handsome gift … that Wilhelm had just offered them the Amber Chamber. With the wealth of these people back in those days, it's hard to imagine … but somehow, I think Elisabeth probably got pretty damn excited. I'm sure ol' Peter described it to her after he first saw it. No matter what, Peter sent a crew down to Berlin to crate this thing up … to make sure nothing was damaged."

"I imagine that was quite a task," Dieter fathomed.

"Yes … I imagine it was quite a chore. I'm sure Peter sent the best-qualified art experts to make sure it was dismantled and properly packaged. It was no small feat, you know. As I understand it, there were 18 large wooden crates specifically made for the transfer. At any rate, it was first delivered to Klaipèda, named Memel at the time, in Lithuania for what reason I don't know. But by April of 1717 it finally made its way by boat to Leningrad, I mean Petersburg, where it was installed in Peter's 'Winterhaus' in 1723."

Dieter slightly chuckled saying they didn't seem to be in much of a hurry to get it installed. Then again maybe they had to prepare a room in their palace and spend a fortune just to get it ready.

"Well, we'll never know. Years later in 1755 the Winterhaus needed to be overhauled, so Elisabeth ordered the room dismantled where it was hauled 25 miles south to Puschkin and installed in Peter's 'Summer Palace' better known as 'Catharine Palace.' This really must have been a complicated puzzle to reassemble because it took until 1763 before it was completed again. And it stayed there intact until 1941 until 'you guys' plundered it."

"You guys?" Dieter felt ashamed his people had done such a thing. But in reality, throughout history, the victorious always plundered something of value from the country they were conquering. Germany was really no different. He just didn't like the idea of being pegged as one of "you guys."

"Well, exactly what did 'we guys' do with this treasure once we got it back?" Dieter sardonically retorted.

"It was brought back to Königsberg, of course just recently renamed Kaliningrad [after Michael Ivanovich Kalinin who was president of the Presidium of the Supreme Council of the USSR] in July 1946 because of the Potsdam Agreement, and reinstalled in the Castle Museum under the supervision of Dr. Alfred Rohde, who I believe, was your Director of Art Collections. But it took a bit of underhandedness to get it there. It seems, even in war, formalities must be preserved.

"In October of '41 after the room was found and dismantled … I might add it only took about 36 hours for that to happen … so I wonder what kind of care it was under during the process."

"Yes … I wonder…." Dieter confirmed trailing off.

"To get this art treasure on the road as quickly as possible, it needed to be signed off on by the 18th Army Commander, General Georg von Küchler. At the time there was a lot of serious fighting going on, so it looked as though that wasn't going to happen anytime soon. There were 27 large crates and the longer they sat in the palace, the shorter time it was possible for the Russkies to risk a full-blown effort to keep the Jerries from taking it."

"You said 27 crates. That's about 10 more crates than what it took in the first place back in the 1700s," Dieter observed.

"Yes … that's true. But the room had additions made to it throughout the years. An extra six-tons of amber from Berlin was shipped to Puschkin and later incorporated into the design … and there was an ornate wooden parquet floor designed and built which certainly added to the weight. They took that also.

"But to get it all out of there as quickly as possible, it seems your East Prussian Nazi Gauleiter Erich Koch had an angle he could pursue that would skirt the issue. In 1933, he made your government, then under Der Führer, come up with a law to protect amber. While the amber *was* in perilous danger sitting in those boxes with fighting going on all around, he was able to have it shipped out immediately."

Dieter was incredulous on the quirkiness of that law and how it was used in this situation. He didn't think it was quite intended to be used that way; but with the Nazis, they could twist anything to their advantage. All Dieter could muster at the time was a sigh of wonderment.

"In any event, the shipment was finally made by boat down the coast of the Baltic Sea to the Gulf of Gdańsk and, by the end of March 1942, was reassembled by Dr. Rohde. A special room had to be constructed on the second floor of the Castle Museum to accommodate the structure. After assembling, it was eventually opened to the public with press releases from Berlin.

"But by late 1943, the war was going badly for 'you guys' on the Eastern Front and by a directive from Martin Bormann, the room was to be dismantled and crated away to some secret location. Of course, any real knowledge of the room was destroyed in August of '44 when allied bombing leveled Königsberg and the Castle Museum. But we wholeheartedly believe there's a map and Bormann probably has it."

Dieter pondered Hildabrand's story. Then he asked, "Well, if this valuable artifact does exist, and it does indeed belong to Russia, why not return it to them if we can find it … or … just give them the map?"

"If you haven't noticed ol chap, we're in a bit of a 'Cold War' with the Soviets, so we certainly don't want to do that now, would we?"

"Yes, but wouldn't the United States be just as guilty of looting as was Hitler?"

Hildabrand stopped walking and looked sternly at Dieter.

"Colonel, look at this as part of our repayment for Lend-Lease. Uncle Sugar poured *millions* of dollars into war materials sent to Russia to help them save their country from your country ... and they haven't so much as made one single attempt at repayment, or even so much as a 'Thank you very much.' Besides, some day the map might become a valuable bargaining chip should we ever need it.

"Nevertheless, before Roosevelt died, he figured ol' Uncle Joe might pull a stunt like this ... so he secretly contacted Wild Bill Donovan to keep an eye on the situation. He told Donovan, if they *ever* refused to pay ... find some recourse in getting back whatever we can. He really didn't specify what, but art works were mentioned," Hildabrand responded rather emphatically.

The two men continued walking.

Dieter looked off in the distance contemplating what he had just heard.

"What is the approximate value of this so-called room?"

"No one really knows other than it's priceless. But, estimates from our art experts have put it at over 100 million dollars ... so, as you can see, we're not dealing with chicken feed here. This is dead-solid serious business," Hildabrand remarked with a critical tone in his voice.

Nearly back at the mansion, Hildabrand told Dieter to be ready to leave within a day's notice—probably by Friday. It was already Wednesday, so that didn't leave much time.

"You'll get your final debriefing right before you board the aircraft," Hildabrand said. "Pack a small bag because you've got to be able to move fast and without notice. You'll be flown to the American section of Berlin where it's easiest to cross into the Russian zone. From there you'll make your way to Dresden. We'll give you Bormann's latest known location. Whether or not it's valid is for you to determine."

The two men parted and Dieter went back to his room. On the way he stopped by the mansion library to look up exactly what amber was. He knew it was beautiful and usually an orange brown color. His wife always thought it was beautiful, but other than that, he knew little.

According to a dusty English encyclopedia on gemstones and other precious materials, *"Amber is a fossil resin used for the manufacture of ornamental objects and jewelry and is often classified as a gem stone. Most of the world's amber range from 30 million to 90 million years old. Because it once was soft and sticky tree resin, amber sometimes contains prehistoric insects and small vertebrates. Semi-fossilized resin or sub-fossil amber is known as 'copal.'*

"Amber occurs in a range of different colors: usually yellowy-orange associated with the color amber, but can range from whitish through pale lemon yellow to brown and nearly black. There also is red amber often known as 'cherry amber,' green amber,' and even 'blue amber.' These are rare and highly sought.

"While the most common amber is cloudy and opaque, the most highly prized is transparent. Opaque amber contains numerous minute bubbles. This type is known as 'bastard amber,' even though it is classified as true amber."

More information than he needed, but certainly just enough to help him realize the value of the prize being sought. If Bormann has possession of such a map it would make sense. He was the closest to Hitler. As the Führer's secretary, no one got past him to have an audience with Hitler. If such a map did find its way to the Chancellery or to Obersalzberg, Bormann would either have it or know where it was.

Even though it was only 10 o'clock in the morning, back in his room, Dieter slipped a sip from a small flask of Jim Beam he had stashed under his mattress. Bourbon was a small American luxury he had acquired a taste. He reached in his desk drawer and pulled out his small Walther PPK pistol. He studied the weapon for several minutes as he took a few more sips from the flask. He thought to himself: *"How in the hell did I ever get myself into such a place? I just want peace ... not to be a pawn between two huge super powers on a giant chessboard. But the stakes are enormous and there's no way of getting around it. Maybe I can pull this off ... maybe I just can."*

Chapter
21

Dieter spent all day Thursday getting briefed on his route to Dresden. Once he crossed into the Russian sector in Berlin, it would be approximately 120 miles from there south to Dresden near the Czechoslovakian border. Dieter had already learned some basic Russian phrases such as Доброе утро meaning, "Good morning," Я ищу отель meaning, "I am looking for a hotel," and Большое спасибо saying "Thank you very much." But since he was to be in Germany, he felt his native language would do nicely.

After some idle chitchat, Hildabrand revealed to Dieter his latest surprise. "You'll now be considered an American citizen sightseeing and looking for lost relatives ... which is true. We don't want the Russians knowing you're a former German Army officer, otherwise you'll be arrested, and god knows where you'll end up!"

Hildabrand then pulled a new United States passport out of his attaché case. The photo was the one taken right after Dieter received a new set of civilian clothes from the Post Exchange when he was in Washington at Fort Hunt. There was no doubt the dark gray suit made him look "American."

Hildabrand continued. "Of course, the MVD [МВД: Министерство внутренних дел (Ministry of Internal Affairs) the forerunner of the KGB] knows exactly who you are and they'll be following your every move, but the passport will at least get you through the low-level security checks."

"Won't the MVD try to arrest me?"

"We don't think so. They're too curious to see what you're up to, so they'll just follow you. That's why you'll need to be cautious once you get to Dresden. More than likely there'll probably be two of them following you … so it's important to identify them as soon as you can. It won't necessarily be two men. One of them could be a woman. And remember this … trust no one … not even any old acquaintances you may run into. You'll need to ditch your tail before trying to make contact with Bormann."

"Tail?

"Damn Dieter … you know what that is! The guys following you … tail you!" Even though Dieter had spent months learning the various skills of espionage, he still had trouble with the American lingo.

At the end of the day, Hildabrand offered interesting information on Bormann and how he came to be in possession of the Amber Chamber map. It had no real bearing on his upcoming mission, but it was good to have a little history regarding his mission.

"As I know you were aware with Bormann's disposition regarding how well he was despised with the hierarchy that surrounded Hitler, he himself was aware of such disdain knowing he wouldn't have too many friends or support if Germany lost the war. He probably figured he was a dead man and needed to make plans for that not to happen.

"When the point in time came that even he knew Germany was lost, he adopted a self-inflected foreign policy of his own seeking accommodations with the Soviets. Of course, he kept this little secret only to himself. You could imagine the consequences if Der Führer ever discovered his little plan.

"But if you think about it, this change of line is not so surprising if you recognize that Bormann and the apparatchiks of the Kremlin had much in common. But Bormann toward the end got cold feet and never carried through his plans to defect to the Russians. He really didn't have that much to offer and he probably figured after the Russians used him for all they could, he'd end up dead."

"Well then, how did he escape and how did he end up with the map?" Dieter inquisitively asked.

"It took quite a bit of investigative work by the OSS and the Brits to figure it all out. But after we interviewed all the survivors captured by our respective intelligence groups, we pieced together what we think happened.

"In 1943 the Brits had an Irish agent working undercover for them in Berlin. Her name was Mata O'Hara and was married to a senior Hungarian diplomat. At the time German – Hungarian relations were cooling to the point the Hungarians believed the Axis powers for world domination wasn't going to happen. Their goal was to extricate their nation from the war and pull their east-front army back to Hungary.

"With Mata's stunning looks, she was able to penetrate the Nazi hierarchy with ease. She was under orders to keep London abreast of what the German reaction would be when Hungary pulled out of the war. At a swank 1944 summer party at Joseph Goebbels posh villa in Schwanenwerder, she got a bit more than what she bargained for.

"It was a known fact that Goebbels and his wife Magda did not have marital bliss because of his philandering with other women. It was at this party that Joseph, in a moment of passion, revealed to Mata the secret whereabouts of the Amber Room. He actually showed her the map."

Hildabrand now had Dieter's full attention. "Mata was fully aware of the Amber Chamber and its value. She secretly radioed London with this discovery and was given orders to stay close to the situation and try to get a fix on exactly where it was located so Allied bombing would stay away from any suspected areas it might be. But the situation within Germany began deteriorating right after the Allied landings and subsequent retreat from France and Mata wasn't able to get very far with her investigation.

"In order to rally the troops and the population, Hitler appointed Goebbels to the title of "General Plenipotentiary for the Mobilization of Total War" and authorized him to gather all the manpower he could muster for a last ditch effort to fight. It was at this time Mata lost contact with Goebbels and the secret information. She had to look for another 'in' so to speak. It didn't take her long before she found her hook.

"At the same Nazi social gathering she had attended in July at the Goebbels' villa, she had the pleasure of meeting the acquaintance of SS General Hermann Fegelein, a skilled jockey and young playboy, who back in June had married Eva Braun's sister Gretl. It just so happened that she was pregnant by a Captain Fritz Darges, an SS Honor Bodyguard, and when Hitler told him to marry her, he refused and Hitler sent him off to the eastern front never to be heard from again. It seems right after that Hermann saw an opportunity, stepped in, and married the ol' gal. He saw it as a quick way for promotion and it worked. Shortly thereafter, he was promoted to lieutenant general and posted as the liaison officer between Heinrich Himmler's SS and the Führer's Headquarters.

"In as much as Hitler was concerned, he was now able to continue Gretl's presence in the social circles that surrounded him which was important because her sister Eva was his mistress. Even though it was "proper" to have Gretl married, she still had the reputation as the nymphomaniac of Obersalzberg.

"Mata was aware of Gretl's reputation and probably figured Hermann's marriage to her was simply for convenience and not for love. With this situation, it seemed to be the perfect 'in' to work herself back to the Nazi hierarchy. She made her move.

"In January 1945, Mata cunningly reintroduced herself to Hermann and it didn't take long before she and the playboy began a romantic affair. He tried to be discreet about it, but that was just about impossible to do. The SS, who he worked for, and the Gestapo picked right up on it ... but surprisingly they kept it secret just within their own ranks. They new of Gretl's reputation and they liked Fegelein, so they just let it go without telling the Führer. They figured if Gretl continued her philandering ways, why not let Hermann do his thing.

"By the spring of 1945 the borders around Berlin were beginning to close-in and any knowledgeable military man could tell the war was just about over. Fegelein had no intention of hanging around to be killed or captured by the Russians, so he plotted his escape and wanted Mata to go with him. We believe it was at this point she confided in him about the Amber Room map that Goebbels possessed. He was no doubt intrigued!

"Now Fegelein had to figure a way to get ahold of the map without Goebbels' knowledge. The 'air' within the bunker was becoming a bit chaotic so he figured he'd probably have a good chance. From what he could tell, Goebbels planned to stay in the bunker for the duration. But regardless, his plan had to be precise. Any misstep and he'd be in front of a firing squad. He knew exactly where Goebbels kept his briefcase."

Dieter was familiar with the stories of the final days in the bunker, but what he was now hearing was absolutely incredulous. He had no idea this event happened. The intriguing part was that what he was now hearing was essentially the story that was going to affect his future. He asked Hildabrand to continue.

"Hermann and Mata had finally arranged their escape plan and Fegelein had devised a scheme to get his hands on Goebbels' briefcase. It was a plan requiring meticulous precision and a bit of luck. Unfortunately, Fegelein's plan immediately went awry and it never got back on track … and that bit of bad luck cost Fegelein his life.

"Hitler was beginning to feel uncomfortable that his SS chief Heinrich Himmler kept making excuses in not being able to get to the bunker. He felt he was up to something that didn't set well with him.

"On April 25, he ordered Fegelein to visit Himmler at his headquarters in Hohenlychen and find out what in the hell was going on and immediately report back to the bunker. This was the first glitch in Fegelein's plan, and he had to make a quick adjustment. Before leaving by car that day, he covertly took Goebbels' briefcase knowing he wasn't coming back to the bunker. But to stall for time, he made the trip to Himmler's headquarters knowing the bunker was still in contact there. When he saw a distraught Himmler, he knew it was time get back to Berlin, pick up Mata, and disappear.

"With the Russians now blocking the roads, he was only able to return the following day by air leaving explicit instructions to the pilot not to leave … that he was going to return with a passenger. He then got into his car and was barely able to return to his flat in the Charlottenburg district of Berlin … about 8 miles from the bunker."

Dieter was told by Hildabrand that his apartment was in the same district as the Charlottenburg Palace where the original Amber Chamber was established. Dieter, of course, had that one figured out.

"When Fegelein arrived at his flat, Mata wasn't there … and there was no note. He had no clue where she was … but he probably figured she'd return because he had the briefcase containing the map. About the only thing he could think of at the time was to take a shower and gather his belongings. Afterwards, he sat on his couch with a large glass of cognac and waited. Before long, he fell asleep waking about mid-morning of the 27th when Mata walked in the door. She made no explanation where she went.

"At this point, the essence of time was important. By now he wasn't sure his plane was still waiting for him … he was forced to make another adjustment in his plan. Getting out of Berlin at this time by car was just about impossible.

"It was also at this time that Fegelein's absence was noticed at the bunker. By now he should have returned. But when an officer at the Brandenberg Gate airstrip called the bunker to let Fegelein know his plane had another mission to accomplish and had to leave, Hitler became suspicious and ordered a small detachment of SS soldiers led by Colonel Peter Hoegl sent to his flat and immediately be brought back to the bunker.

"When they arrived, Fegelein was in the living room half drunk on cognac and partially dressed in his uniform. Mata was drinking a glass of water standing next to a fully packed suitcase. Colonel Hoegl firmly asked Fegelein to return to the bunker ... that the Führer demanded his presence.

"In an effort to ease the situation, Mata spoke up and offered the soldiers a drink of water and disappeared into the kitchen. Within a few minutes, one of the soldiers went into the kitchen where the sink spigot was running and a window was open. Mata was gone. Fegelein was now fully drunk, but stubbornly returned to the bunker. The soldiers brought along the suitcase and also the briefcase holding the Amber Room map.

"When he returned, Fegelein was jailed in the Gestapo cellar to be interrogated later in the day. This cellar was an emergency headquarters set up in the crypt of the ruined Dreifaltigkeit Church on the Mauerstrasse not too far from the bunker.

"Colonel Hoegl took the suitcase and briefcase to the bunker and handed it over to Bormann. He immediately noticed the briefcase was Goebbels' and wondered why Fegelein would be in possession of it. Before giving it back to Goebbels, he would investigate why he had it. In the meantime, he went into the map room and opened the suitcase.

"Aside from a suitcase full of civilian clothes, there was a valise full of expensive jewelry, including a watch that Eva had given to Fegelein to have repaired. Also, there were $40,000 worth of Reichmarks, $800 in Swiss francs, and two passports with the same picture of a woman ... but each one had a different name. One was from Ireland and the other was Hungarian. But what wasn't ken to the Germans ... someone born in Ireland could have had a legitimate United Kingdom passport and still have been a neutral resident in wartime Berlin. Bormann pondered why Fegelein had this valise and further asked Hoegl about it. He of course repeated there was a woman in Fegelein's flat but abruptly disappeared. Now Bormann was stewing mad and demanded he return to the flat area and find this woman.

"Bormann could only imagine that with this kind of loot ... and that he and this woman of British descent must have had some sort of escape plan … the whole situation smelled of treason.

"Needless to say, Bormann got Gestapo Chief Heinrich Mueller involved and he vigorously interrogated Fegelein nearly to the point of exhaustion because Fegelein was still half drunk and talking out of his head denying everything.

"But Fegelein's fate was sealed on the evening of the 28th when a radio broadcast from Stockholm was inadvertently picked up in the bunker claiming that Heinrich Himmler was secretly negotiating with the Allies for peace. Hitler went berserk. He now believed Fegelein was part of the conspiracy. In a fit of anger, he had SS Major General Wilhelm Mohnke, who was the bunker troop commandant, sober up Fegelein, reconvene his panel, give him a fair trail, and then shoot him! And that's what they did.

"But there was an interesting asterisk to the story, as you know Hitler married Eva that night. Before the ceremony took place, Hitler made it a point to make sure Fegelein was dead. By no means did he ever want him to be considered a brother-in-law!"

Dieter chuckled at the notion and asked Hildabrand what happened to Mata.

"We really don't know. The Brits have kept a tight lip about her. Though, it seems she's disappeared from the face of the earth. A woman of her looks in Berlin at that time … no money, no passport … there just isn't a clue. But it's so ironic how close she was to the map. If their plan had worked, it appears the Brits would have it … but they claim otherwise and have no idea where it is. Though, there is one interesting aspect to her disappearance. When she disappeared from Fegelein's flat for some unknown reason, it's possible she was planning her own escape route if the one Fegelein had didn't work out … which we now know didn't. But in all reality … even with all our intelligence secrets … we don't know where this shamrock lady is."

As Hildabrand continued the story, Dieter was getting a good idea now on how Bormann got the map.

"After all the excitement in the bunker during those long hours, Bormann quietly took Goebbels' briefcase to a private room and opened it. To his surprise, he found the map to the Amber Chamber. As he was the one who ordered it to be dismantled and crated away, he now had its whereabouts … and he certainly kept this to himself. This was his safe passage to freedom. Before, he didn't have much to bargain with … now he had something.

"Without anybody looking, he hid the briefcase in a safe place where he could get to it at a moments notice. Goebbels was still oblivious as to its absence. If he did make mention it was gone, Bormann could claim it was stolen by Fegelein and it was never recovered. But to be honest, I don't think he really cared. His wife was about to poison their six children and he and Magda had planned to blow their brains out. At that point, I don't think he really cared. So far as Bormann was concerned, though, it was a great set-up.

"On May 1st, the day after Hitler, Eva, Goebbels, and his wife were dead, along with a few others who decided to end their lives, the remaining people in the bunker made plans for their escape that night. There were roughly 30 people left and they decided to leave in groups of 10 about thirty minutes apart. Each group would take a different preplanned route. Bormann would be in the third and last group because this group was heading off in the direction prevalent to his own designed escape plan, which he had already set in motion. No one else in the bunker had any clue as to what Bormann was up to.

"Late in the war when Berlin was getting a regular dousing of Allied bombs, working-class boys and girls made the ruins their playground. They also used the maze of rat-infested sewers and subway systems becoming quite knowledgeable of its network. Through an off-hand conversation, Bormann overheard one of the bunker's messengers talking of such and calling these children the 'Kellerkinder,' or cellar urchins. This gave Bormann an idea.

"Knowing the end was near, Bormann had a messenger bring one of these cellar urchins to the entrance of the bunker for him to talk with giving the messenger some benign excuse that wouldn't cause suspicion. Within a few days, a cellar urchin was at the entrance to the bunker in the Tiergarten.

"The cellar urchin knew he was in the presence of some high official and showed awe when telling Bormann how he new all sorts of secret passages through the tunnels that even the original work crews had forgotten. This was exactly what Bormann wanted to hear.

"Bormann, using his usual form of deceit, told him that he and some other high officials needed to leave the bunker late at night on a special assignment and needed to make sure to escape the oncoming Russians. He wanted the youngster positioned where Bormann could contact him at a moments notice. The urchin told him of a certain tunnel entrance he would hold vigil until Bormann could contact him. Bormann knew the general location, thanked the boy, and told him to hang tight for the next several nights.

"When the time came to escape, Bormann and his group headed off in the prearranged direction. After several hours of walking through and around burned out buildings, crossing bridges, and generally trying to stay away from Russian tanks … near the Weidendamm Bridge, Artur Axmann, who had led another group that suffered heavy casualties, hooked up with Bormann's group that included General Hans Baur, Hitler's personal pilot; Erich Kempka, Hitler's chauffeur; Dr. Werner Naumann, Goebbels' state secretary; and, SS surgeon Colonel Ludwig Stumpfegger, who replaced Dr. Theodor Morell as Hitler's personal physician in the waning moments of Hitler's life in the bunker only to be replaced himself a few days later on April 21st by Professor Werner Haase.

"Near the Invalidenstrasse, an automobile bridge over a set of railroad tracks, and very close to where Bormann's rendezvous with the street urchin's location was, a commotion stirred a group of Russian soldiers under the bridge to action. They fired off a volley of rounds toward their group killing Dr. Stumpfegger. The remainder of the group hurriedly continued following a concrete bulkhead and disappeared into the darkness … but Bormann ducked behind a pile of debris keeping his eyes focused on the Russian soldiers. They were very near to the entrance to the secret tunnel, and unless they moved, Bormann couldn't get in there.

"In as much as Bormann was concerned, a quirk of fate quickly developed basically saving his life at that point. From around a bend, General Gustav Krukenberg's command of five Tiger tanks opened fire on several Russian tanks about a hundred yards from him. Within seconds, there was a blaze of shells exploding all around and the group of Russian soldiers, blocking his path to the tunnel entrance, immediately disappeared. Bormann gambled on this slim opportunity and made good on his escape. As he entered the secret tunnel entrance, there stood the cellar urchin; and it was at this point that Bormann disappeared not to be seen again until our secret operatives found him in Dresden. So far as the world was concerned ... Bormann was dead."

Dieter thought this doubtful that Bormann could pull this feat off. What he knew of Bormann, he didn't like; but he had to admit, he had to give the ol' boy credit. He was one of the very few of Hitler's henchmen to actually escape the Russians in those last few days in Berlin.

Dieter was also curious as to why Artur Axmann told the story that he personally saw Stumpfegger and Bormann's body.

"As we do know for sure, Stumpfegger really is dead. But to claim he saw Bormann also ... that was to throw us off. Bormann really stuck it to Axmann doing his dead level best to keep Axmann from seeing the Führer ... and I believe Axmann has it in for Bormann and wants to kill him himself. I don't think he has a clue about the map ... he just wants the sucker dead. Though, since we've got him in custody, that's not ever going to happen."

"So now ... when am I going to get the information about Bormann?"

"Not until you reach Berlin. He moves around quite a bit ... but ironically, he stays in Dresden. There's no sense of giving you a location then having to change it two or three times before you actually are ready to push off," Hildabrand explained. "You'll be flown directly into Tempelhof

Air Field in Berlin. You should be arriving around 4 o'clock in the afternoon and will make the crossing at Check Point Charley at eight that night. It should give you enough time to get to the train station and catch the 11:10 for Dresden."

"What'll I do once I'm in Dresden?"

"Good lord, man … we're not a travel agency! We're going to get you on your way, but from there you'll have to use your wits and common sense. You'll have some rubles for spending money, so that'll get you into some sort of hotel you can find until the next day. Dresden's your hometown? You should know of a place."

Dieter thought of the vast destruction left by the Allied bombing missions, but he didn't say anything.

"We'll give you a contact in Dresden. Don't use it unless your life depends upon it. We don't want the MVD to know who it is."

"Maybe I should just ask one of the MVD agents where he'd recommend I stay?"

Hildabrand laughing. "I wouldn't advise that. And, here I didn't think you Jerries had any sense of humor."

Dieter didn't realize he was being funny. The two men spent the rest of the late afternoon going over maps and various escape routes once the mission was accomplished.

After this short session, Hildabrand had a little surprise for Dieter. "I have a little treat for you tonight at a nearby pub," Hildabrand said as he was folding up a set of maps. "My driver will pick you up this evening at 7 pm. Be out front. Tomorrow, I'll be flying with you to Berlin and then *you're on your own*."

Somehow those last four words had a frightening ring to them.

Dieter climbed into the Ford sedan promptly at 7 o'clock for the short trip to the pub. When he arrived, the building looked like something out of "Oliver Twist" or "David Copperfield"—ancient. The front door had to be an original. Dieter ducked as he entered the building; otherwise, he would have scrapped his head on the top of the entrance.

The pub was called "The Grenadier." To the left was a barroom filled with a number of men and a couple of women.

On the right was a dining area that seemed to tunnel back through the building as if it were a cave. The only light emerging from the room seemed to be coming from candle lamps on each table. Back against the wall were three booths. As Dieter walked through the room a familiar face was shining in the far corner booth. It was Greta.

"I was hoping you might be my 'surprise'," Dieter said, embracing his old friend and sister-in-law.

"How have you been?" Greta asked smilingly as she looked up at Dieter.

"Well, I suppose I'm all right, considering where I am and what I might be doing in the near future."

"Well, we won't talk about company business tonight," Greta said, as Dieter pulled her chair back for her to sit.

"Have you heard anything from Marta?"

"Nein. Nothing. I don't know whether to hold out hope or resign myself to realize she's gone," Dieter said pondering his statement.

"Let's have a drink and then let's eat," Greta said, trying to break the solemn mood.

"Is your husband home or is he still on duty?"

"Lawrence was, unfortunately, killed in a training accident," she replied.

"I'm so sorry," Dieter replied, gently taking her hand. "I didn't know."

"How could you? I would imagine they've got you pretty sequestered and away from such things."

"So it's just you and Little Jack?"

"Yes. We're rattling around that big mansion with more servants than we need … but, you know how it is … I must keep up appearances … and, of course, a stiff upper lip. You think the Germans are stoic and traditional, the English take the cake!"

"Take the cake?"

"Never mind. It's one of those silly American lingo phrases I picked up along the way."

"How are you handling Lawrence's death?"

"Fine … of course, he left me his estate and now I'm a very wealthy woman … so I certainly don't have anything to complain or worry about."

The two dined on a roast leg of lamb, one of the few dishes Dieter found acceptable in England. He determined most of the food endured while in this country was barely palatable.

"So, you don't care for the English cuisine?" Greta said with a grin on her face.

"Cuisine? The English have no cuisine. What chef in their right mind would ever try to feed someone kidneys, for god's sake? When I first got here, someone asked me if I'd like some Yorkshire pudding, and I said 'yes,' thinking I'd be getting pudding. Those flopped over biscuits they make are something we used to throw at each other when I was at the university."

Greta laughed and admitted kidney pie and Yorkshire pudding were definitely dishes that required getting used to.

"I've never been much of a beer drinker, but I have to admit I like the English ale much better than some of our beers back home. And they definitely know how to fix lamb but don't let anyone try to feed you mutton," Dieter said, trying to find something of redeeming quality about his host country's food and drink.

Greta just chuckled at Dieter's review of England's culinary delights.

As the time neared 11 o'clock, the pub owner came around announcing he'd be closing within a few minutes.

"That's another thing the British do that is so uncivilized," Dieter observed. "The hours one can buy a drink or a beer in this country is unreasonable. We certainly do it better in Germany."

"Well then … would you like to come back to the mansion for a nightcap?" Greta smoothly asked.

Dieter noticed the tone in her voice was different. Of all the hours the two had spent together, there was never a hint of romance between them, but now their situations were definitely changed.

Dieter smiled back at Greta with a knowing look.

"I'd like to, as the Yanks say, 'take a rain check.' I have to be up very early in the morning."

"Going somewhere? Oops … forget I asked that question," Greta said, putting her fingers to her mouth.

The two old friends gently embraced and gave each other a warm kiss.

"I'll be taking you up on the drink when I get back," Dieter promised.

"I'll hold you to that promise."

Dieter re-ran the entire evening in his mind as he was taken back to the training mansion. When he arrived at his room, a note was pinned to his pillow: "Be at the front door, bag in hand at 0400." It was signed 'H.'

Early the next morning Dieter and Hildabrand were taken to what seemed like the same American air base. There were B-17s still lined up along the taxiway but not as many as before. Dieter thought that odd; but then again, the war was over so why would they still be here. Where did they go? It was unimportant to think about. And, that was the point.

Dieter tried to put his mind on anything but the mission ahead of him. Not only was he going home, he was going into presumably hostile territory. And, then he was supposed to hunt down one of the most notorious war criminals still thought to be alive. Yes, he could think of something else—maybe that wonderful leg of lamb last evening.

That thought directed him to Greta's shining, satin eyes. Was he misreading what happened last night between them? No, her gesture was unmistakable, leaving him in a quandary. He still didn't conclusively know whether Marta was alive or dead. But, he was a man and his physical needs had been suppressed over the past many months.

These were his thoughts as the C-47's two engines winded to full throttle and the plane began to taxi. There's no turning back, or was there? Could he change his mind? Knowing what he now knows, of course not. He had to see this mission to the end—wherever that might take him.

Chapter

22

Although Berlin was a divided city among the four Allied powers, it was deep in the eastern sector of Germany controlled by the Russian Soviet Union. Dieter gazed out the plane's portal as the bombed out buildings passed by while the plane was on its final approach. Tempelhof Airport was in the center of the city and was one of the few recognizable landmarks that essentially remained intact from the war.

Within minutes, the C-47 taxied up to the makeshift terminal. Hildabrand motioned for Dieter to follow, and the two men made their way out of the plane and to a waiting black sedan. As a German lieutenant colonel, he was used to certain privileges, but waiting chauffeured cars was something he had known only while traveling with the Field Marshal.

"We'll be going to an Army office for your final briefing, and then I'll take you over to 'Check Point Charley' to send you on your way," Hildabrand said as he looked out the car's window at the countless bombed and burned out buildings whizzing by. "Lots of work left to put this place back in shape."

Dieter said nothing, but recalled the beautiful city where he once lived. Berlin was one of Europe's classical cities both architecturally as well as culturally. What took centuries to develop was obliterated in the blink of an eye. There simply wasn't much left of the city Hermann Göring declared, "Will never be bombed." It would take years to redevelop and only then would it fashion a far different look.

Dieter couldn't help but notice the hundreds of German men unloading cargo from planes, driving deuce-and-a-half trucks, and performing general all-round manual labor. Most all of them still wore an article of their uniform. Their vestige was all that was left of a once proud army. Along the streets, women and children were sifting through rubble looking for anything of value. It seemed hopeless.

"Most of them are scavenging for something to eat," Hildabrand said, noting Dieter's fixation on what he was observing as they drove along.

"Yes I know … I saw the same scene while I was in Munich. That was several months ago. Why doesn't someone feed them?"

"We do what we can. Those planes being unloaded at Tempelhof are filled with food, coal, and clothing. The Russians are slowly cutting off our Berlin highway supply lines thinking we'll just give up and leave the city to them," Hildabrand replied. "We're doing what we can, which doesn't seem much … but in time things will be back to normal. Though, if the Russkies ever do close the roads, these people *will* starve more so now than they already are."

Dieter pondered on that last statement. *"Things will never be as they were no matter how much money and supplies the Allies pour into this city."*

The sedan passed groups of men, obviously former Wehrmacht soldiers, who smartly saluted as the car slowly passed bearing the American flag on the right front fender. The recognition now was hand-to-brow and not the high-extended right arm that once stood standard for all German soldiers. Dieter thought back to his days with Rommel, remembering how those who didn't work for him would give the "Heil Hitler" salute, while he and the rest of his staff always used the traditional military greeting.

Even though Rommel believed in loyalty and duty, and at first the leadership of Adolf Hitler, the Field Marshal could never bring himself to join the Nazi Party no matter how perversive, corrupt, and misguided it later became. As time has told, it was, for all practical intents and purposes, the ruination of the Fatherland.

"Poor bastards," Hildabrand grunted. "You'd think they'd have a belly full of military protocol."

"It's an automatic reaction from years of training, duty, and devotion to the Fatherland," Dieter replied. "I had to restrain myself from returning their salute. They may be defeated, but they have to cling to something … personal honor and tradition is all they have left."

Hildabrand agreed with a reluctant nod.

The sedan pulled in front of an old government building. Dieter couldn't recall or recognize what it might have been. Armed Military Police soldiers with white helmets stood guard at the entrance. A heavy barbwire fence surrounded the entire structure. Other MPs were walking about the perimeter with German Sheppard guard dogs.

Inside Hildabrand and Dieter climbed the stairs to the second floor and entered an office with just one large window. It looked as though some low-level accountant or such had once occupied the room. It was gloomy with a single frayed electrical cord hanging from the ceiling powering the only bare light bulb in the room. A desk and two chairs were pushed to the corner with a large rectangular conference table dominating the center of the room.

Another man in civilian clothes entered the room carrying a rolled up piece of paper appearing to be some sort of map. His name was purposely not mentioned.

"Gather round, gentlemen," the man said. "I assume you're Colonel Zeis?"

"Yes it is," Hildabrand replied before Dieter could respond. Dieter glaringly returned Hildabrand a staring response.

When everybody was situated, the man indeed rolled out a large map. It was of Eastern Germany—a territory controlled by the Soviet Union. Without hesitation, the unidentified agent began his communiqué.

"After you cross over into the Russian sector of the city, you'll go directly to the train station. You'll have just enough time to catch the 11:10 pm train to Dresden. We don't want you waiting around the station as you might draw attention to yourself. There will be a routine check by Russian guards on the train at least once. They'll have a German official with them helping to interpret anything the Russians don't understand."

"Do I speak English or German?" Dieter asked.

"Speak English as much as you can, but if you get in a bind, give them broken German. Don't try and speak Russian. It's not good to let them know you understand anything in Russian, and certainly not German. You'd be surprised what you can learn just by listening."

Dieter nodded in agreement. That was his forte—listening.

"If you're lucky, you'll only be checked by two Russian soldiers. Half of them don't know what they're looking at when checking your identification papers … but, and remember this … if there's someone wearing a black hat … beware! It's just like you see in the cowboy movies … he's the bad guy … the MVD."

"What do I show them?"

"Your passport and this transit document I'm handing you now. It will give you permission to travel to Dresden only."

"What about coming back?

"It's also a return document, so you shouldn't have any trouble … but never take anything for granted with the Russkies."

"You'll no doubt be followed by at least one MVD agent," Hildabrand interrupted. "If everyone is singing out of the same 'hymn book,' no one should give you any trouble."

"'Hymn book'? Is that more of your Yankee humor?"

"Yeah. It means everyone is on the same page … everybody knows what's going on," Hildabrand replied.

Dieter nodded and laughed quietly. The American language had so many colloquialisms that he finally determined he'd never learn them all.

"Taxis should be scarce at that time of night when you arrive, which should be about 2 o'clock in the morning. Make your way somehow to 43 Piltnitzerstrasse. There is a small hotel on the corner. You'll have a reservation under the name of 'Dean Zimmerman from Roanoke, Virginia, USA,' which is the name and address we've given you on your passport." At that moment, Hildebrand handed him a new passport and told him to memorize all the information it contained. He asked for the original one back with which Dieter handed him.

"Who made my reservations?"

"That's not important. Suffice it to say we have people working for us in Dresden. You don't need to know who they are unless you get into trouble."

"Yes, but if I don't know who they are or where they are, how will they be of help if I do get into trouble?"

Hildabrand and the man giving the briefing looked at each other. Then Hildabrand spoke saying, "They'll be watching you, so don't worry about it."

Somehow Dieter didn't find that information too reassuring.

"Now, pay close attention because this is where you'll first go to find Bormann. There's a small clock shop one block east of your hotel. You won't have any trouble finding it because it's the only building still standing on that entire street, which runs crossways from the hotel. Bormann has been working as a clock repairman. He's been hiding in plain site. You'll recognize him because he dyed his hair gray and has a very thick beard and moustache. He's also lost some weight which makes him a little harder to identify. He does have a mole on his temple next to his left eye. For assurance in identifying him, try to see that mole."

Dieter frowned and looked up at the two men. "You're kidding me … right? If he's that obvious, why haven't you just gone in and picked him up?"

"We don't give a shit about Bormann. It's the Amber Room map we're after," Hildabrand replied. "The Russkies don't know where he is, but they know he can lead them to the Amber Room, so they're looking hard for him. They don't know why we're sending you to Dresden, so you have to be careful. If they ever figure out who the little ol' clockmaker is you're visiting, the game is over and out, and you'll be history.

189

They'll probably send you on an extended vacation to the north of Siberia wearing nothing but your skivvies!"

Dieter had another question.

"What story am I supposed to use for going into the clock shop?"

"You'll be carrying a German mantel clock to be repaired. That's it over in the corner on the desk," Hildabrand said, pointing to a wooden carrying case with a handle.

"It's easily opened for inspection, so if anyone at the Soviet security checkpoints ask you about it … let them look to their heart's content. They'll find a broken mainspring, which is your reason for going to this particular shop."

"Won't they ask me why I didn't get it fixed here?"

"Well, that's the beauty of this particular clock. Everything is handmade … I mean everything, and it was made in that very same shop back in 1835 … so no, it wouldn't be possible to get it fixed elsewhere unless you put new works inside. It's been appraised at over $800 American … so you, as a collector, want to be adamant about making sure everything stays original," Hildabrand explained.

"I'm a collector?"

"Yes you are … and you don't have to know a lot about clocks to be a collector. Just that they're handmade and very old."

"Is Bormann a clockmaker?"

"Naw … he's just the shopkeeper. The clock-master works in the back. He's a distant relative of a girlfriend Bormann had in Berlin. It's such an obscure connection, it's doubtful the Soviets have it figured out. We ourselves would never have known if it weren't for Gehlen," Hildabrand explained.

"Gehlen knows about this?" Dieter asked with wide-eyed astonishment.

"Sure. How do you think we found Bormann?" the briefer said, beating Hildabrand to the answer. "Bormann is waiting for his ticket out of Germany to Argentina or Paraguay. Gehlen is running the Odessa File, which is the 'rat-line' for letting Nazi war criminals escape to South America."

Hildabrand interrupted. "You'll be the courier from Gehlen giving Bormann his travel instructions."

"Just like that?"

"Yes, just like that. You are, after all, a fellow German officer ... and if he does have a way of communicating with Gehlen, the general will vouch for you. We've arranged that much."

"What about the Amber Room map? How will I get him to give it to me or whatever it is revealing its location?"

"Ah, that's the beauty of all this," Hildabrand replied with a big smile. "In order to get his ticket punched to get on the rat-line, he *has* to turn over the map to you before you give him General Gehlen's instructions."

"I thought I was supposed to kill him?"

"Well ... you are ... but first you have to get the map," Hildabrand continued. "We think it's buried in Berlin somewhere near Hitler's bunker."

"That's in the Russian zone, isn't it?" Dieter asked, already knowing the answer.

"Yes. You're going to have to convince him to personally take you to the map. Don't let him get away with just telling you where it's located. Get him to take you there. Once you've got the map in your hands, finish the job, and get back to Check Point Charley as fast as you can."

Dieter looked down at the map on the table, thinking to himself: *"It all seems too easy ... way too easy."*

The unidentified agent wished Dieter good luck, shook his hand, and left the room. As soon as the door was shut, Hildabrand reached into the far desk drawer in the corner of the room and pulled out a bottle of Jim Beam. "How 'bout 'one for the road'," Hildabrand smiled.

"Another one of your Yankee sayings," Dieter said chortling to Hildabrand.

"We have a ton of 'em, son. Maybe one day you'll get the 'hang of it all'."

"'Hang of it all'," Dieter laughed again.

Dieter acknowledged Hildabrand's gesture with the bourbon. He wondered how he knew he liked "Jim Beam" but was afraid to ask. And how in the hell did that specific bottle get in that far desk drawer for this moment in time? Maybe he was in better hands than he thought. Now Dieter was ready for a drink.

"You'll not be getting any of this on the other side of the line Dieter, so enjoy this one while you can," Hildabrand concluded.

At 10 o'clock that evening, Hildabrand took Dieter down to the basement of the building and into a small tunnel. They both were just a bit tipsy but in full control.

"We don't want you being seen leaving the building and going straight to the Soviet sector. At the other end of this tunnel, you go up a set of stairs and into an old bombed out structure. Outside will be a waiting taxi which will take you to Check Point Charley. Once you get through the security checks, there will be a row of waiting taxis. Be sure to take the second one from the end and tell the driver you need to make the train station in time to catch the 11:10 for Dresden. Good luck, ol' man, and Godspeed," Hildabrand said with a smile and an extended hand.

"Thanks ... you know I'll need it."

Chapter

23

At the end of the tunnel, Dieter began climbing the steps to street level only to trip about halfway up. He quickly caught himself before falling forward and knocking out a few front teeth. He knew he wasn't drunk; a bit tipsy, but not drunk. He surmised by the time he got to Check Point Charley, he'd probably be okay.

When he finally got to the top of stairs, an awaiting taxi was there just as Hildabrand had promised. He slid into the back seat and, before he could speak, the driver asked Dieter in German if he wanted to go to Check Point Charley. Dieter slightly chuckled saying, "Sure … why not." Somehow he believed this driver got here about the same way as the bottle of Jim Beam got in that obscure desk drawer.

Check Point Charley, one of the busiest crossings from West Berlin to East Berlin, was well lit with dozens of people crossing between the American and Russian zones. Dieter was carrying his small satchel with a few clothes and the wooden case containing the mantel clock. The American guards were waving everyone through to the Russian checkpoint. Dieter was surprised, almost shocked, that the Russian guards were passing everyone though the same way as their American counterparts.

After crossing over into East Berlin, Dieter walked to the taxicab area where they were all lined up. As directed, he went to the second cab from the end, opened the rear door, and got in. Before he could speak, the driver asked Dieter if he needed to get to the train station in time for the 11:10 to Dresden. This time Dieter looked a bit startled thinking maybe this spy game had gone a little too far. But a lot of things were happening he wasn't aware of, so he continued playing along telling the driver that was correct. It was also at this point he began playing his role as Dean Zimmerman, American tourist from Roanoke, Virginia.

"Why would anyone want to 'tour' bombed out Germany?" Dieter thought as the taxicab passed by rubble-filled streets and bombed-out structures. Since Germany's surrender more than two years ago, there was plenty of cleanup work and rebuilding going on in West Berlin; but here in East Berlin, there was no noticeable improvement of putting things back together.

Dieter's watch read 10:45 as the taxi pulled in front of the train station; a bleak, charred, black and gray structure, which had obviously received its share of damage when the Russians were ransacking the city.

Three cabs pulled up behind Dieter's. The first carried a middle-aged man in a long black coat with a fedora that had seen better days. He was carrying only a newspaper. A couple emerged from the second cab, and a woman from the third.

"Any one of these people could be my tail," Dieter thought. *"The first one was the most likely. Who travels without a suitcase or satchel?"*

Dieter paid the driver in Russian rubles and headed for the tracks going straight ahead through the station to the other side. Even at this hour, there were numerous Russian guardsmen hanging about, but they seemed tired and bored. The train to Dresden was easy to spot as it was the only train left in the station. Besides, there was a sign on the train itself indicating "Dresden."

Everyone emerging from the taxis behind Dieter was also headed for the train. The woman and the couple soon began walking faster than Dieter gradually passing and reaching the train before him. The man in the long black coat and the mashed fedora paced himself well behind Dieter. When Dieter abruptly stopped to retie his shoe, the man following quickly sat on the nearest bench pretending to read his newspaper; albeit upside down. Dieter noticed this and casually thought, *"If this is who*

I'm up against in this spy game, then it's, as the Yanks say, 'a cinch'."

Dieter showed the ticket he had been given to one of the trainman outside the 2nd class car and was directed to climb aboard. Hildabrand purposely put him in this class rather than 1st class, which might have drawn more attention to him.

Dieter had just sat down when he noticed the "tail" get off the bench, roll up his newspaper, and proceed to the train. Predictably, the man climbed into the same car as Dieter, sitting four rows behind him.

At 11:10 sharp, the train started to roll. *"Well, Germany may have been defeated, but punctuality was still a part of what made this country great,"* Dieter thought, gazing out a grimy pane of glass. *"In the old days, that window would have been sparkling clean."*

As the train slowly pulled out of the city, Dieter looked out at the dark of night. Unlike West Berlin, where streetlights and electricity in general were being returned to normal, East Berlin was spotted only with an occasional light or two. It was a desolate place. Dieter wasn't anxious to see what this side of the city looked like in daylight.

Dieter's thoughts switched to Dresden and what he might encounter in his old hometown. His emotions were mixed. The first thing he was going to do before dealing with Bormann was make a search for Marta. While he kept telling himself there was no hope, something in the back of his mind was whispering that she was still alive.

The train car in which Dieter was riding only had two other passengers and, of course, the black fedora man, who was still reading that same newspaper—this time right side up.

Dieter continued staring out the window, but at what he didn't know. The dim lights of East Berlin had faded and there was nothing but pitch black. An occasional single light popped up in the distance—probably a farm, he thought. According to the trainman, there were no stops between Berlin and Dresden. It had been a long day and Dieter realized this was a perfect time to get some sleep. He closed his eyes and rested his head against the window.

He had no more than nodded off before someone was poking him in the shoulder. Dieter awoke finding two Russian soldiers standing by his seat. One of them had been poking him with his automatic weapon.

"Документы," the Russian soldier said in a stern, coarse voice. Dieter learned that word in Russian. He complied and pulled out his passport and transit "papers."

The soldier studied the documents while the other one sternly looked at Dieter. *"Truth be known, probably neither of them could read,"* Dieter thought to himself.

After what seemed like a long minute, the soldier handed the documents back and then left. *"Das ist die eine Hürde aus dem Weg,"* he muttered to himself in German. *"If there were any more hurdles to get out of the way, they'll just have to come tomorrow."* At the moment, he was too dogged tired to care.

Dieter leaned up against the window and shut his eyes. The train was only moving about 30 miles per hour. It was scheduled to arrive in Dresden around 3 am.

Several hours later, the screeching of the train's brakes aroused Dieter from his sleep as the train slowed to what seemed like a crawl. They were finally in Dresden. The moon lit up piles of rubble that once had been a beautiful city. Dieter didn't know exactly where they were, but he'd be able to orientate himself once they were in the station. That took a few more minutes.

The train came to a stop. There were only a few lights and no people on the platform except four Russian guards who were loosely huddled smoking cigarettes.

Dieter grabbed his bag and the wooden clock box and headed for the door. Two elderly ladies were ahead of him. He helped one of them down to the platform. This gesture got the attention of one of the guards who smiled and turned back to chatting with his comrades.

Dieter quickly headed for the main part of the station and found one taxicab waiting outside. He felt bad for taking the lone cab from those old ladies, but the feeling promptly passed. Once inside the cab he directed the driver to 43 Piltnitzerstrasse where the hotel was located and he supposedly had a reservation—or at least was expected to have a reservation. This was all new ground for him. He really didn't know what to expect but was taking each moment in stride.

Within 10 minutes the cab pulled in front of a dark, three-story building. The partial lettering "..tel" was barely legible. It was obvious that it once read "Hotel."

Looking through the glass front door, Dieter could see a night clerk leaning against the check-in counter with his head down resting uncomfortably on his folded arms. A couple of stern raps on the door awoke the clerk and within seconds Dieter was inside asking about his room.

There was no reservation, but the clerk acted as though he was expecting a late arrival. "Dean Zimmerman" signed the registry and the clerk directed him to a second floor room. As he climbed the stairs, Dieter wondered, *"What happened to 'black fedora.' Did he have a room for the night? Would he be waiting outside the next morning still reading that same newspaper?"*

It was nearly four in the morning when Dieter finally drifted off to sleep. It had been 24 hours since he had been in a bed. *"Oh well ... this must be the life of a spy,"* he pondered.

Chapter
24

The dust filled heavy woolen overspread failed to keep Dieter from a yawning slumber, but the bright crisp early morning sunshine emanating through the sullied curtain-less window at seven o'clock brought Dieter to a brief moment of incognizance. He lay there in a fuddled daze wondering just where in the hell he was.

After pulling back the covers and sitting on the edge of the bed, he finally came to his senses realizing he was deep in Soviet controlled territory with a deadly mission on his agenda. He also realized he had to pee like a "Russian race horse" and quickly headed out into the hallway toward the communal facilities wearing only a white tee shirt and pair of olive drab skivvies he was issued months ago. He discovered the night before his own room's bathroom was on the fritz.

When he returned to his room, he felt a lonesomeness he hadn't felt in many years. The best he could figure it was the last time he ever saw his wife in early October of 1944 when the Wehrmacht was suffering major defeats causing them to reposition behind the fortified West Wall. He was stationed in Belgium and had planned on returning, but when he received the missive from Herr Rommel telling him to proceed to England with his plan, it would be impossible to go back. That was three years ago. But today he was back—to what he didn't know. For the first time in his life, he began to shake.

After dressing and descending to the hotel lobby, he recognized the old hotel as the Grand Imperial. At one time, it was the social gathering place of Dresden's elite. Of course, those days are now long gone for the strata of society. Today it is the epitome of depression.

A new clerk was at the desk. Dieter inquired about breakfast and was directed to a small anteroom down the hall where he found strong coffee brewing along with a table of black bread, butter, and raspberry jam. Nothing else. *"Continental breakfast?"* He thought only the French did such things; but these were hard times.

He poured himself a cup of coffee and it tasted like roasted charcoal.

"Chestnuts," said a female English voice behind him.

"Pardon?" Dieter said in his best American accent.

"I overheard you mumble charcoal. No ... the coffee is brewed with chestnuts," said a slender, buxomness, well-dressed blonde.

"Ah ... so that's the funny taste. I thought it was charcoal," Dieter replied.

"Oh ... that's added for the coloring."

Dieter just shook his head. *"Could this be a Russian spy following him? She looked German but her English had a British accent."*

He spread the butter and jam on a big piece of bread and sat down at one of the three small tables in the room. The woman, who was about 30, sat at another table reading a book. Dieter kept glancing over at the woman as he ate his breakfast.

"'Pride & Prejudice' by Jane Austen," the woman said without looking up.

"Pardon," Dieter said.

"I'm reading 'Pride & Prejudice.' You looked as though you were curious," she replied, now looking at Dieter.

"Sorry ... no, I didn't mean to intrude."

"You're not. Are you here on business?" she asked emphatically.

"No, I'm here looking for relatives and to see what's left of the old town," Dieter answered.

"I figured you were some American businessman trying to sell someone something."

"No … I'm afraid not," Dieter said and then asked. "And you?"

"I'm a special agent for the Soviet Union," the woman said coldly but boastfully, going back to her book.

Dieter didn't know how to respond. *"Was she there to spy on him?"*

"Well, that's pretty straight forward. How did you know I was an American?"

"Your shoes," the woman replied, now looking up again. "Only Americans can afford such elegant and expensive shoes."

Dieter looked down at his brown, plain brogans. He had no idea how much they cost, but he knew they weren't very expensive. The shoes were part of the clothes issued to him while he was at Fort Hunt.

"Well, now that we've established who each of us are, what exactly is your position," Dieter wondered.

"I'm watching the Germans. We want to make sure they're working in the best interests of the Soviet Union. The office I supervise has 200 German workers. It's a real job keeping an eye on them. You'd be surprised how lazy the Germans can be."

Dieter was offended by that remark. If they're lazy, then it's only because of their disdain in working for the Russians. As a rule the German people were assiduous and meticulous workers paying close attention to detail.

"Well then … are you Russian?"

"By birth, but I grew up in Holland. That's where I learned English. If you live in the lowlands, you have to be knowledgeable in Dutch, German, French, Flemish, and, of course, English."

"So in effect … you are a spy?"

"I suppose you could call it that."

"Then what made you want to be a spy?"

"It's a better job than anything else I could get here in Europe or in the Soviet Union. Things are very bad all over. Because I speak fluent English and German, I'm more valuable to the Russians here in the eastern sector of Germany."

"Do you speak Russian," Dieter continued his probe.

"Surprisingly very little but just enough to get myself in trouble. It's a dumb language … doesn't make sense. German and English … they're so similar that you can learn them rather quickly. Most of the Russians I deal with speak either German or English, so I don't have to worry too much about speaking Russian."

Dieter finished his putrid cup of coffee.

"Maybe we'll see each other again," Dieter said, standing up and extending his hand.

"I'm sure we will if you're staying here at this hotel. It's about the only thing available that's decent, which isn't saying much."

Dieter left the anteroom. When he passed by the front desk, he noticed a small pile of fresh newspapers as well as his "black fedora" friend dozing on a bench across the street. This gave Dieter an idea.

"Is this today's paper?" he asked the clerk in broken German.

"Ja," he replied. "Ein Rubel."

Dieter laid the money on the counter and picked up a paper. He then walked out the front door and across the street to his friend and, without waking him, dropped the newspaper in his lap.

"Here ya go pal," Dieter smiled. "Have a fresh paper. You must have worn that old one out by now!"

The Russian tail was at first startled and then surprised not knowing what to say. He was caught in an embarrassing situation—asleep on the job.

"If you're going to follow me today … try keeping up. I don't want to have to come back and look for you."

As Dieter turned and started walking back to the hotel, the agent held up the newspaper and with a slight smile said,

"Спасибо." And Dieter acknowledged by half-way holding up his right arm speaking English, "You're welcome!"

After returning to his room to freshen up, Dieter left the hotel walking north toward Konnertzstrasse and the bridge across the Elbe River. Devastation was everywhere. Not only were buildings in large piles of rubble, most of them were charred black from the terrific firestorm caused by the Allied bombings. He hardly recognized anything from the last time he was home. This once cultural center of Europe now lies in ruin.

As he turned right to cross the bridge, Dieter glanced back and, sure enough, his agent friend was a half-block behind, still looking sheepish. His facial expression returned a grin when Dieter saw him. The newspaper he had given him was tucked neatly under his right arm.

After walking for about ten blocks, Dieter came to the first familiar landmark—a catholic church. Ironically it was still in pretty good shape. If his home was still standing, it would be on the street behind the church. Dieter continued walking toward the street behind the church. The whole area was deserted—no one could be seen anywhere; not even women and children picking through the rubble. *"Why? Where is everyone? What's the difference from the Soviet sector and the American sector?"*

Dieter finally found himself standing in front of what once was his home—now it's nothing but a pile of charred rubble. He seemed frozen in place. He looked to his right and his Russian agent friend was at the corner of the block pretending to read the newspaper. Even in all this tragedy that surrounded him, Dieter could still muster a controlled chuckle.

Dieter looked at the pile of stones and bricks, and then stepped forward. He had to climb over a pile of trash, but he realized there wasn't much use in sifting through the debris because someone undoubtedly had already done that. His home had been a three-story brick structure with four other residences on each side. All of them were gone—just heaps of rubble.

Dieter looked around to the other side of the street where he noticed a curtain move in one of the windows.

Someone was alive on this street. He tried to remember who that neighbor was who lived there.

Dieter quickly walked over and knocked on the door. After what seemed like an eternity, the door slowly opened. An elderly woman stood looking at him. But, the more he looked at her, he realized the woman wasn't elderly but hardened. He guessed maybe 35 years old—two years older than himself.

She said nothing, waiting for Dieter to speak first.

He took a chance and revealed his true identity in German and asked about Marta.

The woman continued looking at Dieter, saying nothing.

Dieter asked again, this time with a little forcefulness in his voice.

The woman finally fully opened the door and motioned for him to enter.

"I haven't seen my wife in more than three years," he continued, as he walked into a small sitting room.

A small child clung to the woman's side.

"This is my daughter, Elsa," the woman said, walking over to her and holding her head. "She hasn't spoken since the war."

The child stared at Dieter with saucer-like blue eyes and an expressionless face.

"I'm sorry," Dieter offered, which must have seemed hollow and of little comfort. He didn't know what else to say.

"Do you know what happened to my wife, Marta," he asked again in German.

"Are you Colonel Zeis?" the woman asked.

"Ja, I am. Do you know where she is?"

The woman acted strange, but answered, "Dead. She died in the firestorm."

Dieter's heart sang. He had previously felt something terrible had happened to Marta, but it wasn't until now that he finally realized his wife was, indeed, gone.

"Did she suffer?"

"Colonel, we all suffered. While you were out creating an empire that would last a thousand years, the British and Americans were burning our beautiful city, killing our women and children. All of the men are gone except for cripples and old men. Even our little boys as young as 14 were taken to the front."

Dieter asked where his wife was buried.

"Who knows? There was nothing left but charred bodies no one could identify."

"How do you know she's dead?"

The woman hesitated. "She was working at our hospital that was turned into cinder. Everyone in the building died."

Dieter felt his eyes tearing up, but fought them back asking the woman if there was anything he could do.

"I need food. Not so much for me, but for the child," the woman replied. "Those bastard Russians only give us enough to stay alive unless we work. Those who work are fed better … but I can't leave her … so we starve."

He spent more than an hour telling the woman his story—how he escaped Europe for England and how he became involved with the Americans. Dieter knew he was telling more than he should, but he had to tell someone to help him bring closure with Marta. Somehow he imagined he was talking to his wife, explaining the events that led him back to Dresden. Dieter did not mention the spy part of his story.

Dieter promised he would somehow try and find them food. As soon as he said it, he knew he had no idea where he could find such or any other life sustaining supplies.

He walked out the door, biding good-bye. He promised to return. The woman passed a slight smile and then closed the door.

Dieter walked away.

The woman stood there looking out the sitting room window, watching Dieter leave.

"Do you think he believed you," a voice from another room said.

"Yes … I think so," said the woman.

The curtains separating the two rooms parted and a grotesquely disfigured woman walked in. One side of her face and head had been severely scarred. She wore a scarf on her right side where flowing blonde hair once grew.

"Dieter must never know about me," Marta said, looking sternly at her friend with tears in her eyes. "It seems he has a new life and I don't want his pity. But knowing my husband, he'd be by my side no matter what. Can you imagine what I must look like to him—what it would be like to see this every day."

Marta had become harden by the events since the fire bombings. Elsa has only known her mother with such a face. She'll never know how beautiful she once was.

Dieter's eye's suddenly moistened as he headed back in the direction of the hotel. His paced quickened to where he passed his Russian tail sitting on a row of cinder blocks again pretending to read his newspaper. "Come on … let's go … we've got to find some food," Dieter grunted as he walked by. "And try to keep up!"

Chapter
25

Dieter was beginning to see the diverse differences between the Soviet controlled East Germany and the Allied controlled West Germany, and it wasn't exactly setting all that well with him. What he has been observing is something that was not going to change anytime soon.

Dieter's mind was muddled and confused as he headed to the hotel. He had no idea where he could find the food he promised his neighbor and her child. He felt totally lost and frustrated.

The further he walked, the faster he paced, the more belligerent his mind became. He had to do something and it had to be done now! In a moment of paroxysm, he turned completely around and stormed directly at the agent that continually followed him at the usual half block distance. The agent was stunned when he saw a scornful Dieter bearing straight for him. He froze in his tracks.

Within seconds Dieter was standing there prodding with a puffed-up red face and angry scowl. "Do you know what your people are doing? Do you not know that you are *starving* these people to death? The goddamned war is over … they have already suffered enough! Do you people not have any *compassion* at all?"

"Please … please," the agent said holding up his arms with palms outwardly faced barely touching Dieter's jacket. In broken but understandable English, he quickly retorted, "I am fully aware of what our government is doing and can assure you that not all of us are as hardened as you might think. Many of our own people are suffering the same fate and there are a few of us who understand and are compassionate," replied the agent in a now more rueful tone.

"When you passed me a few blocks ago, I saw tears in your eyes and felt sorrow realizing you must have lost a loved one. I too felt remorse because I have also lost loved ones. The job I have is to follow and observe you and I have observed you in a way with which you might not understand," the agent said with pang.

By now Dieter had quickly calmed understanding the sympathy in this man's voice. After another short exchange, he asked him where he might find food to carry to his friend and child in the house he had just visited. They were in desperate straits.

"Yes … I know of a place where you can get staples for your friend. There are numerous out of the way places in the city, but I know of one station where a friend works that can be of help. Please … come with me and I will show you."

"But … maybe … shouldn't you just tell me where it is so that you can continue following me?" Dieter said concerning he might cause problems with the agent.

"At the moment it is no problem. I am not currently being followed myself and everything is okay. Besides, you will need my help when you get there. The lines are very long taking many hours to retrieve the food. As you Americans say, I can 'cut through the red tape'."

Dieter just nodded in agreement. It was another one of those damned American colloquialisms he didn't understand, but he surmised it was something good.

As they headed off, Dieter heard, "Viktor … Viktor is my name," with which Dieter subtly replied, "Dean … Dean Zimmerman."

With a glimmer on his face and his head slightly cocked, Viktor replied, "Yes … yes, I know. From Roanoke, Virginia … correct?" Dieter just smiled.

They did not crossover the Elbe River Bridge but headed in the opposite direction cutting through countless burned out alleys and traipsing across acres and acres of rubble-filled streets. After a good half-hour, they came upon a row of intact buildings with snake-like lines of citizens meandering out and around its perimeter. Viktor was right, the lines were long.

Dieter was told to sit tight; Viktor disappeared behind the scarred two-story building. Ten minutes later, Viktor reappeared waving his arm to come forward.

Once inside the building, and in the backroom away from where the food was being distributed, Viktor introduced Dieter to his friend Karl. "Viktor tells me you are an American who has lost loved ones in this city and that you need staples for a friend and her child. You realize of course, she is not alone in her troubles."

"Yes … that is correct … and yes, I am aware of the situation. I did have a 'relative' here who was lost in the firestorm and the friend was her neighbor who has a three-year-old child. She is unable to work and leave the child alone. Their rations are barely able to sustain them … especially the child.

"In a fit of anger and self-pity, I aggressively stormed at Viktor in a hostile way. I should have had better self-control, but my emotions ran amuck. I felt so sad … I just had to do something. Viktor was an easy target … yet he was kind and understanding and said he could help. That is why I am here."

Karl was a big Russian reminiscent of his friend Werner Schroeder—amiable and likable. But Dieter also remembered Hildabrand's warning about 'trusting no one;' nevertheless, this was a case where he had to impart his own instincts and throw caution to the wind. By doing so, he knows his mission might be in jeopardy; regardless, he felt the need to help his neighbor. To him, it was the human thing to do. Though in reality, he knows in the days ahead, he is going to kill Bormann—truly an inhuman act not worthy of thought.

Without further ado and keeping a ruckus from occurring within the working ranks, Karl directed one of the German lady workers at the front serving counter to withdraw to the storeroom and gather a bag of supplies. Dieter followed her into the room saying in German, "Diese für ein schwaches Weib und 'Kind krank'." The woman responded in kind by saying she also had a "sickly child" but was forced by the Russians to work.

Inside the storeroom, she gathered five loaves of bread, a large bag of powdered milk for "das Kind," and four quart tins of raw white beans. As she was stuffing the items into a dingy cloth sack, Dieter noticed a lone bag of sugar propped neatly in the corner with "USA" printed in large red letters on the front. Dieter chuckled to himself how Hildabrand's favorite moniker for his homeland was ol' "Uncle Sugar."

Not trying to sound voracious, Dieter asked the woman if he might have "two scoops" of the sugar. Without hesitation, she looked at him and said, "'Zwei Kugeln,' Ja."

She put the scoops into a smaller separate bag and then carefully placed it into the larger sack and handed it to him. Dieter kindly kissed her on the cheek and said, "Danke." She in turn blushed, winked, and then returned to the front counter wearing a blissful smile.

Dieter walked out of the storeroom and into the backroom where he met Viktor and Karl in tranquil conversation. His Russian wasn't good enough to pick-up their tête-à-tête, but he felt it had something to do with him. Then again it wouldn't be surprising because he had intruded himself on a mission of mercy that could have caused them trouble. But had Viktor anticipated repercussions, it's doubtful he would have followed through.

Viktor and Karl bid their adieu. Dieter, in fine American fashion, shook Karl's hand thanking him for his kindness. Viktor then directed Dieter to the backdoor where they both quickly strode past and away from the lines of people.

Fortunately, no one was cognizant of their antics, and they were able to disappear into the rubble without causing a commotion. Had anyone become aware of Dieter's special treatment, there could have been trouble. Viktor was wise to this and played coy to the situation. Dieter caught on quickly and played along.

When they were finally away from the row of buildings, Dieter pointedly asked Viktor. "Why *are* you following me?"

Viktor simply said, "You know your way back to your friend's house. Be sure to 'walk straight' and 'don't get lost.' I will not be following you back." And with that, Viktor turned and walked away.

Dieter's mind was abuzz as to what he'd just heard and how it was said. Was it a threat? Was it a warning? What the hell was it? He was now confused more than ever. But before Viktor had gone too far, Dieter lightly hollered in his best-broken Russian, "Спасибо," to which Viktor turned around, partially raised his right arm, and replied in his best-broken English, "You are welcome!"

By now it was early afternoon and he had a ways to walk to deliver the sack of staples to his neighbor Hilda. It took him a few seconds, but he finally got his bearings and off he went with the sack of food under his arm. After several blocks, he tossed the sack over his right shoulder and a few blocks later reversed the sack to his left shoulder. Even though he had some physical conditioning while he was training in England for his mission, he realized his stamina wasn't quite what it used to be.

After a few more blocks, he noticed a couple of youngsters playing in the street. As he got closer to them, they stopped playing and stared at him with a curiosity that Dieter noticed.

With a jovial tone to his voice, Dieter said, "Hallo Jungen!" They in turn responded asking Dieter, "Braucht etwas Hilfe Mister?"

"Boys," Dieter said woefully with a playful smile, "I could use all the 'help' you can muster."

The boys in turn said they would gladly carry the sack the remaining two blocks, if it wasn't too heavy. But to Dieter's delight, it was a manageable proposition.

When they arrived at Hilda's house, Dieter reached into his pocket and gave each boy a small packet of American chocolate and two silver coins. They thanked each other, and the boys joyfully took off down the street laughing like kids are supposed to laugh. To Dieter, it was a delightful sound he hadn't heard in many years. He hoped he might hear it more often.

When Dieter was in Munich after the war, there were many children looking for food; and it was from that point on, he always made the habit of carrying chocolate on his person. This was the first time he had the chance to pass it out; albeit for a different reason, but nonetheless for a good cause.

Hilda had been observing Dieter and the two young boys through her front sitting room window. When he grabbed the sack and headed for the stoop, she had already opened the front door greeting him by the steps. She surmised Dieter had returned with a bit of fare; and when he confirmed he had by putting his hand on her shoulder and lightly nodding, she broke into tears putting her fingers to her quivering lips.

She then hugged Dieter profusely thanking him for his kindness and that they "all" would enjoy his wonderful gift of thoughtfulness. It was a meaningful moment for Dieter whose own eyes were beginning to moisten from the moment. Such a small and simple gift to mean so much. It's doubtful this trice would ever be forgotten.

Walking back to the hotel, Dieter felt good about what he had done. But now he had many new questions that needed answering. *"How does Viktor know I'm from Roanoke, Virginia? I made no mention of that when I registered. It's only on my passport and I haven't shown it to anyone except those two guards on the train. Naw, they weren't that smart. 'Check Point Charley,' I don't think so ... it was too busy. Nobody really paid attention. It was move ... move ... move.*

"Is Viktor just leading me on ... does he know my real name is Dieter Zeis and I'm on a mission of death? If so, why is he playing it so mum ... and his compassion towards my German friends? Surely the Russians have disdain for the Germans. Maybe this spy business really is the 'cat and mouse' game they taught me in England. Maybe I'm the mouse right now. But his help did seem genuine. He really did seem compassionate.

"But what of his statements: 'not currently being followed himself,' 'walk straight,' 'don't get lost,' and 'I won't be following you back to your neighbor's house.' All those comments had a scary ring to it. I wonder if he'll be following

me at all anymore? Or will he follow me and stay in the shadows? Will somebody else be following me? Hell, I don't know ... I guess I'll just have to play the cards I'm dealt."

There was one interesting note Dieter heartily picked up on when he delivered the food. *"Hilda said 'all' of us will enjoy the food. That's queer ... there were only supposed to be two in the house. 'All' would seem to mean more than two. Maybe ... naw, that couldn't be."*

It was late in the day and Dieter had so much on his mind that he paid little attention to the several shops and stores that were sprinkled throughout the rubble-strewn area. Unlike German cities in the western sectors, particularly the American zone, Dresden had made little progress in rebuilding since the end of the war.

As Dieter made his way to the hotel from a different directon, he noticed a small beer garden with an attached restaurant, a grocery store for those with money, a cobbler's shop, and a rather large department store housing a vast array of new and used clothing. Dieter reckoned those Germans working for the Russians were about the only ones with adequate currency to buy any goods.

An occasional Russian Army vehicle could be seen at some of the cross-streets but very few soldiers were present. Dieter thought most of the Russians were surrounding the city controlling who comes and goes; but that was only a guess. At one of the main streets of the downtown area, a German Polizist was directing traffic at a four-way intersection. It was the first sign of a German civil government he had seen since getting into town.

These shops and surrounding areas of bustling commerce were situated two blocks from the clock shop's location. Viktor was nowhere to be seen; Dieter thought it was a good time to check the shop to see if there were any signs of Bormann.

Dieter casually studied the clock shop building. It once had been a three-story structure; it now barely had two. The top floor was gone and most of the second floor was missing. A makeshift roof had been constructed to repel the weather. It appeared there was enough of the second floor left for a small apartment, but it was hard to tell from walking on the street.

An old brass train station clock, once serving as the grand marquee, hung slightly askew above a shabby front door. There had been two windows on either side, but one had been bricked. The other had displayed various old clocks; nothing was there now. The past proud ornate glass entry was now nothing more than a worn-out insect infested dark gray wooden door that was structurally fitting only for an outdoor privy. It was all depressing; the inside was another matter.

Dieter hesitantly walked in ringing a small brass bell overhanging a chewed-up, misaligned doorframe announcing his arrival. After a few short footsteps on a well-worn wooden floor and then slowly shuffling in a circle, Dieter marveled at how many clocks were hanging on the walls wholly ticking to their own characteristic rhythm. Aside from the splendid array of fine and stately pieces, there were many mantle clocks, bracket clocks, desk clocks, grandfather clocks, and, as well, a large assortment of French, German and Austrian carriage clocks displayed in a superbly crafted curio cabinet that must have come from eighteenth century Prussia.

After admiring the beautifully crafted works, Dieter meandered to a stately old wooden and glass counter that had seen better days. Inside the case was a display of at least a hundred watches. While looking at the watches, he observed a short stooped elderly man crumpled over a cluttered watchmaker's desk gingerly working on a well-used pocket watch.

His full head of hair was silvery gray and his age-spot skin was unusually wrinkled. He was wearing yellow-gold wire-rims with forcibly bent temples wrapped loosely about his ears. A small jeweler's magnifying optic was attached to his right lens allowing for better magnification. Many special tools of the trade lay scattered about the table. He also noticed a half-empty bottle of schnapps in a hutch behind his table. It was Doornkaat—Dieter's favorite.

The old man heard the bell but bided his time allowing a moment for his patron to browse the shop. But now he was at the counter. "Darf ich Ihnen helfen, Sir?"

Dieter, in his purposely broken German accent with an American English flare, tried to explain the antique mantle clock he needed repaired. Before he could finish, the old man interrupted in good plain English—but with a German Bavarian flare. "It appears your English is much better than your broken German. Perhaps I should speak English so that we may communicate a little better." Dieter couldn't agree more. His ruse worked well.

"Dean" explained he was an American from Virginia who was a clock collector. The one he had was a family heirloom from a favored great uncle who claimed he bought the clock from this exact shop in 1835. It had remained in good working order only up until 1942 when the main spring finally broke.

Now that the war was over, and with his high-ranking "position" within the family owned business, he was allowed the freedom to travel. To keep the clock original, he wanted it repaired from the original clock shop. This was that shop.

The clock-maker was intrigued with Dieter's story and was anxious to see the timepiece asking him to bring it in. Before he could finish the conversation, the phone rang and he excused himself. This gave Dieter an opportunity to snoop around.

As the old man talked on the phone, Dieter noticed someone else in the shop milling about the backroom. He couldn't get a good look because of the thick dark green velvet curtain blocking the view. But his feeling was it was another man. He could tell by the footsteps.

The situation was such that Dieter couldn't pry because it would have aroused suspicion; he just continued walking in front of the counter with his hands clasped behind his back hoping to get a glimpse of the figure. It would have been too much to hope he would just open the curtain and come to the counter. That would have been too easy. Spying was supposed to be hard.

When the clock-master returned, Dieter told him he would come back in the morning with his clock. In the meantime, he initiated small talk to see what he could learn. "Your shop seems to have come through the war pretty much intact," Dieter said trying to be complimentary.

"My clocks fared better than my family. I lost my wife and daughter. They were on the top floor during one of the bombing raids. I couldn't tell whether it was English or American bombs that killed them. I guess it doesn't matter. I don't know whether my son is still alive or not. He was in the Sixth Army on the Eastern Front. Hans is either dead or in some Russian gulag. Either way I will never know." There was a tone of sad resignation in the old man's voice.

Dieter was sympathetic to the man's story. He himself was initially resigned from telling the old man about his wife's demise but had a soft heart and reiterated his tale; albeit, a modified version with numerous twist and turns avoiding anything unusual for fear it might come back to haunt him. Nonetheless, he gained the man's confidence and his sympathy. He mentioned he just found out this morning. He made no mention of his mission of mercy.

With the loss of the man's family, who also helped in the shop, Dieter subtly asked if he had hired any help. He replied he took on an older gentleman about a year and a half ago to sweep the floors and keep the shop in order. He had no family. All were lost in the war—or so he said.

But as time moved on, the old clock-master tried to teach him to make minor repairs and simple fixes on some of the lesser expensive clocks. He remarked he was making mediocre progress; but his mind always wandered to "far away places."

Dieter thanked the old gentleman and bid his farewell saying he would return sometime in the morning. The man replied he'd be there as long as the sun would rise. Dieter gave a genuine humorous laugh and walked out the door.

On the way to the hotel, Dieter's mind was clicking a hundred beats a minute. By all indications, it appears that

Bormann is working in that shop. He doesn't know for sure, but he has a good feeling.

There was nothing else he could accomplish this late in the day—for it had been long and exhausting. Maybe he could find something interesting to do; yet, not too strenuous. Maybe he could just find a bottle of schnapps, a soft chaise lounge, and get controllably drunk. Yes, maybe he needed that; or maybe even a tub of hot soapy water. Either way, it was an inviting idea.

As the sun crept downward over a ragged strewn horizon, Dieter approached the Grand Imperial Hotel where he noticed Viktor sitting on that same wooden bench across the street. They each made eye contact nodding with a pleasant smile. Then Dieter disappeared through the large double glass doors. Inside the foyer were numerous people milling about, talking, and shaking hands in a greeting sort of way. It was good to see the place alive, but he had no idea as to where all the people had come from. When he first got here yesterday, it seemed as dead as a dodo bird. *"Maybe there's a clock convention or something. Who knows?"*

Passing through the groups of people and by the front desk, he headed for the large spiral staircase to go to his room. By happenstance, he spotted the spy lady he had met earlier that morning. She was sitting in a heavy, red leather, wing-back chair near one of the beveled glass front windows across from the staircase. She also noticed him; laying down her newspaper, she motioned for him to come over. He wondered, *"Is she there on purpose and is this some kind of set-up. After today's activities, it could be anything. Maybe I should just say hello, excuse myself, and go find that bottle of schnapps ... or find that hot bathtub! Then again, she is pretty to look at ... so, what the hell! I guess it's time to go see what's in this deck of cards'."*

"Guten Abend, Herr Zimmerman," she greeted warmly in German.

Without missing a beat, Dieter replied in good solid American English, "And *good evening* to you! But, I must say, you seem to have the advantage on names. May I play along?"

217

"Yes ... I was a bit sneaky this morning and looked at the desk register. I hope you don't mind. I'm Raisa Yana ... but I go by Reese because it sounds more European and I have less explaining to do. As you *may* have experienced today ... the Russians are not very fond of the Germans." Dieter quickly pondered that statement. Maybe that was true as a whole, but what he saw today was just plain good old human kindness. Though, he had no desire to expound on that with her. He thought it best to stay quiet.

"Well Reese ... it is a pleasure to formally meet you!" Dieter said with a smile.

Rees then forwardly asked Dean if he would join her for an aperitif in the hotel's lounge. He thought that might be a good idea. It had been a long day and he was thirsty for schnapps; but he thought it might be best to play "American" and go for a frothy beer. He didn't want to tip his hand he was German—and all Germans like schnapps.

Dieter was surprised to see the hotel's lounge was open. Reese explained it had just gone through a renovation and merely opened today for the first time in well over a year. After taking their seats at a corner table, Reese ordered Russian Kubanskaya Vodka over ice, and Dean ordered a draft beer in a cold mug. He was told the beer was cold but the glass wasn't and nonchalantly said that would be fine.

After the drinks were served, Dean casually asked, "And ... so ... how was your day at the office."

"The same as usual just like it always is. These Germans will do anything to get out of work," she replied in English.

"Maybe it's what you're having them do. What exactly is it that you are having them do?" Dean asked inquisitively.

"I'm afraid I can't talk about that," she countered with a slight smile.

Dieter decided not to pursue that line of conversation anymore and changed the subject to something simpler. "Well then ... how long have you been in Dresden? Surely that's not prying."

"No ... of course not. I've been here for almost a year. My government saw a good fit for me and I decided to take it. As I mentioned this morning, my language skills gave me this opportunity and I thought I'd take it. Yes ... times are tough everywhere, but this job seems to be the lesser of two evils. But because of what I do ... I really can't and don't want to talk about it. Besides, it's simply *none* of your business," Reese said matter-of-factly taking a sip of her vodka.

"Yes ... I think I understand that. Well then ... where are you living ... if I should be so bold to ask?" After several good slugs of beer, Dieter was beginning to relax just trying to have a pleasant evening without stressing his mind. Simple conversation at this point was good therapy.

"Actually, I'm living here at the hotel ... I have a suite on the third floor. It's been renovated ... it's very nice and comfortable. After the war, Russia demanded reparations from the Germans. The hotel, among many, many other assets, was part of that deal. They give me my room and service and also pay me a salary. So tonight, the drinks are on me!" Reese said slightly boasting.

"And what about you Dean Zimmerman from America," Reese said working on her second vodka.

Dieter had to be cautious and keep his ruse simple and in order. While he and Hildabrand were drinking Jim Beam in the old rustic office in West Berlin before coming to East Germany, they discussed various scenarios to thwart prying eyes and ears. The one piece of advice Hildabrand told him that wedged in his mind: *"To be a good liar, you have to have a good memory. Stay within those limitations and you'll be just fine."* Dieter knows his limitations and has taken the advice to heart. *"It'll probably save my life someday."*

"My family owns a small manufacturing firm in Roanoke, Virginia, and because of my position within the organization, I'm afforded the opportunity to travel. I have always wanted to see Bavaria, and a chance recently arose for that to happen. Before going there, I was asked by family members to find the whereabouts of a favored great aunt who was living here in Dresden. Since the end of the war, they haven't heard from her. So ... that is why I'm here. Unfortunately ... today I discovered she perished in the firestorm."

Reese showed little outwardly emotion. She prodded a little deeper. "And … you are from German descent? "Yes, my great grandfather was from Bremerhaven before emigrating to America and settling in Central Virginia. He then started a small manufacturing firm making door parts for Henry Ford's automobiles. As time progressed, he diversified to other types of components."

By now Dieter was on his third mug and feeling relaxed. At this point, he felt it was a good time to have a little fun with Reese and her little game of "cat and mouse." He was keeping his ruse simple and to the point. Though, he didn't think he could forget this. Much of it was true!

"Before America got involved in the war, Roosevelt worked out a 'Lend- Lease agreement' with Stalin. At that time, we, the company, were asked by our government to retool and make parts for the military. By now my father was running the company, and he wholeheartedly felt the need to work for ol' Uncle Sam in helping Mother Russia. He well knew they needed it because the Germans could very well overrun your country and create more trouble for the Americans when they joined the war, which they knew was eventually going to happen. It was a nice arrangement for us."

Reese had just ordered her third Kubanskaya and was paying very close attention to what Dean was saying. Her Russian accent was becoming more pronounced. "What type of military parts did your company supply us … if I may ask so boldly?"

"Yes … well … that would be a secret now wouldn't it? But we're still not allowed to discuss it. Just suffice it to say it simply isn't *any* of your business!"

Reese clearly got the message. She cleverly smiled, picked up her vodka, and lightly toasted her companion in a strong pronounced Russian accent that was ever so slightly slurred. "Dean Zimmerman from Virginia, you are okay! Finish your beer and let us go get something to eat. I know a nice little out of the way Italian restaurant on the other side of the river. It is in a section of town that is being rebuilt. Why don't we each freshen up and I will meet you in the lobby at 8 o'clock. I will have a cab waiting for us."

As they arose from the table and straightened up, Reese lightly grabbed Dean by the arm, looked up, and softly kissed him on the cheek. "Don't be late. Russian cab drivers hate to wait!"

Dieter went to his room forgetting his bathroom was out of order. After grabbing a washcloth and hand towel, he went to the communal facilities at the end of the hall. While shaving he looked into the mirror pondering whether Reese had "interest in him" or whether she was "interested in him." There seemed to be a little of both; but as much as he was concerned, he played those cards with remarkable confidence. Maybe he should continue and see what his new hand was like. So far it's been fun. But there is one thing for certain: *"She sure is pretty."*

Just before 8 o'clock, Dean was standing in the foyer by the front desk. A few minutes later, Reese descended wearing a beautiful crimson outfit snuggly fit to her lovely hourglass figure. She was ravishing!

Dieter was overwhelmed at how quickly she had transformed herself from everyday plain clothes to awe-inspiring beauty. The best Dieter could perform during this same time was shaving and donning a clean shirt. Anything beyond that Reese and the cabdriver would have already split.

Reese greeted Dean with a light kiss on the cheek and they headed out the door to a taxicab that had just pulled in front of the hotel. The timing seemed impeccable. He opened the rear passenger door for Reese and he in turn made his way to the driver's side passenger door. Before getting in, he noticed the driver was Viktor (!) who had his left forefinger pressed to his lips warning Dieter to be discreet. *"What in the hell is going on now!"* he thought.

Dieter didn't know what to think but remained quiet as Reese directed the driver to "Gino's" place in the northwest section of town across the Elba River. She asked the driver if he knew where it was.

"Да, Все водители такси знают Gino место," he replied in Russian.

"What did he say?" Dean asked Reese.

"'Yes, all cabdrivers know Gino's place.' Well, they should. It's where most all our senior staff members and military officers hang out. It's one of the few places in town they can go and relax, drink, and have a good meal. It's generally off limits to the public, but I know many of the officials, and I know Gino quite well. You'll be all right with me.

"Gino is from the Ukraine and considered one of the best chef's in Kiev. One of our army generals discovered him during the war and brought him down here to Dresden to cook for all the officials when our armed forces moved in towards the end of the war. He's become a big hit ... everybody loves him."

"But Gino can't be his real name if he's from the Ukraine!" Dean remarked.

"Oh ... we all know that ... but nobody cares what his real name is. He picked up that moniker rather quickly because of his wonderful flare for Italian cooking."

The cab finally pulled in front of a small nondescript brick building with no windows and an old style street lamp overhanging the front door. There was no signage anywhere describing the place as "Gino's." Reese simply announced, "Ah ... we are here." She quickly opened her door and got out.

Dieter slowly followed but before exiting, brusquely tapped Viktor on his shoulder loudly whispering, "You stay right here! I'll be right back as soon as I get the lady inside the building. Don't leave ... you understand!"

The door to Gino's was locked but after a few raps, the door opened into a small wooden foyer leading to the dining area. The man at the front immediately recognized Reese and began chatting. Dean saw an opening and told her he was returning to pay the cabdriver. She nodded and continued talking to the doorman.

When Dieter returned to the cab, he went directly to the driver's window. "Viktor, what in the hell is going here. Something tells me you're not exactly moonlighting to pick up extra Rubles!"

Viktor looked at Dieter and said, "Shut up … now listen quickly … she doesn't know who I am but I know who she is. Be *careful* around her and 'walk a straight line.' She knows many of those officials intimately and some are very ruthless. Play it cool and act stupid.

"Gino and Karl are brothers and they are friends of mine. Gino knows that you are coming tonight and he will steer you away from the nasty officials that are always looking for trouble. He will look after you … remember that! Now go have a nice meal. I will come back at 10:30 to pick you up. Be ready! And by the way, try the Campania Spaghetti topped with Pommarola sauce and the Mozzarella di Bufalo cheese." And with that, Viktor drove off.

Dieter re-entered the restaurant and met Reese who had already taken a seat at a table by the far wall. She inquired as to why he had taken so long. "Was it that long? I was just having a little chat with him about the weather. Anyway, he said he would return at 10:30 to take us back to the hotel, which I thought was a good idea." Reese agreed.

The restaurant that night was about half full with Russian officials. There was a lot of chatter, general noise, and plenty of blue haze cigarette smoke curling about the ceiling. Reese asked Dean if he smoked.

"No, but I have a pack of American cigarettes. I figured they might come in handy on this side of the line," Dieter said jokingly.

"American cigarettes are like gold over here," she replied. "Those shit sticks they make in Russia are terrible. What does a girl have to do to get one from you?"

"Oh, I'll think of something," he wryly said as he pulled out a full pack of Chesterfields.

Reese took a cigarette from the pack and Dieter had a match lit before she could ask. She inhaled a long deep drag and slowly exhaled through her nose. "Ah … these cigarettes taste so much better than the weed back home," she said deeply and slowly with her Russian accent returning.

Gino had just walked out of the kitchen and recognized Reese and her new dining companion. He knew right off it was the gentleman that Karl, his brother, had told him about who visited his bread station that morning. He immediately went over to greet them and take their drink orders.

"Raisa … welcome and so good to see you again! You look so ravishing tonight. And who is your dining guest?"

She introduced Dean as an American citizen who is in Dresden looking for relatives lost in the firestorm. Dean in turn finally spoke telling Gino that it was a pleasure to meet him and also how he had heard from Reese many good things about his restaurant and his wonderful Italian cooking.

Gino gave a big bursting Russian laugh and asked Dean what he would like to drink. He already knew what Raisa wanted.

"I would love to have a tall chilled mug of your finest draft beer," Dean said in a jovial sort of way.

"Our finest draft beer is Hefeweizen and it will be chilled but, unfortunately, the mug will not. I hope that is not a problem," Gino said almost apologetically. Dean of course has expecting the mug to be warm but told Gino it wasn't a problem. As far as he was concerned, all beer tasted the same. He really didn't care. He was a schnapps man.

Within a minute, Gino returned with Dean's draft beer and Raisa's Kubanskaya Vodka over ice. They each picked up their glasses, made a simple toast, and took a sip. Reese took another draw off her Chesterfield this time exhaling through her lightly pressed lips.

After a half-hour of broad conversation, several more drinks, and Reese moving closer to Dean, Gino sensed he was ready to eat and appeared at the table with a big and robust smile. Raisa was a little incensed at the timing, but Dean remarked he was getting hungry and ready to order.

Dean inquired to Gino as to what region of Italy he preferred his cuisine. He unquestionably said he preferred the southern area because of the tomato type sauces that suited his liking.

This comment surprisingly filled an "inside straight" for Dieter given Viktor's food recommendation just before driving off! Dean's only knowledge of Italian food was that Southern Italy *was* known for cooking with tomato paste.

Dean therefore suggested that he was quite fond of the Campania Spaghetti topped with the Pommarola sauce with Mozzarella di Bufalo cheese. Gino lit up like a firefly on a warm June night telling him that it was one of his specialties and that he had just received a shipment of Buffalo cheese that afternoon! "Excellent choice my friend … excellent … and Мисс Raisa, what would you like to have tonight … the usual?"

"No Gino" she said half crocked, "My friend here from America has just impressed me with his knowledge of spaghetti … and I've yet to have your spaghetti … so tonight I think I will have your spaghetti … and of course you can bring me another Kubanskaya and another beer for my friend. He looks thirsty!" she said in the same deep voice.

Dean interrupted the beer order and told Gino that he would really like to try schnapps. "I've never had one. All my friends back in the States say it tastes like nitroglycerin, but tonight I would like to give it a *shot*, so to speak. And besides, from what I hear, 'when you are in Rome, you do as the Romans'!"

Gino laughed again and with his strong accent said, "That will be one schnapps and another vodka … coming right up!

Dean quickly stopped Gino before he left the table, "By any chance do you have Doornkaat Schnapps?

Gino told him it was a favorite among his customers and he had a full stock.

Reese moved closer to Dean and put her face close to his. "My … my … aren't we getting brave tonight." And so as nobody would notice, she moved even closer and put her left hand on Dean's upper thigh whispering, "I think tonight, I will be helpless and you will have to save me from danger!"

Dean played along as best he could, but he was becoming slightly embarrassed as to how Reese was acting. But the more he played coy, the worse she got. Fortunately he was *saved* when the spaghetti arrived—it smelled delicious.

Reese finally slowed her vodka intake and started acting a little more mature; but not too much more. She was able to eat her meal and not spill anything; though, she did drop some Pommarola sauce in her lap; but as it turned out, it blended nicely with her crimson outfit.

Dean on the other hand was overwhelmed with his meal trying to compare his good friend Werner Schroeder's cooking when he was with Herr Rommel. Werner never cooked spaghetti, but the sauce he ate certainly brought back good memories.

After they finished their meal, Dieter noticed it was getting close to 10:30 and suggested to Reese that maybe they should have a digestif back at the hotel. She in turn excused herself to the ladies room.

Dieter went to the counter and complimented Gino on an excellent meal. He reached into his pocket to pay the bill. In his broken English and magnified Russian accent, Gino said. "There is no charge for you tonight my friend. It is paid for courtesy of Herr Hitler and his former band of thugs. But there is something you can do for me. I have to get message to Viktor, your cabdriver. Please take this note to him. He will understand. And just for your own curiosity, it does not concern you but another matter of importance. We have to communicate discreetly. You seem to be nice man who will help me." Dieter covertly took the note and put it in his pocket looking none the wiser.

"Мисс Raisa is nice lady who likes to flirt and have good time. She can be hard nosed at times, but she is basically good person. But be *careful* what you say to her! Go back to hotel tonight and have fun. She will more than likely accommodate your desires!"

Raisa appeared from the restroom looking much fresher and ready to go. Dieter was astounded as to how this lady could restore herself so quickly. But at the moment, it was too much to figure out. He had way too many other things on his mind. Trying to figure out how she restored herself wasn't on the list. Getting her to the room was!

As they walked out the door, the cab was just pulling up. Again Dieter was overawed at the timing. Maybe these cab drivers took lessons from the train engineers. As expected, when he and Reese entered the cab, Viktor was still driving.

When they reached the hotel, Dieter walked Reese to the foyer excusing himself briefly to return to pay the cabdriver. Reese said she would meet him in the lounge. Dieter went back to the cab, handed Viktor $20 in Russian currency along with the note from Gino. Viktor tried to return the money, but Dieter refused.

"Thanks for the tip on the spaghetti ... it was delicious! Even Raisa enjoyed it instead of ordering her usual ... whatever that was!"

Viktor laughed. "Her usual is a small shrimp salad on lettuce with a touch of sweet mustard on the side. How do you think she maintains that hourglass figure? If she regularly ate what you had tonight, she would be as big as the work horses back in Moscow!"

Dieter chuckled and reckoned so. "I better get back to her before she falls asleep. She's in the lounge."

Viktor reiterated his strong advice to Dieter before driving off. "Remember ... 'walk straight' and have fun tonight ... but be *careful* what you say to her! And think about leaving Dresden in a few days. Situations rapidly change around here and you must not be here when that happens!"

Dieter again became confused; but then, the entire day was confusing. And the guy confusing it all was Viktor. *"Who is this guy and what in the hell is he up to?"*

Surprisingly, numerous people were still in the lounge when he entered. Reese found the same table they had earlier that evening. She had also ordered each of them a snifter of Doornkaat Schnapps. When Dieter walked closer to the table, a man in uniform she was talking to excused himself and went to another table with a woman in uniform. He tried nonchalantly to look at their rank, but it was too dark to notice. It really made no difference; he was just curious.

Inside the newly renovated lounge, there was merely the sound of low hum chatter with occasional soft laughter followed by girly giggles. It was certainly far removed from the noisy clang of glasses and boisterous conversations echoing from the brick and mortar walls at Gino's. It was a pleasant setting for cozy conversation and sipping of schnapps.

227

For all the day, Dieter lastly found a quiet moment where he could finally hear himself think and concentrate on Reese's eyes—and her breast.

Dean quietly started to talk when he began to sit down. "Had we not crossed each other's path tonight, I was planning on a rendezvous with a tub of hot water and soapy suds. Since I left the States, I've been so much on the go … that my *aching* body needs refreshing. But after leasing my room, I discovered the water in my lavatory was on the fritz. With your connections, you think you can get it fixed?"

Reese knew Dean was being playful; and she also knew what he was alluding. Though, for the short while, she'd be coy. Maybe a little payback from earlier this evening. "Yes … the bombings did loosen a few of the pipes in this old place. Some rooms have been repaired … others haven't … mine's been repaired. Do you know if they gave you a discount on your room?"

"No … I really don't know. I'll have to check on that tomorrow."

"Yes, that might be a good idea. But no … my connections wouldn't work very well for bathroom repairs," she stated coyly and continued.

"Perhaps if you had some tools, you could fix it yourself. You look like a guy who is handy with his hands!"

"You know, I was quite handy when I worked in the plant … I fixed *plenty* of broken pipes. Maybe I can fix this one too," Dean said playfully.

"Some workmen who were in my room the other day left a large bag of something or other in my spare closet. Maybe they left some wrenches in it?" Reese suggested.

"Yes … maybe they did!" Dieter said.

After they finished their schnapps, Reese suggested to Dean they should go to her room and search for the wrenches.

Both looked at each other grinning and in unprovoked unity said, "To the wrenches!"

Chapter

26

Early the next morning prior to the rising sun, Dieter suddenly awoke. He lay there on his side away from a very sleepy Raisa. His eyes were open and his mind was racing. He knew that today was a day of reckoning. He was going to confront Martin Bormann, the private secretary to Adolf Hitler.

Today, Thursday, October 16, 1947, was the one-year anniversary of Bormann eluding the hangman's noose in a prison gymnasium next to the Nuremberg Palace of Justice. The "Trial of the Major War Criminals before the International Military Tribunal," later known as "The Nuremberg Trial," put twenty-two of Nazi Germany's most notorious leaders on trial. This number also included Bormann who was tried in absentia and actually given a trial lawyer named Friedrich Bergold.

The trial proper began on November 20, 1945 and lasted until September 2, 1946 when the eight judges, two each from the four allied countries, met to decide the fate of the defendants. On October 1st the judgments were handed down where twelve of the defendants were given a sentence of death by hanging. Only ten made it to the gallows.

Hermann Göring, the disgraced Reich Marshal and Commander in Chief of a once proud and powerful Luftwaffe, was one of two who cheated the noose. He was to be the first defendant executed; but two hours before that was to happen, he begrudgingly bit a stashed away cyanide capsule and was dead before the guard outside his door could react. Later inquisitions could never prove his acquisition of the pill and it quickly became a news media frenzy.

Martin Bormann was unanimously convicted of Count Three of the Indictment, War Crimes, and Count Four of the Indictment, Crimes against Humanity, and sentenced to the gallows; though, he was nowhere to be seen. He *read* about his fate several days later in a newspaper article while he was safely tucked away in an obscure clock shop in rubble-strewn Dresden. After reading the worldly news, he casually lowered the paper and swept the floor as the shop owner had requested.

The world's best-known fugitive from justice was the son of a sergeant in a cavalry regiment who later became a civil servant. After one year in high school, he dropped out to work on a farm. After serving a brief stint in the army as a cannoneer in a field artillery regiment in the waning days of World War I, he returned to the farm. A few years later he joined the newly formed Freikorps.

The "Free Corps" were paramilitary organizations that sprang up all over Germany fashioned from World War I military adventurers, fanatical nationalist, unemployed youths and demobilized soldiers, who felt disconnected from civilian life with the need for stability in a military structure.

The Freikorps, rightist in their political philosophy and blaming Social Democrats and Jews for Germany's appalling plight, called for the elimination of "traitors to the Fatherland." At first, Paul von Hindenburg, Supreme Military Commander of German forces in World War I supported these "freebooter squads." But because of their boorish and obnoxious behavior against the old military guard, he and his colleagues withdrew their support.

Since the Treaty of Versailles officially limited Germany to a 100,000-man army, called the Reichswehr, the Freikorps were allowed to exponentially grow eventually sustaining a force of three million men. Though the Freikorps was officially disbanded in 1920, Adolf Hitler, who was just beginning his political career when he transformed the little known German Workers Party into the infamous National Socialist German Workers Party (NSDAP and known as The Nazi Party), revamped the Freikorps the following year into an organization called the "Sturmabteilung" which was better known by the names "Brownshirts" and "Storm Troopers," but even more commonly by the initials "SA."

Hitler considered the SA as a political force and not a military force. His intent was to use this group as *shock troops* to keep the German people in a permanent state of excitement. Though, his biggest problem was maintaining the spirit of the SA without allowing them to move into a revolting state. He also used the SA as protection against other rival political parties prevalent at the time.

In Munich on November 8, 1923, Adolf Hitler, Rudolf Hess, Hermann Göring, and many other early Nazi Party members attempted the take over of the Bavarian and Berlin governments in what was known as the "Beer-Hall Putsch." The rebellion failed and Hitler and many of his cohorts were sent to prison. On the surface, the coup d'état was a colossal defeat; but in the short-run, it quickly and earnestly evolved into a dazzling triumph for the political unknown. In the days to come, Hitler catapulted his scarcely known unimportant political party into a worldwide headline.

While in Landsberg Prison, Hitler quietly pondered that the direct and confrontational approach was not the means to political power; the way to political success and winning the masses was by attracting the support of wealthy industrialist; therefore, easing his way to party-political supremacy by legal and licit means. But perhaps the key ingredient to Hitler's success was his arousal of geopolitics instilled by Rudolf Hess, also imprisoned at Landsberg Prison. Hess had studied geopolitics under Professor Karl Haushofer at the University of Munich and was vastly impressed with his theories. He passed this knowledge to Hitler.

With Hitler's rise to power and Hess's devoted loyalty, he was promoted to many high-ranking positions within the Nazi Party. And because of his faithfulness, in April 1933, two and a half months after Hitler was installed as Chancellor, Hess was appointed to Deputy Führer.

Martin Bormann's rise to infamous fame occurred shortly after he joined the Mecklenburg Freikorps Group commanded by former 1st Lieutenant Gerhard Rossbach. This faction resorted to killing for the cause those traitors to the Fatherland. Bormann, a devout believer, was no exception. He was accused, along with Rudolf Höss, the future commandant at Auschwitz concentration camp, of killing Walther Kadow, Bormann's former elementary school teacher, when he betrayed Albert Leo Schlageter, a young Freikorps officer living in the French occupied German Ruhr region after World War I.

Schlageter opposed French authority and the French criminal police, acting on Kadow's information, arrested him for espionage and sabotage. He was soon found guilty and executed in May 1923. Bormann and Höss were later arrested. In March 1924, Höss was sentenced to ten years in prison; Bormann, convicted as a collaborator, served one year in Leipzig Prison. Shortly after his release, he joined the Nazi Party and rose steadily through the ranks eventually becoming a member of the Supreme Command of the SA. With this position, he came into intimate contact with Adolf Hitler.

In 1929 Hitler witnessed the marriage of Bormann to Gerda Buch, the daughter of a Reichstag deputy. She was well regarded by Hitler who shared his beliefs of the Nazi ideology. In the years to come, she bore her husband ten children with which she named the first child after Adolf, the Führer himself. He would become godfather to this child.

In due time, the antics of the SA became harsher and harsher using terror and scare tactics to frighten anybody opposing the NSDAP, especially the Communist Party. Bormann in 1930, with Hitler's permission, created and administered the "Hilfskasse" (Relief Fund) to help party members who had been injured in the ongoing street fights.

But Bormann's biggest break came in 1933 when Hitler appointed him Chief of Staff to Deputy Führer Rudolf Hess. From this point on, Bormann was unstoppable in his rise to the top. A few months later, he was again promoted to "Reichsleiter" (Reich Leader) of the Nazi Party and also to the post of NSDAP deputy to the "Reichstag" (Parliament), which was the German legislative body. But by then Hitler had deprived it of all legislative power by enacting the "Enabling Act" on March 24, 1933. By now, Hitler's rule *was* the rule.

It didn't take long before Bormann became a master in the art if intrigue and political infighting and working his way closer to Hitler. He took control of Hitler's financial affairs and functioned as the administrator of the "Adolf Hitler—Spende" (Adolf Hitler Fund): Bormann believed that businessmen who profited from their association with the NSDAP were expected to *voluntarily* contribute to Hitler's favorite projects. By Bormann administering this fund, it gave him untold power status within the Nazi ranks.

On orders from Hitler and with these funds, Bormann purchased the Pommer Inn in Braunau, Austria where Hitler was born; his parent's house in Leondig, Austria; and the entire Obersalzberg Mountain plateau near Berchtesgaden, Germany where the German hierarchy positioned themselves for preservation and privacy.

Perhaps the most ostentatious purchase with these funds was Bormann's *gift* to Hitler on his 50th birthday on April 20, 1938 on behalf the Nazi Party. Bormann had built atop the Kehlstein Mountain, just above the Obersalzberg plateau, a "Tea House" of sorts that eventually became known as the "Eagle's Nest." It was a modern era marvel that rivaled virtually anything ever built simply because of the logistics of where it was positioned—on a rock edge just below the 6,015-foot summit.

Getting to the house required walking through a 415-foot tunnel to a solid brass elevator car and ride 425 feet skyward through a carved granite shaft to the base entrance inside the house. But as close as Bormann was with Hitler, there was one thing he didn't know—he had a fear of heights; and because of this, Hitler made rare appearances never going back after October 1940.

On May 12, 1941, Bormann was promoted to his highest level when Rudolf Hess, the Deputy Führer, secretly flew to Scotland two days earlier on a forbidden 800-mile journey to arrange a peace with Britain. Since the beginning of World War

II, Hess's position with Hitler began to wane, and he was relegated to background duties. To regain Hitler's attention, he sacrificed himself to stop the unnecessary bloodshed between the German and British "Aryan blood." Unfortunately the strategy failed, and he was confined for the remainder of the war later being sentenced to a life in prison.

Hitler was furious and immediately abolished the title of Deputy Führer and appointed Bormann to a new political position as The Director of the newly created Party Chancellery where he was to work reinforcing The Party against both the Wehrmacht and SS (Schutzstaffel: Elite Guard). Originally the SS was the guard of Adolf Hitler, but it later transformed into a mass army serving as the political police and also serving as the administrative arm of operating the concentration and extermination camps—later known as the death camps.

Aside from this duty, Bormann also found time to supervise unprovoked attacks on Christianity, write extensive memorandums dealing with Jews and Slavs, prisoners of war, and the unnecessary behavior by the Gauleiters: Nazi district officials below the top Reich leadership. Party allies called him the "Brown Eminence" where as Party detractors called him "a Machiavellian in a ill-fitting civil servant's uniform sitting behind an office desk working to advance is own interest."

When virtually all the Nazi hierarchy abandoned Hitler in the final days, Martin Bormann remained loyal to the very end. His last act as a purist and loyalist was personally hauling Hitler's dead wife, the former Eva Braun, out of the bunker and laying her next to her very dead husband Adolf. After their bodies were engulfed in flames, Bormann stood at attention and gave the Nazi "Heil Hitler" salute with a very loud heel-click. When he returned to the bunker, he set his escape plan in motion. He wanted out of there in a very live sense of the word. Two days later, that happened.

The pre-glow of sunrise was beginning to lighten the early morning sky. Dieter's thoughts now drifted to the bathroom, getting dressed, and heading for his own room. He was hoping this could be done without waking Reese.

As quietly and softly as he could, Dieter slid from the lofty pencil-post bed and tiptoed out of the boudoir and straight through the living room to the other side of the suite to a hallway adjacent to a small sitting room. In passing, he noticed a piece of Reese's undergarment hanging from the chandelier. He had completely forgotten how that episode happened.

In the bathroom, some memory was returning. He did recall the oversize bathtub where he and Reese enjoyed a hot soapy bath somewhere around midnight. There was an empty bottle of Kubanskaya sitting on a marble table next to the tub along with an ashtray with several half-smoked cigarettes. He wondered where the remaining pack was then noticed them in the trashcan under the sink—wet. Dieter thought as he stood in front of the toilet. *"I think a have a few extra packs in my valise ... might come in handy again."*

After finishing, he searched for his clothes finding some of them in the sitting room along with a crimson outfit with Pommarola sauce stain visibly showing. He put on his undergarments and headed into the living room where he found his pants, shirt, and jacket. He found one shoe under a chair and another under the sofa. *"Now ... where are my socks? I can't remember where my socks are! They have to be around here somewhere ... can't be too far away ... let me think."*

Dieter was now dressed except for his socks. He continued looking. Finally he remembered. *"Shit ... Reese has them on! The damn temperature dropped last night and her feet got cold ... she put them on. Damn ... well ... I really don't want to wake her for a lousy pair of socks. If I do, it might be another hour or so before I get out of here! Well ... fortunately I got a few extra pair. One thing I learned about being in the army was you can never have too many pair of socks. We were always told you'd never know what you might get into ... boy, were those generals right!"*

Dieter quietly slipped from the suite and headed for his room. Maybe he'd see her in the anteroom for a hot roll and some of that awful chestnut and charcoal coffee. But right now he wanted to return to his room and gather his thoughts. It was going to be a long day and he had to figure an angle of attack.

Last night was a ball of fire; today it's going to be the whole ball of wax.

When Dieter opened his door, he noticed someone had previously been in there. He quickly looked around and made sure his Walther PPK was still hidden. It was. Then he noticed a handwritten note on the dresser. *"Sorry für die Unannehmlichkeiten. Ihre Toilette ist jetzt betriebsbereit."*

Dieter laughed aloud, "Well … what do you know … the water's back on!"

Then he pondered, *"I wonder if Reese had anything to do with this. Naw … there wasn't enough time … she couldn't have. When would she have had time to talk to somebody? Maybe it's just one of those quirky coincidences."*

Out of curiosity, Dieter went to the lavatory and turned on the sink faucet. A gush of air was followed by a burst if spitting water, a clanging of the pipes, and then a regular stream of water. The tub faucet did the same. Dieter thought, *"Maybe a fresh bath this morning might sooth my aching head. It's still early … I've got plenty of time before heading to the clock shop. Besides … I've got to figure this scene out. Some things have gone too easy. I've got to figure where the screw-ups are going to occur."*

Around 9 o'clock Dieter left the room carrying his Walter PPK and the clock he was taking to the shop. He stopped by the anteroom for something to eat and try to tolerate that awful coffee. Reese was nowhere to be seen. *"Maybe she's already come and gone. Maybe she's still in her room. She drank a lot of vodka last night … she's got to be tired. She wasn't of this world when I left."*

Dieter walked out the hotel and it was cold and gray. It wasn't cold enough to snow; but if it rained it was going to be miserable. He continued walking toward the shop. Viktor was nowhere to be seen. *"Maybe the weather was keeping him from his appointed round with me today."*

Around the corner was the clock shop and the moment of reckoning. Dieter's heart began pounding and his stomach was churning. He had to quickly regroup if he was going to handle this situation with authority.

He walked into the shop hearing the familiar sound of the small brass bell hanging on the doorframe. The shop owner was behind the counter rearranging a few of the used watches he had for sale. He immediately recognized Dieter and in his fashioned English accent welcomed him good morning with which Dieter returned the salutation.

"Ah … I see that you have brought the mantle clock. Good, I will take a look at it."

Dieter took the clock out of its wooden case and set it on the counter. The clock-master turned it around, opened the rear cover, and looked inside. After a brief moment, he excused himself returning with a lightly crumpled piece of folded paper. Dieter seemed slightly befuddled taking on a blank look.

The shopkeeper looked at Dieter, "My memory is not so good these days … I have to write things down." He then unfolded the note and softly read aloud, "The water in Munich makes better beer … don't you think?"

The look on Dieter's face turned to incredulousness and then to surprise. "My god man, where did you get that," to which the old man replied, "That is not the answer."

Dieter said, "I know what the answer is … it's 'not as good in Düsseldorf!' Who gave you that message?"

The clock-master told Dieter that when he looked inside the clock, he noticed a unique symbol he had secretly etched when he handed the clock over to a secret operative many months ago. The old man was told that whoever returned this clock was to be trusted and to follow his instructions. He has not seen or heard from that operative since. As a matter of fact, he hadn't heard from anybody until this very moment.

The clock was original to the shop and the clock-maker was directed to mark a symbol to verify its originality. This was unquestionably that clock. The so-called question and answer ploy was to further verify its receiver. Had someone stolen the clock, it's doubtful they would have known the secret answer to the question.

Dieter now fully realized he was playing a powerful game with powerful people and that absolutely nothing from here on out can be taken lightly. So far, he's been lucky and he knew it. The knot in his stomach tightened.

The old man introduced himself as Fritz Stocker. Dieter, not expecting this change of events, continued his ruse by introducing himself as Dean Zimmerman. Everything he had earlier predicted as to what could go wrong was beginning to unravel; but the best course of action was continuing with the plan—get Bormann out of the shop.

Fritz offered they should continue their conversation in the backroom behind the thick green velvet curtain. Prying eyes might be lurking through the only window in the shop.

"Would you like a cup of fresh coffee, Dean?"

"Well … to be honest, the coffee I've had so far hasn't suited my taste, but given the circumstances I've just encountered … I'd really like to have a snifter of the Doornkaat I saw in the hutch!"

Fritz replied that maybe that was a good idea and went to the front counter area and retrieved the bottle and two glasses. He poured each of them a drink when he returned.

Without provocation, Fritz inquired to Dean. "I suppose you are here to relieve me of my responsibility of Herr Bormann?"

By now Dieter's character turned serious. "Yes … I am. Hopefully this will happen by tomorrow morning and you will be rid of him for good. But may I ask how it came to be that he ended up here in your shop. My informer directed me here but was not told of your involvement. That is why I looked so surprised."

"I can understand that but cannot answer your question as to why you weren't told. I suppose in these trying times it is best to just pass the basic information. Too many people with too much information have been known to disappear.

"Many months ago I was approached by a secret German operative working for the allies. I was to be given a large sum of money if I would hide a former high-ranking German official. I was simply told that sometime in the future, someone would take him away. I was told that it was of the utmost importance that this be kept secret. But because of the money they offered, I felt I had no choice. And if I turned them down, I would be afraid for my life … and I agreed."

Dieter inquired further. "When did you know it was Bormann?"

"At first, I did not recognize him because of his beard and he had lost some weight. After a few days, he began to act belligerent toward his secret confinement and started talking in such a manner I felt he had come from wealth and comfort. It really wasn't until after the war criminal trials in Nuremberg started that I read where Martin Bormann was to be tried in absentia because he had disappeared and nobody knew where he was. It was believed he was still alive.

"They had a picture of him in the paper and it didn't take much to make the connection. I can assure you that when I realized who I had living in my basement, I became quite nervous. I can now see why they gave me so much money."

Dieter could only surmise that General Reinhard Gehlen had his hand in this. He knew that Gehlen's "Odessa File" had established "rat-lines" to South America for many of the former high-ranking Third Reich officials. Because of Bormann's dislike within those ranks, it was a wonder how he rated any seniority to get in that line. But Dieter knew he wasn't ever going to make that rat-line and thought it was best not to mention this to Fritz. The less information he knew, the better.

"Do you think Bormann knows that you know who he is?" Dieter asked.

"I really don't think so. He has portrayed himself as Günter Keppler, an official from the former Krupp Manufacturing Works and says he needs the time for things to simmer down before he returns home.

"He claims he worked at the plant making household items before the war. When the war started and the firm retooled to make war parts, he left in anger. He was afraid his name was on a list as a criminal who was building these war parts. That is why he needs to bide his time to later give him an opportunity to prove his innocence. I accepted that as his answer … but of course I know different.

To pass his time, I have also tried to teach him how to repair clocks. He shows very little interest but pacifies me with an effort. We have had some moments of laughter, but I am still cautious."

"Where is he now," Dieter asked inquisitively.

"He has run an errand for the shop and should return shortly. It is good that you came by when you did so we could have this talk. Would you like another shot of schnapps?"

For some reason, Dieter was beginning to feel more relaxed, and it wasn't because of the schnapps. He was getting a better handle on the situation thanks to Fritz. After lighter conversation and another schnapps, Dieter excused himself to the lavatory. Fritz went to the front counter.

As Dieter was prepared to walk from the lavatory, he heard the brass bell on the front door. He was able to peek out and observe that Bormann had just returned. Dieter's heart took an extra beat. Now was the moment.

Bormann briefly spoke in German with Fritz and went behind the curtain. Dieter quietly walked out and around some clock displays and back to the counter where he met Fritz. They both nodded at each other. Fritz intuitively walked to the curtain and speaking German told Günter that someone was there to see him. Fritz motioned for Dieter to go behind the curtain.

While Günter was busy storing the items he had picked up from his errand, Dieter walked into the room. Günter turned around to greet his visitor. Fritz had returned to the far end of the counter.

Dieter, in German, spoke firmly and directly. "Herr Bormann, I am here on a mission from General Gehlen to remove you and position you so that you can make your trip to South America. These orders come directly from him."

Bormann did not appear stunned but stood there with blankness on his face. He curtly asked. "And who might you be?"

"That is none of your concern. If you do not comply, I will leave and you will no longer have the necessary help in getting to South America. If you agree, I will make the proper arrangements and you will be on your way. But there is one item of interest you will have to attend before this happens. We require that you return to me the Joseph Goebbels's briefcase containing the map to the Amber Chamber. This is a prerequisite for your safe trip."

Bormann acted stupid and replied with disdain, "But I do not have such an item. You must be mistaken."

Dieter was not swayed by his blatant lie. "In that case, we have nothing else to discuss. If you will excuse me, I will go now."

Bormann immediately began backtracking. "No … wait! I do have it. I have it hidden in a safe place."

"Yes then … you must put this map in my hands before we go further," Dieter deadpanned with absolutely no emotion.

"But … it is in East Berlin. It will be hard to get now that the Russians have taken over that sector."

"*Where* in East Berlin," Dieter abruptly asked.

"It is near the Führer bunker … it should still be there. I hid it well."

"Then you will have to take me there and retrieve it. Once it is in my hands, we will get you to safety so that you can be on your way. It is a *must* that it be there. If it is not, we cannot help you," Dieter said firmly with an authoritative voice.

"Yes … yes … it will be there," Bormann said weakly with sweat dripping from his forehead. He knew it should be in the same place where he stashed it but much time has passed. He had no idea what has happened in that sector since the end of the war and the Russians moved in. He knew at this point his life was under threat. He silently prayed for the first time in his life.

Dieter believed his story. He saw the sweat emanating from his forehead. "Tomorrow morning … I will pick you up in front of the shop and we will go to Berlin by train. I expect you to be ready by 8:30 and we will make the 9:05 train. Bring what you will … but I suggest you travel light. No matter what … you will not be coming back to Dresden. Your own fate is in your hands. Do you have the proper travel papers?"

"Yes … I do."

"Then I suggest you be on time. Tardiness in my business is not tolerated!" And with that Dieter turned, pushed the green velvet curtain aside, and entered the shop. As he walked by the counter, he shook Fritz's hand, blinked with a smile, and said, "Danke."

When Dieter walked out of the shop, it was drizzling. He donned his fedora and started walking back to the hotel feeling good. He had handled the day of reckoning with much ease and authority. He had a feeling of confidence. He also looked around seeing if Viktor was lurking in the rubble. No, there was nothing. Dieter thought, *"Maybe he was at home with his wife taking the day off. Yes, that's probably what he's doing."*

Dieter felt his best course of action was to return to the hotel and stay out of sight. A good part of the day was still left and maybe he thought he'd get some sleep. He figured in the last couple of days he hadn't had much more than a few hours. But the one thing that still puzzled him while walking through the rubble: *"How in the hell did Raisa's undergarments get in that chandelier?"*

Chapter
27

The following morning, Dieter awoke to another gloomy day of clouds and light rain. The temperature was in the mid-thirties and it was doubtful it would go any higher. For Dresden, this was a typical day for the middle of October. For what the day was to bring, it was probably fitting.

The thought of his deadly mission weighed heavily on his mind; today was the day he was going to kill Martin Bormann—a fugitive from justice. But whose justice? His stomach began churning as he replayed in his mind how it was going to happen—up close and he hoped impersonal.

The last time Dieter killed it was up close; but he thought too personal. Fellow German soldiers in the wrong place at the wrong time. Two SS officers pleading for their lives. One bullet each to the back of their heads. Their slumped bodies and cold gray eyes. It was the cold gray eyes that Dieter remembered—not pulling the trigger. Dieter justified the killings as mercy. His mission for Heer Rommel was paramount and nothing was to stand in its way—nothing.

By eight o'clock, Dieter had made his way to the front desk. He requested to the clerk he needed a cab in twenty minutes. After paying his bill, he went to the anteroom for something to eat. He had slept all afternoon yesterday and all through the night. He was well rested finally catching up on his hours; but now he was quite famished. He needed something to stop the churning in his stomach. The bread and jam were good. He stayed away from the coffee.

"I wonder where Reese is this morning," Dieter pondered to himself. *"Surely by now she would be up and about. For the most part, she was fun to be around and the sex was anything but lifeless! But she kept prying into my affairs asking all sorts of subtle questions. Maybe she picked up on something I was doing that gave her the impression I was someone other than who I said I was. Of course, that is true, but I was being careful in what I said ... and I remember everything ... except those damn undergarments! Then again, maybe I did indeed say something to spark her curiosity. On the other hand, she is a spy and that's what spy's do ... keep a sharp eye and ask question. Perhaps it's best she's not around ... yes I think that's best. It's time for me to move on. I don't have the need to see her anymore."*

The cab arrived on time. Dieter entered the black sedan halfway expecting to see Viktor. No such luck. Somehow he missed his little buddy hoping to chat with him about his role in Dresden. He had imparted just enough information to keep Dieter's mind cluttered. But Viktor was nowhere to be seen and it's doubtful he'd ever see him again. For in less than 40 minutes, he and Bormann would be on a train to Berlin.

At exactly 8:30, the cab pulled in front of the clock shop. Dieter could see through the lone window Bormann standing by the old wooden and glass counter shaking hands with Fritz. Within seconds, Bormann was in the cab.

"Guten Morgen," greeted Bormann. Dieter made no response.

The cab pulled away and headed toward the train station as Dieter had previously directed the driver to do when heading toward the shop.

"Do you have your travel papers?" Dieter deadpanned.

"Yes ... I do."

"May I see them?"

Bormann reached inside his inner coat pocket and handed over the papers. It was hard to tell just how old they were. From what Dieter could tell, everything looked in order, but he did notice the papers allowed him to travel to West Berlin. *"That's a bit odd,"* Dieter wondered. Nonetheless, an added bonus if they had to travel there; although, he saw no reason for that to happen. He then handed the papers back to Bormann saying nothing.

Bormann quickly picked up that Dieter wasn't interested in conversation. The ride to the station was quiet and uneventful.

As both exited the cab, Dieter, in German, firmly told Bormann, "Don't do anything stupid to bring attention to us. The Russian guards this morning seem nervous like they are looking for someone. That someone may just be you!" If there was anybody in Dresden at that moment who didn't want to attract attention, it was Martin Bormann. He wanted his life and South America. He wasn't stupid.

After Dieter purchased two one-way second-class tickets to Berlin, they strode to the loading platform where several morose looking characters wearing black fedoras quietly walked about staring dourly in their direction. Dieter whispered to Bormann not to look in their direction but to stand still and stare at the tracks. Within five minutes, the Berlin train slowly pulled into the station.

Both were directed to the fifth car where a dozen other second-class passengers boarded. This car was arranged so that passengers could sit facing the other. Dieter directed Bormann to the middle of the car where the majority of the passengers gathered. *"Safety in numbers,"* Dieter thought.

Dieter sat forward facing the front-end door hoping at a first glance of the guards and ticket handler heading into the compartment. At exactly 9:05 the train slowly pulled from the station. Within minutes, the train speeded forward at 50 miles an hour smoothly pitching side to side making the familiar click-clack sound with metal against metal. Bormann remained quiet. Dieter kept a close eye on the entrance door.

Sitting face to face, Dieter studied Bormann's visage finally noticing the life-long mole protruding from his left temple assuring himself that this was in fact his target. He also noticed

Bormann's gaunt appearance comparative to the photos he had seen of him during the war. Then again, the two and a half years on the run and hiding from the hangman's noose could cause this veneer. For a man of 47, he looked much older. Then again, war had a tendency to pounce on a person—regardless of his position within the German ranks.

With a hint of a smile, Bormann subtly glanced Dieter's way suggesting the opportunity to question his arrangements about South America; Dieter continued his silence with coldness. Bormann perceptively returned his eyes to the barren countryside quickly passing before him.

After 30 minutes, the train conductor and an armed Russian guard slowly accessed the forward door checking passenger tickets. After a few minutes, they stood in front of Dieter. Bormann, without hesitation, handed his ticket for stamping when suddenly the guard requested his traveling papers. Bormann nervously passed them over where the guard examined the information. After a seemingly long time, he handed them back then motioning for Dieter's papers. After looking them over, he further requested to see his American passport. Dieter confidently complied.

After several anxious moments, he returned them asking in Russian if he knew the gentleman sitting across from him. Dieter acted dumb to the Russian language by shrugging his shoulders, slightly cocking his head, and turning his palms skyward insinuating he didn't understand. He then played coy shaking Bormann's hand in a greeting sort of way as though he was introducing himself for the first time. Bormann perceived the act and introduced himself to Dieter followed by a hearty laugh. This seemingly simple act pleased the guard where he and the conductor casually moved forward to the next set of passengers.

Dieter realized Bormann's act was the coup de grâce keeping the guard from further supposition in their flight to Berlin. His dumb American act could only go so far. But Bormann's ploy was the kicker. Maybe it was time to cut the old man some slack. No matter what questions he asks, the answers would be bold face lies.

When the guard passed to the other car, Dieter, in German, asked Bormann how long he had hidden in the Berlin tunnel system before escaping to Dresden.

"How do you know such facts? Only the cellar urchins [Kellerkinder] and an operative working for Gehlen know specifics! Who are you?"

"My identity is not relevant ... but suffice it to say the Gehlen Org is one big family and I am part of that family. Let's just say I was aware of your disappearance inside the tunnels ... beyond that, I wasn't privy for how long. But it makes no difference as to how long you were in the tunnels. I was simply curious. Though, I've known of your 'clock shop' disguise for sometime."

Bormann was miffed. Not because he had no control, but his life was on the line and, to him, too many people knew too much about his doings. He was being forced to trust people he didn't know. This is what made him edgy; but, he finally got Dieter's attention, and he saw no harm in passing on worthless old information.

"I was in and out of the tunnels for seven months. The urchins treated me well ... and they gave me food and kept my spirits alive. One of them had a relative who was with the 'Werwolf' organization in the closing days of the war. Even though they theoretically were disbanded right after the war, there were still secretive bands spread throughout the city. To keep their actions alive, they changed tactics from resistance fighting to removing high-ranking officials to safe-houses for later transfer out of Germany. Because of my position with the Führer and the Third Reich, I was able to filter inside their organization. Through various connections, I was able to transfer to the Gehlen Org who had me transferred to Dresden. I was told that one day I would be removed when the timing was right. So ... I suppose now the timing is right?"

"Yes ... yes it is. As soon as you place the map into my hands, you will be transferred to another agent where you will be processed to South America. To what part … I have no such clue. Perhaps they will give you options."

"If I may ask, how did you know of the map?"

"Yes … you may ask but that information is secretive. It is not necessary for you to know how I know. It is only necessary that you turn it over to me. That is all you need to know. It is that simple."

"What happens if, by happenstance, I cannot produce the Amber map? Will I still be able to escape?"

"No … you will not. You will no longer see the light of day. You will immediately be shot. Though, for your sake, I hope it is still resting where you placed it," Dieter said emphatically with cold emotion. It was as serious as he had ever been.

Bormann's expression instantly blanked with a bead of sweat forming on a snow-white forehead and red-flushed cheeks. His eyes widely opened fearing the spirit of Mephistopheles. Dieter thought he'd seen a ghost. But that was his problem.

Sooner or later, Dieter would know the location of the map. But in the interim, after Bormann had uncontrollably swallowed several gulps of air, he asked him for a general location of the map. Dieter was emotionless.

"As I recall, it is approximately one mile from the Führer bunker on the other side of the Spree River. On the night of the escape, I entered a service tunnel with my group from the bunker. From there we took a subway tunnel running north under the Friedrichstrasse to the Friedrichstrasse Intra-Urban Train Station … a few hundred yards south of the Weidendamm Bridge over the river Spree. From there we followed a set of local rail tracks over the river to the Lehrter Train Station on Invalidenstrasse. It was here I met up with my cellar urchin contact where we found another tunnel leading to a large underground area underneath the main floor of the station. It is in that space I hid the briefcase. We must get to the Lehrter Train Station."

To Dieter, this was good news. The Lehrter Station was in West Berlin and had been severely damaged by allied bombings. The building had been cordoned off and no trains were using the station because of the low volume of traffic that was created when Berlin was subdivided into sections as set forth by the Potsdam accord. It was the last station in West Berlin before entering East Berlin.

Throughout the 120-mile trip, the train on several occasions slowed to a sluggish crawl as constant work was being performed on the tracks. When slowing, workers were seen standing along the track's embankment holding various kinds of railroad hand tools. What else could be seen were Russian soldiers kibitzing about in the nearby distance with automatic machine weapons strapped to their shoulders. Dieter believed the workers were former German soldiers captured before they could escape to the west. It was doubtful any of them would ever be absolved to freely return to their homes and family. So far as the Russians were concerned, their lives were doomed to hopelessness and misery.

With information Bormann had imparted, Dieter plotted his next moves. The train would arrive at the Lichtenberg Station. From there, it was to Check Point Charley at the junction of Friedrichstrasse with Zimmerstrasse and Mauerstrasse—a five-minute walk. Assuming Bormann's travel papers were in order, they should whizz through to the west side.

But from there across the Spree River to Invalidenstrasse and then to the Lehrter Station was entirely another matter. It was too far to walk in broad daylight without arousing suspicion; they would have to hire a cab. Dieter couldn't plan beyond that. When he got there, he would visually reconnoiter the area and make his plans. There was no other choice.

Around the hour of noon, the train began slowing with each car lightly pitching forward every time the engineer applied the brakes. From Dieter's point of view, he could see the outline of the once great German city. From this distance, it looked far more impressive than it did up close. But in the next ten minutes, the reality of rubble in a burned out city would clearly come into focus.

Dieter didn't talk much further over the previous hour. Any conversation was kept as light as possible. He had finally gained the necessary information he needed, and he saw no reason for further chatter. He now had a good idea where the map was stashed; Bormann's part was providing the final details. That's all he wanted to hear. While contemplating Bormann's fate, Dieter finally decided how he was going to kill Bormann.

The train finally halted with one last jerk. Each man stood and reached for their satchels in the overhead open compartment. Bormann's satchel inadvertently got stuck on a protruding rod, and he was struggling to break it loose. Dieter had to help.

Once leaving the train, they walked through the station and out the large front door. The numerous Russian guards standing about paid no attention. From there they turned north strolling the short distance to Check Point Charley. There was a crowd of people milling about moving in and around the buildings. It was the lunch hour and people were entering the several local restaurants. Dieter was beginning to hunger himself but decided it was time to keep moving. Besides, he really wasn't in the mood to sit with Bormann even over a sandwich and a drink. He was soon to be dead. It was not necessary for him to eat.

Getting through Check Point Charley was about as easy as it was several days before when he entered from the American side. Bormann's papers gathered no ones attention, and he was able to breeze right through. But timing was everything. Several months after this departure, the East German government ordered the Commandant of East Berlin, Aleksandr Kotikov, to make it very difficult for its citizens to pass through the gates. They apparently discovered over three million of its population had simply abandoned their homes and families for a free world in the west. It was their intent for that not to happen again and closed the entire border.

Once through Check Point Charley, Dieter hailed a cab. He told the driver to take them to the corner of Chausseestrasse and Invalidenstrasse, which was two blocks north of the bombed out train station. On their way, Dieter quizzed Bormann if he recognized this location. Bormann lightly nodded waving his hand and forefinger in a forward motion. He could sense his freedom was not far away. He had a smile on his face.

Once out of the cab, Dieter paid the driver in United State's currency. The driver looked at Dieter, thanked him in German and with a slight smile and a wink, he drove off. No sooner had the driver pulled away, Dieter's mind clicked realizing he was the same driver who had originally taken him to Check Point Charley the night he and Hildabrand had sipped Jim Beam. At least he thought it was. It was dark and he really didn't pay much attention to his face; but the voice sounded familiar—he thought. Dieter began nervously wondering if his own life was at stake. Too much was going on beyond his control. And if that was him, how did he know he was back in Berlin?

Bormann was totally oblivious to what was going on. He gazed about the district and, for the most part, recognized the area. He was beginning to feel his own ordeal was over. Now all that was left was finding the tunnel entrance leading to the basement of the station. He was confident the map was there.

When Dieter turned around, he saw a glow on Bormann's face. He knew he was in the right place. But Dieter himself surveyed the area with glances. There were more people in the area than he expected. Across the street was a good deal of activity clearing a bombed out structure; and across the other side of the street was similar activity. Looking south down the Invalidenstrasse, there was less activity. He motioned to Bormann they walk in that direction. They headed south. Dieter pondered. Bormann smiled.

Upon reaching the Lehrter Station, there was no activity. The structure itself was in total disarray with a barbwire fence surrounding the building. Bormann said there was no entry into the basement from that direction; they would have to venture one hundred yards behind the structure and find the entrance from there. At the time he escaped, the tunnel was vastly overgrown, and it was dark with exploding tanks all around. But he thought he could find it. He knew he could find it.

After walking an acre of rubble, Bormann stopped to gain his bearings. His head weaved and bobbed in the general direction he thought the entrance to be. He continued stomping over chunks of concrete working himself into a high-pitched frenzy reminiscent of a panic-stricken state. He stopped and cursed yelling, "Where are you … where are you?"

Dieter was patient giving the old man time to gather his emotions. Within Bormann's mind, he knew freedom was close, and the anxiety of not finding the entrance was praying on his mind. He was frustrated. Without compassion, Dieter said, "Calm down … calm down … give yourself a second. You will see it in a moment."

After several minutes, Bormann stood walking left behind a mound of dirt. There was that empty musty smell he could detect. He looked right following the scent and peering before his eyes was a hole no bigger than a common automobile tire. That old damp smell was emanating from the hole. He dropped his satchel and fell to his knees frantically digging with his tender bare palms. Within seconds, blood oozed from his hands; but tenaciously continued like a dog for a bone. He found it!

Over the last several years, weather had caused the surrounding dirt to fall around the entrance almost to the point of enclosure. With a little more digging, they were able to enlarge the hole enough for them to scuttle through. It was predictably dark, but Dieter had the presence of mind to carry a flashlight in his valise. He pulled it out and handed it to Bormann telling him to lead the way.

Once fully inside the tunnel, it enlarged to a height of six feet making walking much easier. Dieter had to slightly bend, but Bormann was short enough he could stand tall and not rub his head. They continued forward stepping over small objects left by the cellar urchins. About halfway through, a glimmer of light was visible at the other end. It was probably the basement of the station. But how could there be light there?

When they reached the end, a large basement opened before them. The light illuminating the room was dim and was coming from large cracks in the station floor that occurred during the bombings. The entire room had solid concrete walls with numerous pillars holding up the ceiling. There was much debris strewn about.

Bormann had spent much time in this room and seemingly knew every nook and cranny within its walls. But it had been two years since he was there, and he had to readjust his bearings and remember just exactly where he had hidden the briefcase. Time had a way of distorting the memory.

After a brief moment of standing by the entrance, he slowly walked about the room flashing the walls from ceiling to floor looking for a clue to refresh his memory. When he worked his way to the far side of the room, he noticed a large chunk of concrete forcibly stuffed into a fairly large hole. It was as though that exact piece had originally come from that hole; some large force, such as an exploding bomb, had broken it loose from the wall. Bormann knew this was it. He asked Dieter for help in dislodging it from the wall.

Each of them was able to wrestle their fingertips to the topside of the chunk and pull it from the wall. It quickly fell to the ground with both men jostling to the side keeping their toes from being crushed. Bormann grabbed the flashlight and peered inside. For his sake, it was there!

Bormann handed the flashlight to Dieter. His eyes glistened with hope as he removed the briefcase. Not far from the hole was an old wooden table. He took the briefcase and laid it there fumbling to open the latches. Within seconds he had it unlocked displaying numerous papers, a large envelope containing the map, and also the currency he had pilfered from Fegelein's valise when he tried to escape with Mata. Dieter reached for the envelope and opened it. It did indeed contain the Amber Chamber map. The second part of his mission had been accomplished.

Dieter returned the envelope to the briefcase, closed it, and picked it up. He handed the flashlight to Bormann and directed him to the tunnel entrance. Bormann quizzed Dieter in a demanding tone. "I have lived up to my part of the bargain. You will now take me to the authorities for my transfer … yes?"

"Yes … that is correct. We will now go in that direction. You lead us back through the tunnel."

Dieter knew this was the moment. As Bormann ambled across the room, he reached for his weapon intending to plant one shot to the back of his head. The spacing was good. The timing was good. But just as Dieter removed his gun from his inner coat pocket, a muffled thump caused Bormann to drop the flashlight and grab his bloody throat. There was gurgling and a gasping for air. Bormann's face went skyward. His mouth and eyes vividly open.

Within milliseconds Dieter fell to the floor right behind a concrete pillar. Inside that time, another muffled thump sent Bormann crumpling to the floor with a bullet to his forehead; his body violently shaking and twitching. It quickly stopped. He was dead.

Dieter was stunned. *"Ah shit … I'm in deep trouble now. Just who in the hell fired those shots … or does it even matter. I'll probably be dead in a second anyway. Somehow I've got the keep my wits … yes my wits!"*

After a few seconds, he could hear movement. Then, "Zeis … Zeis! Do not fire! You are safe. It is I, your friend!"

"Well … just who in the hell are you, my friend? You scared the shit out of me!"

"Step from behind the pillar and you will see me. My gun is lowered. You have no fear."

Dieter was cautious. He got to his feet clinging to the pillar. He peeked around its edge. He saw a black fedora. It was Viktor!

"Goddamnit Viktor … where the hell did you come from. I thought you worked for the Russian Secret Service? You know … you scared me to death!"

"That certainly was not my intentions … but I had to stay close. Your life was in danger. At some point, you were to be killed"

"My life! How was that? Who was going to kill me?"

"I was hired by Hildabrand to keep close eye on you. I was told to let you recognize me so you would think I was Russian agent. In truth, I am … but also CIA agent. You did terrible job in shaking me. You need to work on that job aspect!"

"But there were many times you weren't around," Dieter said in confusedness.

"Yes … that was by design. I wanted you to get just so comfortable. Actually, I was always near you. You never left my sight. I too had to be careful. Other Russian agents were tailing me, but I did good job in shaking them.

"The Russian MVD was aware Bormann was in Dresden but confounded as to his whereabouts. They got wind from a secret source you were coming to town with mission of removing him. Once they identified you, I was sent to protect you. They suspected at last moment that Bormann had knowledge of the Amber map. Had they not had that information, you and Bormann would have already been killed. But they got greedy and wanted map. After they got map, they were to kill him and you."

"Well then … who was going to kill me?"

"Come here … I will show you." Viktor walked Dieter over to a small anteroom in the darkened corner where there was a hidden staircase to the main floor of the station.

On the stairs about halfway up was a body. With their flashlight in hand, they went to it. Viktor shinned a light on the face.

"My god … it's Reese!" Her throat had been slashed.

"Yes, she was assigned to kill you. She was one who was given orders to retrieve map and assassinate you and Bormann. I received information last night. I pulled off you and started tailing her … it was a safe move because we all were going in same direction. She saw you and Bormann head into tunnel. I think by accident she found this staircase. She was just heading to basement when I caught her. She rolled down rest of way. Why don't you look in coat pocket? You will find weapon she going to kill you with."

Dieter reached down and pulled out a Russian manufactured Tokarev TT-33 semiautomatic pistol; standard issue for Russian officers. He looked it over and decidedly put it into his own coat pocket.

"Well … all's fair in love and war! I think I'll keep it specifically for her remembrance. Though, I would liked to have remembered her in a more lovingly way. But I don't think that'll happen. She'll play hell recovering from this condition," Dieter said with a slight chuckle remembering how quickly she could transform herself.

Both walked back down the stairs to retrieve the briefcase and also Bormann's satchel. Viktor and Dieter continued to talk.

"Why did you shoot Bormann? I had my gun ready to go. I was just about to put it to the back of his skull and pull the trigger when you fired."

"Yes … but from my angle, I could not see that. Hildabrand had always feared you'd never pull trigger. It looks like he was wrong … nevertheless; I was instructed to make sure he was killed. But it makes no difference … he is now dead and blood from this murder is on me … not you. If that eases your conscious, so be it. But remember … Bormann was nasty person and he was convicted in Nuremburg of terrible war crimes. Whether he died swinging from his neck or gunned down in old smelly cellar, it makes no difference. One way or another, he was going to pay for his crimes … and he has."

"What now?" Dieter simply asked.

"When Russian MVD discovers this, you will be a marked man. They will know what happened and you will always be wanted … make no mistake, one day they will find you and kill you.

"They suspect you will turn map over to your superiors and they know it will be almost impossible to retrieve. Because of its value, individuals will no longer be involved … it will now be nation against nation … and as you know all too well, wars have started on subjects of less concern. Once that map is turned over to your government, it will cause nothing but pain and misery for generations to come. I think you know what to do, and as your friend in the shadows, I can cover for you as best I can. But the decision is entirely up to you. From this point on, no matter *what* your decision will be, your life has changed. Here, have American Pall Mall cigarette … you look like you could use a drag!"

By no means was Dieter a smoking man, but what information Viktor just passed on caused him to light up. Viktor lit one up too. They picked up the briefcase and satchel and walked over to observe Bormann's body. Viktor calmly reiterated to Dieter, "Remember my friend ... even though this man worked behind the scenes of the German Third Reich, he was one of Germany's most despised humans ever. Even Gehlen wanted nothing to do with him. That is why he turned him over to us."

"And what of you ... where will you be going?"

"Fortunately Russian MVD does not know of my role in this plot ... for time being I am ok. But I am thinking of working full time for CIA ... they pay better! Now, let's stop chit-chat and go."

As they walked to the top of the stairs and into the main rubble filled foyer of the rat infested station, Dieter saw another body. He was a bit startled. Viktor said, "Good ... I see that Raisa's tail met same fate. Would you like his weapon?"

"Who is this guy? You said Raisa's tail?"

"Yes ... Russian agents always work in pairs, as do most CIA agents. We were expecting him and planted an agent nearby to kill him. I am good to see my better half wasn't asleep or we might have been in jam ... as the American's would say."

"And who was following you?"

"The cab driver who took you and Bormann to intersection two blocks up a while ago. He thinks you recognized him. He parked cab and kept eye open for second agent. Like I say ... good he not asleep! He good with gun though. Two bullets into back. Just as ordered!"

Dieter continued to be astonished as to what he was seeing. He declined the offer of the dead agent's gun. Victor on the other hand obliged himself to it.

"Ok ... let us go. Car waiting out front."

As each of them worked their way to the front of the station, Dieter noticed a black sedan parked near the curb. Again he was totally amazed realizing he was playing with super heavyweight spymasters. This *was* serious business.

As they walked over to the car, Viktor said to Dieter, "Hildabrand good man ... he think of everything. Let us go grab beer. I am thirsty!"

Chapter
28

The drive with Viktor back across the Spree River caused Dieter to ponder what had just occurred. The anguish of it all churned in his stomach almost to the point of being sick. It was a feeling he hadn't felt since the day on the battlefield where he killed his fellow countrymen.

Even though he didn't pull the trigger on Bormann, somehow he felt responsible for the other two deaths. But in reality, Viktor saved his life. Had he not been there, he would be lying next to Bormann ready to rot away. But Viktor was there because leading spymasters told him to be there; and that was the part that scared him the most. Secretive eyes in the shadows of gloom.

"You will be all right my friend. You were never in danger. There were too many factors keeping you alive. You accomplished a great feat today that very few agents could perform. Even though Hildebrand was afraid you'd never pull trigger, he knew you were only one who could fully accomplish this mission. He had tremendous faith in you because of your character. He told me this and I believed him when you confronted me that second day. You are a man of means who will accomplish a mission regardless of cause. I also know you are a man of compassion with a heart of gold who is struggling internally. As you probably know, that is not a good trait for this line of work. I know this bothers you."

"I had no idea I would end up in this particular field of spying. While training in England, we took many psychological tests to detect our field of duty. One day I was positioned into a new field of training. After a few days, I knew it was that of a hit man and not one of hiding in the shadows. But I had no idea my test would steer me into this direction. Perhaps my inner reactions were beyond my conscious ability. There is no doubt I am torn with this profession."

"Let us go have a beer and rest aside these actions. I have discovered this lessens the anxiety of trauma. It never fully goes away but drinking seems to help."

With that Dieter and Viktor found a beer garden near Check Point Charley bustling with business. It was mid-afternoon and many people were taking an early Friday to start their weekend. The weather was still cold and the rain began pelting. To Dieter, it seemed a cleansing of the soul. To Viktor, it washed the blood from his hands.

Sitting down with a Russian spy was an interesting experience. But sitting down with a Russian spy who also worked for the CIA was a true experience. Depending on who hired him for what job determined whether you lived or died. And to Viktor, it made no difference. Today Dieter lived. Next week he may die. Same gun—same finger.

After their beers had been served and several good slugs had been taken, Dieter asked Viktor a pressing question. "You knew the value of your target today, why didn't you just shoot me also and take the map for yourself. It would have made Mother Russia very happy!"

"Yes … that may seem so … but that not how it works. For this job I work for CIA and I do what they ask. It is that simple. I was to protect you … not shoot you. If I work for MVD and given this mission … I shoot you. But this week … you lucky," Viktor said with a laugh.

Dieter wasn't laughing. He had a deep concern knowing he was lucky this day. But Viktor followed up.

"Don't worry my friend. Even if I was working for MVD at time, I still not shoot you. You have too big a heart and I notice. I would still shoot Bormann, take map, your gun, and let you go. You probably would have lot of explaining to do without map … but you would be alive and map would be back with Russia.

"But that not case. You have map and you must decide what to do. That map will cause many problems in years to come. My country … your country … it could cause war. Russia beat Germany with American support and Russia does not reciprocate with agreement. I can understand America predicament. America can use map against Russia for repayment. America proud … Russia proud … but stupid. It is best that map not be in either hand. It is best map go away. Neither country should have it … then … only fistfight can occur."

Dieter couldn't say much because he knew what Viktor was saying was true. What he has learned and what he knows, he knew Viktor was right. But how was he going to cause the map to disappear and also protect himself? This was a concern. Too many people knew too many things about his mission.

He knew if he returned without the map, he'd be locked away in the basement of some castle with the keys thrown away. It wouldn't be like it was during the war where he was given the comforts of an English mansion. And there'd never be a trial— too much publicity and that's the last thing the CIA wants.

Then again, *"Maybe I can get the comforts of an English mansion."*

"What would you do if you were in my position?" Dieter asked.

"My position probably no better than your position except I die a lot quicker. The best thing for you to do is disappear along with map … and disappear for good! That is your only option if you decide not to turn it over. Do you have a good friend you can trust?"

"Yes … I have two very good friends I can trust. One is here somewhere in Germany and the other … well, let's just say that person also has a heart of gold. Perhaps I should see my friend here in Germany first. He has become a solid rock … someone I can trust with my life … someone who has a good head on his shoulders. That's the person I need to see!"

"Then let's order one more beer for road and toast to your friend and to the right decision you must make. I can hold Hildabrand off for a few days, but beyond that … there's not much else I can do. I was to tell him I saw you off on your trip back to England. I can give you a few days head start before they start looking for you. Make your decision fast … or you'll have a lot of explaining to do."

The beers came and they toasted. Each shared a laugh as to how they were treating a delicate topic with such mundane air. After a few more laughs, Dieter asked Viktor what of his plans. "The first thing I do, when it gets dark, I will go with cab driver back to train station and bury Bormann's body. This should also buy you time. When MVD find Raisa and her backup killed and no Bormann, they will speculate he was captured with map … and will begin looking for him … and eventually for you. But this should give you a good head start in any direction you take. Use this time wisely, my friend! Right now, time is on your side. Do not waste it … or it will kill you."

After Dieter and Viktor bid their farewell, Dieter walked to Check Point Charley and asked for directions to the Office of Military Government Detachment A1A1. He was hoping from this office he could locate his friend John Krauss. After leaving Paris, Dieter caught wind John was working for the American Farm Bureau helping the German farmers procure the maximum yield from their fields. Even two years after the war, the German populace has been struggling with food production. John has been helping.

Dieter was told the detachment was eight miles from there to the Zehlendorf section of Berlin just a few miles south of Charlottenburg. It was too far to walk, so he hailed a cab getting there just in time before the office was leaving for the day. By happenstance, he met with an officer willing to help him.

John Krauss was working in the Bavarian small town of Schrobenhausen about 30 miles north of Munich. The office he was dispatched to was the 364th I Detachment, Company F of the 3rd European Civil Affairs Regiment. Captain Beirman was in charge. Dieter then asked where the nearest train station was so he could travel in that direction. It was the Zoologischer

Garten Station about three miles north back toward Berlin. The young officer told Dieter if he could wait about 15 minutes, he would be glad to give him a lift to the station.

When Dieter arrived, he was told the train leaving for Munich departed at 10:05 and had numerous stops along the way. Schrobenhausen was not one of them. He would have to backtrack the 30 miles by car or cab. Dieter purchased a ticket, walked to a nearby restaurant, ate a solid meal, and returned to the station where he grabbed a well-worn wooden bench to wait out the next two hours. It had been a very long day and he was exhausted. The ride to Munich was 308 miles and it would take all night. He was unable to get a sleeper car and was hoping the seats would at least have some comfort.

For the most part, riding a train in West Germany was pleasant. There were no guards with machine pistols and the trainmen were all very pleasant. The general attitude among the populace was friendlier and the air seemed fresher; although, he knew that was just a perceptive sense derived from the stench of communism.

In the trip to Munich, the train would pass into East Germany as defined by the Elbe River. Fortunately, this set of tracks would allow them unobstructed passage into West Germany as defined by the East German Government. But in the months to come in 1948, that practice would cease to exist and there would be no free passage from East to West Germany. It would be a very sad day.

Dieter grabbed a window seat at the back of the car. The cushion was worn but it was comfortable. No one sat beside him. He put his hat and valise there but did put the Goebbels briefcase under his seat for better safekeeping. He knew there were common thieves thriving about and a stolen briefcase— this briefcase—would be hard to explain.

With the train bobbing at a rhythmic beat, Dieter harbored his thoughts and actions and short tenure as CIA assassin. It was all a blur and hard to focus. Bormann gurgling and gasping, collapsing and twitching. *Even though it wasn't my bullet and the blood is off my hands ... do I feel better ... do I feel solace?*

It makes no difference. I was within seconds of pulling the trigger ... within seconds of braining the poor son of a bitch. Even if I didn't kill him ... I was prepared to kill him. Only split second timing out of my control prevented my blood from staining his. No ... I didn't pull the trigger but it was as though I did. Either way ... I am responsible. Do I feel better? No. Do I have solace? No. Just what do you feel? I feel terrible! I want no more ... no more ... no more...."

The following morning at 7:15 the train glided to a stop at the main station in Munich. Dieter had been awake for an hour just staring out the water-streaked window with thoughts of meeting his friend John. Through the years, he and Dieter had become fast friends.

Dieter first met John when he was renting a room from his sister-in-law, Greta von Carlsen, while he was studying medicine at the University of Berlin. Through a quirk in Nazi Law, John, an American of German descent, was drafted into the German Army. Because of Greta, Dieter had him transferred to the Army Medical Depot based on his medical schooling.

In another quirky sort of way, Dieter unintentionally impressed General Erwin Rommel, later known as the Desert Fox, at a high-ranking cocktail social in such a way that Rommel eventually brought him into his staff. To complete the staff, John was chosen as Rommel's personal valet, and Sergeant Werner Schroeder was brought in as his personal chef.

Dieter and John's path separated when Rommel was recalled from Africa to Germany by Hitler. Dieter followed. Shortly thereafter, the German Army surrendered and John was captured. His group of soldiers was shipped to the United States.

In a revelation unknown to John, he was allowed to escape, with the blessing of the OSS, near his home in Broken Bow, Nebraska. John then was conscripted into the US Army. Because of his knowledge of the German language and his position with Herr Rommel, he was handpicked to perform a secretive mission at the end of the war. While in the performance of this mission as a CIA operative, he was betrayed, captured, and severely tortured. Before he could be executed, the American Army overran the German town and John was saved.

It was two years later before they met again. While in the city of Munich, John reunited with Dieter in a rundown bar next to an old hotel where Dieter was staying. John's mission was working in supplying the German people with food; Dieter was observing criminal war trials in war-torn Dachau. The following day they again enjoyed each others company at a family owned beer garden until they each had to split for further duties. That was one year ago.

Dieter exited the train and it was still cold, but the rain had dissipated into a fine mist. It was gloomy. Upon entering the station and walking through to the front entrance, Dieter hailed a cab for the 30-mile ride north to Schrobenhausen. It was a straight shot on a small two-lane highway taking about 45 minutes. It took another 15 minutes once in the town for the cab driver to locate the US Military Government Office. The driver finally found it and apologized for the delay. It was his first time to the small town.

It was Saturday and it was questionable if anybody was on duty. Two years after the war, activity had calmed to normalcy and the two-day weekend was now considered customary. But Dieter didn't have much choice in the matter and decidedly gambled to give it a shot.

Surprisingly the office was open where a dyed-in-the-wool sergeant was sweating over a heating system malfunction. Dieter could smell a fresh pot of coffee emanating from somewhere in the building. And it smelled like real coffee and not burning chestnut shells roasting on an open fire. Dieter yearned for a cup.

Dieter entered a hallway from the foyer. With good American English, he lightly hollered, "Good morning ... good morning! Anybody home?"

"Yeh Mac ... hang on a second. I'm trying to get this damn heat back on. Whoever left last night cut the damn thing off and it takes a modern day miracle from a stubborn mule to turn this sumbitch back on."

265

Dieter walked into the room from whence the voice came. Within seconds Dieter heard a loud poof from a gas-fired furnace. "Gotcha you lousy sumbitch. I weren't gonna let ya *whoop* me this time," the sergeant said standing up brushing his hands on his dark green woolen army slacks then brushing his slacks again to remove the dirt he just put there. They looked as though they hadn't been washed in a while so it really didn't seem to matter. Dieter thought it was humorous.

"What can I do for ya Mac … you look like ya just been put through the tit ringer."

"Well … actually I feel like I have. I just spent nine hours coming in on the Berlin train and another hour in a cab getting here. But a cup of that fresh joe will probably do the trick and fix me right up!"

"Sure thing Mac … let's go grab us a cup. Just made it fresh. First things first ya know … gotta make the coffee and then fix the damn heat. I can live without heat … can't live without a fresh cup a joe! Hell … even on the frontlines we had fresh coffee … probably what won the war for us! I hear tell them Germans drank chestnuts and charcoal … no doubt they spent more time shit'en than fight'en!" Dieter let out a hearty laugh knowing the sergeant was just about right on the money.

After about ten minutes of idle chin waging and warming up, Dieter explained he was a friend of John Krauss and wanted to come by. He kept his ruse very simple as a private American businessman on holiday and had the time for a visit.

"You buddies with ol' Loo'tenat John … boy, now there's a great guy! Hell, he'd do anything for ya … and he sho is smart … knows his farmin' like you ain't never seen! He's been doing a great job with these Krauts helping bring in their crops. I sure as hell hope these ol' boys pay attention to what he's teaching 'em, cause they sho as hell gonna miss his young ass when he's gone! I hear tell he's come up with some new farming technique that's making its rounds all the way to the top brass. He's got their attention pretty good … yea he does … and that ain't no lie I tell ya!

"He got in late last night from a farming trip *way* out in the county. I reckon he's damn near wore out. I'll giv'em a call over to the house … probably wake his ass up … but I'm sure he'll be glad to see ya. Here now … go on and get yourself another refill … we got plenty around here. That's the one thing we got plenty of … no doubt about it. I'll just mosey on over into the office here and buzz 'em over at the house. Now … go on a get'cha another fresh cup now, ya hear."

While the sergeant was on the phone, Dieter grabbed another cup of coffee and pondered his conversation with this humorous person. Of the many Americans he had met, he'd never crossed paths with someone of his nature. He guessed that in America, he'd be known as a "good ol' boy."

The sergeant returned saying he had awoken John but he wasn't mad. As soon as he had gotten dressed, he'd come down in the car and pick him up. John did ask the sergeant if he had made a fresh pot of coffee. Another fresh pot was in the works. It was a cold day and the sergeant didn't want to run out.

The sergeant excused himself to finish up some paperwork for Captain Beirman who would be coming in shortly. Dieter casually walked around the office finally feeling the heat from the radiators. It was now beginning to feel comfortable. He looked out the window thinking he saw snowflakes. It would be the first of the season as far as he knew. While moving to the large front glass door, Dieter saw a black German made Opel Kapatan pull inside the compound and circle to the front steps. It was John.

John was excited to see his friend Dieter but had a gut felling something was wrong. He felt it had something to do with his job. For him to travel all this way to Schrobenhausen was indication enough. He would be careful in what he said when they greeted. He didn't want to alert the sergeant that Dieter was German.

John greeted Dieter warmly shaking his hand and giving him a light friendly hug. There was the usual small chitchat; then the sergeant hollered to John he had a fresh pot brewing.

"Sergeant, just *where* do you get this delicious coffee?"

"Now loo'tenat … I done told ya I can't give away my secrets. I don't ask ya where you get them mighty fine vittles we eat … so let's just leave it at that … ok?"

"Okay sergeant … but before I ever leave … you going to tell me?"

"Maybe!"

"You got that paperwork ready for Captain Beirman?"

"Yes sir loo'tenat … all ready for his signatures."

John looked at Dieter knowing something was bothering him. After a few more minutes in the office and a quick cup of coffee, he suggested they head back to the house. The cook was preparing breakfast and he knew Dieter was hungry.

"Come on … let's get back to the house. The sausage should just about be ready. You look like you hadn't eaten in a while."

"I did have a good meal last night before I boarded the train but haven't had much since your sergeant filled me up on this delicious coffee."

"Yeh … it is good. He won't tell me where he gets it but one day I'll find out! You hear that sergeant?" John said gradually getting louder for the sergeant to hear.

"I hear ya loo'tenat. Now you take your friend on back to the house for some filling vittles. I bet this'll be a breakfast he won't *ever* forget!"

John head motioned Dieter to the front door. Dieter had a slight look of enjoyment on his face. Just being around John had already made him feel better. He was also ready for a plate full of eggs. He was starved.

Dieter put his valise and briefcase into the back seat and hopped into the front. "Looks like you and that sergeant get along quite well. He sounds like a real character."

"Sergeant Wiggins is a good man and don't let that Deep South southern twang fool you. He does a great job in keeping this office shipshape and performs the work around here nobody else wants to do … he always does it willingly with a smile. And … he does a great job keeping all the files organized and in the right place. That in itself is an accomplishment!"

"We know all about good sergeants … don't we John?"

"That's a fact and you absolutely won't believe this German cook we have … looks and acts just like Werner … we call him Cookie. Dieter, I swear to god, you're just not going to

268

believe it. The only difference is he has a wooden right leg. He lost it fighting in the Hürtgen Forest against our US 8th Infantry Division in late November 1944. He ended up in one of our medical facilities until the end of the war. After the surrender, we returned him home … this being his home. Some lieutenant before our group moved to this detachment found him and brought him in. Dieter … he is one helluva a cook!"

"As good as Werner?"

"He hasn't cooked the leg of lamb yet, but he makes the all-time best American meatloaf you ever tasted. Seems this same lieutenant taught him when he brought him in."

"American meatloaf I have never had," Dieter said with his mind clicking.

"Dieter … it's somewhat similar to that Leberkäse we had in Munich last year when we met at that family owned beer garden. Instead of using corned beef, you use ground beef and whatever suits your fancy along with onions. It is some kind of good!"

The trip to the house took only a few minutes. John pulled the car into the driveway that circled in front to a very large two-story six-bedroom stucco house with a large four-column portico attached to the front. By now the snow was falling at a good clip. John pulled under the portico.

"John … it looks like you are living well! How many live here?"

"Myself, the captain, and two other lieutenants. We have a room near the kitchen for Cookie. Sometimes he stays … sometimes he doesn't. Pretty nice … huh?"

"Yes … I think so. How did all this come about?"

"Towards the end of the war, the American Military Government moved to hundreds of German cities throughout for the soul purpose of restoring law and order. Shortly after the Potsdam Conference, allied forces subdivided the entire country and the Americans were assigned to Bavaria. We then moved all our forces into our sector and set up shop … so to speak.

"Aside from establishing law and order, the Military Government was ordered to remove all Nazis from positions relating to civil service … you know, the running of the cities …

all the way from the mayors on down to the guy who flips on the light switch. It was a tremendous chore trying to find qualified individuals to accomplish this work who weren't Nazi sympathizers. But after a while, they were found, trained, and put to work. The police were finally established and a little over a year ago we turned over the court system. About all we do now is monitor these functions and make sure it runs the way it's supposed to run. Hell … their own people are tougher on themselves than we were!"

"And where do you fit in?" Dieter asked probably knowing the answer.

"Actually my position is now with the American Farm Bureau … I'm trying to retrain these people on how to farm … gain maximum yield from what acreage they have … use better techniques, and most of all how to pay attention! I really worry about their knowledge. Now I know these people aren't stupid … they're just hardheaded as hell in changing tactics. A lot of farmers I've gotten through to … many just make me beat my head up against the barn. Talking to the cows is a lot easier. But one day I think they'll come around. When one farmer sees another out-producing him … he's going to find out why. Money talks … when he starts seeing the profits … he'll change. By then … I'll probably be back in Nebraska with my own set of problems."

Dieter laughed. "Well … what about your CIA status? Doesn't look like you're doing too much spying here!"

"When I left you at the beer garden, I went back to France to deal with French collaborators working for the Germans. For me … it was boring … I spent six months interviewing some real scum bums. I finally got with Hildabrand and begged him to assign me somewhere else to where I could be useful … or else send me home.

"I got wind about the farming issues in Germany and asked to be assigned there. He, of course, knew of my farming background and finally relented thinking that might be a good fit after all. It didn't take long after that before I was reassigned and sent here … been here now for about six months.

"My CIA status? Yea ... I still have it. I suppose once CIA always CIA. To me ... it makes no difference. At heart, I'm really nothing but a farmer ... so I guess I'm farmer status now! Captain Beirman knows I'm CIA but doesn't care. He's got his own agenda. He does his job, and I do mine ... we get along just fine. He's a good man."

Dieter laughed again. "How about this house? How did this happen?"

"I had nothing to do with this proposition. I just moved in. That was done by the original detachment that came here. Not only did the Military Government remove Nazis from prime city government positions ... they were also removed from their houses. The idea was to let them know that Eisenhower and Truman meant business ... that is ... lower the Nazi bastard standard inferior to the way they had set the standard for the Jews. Make him eat dirt ... and that by god is what we're doing.

"The Nazi son of a bitch that owned this house is now living in the basement of a Jewish bread-maker's store ... and he is absolutely livid! Still is to this day! He often approaches Captain Beirman begging for his house back ... Beirman literally turns him around and kicks his ass out the door. Beirman doesn't put up with his shit!

"Captain Beirman, as you may have recognized from his name, is Jewish. It was speculated he was specifically brought in here to re-establish the Jewish business owners back into the business they originally owned. This has been a hard row to hoe. He's had his hands full and has had a heck of a time doing it. But you know ... ol' Sergeant Wiggins is actually one mean son of a bitch. When he hears that Beirman is having a little trouble, Wiggins seems to make things right. Not too many non-Jews mess with Sergeant Wiggins ... but all the regular Jewish folk around here love him to death. That's probably where he gets that damn good coffee!"

"Yes ... I would think so."

"Dieter ... I know you've *got* to have something on your mind or you wouldn't be here ... but sitting out here in this cold car is beginning to chill me a bit. Let's first go in for a nice breakfast and then we'll go into the house-office and talk out your problem. I know you've got to be hungry!"

Dieter was totally oblivious as to what John had just described about the American Military Government. While he had been around many Americans after the war, he was totally unaware of how the occupation actually worked. Maybe he did know but was being naïve to the fact. But for Dieter, since his capture, he was always sheltered and coddled and then inherently thrust into a secretive system keeping him away from such realities. This was one of those realities.

From the past, he knew the Nazis bastards were bad; and he was glad to see them pay for their acts. It was fitting that dirt eat dirt. But he was also pleasantly pleased that conscientious Americans were making assiduous efforts in supporting the common German who wasn't tied to the Nazis Party scheme. He was pleased to hear all this; but he was also sad that it had to come to this. To him, it was all just very, very sad.

"John … that was about one of the finest filling meals I've had in a long time … I think about as long ago as Fort Hunt in Washington. Your Cookie, as Sergeant Wiggins would say, 'Sho does know how to cook them vittles'!"

"How did you like Cookie … about the way I described?"

"He couldn't have made a better Werner Schroeder than ol' Schroeder himself. You lucked up when you made it to this office. I commend your persistence with Hildabrand!"

"Dieter … lets go into the office in here and get down to business. Let's straighten you out. You look like you're all bent out of shape."

This was one trait Dieter always liked about John. He was no nonsense: get to the problem, work it out, make a decision. During the war, this was also Dieter's trait, but now the problem lies with him, and he needs to reverse the advice. John was that man.

After settling into the house-office where a fire in the fireplace had already been established, Dieter went straight to the point. "John … my last mission … the one I finished just yesterday … well, it has put me into a moral dilemma…."

And with that Dieter spent the next hour diligently telling John all the details relating to his mission. John was concentrating on every word, intently listening and watching the anguish encompassing his body. It was an incredible story.

"Dieter ... in as much as Bormann is concerned ... I wouldn't worry too much about his fate. Whether you pulled the trigger or not makes no difference. He was bad and he was scheduled to die anyway. Regardless, you knew you were going to kill him. When you took this mission, you knew that was part of the plan. You accepted that. You dealt with it. If I were you, I'd rest my thoughts and not worry about that son of a bitch.

"Raisa and her backup ... same thought. Hell Dieter ... they were going to kill you! Does that not prey on your mind? Would it make you *feel* better if you were lying there next to Bormann? I think not and you know it! The good news is Hildabrand had the presence of mind and forethought to keep an eye on you ... and for your sake, you better be glad he did! Hell buddy ... you're about one of the luckiest son of a bitches I know! This CIA/MVD game is for real ... this is serious business. You knew that when you made the decision to stay in the program.

"Hildabrand did give you an option for another mission ... god knows what it was, but I believe it probably entailed something a whole lot less stressful ... probably interviewing French collaborators for all I know! But the fact is ... you took the more dangerous mission. Those test in England proved right. I took the same damn test after the war. Outside of my first and only real mission ... my test proved otherwise. Aside from my short stint in Paris, I'm plowing fields. Whether you know it or not Dieter ... you're supposed to be as ruthless as Viktor or Raisa!

"But in reality ... your outside emotions are fighting with your inner deep desires and that alone is a dangerous game. If you stay in this business long enough ... you're going to die. You want my advice ... go find a nice Jewish girl and marry her. Maybe her father will let you work in his store!"

Dieter nervously smiled at his last comment. This was the first time in his life he had ever been talked to in this manner.

He was always the strong rock in the family and among friends and colleagues. At the moment, he felt like a whipped puppy. But John was right. He knew John was right. Though, he pondered the Jewish wife thing believing John was interjecting a slice of levity. A good trait with him.

"Now Dieter … this map thing is a horse of a different color. You and I both know it … and I know this is your moral dilemma. This is international big that can cause some serious problems. With the Cold War just now heating up and tensions flaring … all hell could break loose."

"Yes … yes … I know. That's why I came, John. Viktor suggested I don't turn it over because of just what you said. But if I show up without the map … hell I'm a goner! If the map goes, I have to go with it … my life as I know it today will just evaporate … it'll never be the same. I'll have to disappear for good so that nobody … and I mean nobody will ever find me. John … is it worth it … I mean is it really worth it?"

"Big question Dieter … you do have a dilemma. But let's look at the moral side of it. If you plan this just right, you can continue to live some type of secretive life that actually may well suit what you really want. You're smart enough to do that. On the other hand, you'll also probably be saving millions of lives if war breaks out. Under those circumstances … you have no choice."

"John … it's just like the way your sergeant told me this morning, 'you sho is smart'! You certainly have a way of putting matters in perspective. Yes … my head is unclogged and I can think a much better now with more authority. I see things more clearly!"

"Where will you go?"

"John … we both know that answer!"

"Dieter … why don't you spend the night and get a fresh start in the morning. I'll go get with Cookie and see if I can get him to cook up a special meatloaf for dinner tonight. It'll be a great going away meal!"

"Yes John … that sounds good … that sounds real good."

Chapter
29

"I'm tired my dear," Greta said. "Would you help me back to my room so I can take a short nap before dinner?"

Cindy arose to push her wheelchair back to the house. No wonder the old woman was tired, she had just spent the last three days telling Dieter's story and it was wearing her out.

As they walked, Cindy couldn't help but to ask one last question.

"So ... did Dieter make it safely to England?"

"Oh yes," she chuckled. "It took him about two weeks, but he finally made it. He left John in Schrobenhausen the following day and caught a train to Bremerhaven. He was able to get a sleeper car this time with the help of Sergeant Wiggins who had became quite fond of Dieter because of his friendship with John. He made the arrangements and drove him to the station. He chuckled as they drove that he purchased the coffee from one of the Jewish merchants he helped who was having trouble. But that was supposed to be a secret! He always suspected John knew but was just playing a little game with him."

The 410-mile trip took Dieter until early morning Monday to get to the seaport. The sleeper car had given him the extra rest he was unknowingly going to need crossing the North Sea.

The weather out there could quickly change and the seas could get rough.

When he got to Bremerhaven, he finally located a rather large fishing vessel that would take him to an area near Harwich, England, a large seaport. He figured by now Hildabrand was looking for him and he thought this might be a good place to enter the country. He still had to be cautious in what he said and how he acted. Prying eyes just might be lurking.

The captain of the fishing vessel, an English bloke, requested 200 shillings to get him into the British port. The train ticket from Munich pretty much wiped out Dieter's funds he had received from Hildabrand. The only money he had left was the Reichmarks and Swiss francs stashed in the Goebbels briefcase. The captain was pleased to take the equivalent in Swiss francs.

"In early November," Greta continued, "Dieter showed up on my doorstep and was he a sight for sore eyes. He was quite disheveled. His clothes were a mess, he was showing a beard, and he was on crutches!"

"Crutches?" Cindy said surprisingly.

"Yes … the poor dear had broken his leg."

"Broken his leg? How did that happen?"

"Silly him. He was trying to be of help to the fisherman who brought him across the sea. They ran into a big school of cod and there was nothing to do but go after them," Greta continued chuckling. "Dieter got caught up in a net and somehow broke his lower leg. The crew set it as best they could, but it never mended properly leaving him with a slight limp."

When reaching Greta's room, Cindy helped her into bed and covered her with a beautiful hand knitted afghan from the foot of the bed. Greta asked Cindy to wake her at 7 o'clock so she'd be ready for dinner.

Cindy went into the library and found a comfortable chair. She herself was a bit tired from listening to this incredible story and all she could do at the moment was sit, stare, and ponder everything she had heard. There were still many questions that haven't been answered. But several questions were answered. Her Grandpa John really was just a farmer, but he had CIA status and that's what kept him from revealing any information about his work, regardless of how mundane it appeared. He did help the German people revamp their farming system which was a great help to their war-stricken economy. But she also discovered how close to death he came on his first and only mission inside the Third Reich. It sent chills up her spine hearing of the torture details.*

"And what of Dieter and that Amber Room map? That's what this whole saga is about in the first place. Where is he and where is that map? About the only answer so far is that Dieter wasn't a double agent working for the Russians. I guess that in itself was a good piece of information to discover. I wonder why Greta was reluctant not to tell her own son? She'd tell me ... but not him ... interesting. Maybe it simply was that girl-to-girl thing that men don't understand."

A few minutes later, Somes entered the room and asked Cindy if she would like something to drink. "You know Somes ... yes ...I believe I do! Right now I've got a desire for a glass of whisky and ice if you have some around. And listen ... why don't you fix yourself one and join me. I'm sure Miss Greta wouldn't mind. Right now she's taking a nap before we have dinner. You're about the only one I haven't chatted with around here, and I'd like that very much."

"Yes Miss Cindy." And with that Somes left the room with his usual slight limp returning with two glasses of bourbon on a tray. He offered her glass first, set the tray down, and sat in a chair across from her. As if on cue and without provocation, each slightly raised their glass and toasted the other, and took a sip.

"Somes ... how long have you been with Miss Beckham?"

"I have been with her for many ... many years. Perhaps so long I have forgotten the years. It has been such a pleasure working here that it really makes no difference. Miss Greta has made me feel as though this is also my home."

---

* "Nebraska Doppelganger," Chapter 22.

After a few sips of the bourbon, Cindy recognized a familiar flavor. She asked Somes what brand. "Yes … it is Jim Beam from America. Her son usually brings back a few bottles from the 'Colonies' when he travels there. For many years, Miss Greta occasionally has a glass in remembrance of Colonel Zeis. She was very fond of him and this always made her feel close to him."

"Somes … let me may ask you … were you here at Beckham when Colonel Zeis returned from Europe with his broken leg?"

"Aye … yes… I remember it very well. Miss Greta was quite overcome with joy. She last saw him just before leaving on his dangerous mission. They had a nice quiet dinner. She was deathly afraid he wouldn't return. But yes … he returned and he was quite the mess. The broken bone in his leg had already started to mend in a crooked fashion. For it to heal properly would have required re-breaking it and setting it straight. Colonel Zeis didn't want to experience that sort of pain again and just allowed it to mend crookedly."

"How long was the Colonel here at the mansion," Cindy now being inquisitive.

"After his leg healed, he changed his persona with the help of Miss Greta. Neither the Russians nor the Americans ever found him. It was as though he had just evaporated into thin air."

This answer seemed to suit Cindy, but it was presented in such a way it left open more questions. She would continue to observe.

"Somes … if I may be so forward to ask … how old are you?"

With a big grin on his face, he happily replied, "I just turned 93 years old this past April and I feel fine. Of course, I am not as agile as I used to be as you can see. I have asked Miss Greta to allow me to continue working as long as I can stand … and she has agreed. As you have noticed, there are several younger faces about the manor that perform the necessary house functions. I guess you could say I just manage them … but everything is so well organized, there isn't much for me to do.

"Now if you will excuse me … I have a conference with the chef. He has prepared a *magnificent* leg of lamb and I must assure it is properly baking. I have enjoyed your company and *thank you* for allowing me to chat with you!"

Somes stood, slightly bowed, and gave a very light click of the heels. Cindy remained quiet. She took another sip of her whisky and carefully pondered the conversation. She then stood herself and slowly glided to the large window overlooking the front of the grounds. The grass had just been mowed and it was especially pretty.

That night at the dinner table, there was only Greta and Cindy. Jack had left the country for Japan to conduct corporate business. He would be gone for a week.

The dinner that evening was delicious and cooked to perfection exactly the way Cindy preferred—medium rare. After the meal, Somes entered asking where they would take their coffee. Greta motioned to the library.

Cindy still had three weeks left of her stay at Beckman Manor and felt as though she had most of her story. Jack did have it approved with her New York boss that she didn't have to return until the first of August. She thought she could probably wrap everything up in a day or so. When that was done she thought she might explore the countryside if that was okay with Greta. The last time she was here, all time was spent at the manor other than one night to a restaurant.

Soon after they settled into the library and had their sips of coffee, Greta presented a revelation to Cindy that would change her life forever.

"My dear … how would you like to spend more time here at Beckham Manor?"

"Well … yes that would be nice. I do have about three more weeks left here before I have to report back to New York. How much more time would you like for me to stay? I would have to get Jack's approval though."

"Darling … listen to me. You don't have to get Jack's approval. Jack gets approval from me. You see my dear … I am the owner of the Beckham World News Service. Jack works for me!"

Cindy's eyes and mouth flew wide open. She was astounded. She was speechless. Stuttering was her only response.

"But ... but...!"

"Yes ... I knew you didn't know. Only the top people in the organization are privy and a few very longtime employees. It is not something I really care to share with the world. I like it just that way."

"But ... how ... how did...."

"After Lawrence died in the training accident in early 1947, he left me a very wealthy woman. I had no desire to follow the high social tea parties and get involved with the upper crust of society.

"In the late 1950s, I purchased a fledging newspaper from a gentleman I had known for years. He was elderly and his children had run the company into the ground. I offered to help him financially but he wanted completely out just to punish his children. It was quite ironic actually, because Little Jack, my child, had by then graduated with honors from Cambridge University in business. I was thinking all along of putting Jack to work there.

"After taking over the paper, I put Jack in control to see if his education would pay off ... and he did a wonderful job. As you can see, it has paid off quite well. But all through the years I have maintained full control. Jack really doesn't seem to mind ... today he pretty much does as he pleases ... which is make money! But he takes the time to enjoy life too. And he *does* take care of his dear old mother!

"I have already made preliminary arrangements with Jack and if you agree, I will complete the arrangements. The first, of course, will be that you will now be working out of our London office taking care of the international accounts. I would also like for you to stay here in the house with me, but we can also arrange an apartment for you in London. It is up to you. Why don't you think about it tonight and we'll talk further in the morning."

Cindy was completely dumfounded. She could hardly speak. So much had just happened that her head was spinning like a top in a child's hand.

"Darling … it has been a very long day and I am a bit tired. Let us retire for the night and we will talk further in the morning. Tomorrow we will *take the day off* and just enjoy each other's company. Perhaps we will ride into the countryside and enjoy its beauty!"

Cindy lay in bed with tears moistening her wide blue eyes. She could hardly believe what had just happened. She did believe at that moment she was the luckiest person alive. But now the big decision had to be made and it was going to take every ounce of her being.

The following morning, Cindy arose a little later than normal. Her mind that night had clicked away until it physically exhausted her. Her body felt refreshed, but her mind was tired. She felt a warm shower and a cup of Somes' fresh coffee would smooth the clutter.

As Cindy descended the staircase, by happenstance she noticed a long black windowless car heading from the driveway. Her heart began pounding fearing something had happened to Greta. At the foot of the staircase, she turned into the library. Greta was sitting there in her wheelchair staring out the window. She instinctively knew something was wrong. Cindy cautiously entered the room moving in slow short steps. Greta's head turned towards Cindy. Her eyes were moist with tears.

"It was Somes dear … it was his heart. He died sometime last night. The cook found him early this morning when he saw the coffee wasn't brewing."

"Oh Greta … I am so … I'm so sorry."

"Please dear … roll me by the fireplace. I want you to do something for me."

Cindy moved her near the fireplace and then took a chair close enough to clasp her hands. "Sometime this morning, I want you to go into Somes' room and pick out the navy blue wool suit I bought for him several years ago. It is hanging on the rod in the far left side of his closet in a suit-bag. Perhaps you would be kind enough to pick a pretty tie against a white shirt. Later today, I would like for you to take these items to him. The driver will escort you. In the meantime, I will make the burial and other arrangements. I also have to make one important phone call. We will entomb him in the family burial plot on the grounds in two days.

"Now … why don't you get a cup of your morning coffee so that you can be fully awake. I will need your support over these next few days and then after the funeral, we will continue our conversation from last night. The situation has changed and I want to discuss it with you."

Chapter
30

The following two days were very calm and somber around Beckham Manor. Greta took her meals in her bedroom only visiting with Cindy briefly about the arrangements. Cindy spent her time walking about the estate, talking with the service help, and listening to the humorous tales about their friend. Cindy stashed her pen and was taken to the stories of this wonderful man. There was no question he was a much-loved person.

On the day of the funeral, the burial was set for 11:30 on the family grounds two hundred yards behind the manor. Earlier that morning Cindy recognized the funeral service excavating the hole for the coffin. She noticed the efficiency in which they came and left.

A half-hour before the service, Greta, with the help of the housemaid, lowered themselves on the elevator where the maid rolled Greta into the foyer greeting Cindy and clasping her hands. With what seemed like military precision, Greta's Rolls Royce Silver Cloud slowed to a stop in front of the house. The maid opened the large front door to the house. Greta motioned for Cindy to follow to the front of the steps.

"Cindy ... there is someone here I'm sure you'll be glad to see. Perhaps you will open the door for him," with which Cindy obliged but was terribly confused.

"Grandpa!"

"Don't look so shocked. Did Greta not tell you I was coming?"

"Grandpa ... I ... no ... are you here for Somes' funeral? You are...!

"Yes ... yes I am. Though for a while there it was questionable if I would make it. We ran into some bad weather over the Atlantic. The pilot went around the storm and then put the 'pedal to the metal' to get me here on time. Greta, I commend your pilot ... maybe you should give him a raise or something!"

"Gramps ... it is so good to see you again even if it has only been two weeks!"

"Yes this is an unexpected visit and a sad one at that. Greta I am so sorry," as he walked over and gave her a light hug.

"It was his heart John ... it just stopped. But yes ... I am doing well. Did you bring it with you?"

"You know I did!"

Cindy continued to be puzzled with conversation that made no sense.

A few minutes later, the butler came to the front stoop and nodded. Greta knew this was the signal it was time to precede. John went to the front seat while Cindy and Greta entered the rear. A servant put the wheelchair in a following car.

As the car pulled into the freshly mowed grass heading to the plot, Cindy asked Greta a question. "I thought Jack had the Boeing 737?"

"Yes, he does. We picked your Grandpa up in the corporate Lear Jet. It's considerably faster ... and in this case, as you well know, the essence of time was indeed important."

When the car pulled beside the plot, several funeral servicemen opened the doors and prepared Greta's wheelchair. They then carefully rolled her beside the coffin positioned over the freshly dug hole. It was a very plain simple wooden pine box. This he told Greta he always wanted.

Once Greta, John, and Cindy were in place, all the service personnel, except one, moved to the far side of the field. Greta then spoke extemporaneously from her heart.

"My dear friend, you are now gone from me and I am sad … but yet I am happy, for I now know that you are at peace.

"We have had many good years together where we have shared our souls. We have laughed together and we have cried together and we have avowed our love. It is only now that I shed a tear, for those who live in the hearts of others, their spirit never dies.

"Good-bye my friend…."

As soon as Greta finished, John stood. The serviceman opened the lid of the casket. John approached carrying a small cloth sack. He reached in and pulled out a flag. With the help of the serviceman, they unfolded a 1932 German flag and draped it over the body. At that point, Cindy instantly recognized that Greta's Somes was Dieter Zeis! She broke into tears. Greta gently put her hand on Cindy's knee and affectionately patted it.

When John returned to his chair, he stood at attention. A Black Watch trumpeter then played "Das Deutschlandlied (Deutschland über Alles):" The German National Anthem. Cindy quickly gathered herself and also stood at attention with heavy tears streaming down her cheeks. When the trumpeter finished, the serviceman closed the casket.

Dieter Zeis now lay at rest. He lies next to Paul von Carlsen, Greta's first husband, and Lawrence Beckham, her second husband.

When the trio returned to the house at 12:15, Greta released the staff to the plot to pass their final farewells. When they returned at 12:45, they served a table full of freshly made sandwiches. It was how he would have wanted it—simple. They also had a large bottle of Jim Beam bourbon for anyone who would like to serve a toast. At 1:00 sharp, Greta, her guest, and the entire house staff each raised their glass to Dieter's honor.

An hour later, the staff had cleaned up and disappeared behind the scene. Greta excused herself to her bedroom requesting that Cindy come to her room at 6 o'clock later that afternoon. She thought it would be a good time for she and her Grandpa to spend time together. They in turn retired to the library for conversation.

After getting comfortable, Cindy asked John, "You've known all along … haven't you Grandpa … about Dieter?

"Yes dear I have. When he left me in Schrobenhausen, I knew he was coming here. Given his predicament, it was his only choice … he had nowhere else in the entire world to hide. When he disappeared with the map, the entire CIA and other forces went looking for him. They even came to see me, and it was the first and only time in my entire life I didn't tell the truth. I think they believed me because they never gave me any trouble.

"They even came here to Beckham Manor, but Greta was smooth as silk in portraying her story, and they eventually moved elsewhere trying to locate him. It was as though he just vanished into thin air … just plain disappeared. I made no contact with Greta for years because I was afraid there might have been a tail on me. If there was, I didn't know it. But eventually we got in touch with each other and she would plant little tidbits of information in her letters implying that Dieter was well. In the years to follow and things slowed down, I made many trips here."

"And what of the butler act … how long had that been going on?"

"Oh … that was just one of his many ruses he played to stay out of trouble. From time to time, he played every character in the house … and then some. He and Greta shared a relationship that very few people would ever understand. To me it was a beautiful relationship. But simply, they protected each other as though it was their last moment on earth. Nothing would stand in their way in that devotion … nothing."

"What of the map?"

"May I remind you that I'm still under oath from the CIA!"

"You're not going to tell me?"

"As I said … find another subject. That is none of your business!"

Now John asked a question. "I understand Greta has made you a new offer on you employment?"

"Yes Grandpa … she has. But on the day Dieter died, she told me the situation had changed. I don't know what that entails, but we're to talk later this afternoon in her room. I suppose then she will enlighten me … we'll see."

The afternoon slipped by and Grandpa John escaped to his room for a 'power nap' so he would be refreshed for the evening. He had certainly had a long day and he was quite tired. Though at his age and with jet lag, it was doubtful Cindy would see him until morning.

Cindy herself was getting tired, but it wouldn't be much longer before she would make her way to Greta's room. She didn't want to accidently fall asleep, so she went into the kitchen and found a freshly uncorked bottle of wine. She poured herself a glass and walked about the pool area enjoying the countryside. From there, she could see the location of the family plot. It didn't take long before tears again filled her eyes reminiscing over the days events. Of all the funerals she had ever attended, this was the saddest.

At 6 o'clock Cindy lightly tapped on Greta's slightly cracked bedroom door. "Greta…?"

"Yes dear … please come in."

Cindy gingerly walked into the room. Greta was already out of the bed and sitting in a chair near a large built-in bookcase. Another chair was next to her.

"Please come and sit next to me so that we may talk."

Cindy now had with her a full glass of wine. She was afraid to hear bad news and felt the wine could be her crutch. She sat next to Greta. Cindy still had a tear in her eye."

"Oh please dear … don't be sad. Dieter is now at peace with himself. He professed this to me years ago. Yes … I am sad too, but it is now time to move on. Now dry your eyes and put a smile on your face. My news is not what you may think!"

Cindy dried her eyes and put the wine glass upon the napkin she had with her. Greta clasped her hands with Cindy and smiled.

"The reason I want to keep you here, is so that you'll be happy."

"But, Grandma why wouldn't I be happy?"

"Grandma…! Yes I like that … and you are my 'granddaughter' which makes this proposition so much easier!"

Cindy was now totally confused.

"You see my dear … I have decided to leave my entire estate with you … Beckham Manor. Regardless of your decision, she will always be yours."

"And I have also dictated that, upon my death, you will receive fifty percent of my shares in Beckham World News Service. You will now be working directly with Jack … Though, I might suggest, you listen very carefully to him and let him teach you the business. It is mighty big and it will take some time … but you will learn … and you will be successful. You won't turn out like my elderly friends children."

Cindy was floored. She put her arms to her chest and gasped.

"But what of Jack? The house … what will he say? What are his feelings of the News Service? Oh Greta…!"

"Jack is in full agreement. He is now beginning to reach the age where he wants to slow down and play more golf in Scotland. He has the desire and energy left to teach you. He likes you very much and thinks it will be a good match!"

"But what of Beckham Manor. He is your birth son. Would you not want to leave it to him?"

"Oh Cindy … Jack really doesn't care too much for this old place. Oh sure, he comes to stay occasionally … yes … but that is only because of me. He has a penthouse in London and a summer home in Scotland. When I am gone, he'll probably just sell it to the highest bidder. It will probably go to someone who won't appreciate its history."

Cindy was trying to understand what Greta was saying. She continued to listen.

"You see ... there is something else more to this house than just the walls and the landscape. It is a piece of history only three people know ... me, Dieter, and your Grandpa John. Of course, you will be the fourth person to know ... and I would like for it to stay that way. It is way too important."

Cindy took a large gulp of wine waiting for the bombshell.

"Dear ... if you will. On the bottom shelf of this bookcase, I would like for you to pry it open. It's lightly attached. Underneath, there is something there and I want you to pull it out. At my age, it is hard to do these days!" Greta said with a light grunt to her voice.

With little effort, Cindy got onto her knees and slowly pried open the shelf. She set it aside. Inside was a very dusty well-worn black briefcase. She gingerly pulled it out, returned to her seat, and put the briefcase on her lap. Underneath the rough leather handle were the initials PJG. Cindy now knew exactly what Greta was saying. This was the briefcase containing the Amber Room map.

"Paul Joseph Goebbels. This is it ... isn't it Greta?"

"Yes dear ... yes it is!"

Sitting on Cindy's lap was a major piece of world history known only to four people. She knew with the ages of her Grandpa and Greta, she would in due time be the only bearer of this artifact. If only these walls could talk of its secrets.

"I am getting tired my dear ... please help me back to the bed. And take the briefcase to the library and open up the map. You might be surprised as to know where it is hidden!"

While helping Greta into bed, she had one more pressing question. "Did Jack know that Somes was Dieter?"

"No ... he did not. When Dieter came to the house, Little Jack was at prep school. When he came home for holiday, he recognized only that I had hired a new employee. He was never to the wiser through all these years. He of course knew of Dieter but not of his identity. I hope you will maintain that thought."

"Now let us all get some rest. Tomorrow I would like for all of us to take a ride into the country. There is a *special* place that Dieter and I used to go. I would like to see it one last time before my time is up."

Cindy closed the bedroom door leaving it partially cracked. She followed the stairs to the library and set the briefcase upon a table. Her wine glass was empty. She went to the kitchen, refilled it, and returned to the library. She sat in her usual chair with world history staring her back. The house was very quiet. She lightly thought to the briefcase.

"I will open you tomorrow. There will be plenty of time."

About an hour later, Cindy returned to the kitchen and looked for a pair of scissors. She then strolled to the garden overlooking the beautiful row of rose bushes. She knew Dieter liked roses. With the scissors, she cut the stem of a full bloom Fair Bianca.

From there, she passed through the garden and walked across the freshly cut manicured lawn towards the family burial plot. Her thoughts were still reminiscing with Dieter.

"It was a pleasure to have chatted with you. I wish we could have had more time. I now know it wasn't your place to identify yourself ... but you knew that all along knowing Greta was going to tell me ... and she did so in her own way. I guess that's the way it was supposed to be ... and I am glad that was the way it turned out.

"Though in her story, she brought your life to me and I felt as though I have known you forever ... and in a sense that is true. She was very fond of you. Her eyes always lightened when she mentioned your name.

"I appreciate what you did for my Grandpa John and I'm sure you appreciated what he did for you. That is friendship ... and in this cold world today ... that is a very rare thing to happen. You must be proud!"

Cindy had now approached the gravesite. New fresh sod had been well placed over his grave as though it had never been disturbed. She walked to the side of the plot. At the head was a simple plain granite marker embedded in the soil. Upon it simply read: "Somes – My Dear and Loyal Friend, Love Greta." She took the rose and placed it on the stone. She then looked skyward and said. "So long too my friend."

The End